Threatening Sky

S Jade Castleton

Danseibi Press

ISBN 978-0-473-48378-4 (soft cover)
ISBN 978-0-473-48379-1 (ePub)
ISBN 978-0-473-48380-7 (Kindle)

Owen, Andrew and Jamie — *thank you once again.*

THREATENING SKY

[*One*]

Owen

Dad ruined the quiet April afternoon by not being dead.

Ruined wasn't as cold as it sounded, given that he'd gone to work one day more than a year ago but not come home. With his bank accounts untouched and the authorities unable to trace him, we'd presumed he *was* dead and that's how we'd coped and lived.

And now we were a better, closer-knit family for the experience—my brothers and sisters, and me and my partner Andrew.

Sitting on the bench under the oak tree, I was enjoying the fresh air while proofreading a bunch of reports for Andrew. He was in Springfield with a client, and on days when he wasn't in the office I usually worked from home because I'd be there when my youngest brother and sister got out of school. Except, today they were out enjoying their usual Friday ice creams with our amazing neighbour.

Jamie, with black earbuds plugging his ears, sat on the deck, fingers tapping his knees as he mouthed lyrics. He'd stopped singing out loud so much after Megan had told him he should do Show Choir. He was actually pretty good but I'd been appreciating the silence.

Megan stepped out onto the deck behind him. Seeing the total shock on her face got me immediately onto my feet. As I was starting to ask what was wrong, she said, 'I… I was just talking to dad.'

'Who?' Because that word wasn't really on the list of people

I thought of these days.

Jamie obviously missed her words because he pulled out the closest earbud. 'What?'

Megan shouted the repeat, making him hustle to his feet, stooping to pick up his phone when it dragged the other earbud out of his ear. He looked at me but I didn't know what to say.

Our sister sat, hands gripping her knees. 'I don't even think he knew it was me and not Lisa.'

'What… did he actually say?' My gut was churning. Shit, dad was alive! And he'd contacted us! 'You sure it was him?'

'Yeah,' Megan said, dully, and put her face in her hands.

'Dumb ass,' Jamie muttered but I reckoned it was a valid question, and my gut twisted further that it seemed like dad really *had* abandoned us back then.

Megan drew in a breath and looked up. 'Can you guys sit?'

Jamie and I glanced at each other. Usually she'd just get on a higher step for the advantage, but she was obviously thrown. We sat either side and she said, 'He said, "Hi kiddo, it's your dad. I'm back."'

'Back?' Jamie and I blurted together.

'What did he mean "back"?' I added.

'I don't know, he didn't say. He asked how I was and said he'd call again later. And… hung up.' Her indrawn breath shook.

For half a minute all we heard was our own breathing. Then Jamie asked when Andrew was getting home.

'Really late,' I said. 'So he's gonna go to the apartment then come over in the morning.'

'No way he could come earlier?'

I shook my head.

Jamie nodded. 'Well, okay, we're on our own then. Done that before. Megs, did dad—' He broke off and pulled a face. 'Weird, saying that word.'

Megan bunched her shoulders.

Jamie finished his question. 'Did he say he was here?'

'Here?'

'Yeah, in the area.'

Megan swallowed. 'Didn't say. God, what if he *is?* What if he comes around?'

'He won't,' I said.

They looked at me.

'Well, wouldn't he have done that instead of phoning?'

Jamie shrugged. 'Guess so.'

Megan was biting her lip. 'What if he wants to live here again?'

'No way!' Jamie shot out, scowling as we both looked at him. 'Oh, come on! You guys *want* that after so long?'

'No,' I said.

Megan shook her head with such force that we had to lean back from her whipping ponytail.

'Then don't look at me like that,' Jamie growled, rising.

I got up too. 'Calm down, we can't overreact before we know what's going on. Dad contacted us, that's all.'

Jamie's mouth opened but he didn't echo, 'That's *all?*' in an incredulous voice. I was as thrown as they were but somehow I was also being sensible. 'Let's just… be normal right now. Not tell Lisa and Matty yet.'

Right on cue, we heard the front door unlock and open, followed by the noise of happy kids. Megan leapt up and hurried inside.

Jamie and I looked at each other.

'If this is a Friday the Thirteenth prank,' he said, 'I'm not fucking appreciating it.'

I cocked my head briefly, then realised it *was* that date. 'Shit,' I breathed.

'What if he *is* coming back?' Jamie asked hollowly.

I just shook my head, unable to get my thoughts and voice to work together.

Knew one thing though—I didn't want dad back.

We'd gone through hell last year after he left us on our own, but after a hard slog we'd come out right side up. Now we were fully settled in our new life with Andrew as my partner and he as my siblings' official guardian, and everything was really good.

Dad had the power to mess it up. Quite apart from what his return would do to everyone emotionally, my gut flipped at the possibility his return might sever Andrew's guardianship. *We'd* still be partners but if that guardianship link was gone, what would happen to the others?

I nearly reached for my phone, but calling Andrew right now would only worry him. And I didn't want him to cut his meeting short, like I knew he would.

Jamie was still with me on the deck, and he jerked when I said, 'Do you think I should call the sergeant and tell him?'

Sergeant Morrison was our contact after dad failed to come home, and had remained so all through last year when I'd done some dumb things and ended up in hospital. We hadn't had to contact him much these last few months.

'What could we say? It was just a phone call.'

Jamie had this weird tone thing going on so I just said, 'Yeah, okay' and left it.

He fiddled with his earbuds and then went inside without

another word.

I stood on the deck listening to the sound of Megan trying to corral sugar-dosed kids into a sort of calm. Probably should have helped, but instead I crossed back over to the bench and picked up the report and pencil.

Looking down at the papers I held I really didn't see the words, just kept hearing Megan say she'd been talking to dad.

It really did feel like dad being alive had ruined the day. We'd been having a peaceful Friday afternoon, each doing whatever, and now I was sure that my brother and sister had dad on the mind as much as I did, totally forgetting their afternoon prior to the phone call. Pain and loss and anger were starting to break through the barrier that had kept me from even bothering to think about him recently.

Knowing he was alive and that he hadn't contacted us made me sick.

Didn't help that a tiny nag wiggled to life in my stomach about how he'd be when he heard about me and Andrew. I couldn't recall dad showing any homophobia but a lot had happened since we'd last seen him so the little bundle of nerves remained.

I had to work hard not to ring Andrew just to hear the sound of his voice. In the end, I didn't because I probably wouldn't be able to keep the fact that something was up out of my own voice, and I really didn't want to tell him over the phone what had happened.

And Jamie was right about not ringing Sergeant Morrison. It *had* just been a phone call, wasn't much the police could do. And if he showed up…

I swallowed, tried not to let my imagination play out that scenario. To block it, I let recall unwind that Friday last

January when dad left us.

We'd had no clue.

He'd dropped Lisa and Matty off first that morning, then the rest of us outside the high school. As I'd started to close the door with the usual, 'See you later, Dad' he'd called my name. Once I was leaning back in the car, he told me he was working late again, so we'd be on our own for the evening. He sounded apologetic, even though we were used to it.

'Okay.'

'Don't bother saving any dinner for me,' he said. 'I'll eat at work.'

I nodded.

'Study hard.'

'Don't *work* too hard,' I replied. 'We'll see you tomorrow.'

I hadn't even watched the car pull away.

This was the same car in our garage now; a big lump that we passed each time we did the laundry. We hadn't discovered it until later on Saturday. By then we'd just thought dad had had to stay even longer. He'd often said that being head-hunted for the role put the pressure on him to really perform, so extra extended hours weren't new to us at all.

We weren't that worried, either, when we tried to contact him and his phone went straight to messaging. It wasn't always surprising. However, finding the *car* sort of nailed the point home that the absence wasn't normal.

After a while we'd given up looking for the keys; didn't matter anyway, since back then none of us could drive.

Still couldn't, though Andrew had offered to teach me in his Mercedes. A smile curved my lips as I remembered his expression when I'd declined, telling him I was too afraid I'd put a ding in it. A sort of relief alongside amusement.

He hadn't offered again.

The indrawn breath was ragged enough to startle me back to the present, and I sucked in a lungful of fresh air.

I tried to get back to the report but dad had destroyed my concentration. Crowding in my head were memories of how distant he'd been before he left, how miserable and hard that Christmas had been without mum, and how his disappearance had wrecked the fragile lives we'd still been putting back together.

Tagging along with those were the definitely unwanted memories of where *I'd* ended up in my attempt to keep my brothers and sisters and I together.

Dad would ring again, Megan had said, so I told myself to stop thinking about him until that happened. I took the report and pencil inside, and gave myself over to Lisa and Matty distracting me with their rambling, excited babble about their day. Which seemed twenty percent school and eighty percent ice cream.

Andrew

Jamie didn't quip when Owen and I showed up in the kitchen—him in PJs with a sweatshirt over top, me dressed.

Probably because he knew I'd gone to my apartment last night instead of coming here and disturbing everyone with my late arrival. In any case, Owen and I didn't always share the big bed when I stayed over; we kept apart so as not to make things awkward.

Though, in fact, Jamie didn't mind us sharing since he'd usually take Owen's room. I realised he really ought to have space for himself now, rather than continue to share with

Mathew. Perhaps we needed to make some official rearrangements.

In any case, Jamie just asked how my meeting had been down in Springfield. While I answered, Owen tinkered with organising a pot of tea.

After a moment, Jamie said, 'So, what do you think about dad?'

'Pardon?' I answered, fully surprised.

Hearing a clink of crockery, we both turned to look at Owen, and I realised there was something to that way-out-there question. Owen set a cup right side up then mopped up milk. His gaze caught mine and then swerved to his brother, who seemed kind of surprised.

'Um,' Owen said. 'I haven't…' He pulled a face.

'What's this about your father?'

Owen came to the table but didn't sit. 'He rang yesterday. Megan spoke to him.'

I heard him, but also didn't, since a sort of alarm was clanging in my head. Somehow I said, 'I see.'

He and Jamie shared a glance, but for a long moment I didn't know what to say or how to react. Their father had been gone well over a year, without any contact whatsoever, and suddenly he'd *phoned?*

I sat straighter. 'Did he come here?'

The boys both shook their heads. Jamie indicated himself and Owen. 'We didn't speak to him. Just Megan.'

'Okay,' I said. 'And what did he say?'

It was Jamie who told me what Megan had heard. Owen continued to stand at the end of the table, fingers pressing into the edge of it.

I was surprised no one had called or texted me about it,

maybe even a little hurt, though I realised that I wouldn't have been able to do anything anyway. And… the kids did have right to talk to their father. Holy hell, their *father…*

'Andrew?'

I shifted, realising Jamie had stopped speaking. 'Sorry, Jamie, I… I'm shocked,' I said, expected they could tell. 'How's Megan? Do the kids know?'

'Megan seems… okay,' Owen said, though his blue-green eyes were dark with concern. 'And we haven't told Lisa and Matty. Megan said that *he* said he'd ring again, so we decided we shouldn't tell them until we knew more.'

By his stiff stance, I could tell that Owen hoped his father wouldn't make any further contact. I sensed nerves and fear, but wasn't sure what over. Though… their father calling out of the blue after so long with them believing he was dead was certainly enough of a reason.

None of the kids had actually revealed to me what had gone on the day they'd been abandoned, so I put it on a mental check list to ask. I had a feeling that forewarned was to be forearmed in this instance.

I pulled in a quiet breath. 'Did he leave a number to call?'

'No,' Jamie said. 'Well, Megan didn't say he did.'

He looked at Owen who just shrugged.

'And no time frame for when he'd ring again or visit?'

Jamie shook his head. 'Sorta sounded like he wasn't actually in the area.'

'No,' I said. 'Presumably, if he was then he'd have dropped by.' I felt incredibly uneasy over that.

Owen shifted; neither he nor Jamie looked comfortable either.

After a small silence, Andrew asked if we'd contacted Sergeant Morrison.

'Why would we?' Jamie asked. 'It was just a phone call.'

Andrew raised a brow. 'Didn't he have resources looking for your father?'

Jamie and I shared a glance.

'Give him a call, Owen,' Andrew said.

I gave a nod but didn't move, it sort of felt like doing so would make this whole thing true. He arched a brow at me, making me spout, 'What, now?'

'Better sooner than later.'

I hesitated a moment, feeling waves in my gut pick up like yesterday, then sighed and turned for the phone. I half hoped Sergeant Morrison wouldn't be in the office on a Saturday morning, but the reception guy put me straight through.

'Hello, Owen. I haven't heard from you in a while, what can I do for you?'

'Um, hi,' I said. 'Uh, dad's back.'

'Pardon?' He sounded a lot more alert suddenly.

'Um, well, not back back. He's not *here*. And Jamie and I haven't—' I shut up a second to sort myself out, turned my back so I couldn't see Andrew and my brother watching. 'He phoned yesterday. Megan spoke to him. He said he was back. Did you know?'

Silence on the other end and I knew it wasn't Sergeant Morrison just figuring out how to bluff. He sounded tired when he said, 'Owen, if I knew your father was around why would I keep that from you?'

I imagined he had a hand over his face as he spoke,

shoulders slumped. 'I don't know. Sorry, but... well, it's a bit of a shock.'

I heard his indrawn breath. 'I take it Mr Gordon is with you?'

'Yes.'

'Can I speak to him then, please?'

'He wasn't here when—'

'Owen.'

'Okay, okay.' I turned, setting the phone on the bench. 'He wants to speak to you, Andrew.'

Andrew's brows rose in surprise, but he got up from the table. I wanted to linger but he told me to get the others out of bed, that he'd make pancakes. He didn't send Jamie off, but then my brother probably didn't freak out as much as I did whenever the sergeant talked with Andrew.

He was done, of course, when I came back from ordering my brother and sisters up, and already involved in making the promised pancakes. Jamie was in the lounge on his phone, sorting something or other, but Andrew didn't take the opportunity to fill me in.

I chose not to badger, instead set the table and then remembered that I'd earlier been making a pot of tea.

When Megan arrived out, Andrew didn't ask her about the phone call, just checked that she was okay. She said she was, would know that me and/or Jamie had already filled Andrew in. She probably knew, though, that he wanted to hear her own thoughts at some point.

He didn't reveal that we'd phoned the Sergeant, so Jamie and I kept mum on that too.

'Owen.'

I glanced over my shoulder. Jamie jerked his chin at me and then sideways. 'What d'you think he looks like now?'

'What?'

He flicked a finger at the large portrait photo on the wall, I shifted so I could see it more clearly.

Whenever I actually thought of dad, I didn't picture him any different from the photo. Except maybe tired, because he'd seemed that the last time I'd seen him. I looked now at his dark hair—mine, Jamie and Lisa's shade—cut short, the bristles at his jaw. Mum had liked the five o'clock shadow. Dad was smiling, lips slightly parted, and his brown eyes seemed just as happy as his lips.

It hurt to look, to remember that just a few weeks after this moment we'd lost mum. *And* dad. I let out a breath and glanced at Jamie standing beside dad—same hair, same eyes, same sort of smile even. I hadn't really noticed the resemblance until now. Well, probably we all resembled mum and dad in some way, but Jamie was suddenly very like him.

I turned to my brother; he stood looking at me like I was a bit slow or something, got an even more set expression when I looked him up and down. He'd been fourteen back then and looked so young, just a kid. Now he didn't, even if he was still only sixteen. The hard lines in him were partly my fault. His teeth ground under my scrutiny and I said, 'You could do with a haircut.'

Jamie's gob dropped; he caught his breath and responded, 'You're the one wearing a freakin' mop!'

Yeah, my hair in that portrait *had* been pretty sharp. I ran fingers through the mess now, grimacing when I hit a knot. Should probably get it cut some time.

Then Jamie said, 'We look different—you and me. Guess

dad will too.'

He probably would but I didn't know quite how. Maybe grey hair or a full beard?

'Reckon you have a different father, with those eyes.'

"Those eyes" went wide a second and Jamie clapped a hand over his mouth. That had been a joke long ago—the fact my blue-green colouring kinda came out of nowhere. Mum's eyes were sky blue. Matty had them too, but mine were definitely more on the green side, darker.

I cleared my throat. 'That'd be kinda handy.' Still came out like a rasp.

Jamie mumbled an apology. I just shook my head.

We turned from the portrait as Lisa and Matty chased each other in one kitchen entrance and out the other. Megan hollered for order, having nearly dropped a plate of pancakes.

Andrew

Megan was calm talking about her father's call and, when I asked, she told me he hadn't been threatening. 'Nothing like that, Andrew, though we…' She pulled a face. 'Probably we all acted like it. I don't think Owen and Jamie want to see him any more than I do. Even though I do.'

'Hon, it's okay if you want to see him,' I said softly. 'He is your father.' As much as that hurt to say, since even in this short time I really felt like Owen's brothers and sisters were my kids. But, in fact, I wanted to meet the man too. I had my own opinions about him, but they were based on the belief that a man who abandoned his young children was no-good and had a lot to answer to.

What I'd gleaned from the kids themselves hadn't openly

painted him as mean and cruel in a physical or emotional manner. There'd been a few loud arguments with their mother in the month before she died but nothing they'd felt greatly worried about. And I understood that her death had been a terrible shock, but Mr Tremayne hadn't been the only one dealing with that loss.

I suddenly realised Megan was looking at me. 'Sorry, Megan, what did you say?'

She shrugged a shoulder. 'Just that… well, I'm scared he'll just come back like he hasn't been away. He didn't seem bothered by the gap when we talked.'

I drew breath. 'We'll just have to see how it pans out. I'll remain your guardian. Sergeant Morrison confirmed that this morning. That sort of state doesn't just dissolve. And,' I added, 'you'll always have me, no matter what.'

Megan chewed on a fingernail, nodding, all the while looking like she struggled to hold back tears.

I found myself flattered that the three older kids didn't seem enthusiastic about their father returning. It had more to it than just *me*, I knew, but I was still flattered.

Then Megan said she didn't know how Lisa and Matty would be.

I inclined my head; her gaze was directed outside where her brothers and sister were playing tag. The younger pair had such endless energy! As we watched, I caught Megan's quaking breath.

'Honey.'

'It's thanks to you they're like *that*,' she whispered, lifting a hand briefly.

'I didn't put those piles of sugar on their pancakes.'

A tear slipped down her cheek, but I knew she meant them

simply being happy and playing, and probably meant the older brothers more than Lisa and Mathew. I squeezed an arm around her shoulders. 'It'll be okay. We'll work it out.'

As we watched, Lisa jumped onto Jamie's back and he piggy-backed her around as she ordered him one way or the other after her laughing brothers.

My throat tightened as I hoped I wasn't saying empty words.

- # -

Owen was rapidly losing ground in height to Jamie, but he was still tall enough to be scrunched on the bench. Possibly because he lay with his head on my thigh, a chin-to-chest angle that would likely give him a cricked neck. One leg was hooked up over the back of the bench and toes of the other foot were wedged into the ornate iron seat end.

Ostensibly, I was reading over notes from yesterday's meeting but mostly I just watched Owen's hair kinking on my leg when he shifted or his fingers folding creases in his sweatshirt. After all these months, I still had a total fascination with how he and his clothes interacted with each other.

And, though my left leg was going a little numb under his head, after being separated from him yesterday I appreciated his closeness now.

Especially after what I'd heard this morning.

'I'm looking forward to meeting your father.'

Owen tilted his gaze up, ocean eyes more blue than green in the partial shade. He looked puzzled for a second, which wasn't surprising since we'd both been silent the last twenty minutes or so and I'd spoken out of nowhere.

'I won't let you kids meet him alone, Owen,' I murmured. 'Not the first time anyway.'

'Hunh.' He began the careful process of gathering himself into a tidy sit beside me. Poking a finger into his jeans, he said, 'You don't have to if you don't want to. We'll probably be alright.'

I managed a small smile when he lifted his face to me. 'I want to be present,' I said. 'And I am the kids' guardian.' That gave me legal right to keep an eye on proceedings.

Owen cocked his head, one eye closed as he obviously read around and beyond my words. Didn't speak, just nodded. Then he twined fingers with my paper-free hand. 'Thanks.'

After a short moment I ventured, 'You don't want to see him, do you?'

His fingers tightened on mine just a bit and I wasn't really sure he'd answer. His gaze remained somewhere on the grass, but then he let out a short sigh. 'It's stupid, I guess, but I'd rather not know where he was, pretend instead that he was just... dead. It's easier.' He inclined his head. '*Was* easier. Now all that stuff keeps coming back, the time after mum died. It's... hard.'

I released my hand so I could hug him to my shoulder, pleased and worried he'd told me that. Pleased because he was such a hoarder of his feelings, worried because this sort of stress could make him vulnerable to nightmares. 'Talk to me, Angel,' I murmured.

He cast me a sort of "your funeral" gaze, but stayed silent. Then he said, 'I'm worried about how Lisa and Matty will be.'

'Megan said the same thing,' I told him. 'Do you think they'll be scared?'

Owen shook his dark head. 'No. Well, actually, I don't

know. None of us talk about him now, not even when mum's mentioned. We've *all* kind of lived like he died.' He looked at me. 'When you and I first met, dad had only been gone two months but Lisa and Matty had already stopped asking about him by then.' He shrugged in my embrace, obviously wasn't quite sure how to think.

After a moment I said, 'But… you miss him?'

Owen eyed me. 'No.'

I lifted a brow.

'Well, maybe,' he said, sounding puzzled about it. 'I don't know. No,' he added, with a head shake. 'Not now anyway, now that I know he's not dead and that he really did just run out on us.' He shifted straighter on the bench, hooked my arm over his head so he could hold my hand in his lap between both of his. 'But… the others .. I don't know, Andrew.'

I'd thrown him with that question. My "you" had been all encompassing initially but I had been interested to hear *his* response.

'It would be no surprise if you or they did, Owen,' I told him. 'Even if you've not felt it openly. But… is that what you're worried about with Lisa and Matty?'

His fingernails traced sharply down my thumb, but he shook his head. 'I guess I just don't know how they'll be. Not scared, I don't think, but to have him show up out of the blue…' His lips curved into a smile and he said wryly he didn't know how he'd be either.

That was understandable. I said we'd tell the kids once we'd had further contact from their father. Hopefully, before he showed up physically, all of his children would be in a better head space about his reappearance.

Owen did his long nod, so I knew his thoughts lay

somewhere else. I just sat patiently and, eventually, he said, 'That day he left he dropped us off at school like nothing was up. Said he'd be late home so not to save dinner for him.'

'And that wasn't unusual, his being late home?'

'No. Not even back home. In New Zealand,' he added after a second. A rueful smile curved his lips. 'We had no clue. He'd been working long hours, said he felt he had to because he was head-hunted for the job. That was even before mum died, actually.' He let out a soft breath. 'Definitely looked tired a lot, but *that* day he seemed somehow better. Remembering's made me think that maybe he'd come to some sort of decision.' I watched his brows knit. 'Don't think he wanted to be around us much.'

I couldn't prevent my breath sucking in at the pain in his voice.

Owen glanced at me. 'You've seen that picture enough. Megan and Matty have hair like mum's, and Matty's got the same blue eyes. I think—' He cut himself off.

Yes, a resemblance would have been tough but to abandon children because if it? The man should have hugged the memories closer. And I *had* looked at that portrait a lot— mostly Owen and his brilliant smile that day—and had noticed how much or how little the kids looked like their parents.

'I'm sure he will explain everything.' Trying to be encouraging even as an uncharacteristically mean thought crossed my mind—that the man get himself rolled by a bus. I winced.

After a while I asked directly something that had been niggling since I'd heard the news and gotten their responses, verbal or otherwise. 'Owen, was your father heavy-handed with you kids?'

'He wasn't around enough to be heavy-handed,' he responded.

I looked at him, ensuring he knew it wasn't a good enough answer.

He inclined his head. 'Yelled like any parent,' he said. 'More after mum died, usually about stupid no-nothing things. Niggled now I think about it, like he wanted us to yell back, but…' He shook his head. 'He didn't hit any of us. At least, I don't think he did. Not me anyway. Jamie pushed him close once or twice.'

I straightened.

'He didn't, Andrew,' Owen said quickly.

'Okay,' I said after a moment. And then I asked if he—or the others—had told Sergeant Morrison what their father's behaviour had been like before his disappearance.

'Yeah, I think so, though maybe not the niggling bit.'

I left it at that, and had a sudden thought about Jamie. If any of the kids could push a parent it was him with his antagonistic, button-pressing attitude. He'd lost that attitude with me, but in those early weeks…

Hell, that kid had pushed *me* close out of sheer frustration. And Owen *had* hit him, I recalled. Not that terrible hallway fight that they'd had, but an earlier argument. Owen hadn't explained what or how, but obviously Jamie had pressed the right button that day.

I brought Owen's hand to my lips. He arched a brow, and I smiled at him.

I would have sat with him all afternoon, but my mind turned toward dinner. We'd have two extras at the table: Alana and Jamie's girlfriend, Sarah. Pizzas would have been a breeze, but I'd decided a good old sit-down roast and vegetables was better. Though the beef wouldn't take forever, it was probably time I prepared it, and get the kids away from the TV and onto the job of potato peeling.

As I started to shift, picking up my notebook from between my knees, Owen said, 'I reckon your storage unit needs a spring clean.'

I found myself stuck in a half rise as if I needed to stay still in order to get my brain working. Didn't help so I straightened and said, 'What? The unit? I don't—'

Owen shook his head at me, lips curving. 'Was that too subtle for you?'

Now I felt somewhat alarmed, casting about in my mind for something I must have forgotten. Owen laughed, got up on his toes and kissed my cheek. Leaned in a little longer than normal and a light bulb flashed on in my head.

He smiled, as if he realised I was finally on the same page. 'I thought maybe...'

'Maybe?' I prompted rougher than expected.

He seemed suddenly too shy to finish the sentence but bit on a finger, staring full into my eyes.

'You're a hell of a tease, you know that?' I pulled the finger away from his mouth, brought it to my own for a kiss.

'Who's the tease?'

I grinned and let him go. When I didn't speak, he cocked his dark head, hair bending against his shoulder.

'Today is very much out,' I said, waggling a finger. 'I've got a roast to concentrate on. But tomorrow... Well, sure, I'm happy to check out the unit if you are.'

Owen stuck out his tongue, looked very okay with that suggestion, then sank back to the bench, apparently content.

I had to get inside before he got me more hot and bothered. We tried not to need to go do something about our wants and needs when others were around.

His chuckle behind me soothed my soul.

[*Two*]

Owen

On Wednesday, we managed to convince Andrew that he didn't need to be around when we told Lisa and Matty about dad's return and that we'd jacked up a visit for this coming Saturday.

It was dumb on the one hand because he was their guardian but good on the other in case my main worry became real— that they'd instantly be all about dad and forget that he'd abandoned them, forget how wonderful Andrew had been. Megan, Jamie and me could handle that if they did, but I didn't want Andrew to have to face it. The little ones weren't going to get the enormity of dad's return straight off, what it might mean for Andrew.

Maybe he wondered all this himself because it didn't take a lot of hard talk from us before he went home (sort of handily, a night when he didn't normally stay anyway). He had us promise to call him if things went awry.

Jamie snorted. 'Owen's gonna call you even if they don't. Just make sure he mentions how it all went.'

I didn't comment but felt my face heating at his side way of hinting that what we talked about didn't involve anyone but ourselves.

Andrew rolled his eyes, then grinned at me, making the heat worse. I told him to go away. He went, chuckling.

Lisa and Matty were squabbling over a puzzle they were completing when I told them to settle down because we had some news.

They totally ignored me, so Jamie released a piercing wolf-whistle. Certainly got their attention, though Lisa complained about the noise.

'Yeah, well,' Megan said, without sympathy, 'if you'd done as Owen said then Jamie would have kept that to himself.' She gave him a push and he exaggerated his stagger.

'Guys, come on,' I said. 'We're not a circus.'

'Yes, Dad,' Matty spouted.

Jamie and Megan went about as still as I did, and we locked gazes. I gave a half shrug. 'Um, about dad. He's coming around on Saturday.'

Total silence in response to that as my youngest brother and sister just looked at me. Then they looked at Jamie and Megan.

'Dad?' Lisa said. '*Our* dad?'

'You've only got one of—' Jamie cleared his throat. 'The one that ran out on us, yeah, him.'

'Jamie,' Megan murmured.

Jamie lifted his hands but clearly wasn't going to apologise. Since I didn't think he had to, I kept silent when Megan lifted her brows at me as if I should be telling him off. My gaze was on Lisa, because she was looking at me, head cocked, like she didn't quite compute.

Then Matty said, 'Dad's back' in this kind of wonder-filled voice, and whacked Lisa on the arm, shouting, 'Dad's back!' in her ear.

She retaliated with a good blow herself. 'Don't hit me, you dork.'

Next thing, they were doing one of those flailing-hand slapping fights. I sat down beside Megan as she said, 'We should probably stop this.'

'Shit, no,' Jamie said, amused, and I shook my head in agreement.

Megan scowled at us both and then stood, crossed to Matty and Lisa and yanked them apart. 'Behave!'

'She hit me,' Matty pouted.

'Because you hit her first, you twit,' Megan said. 'Go sit over there with Owen.'

She probably would have dragged him if he'd not moved, then took his seat. 'Now, honestly, I don't know what that was about but hitting each other is *childish*. You, shut up,' she delivered at Jamie as he opened his mouth.

Jamie grinned but stayed silent.

Then Lisa said, 'Is dad really back? Have you seen him?'

'No, we've not seen him,' Megan said. 'But we've spoken to him.' She didn't say which of us or even when. 'And he's going to come around on Saturday.'

Lisa's eyes widened with excitement and then Matty said, 'But we're going to the museum on Saturday.'

'Yep,' I said, 'and that's still the plan.'

'Are we meeting dad there?' Lisa asked.

I shook my head. 'Dad will be here, with us and Andrew. You guys will be at the museum.'

'But that's... I want to see dad.'

'And you will, Lis,' I told her with a smile. 'But not Saturday. We can't cancel with Mr and Mrs Carter. They've already paid for the tickets, remember?'

'Yeah, and I want to see the sub,' Matty piped up.

'You've seen it a million times,' Lisa complained.

'So?'

There was no easy comeback to that, but Lisa said she

didn't want to see the stupid submarine.

'You don't have to,' Megan said. 'But you do need to *go*, Lis, just to make sure he comes home. Or even manages to get to dinner.'

The Carters were taking Lisa and Matty out to eat after visiting the Museum of Science and Industry. I don't know how they didn't go nuts with such a visit but I appreciated that they'd always been good with our youngest siblings.

There seemed to be only two things that could divert Matty about sub talk, and eating was one of them. Hearing him chatter now, I half wondered if he'd already totally forgotten what we'd been discussing. I looked at Megan and Jamie; they both had a sort of *let's run with this* expression going on and so we did. By the end of it, even Lisa's enthusiasm for the outing had returned.

Thankfully, because I'd be able to report truthfully to Andrew that the reveal had gone okay. Guess we *could* have kept this first visit entirely secret, but it'd be our luck dad would mention it when we *all* got together and then there'd probably be big fall-out from the kids. Easier to manage things *this* way.

Jamie

God, it was like we were attending a funeral or something, the atmosphere was that grim. And we looked it too—Owen, Megan and me. No one seemed able to call up any enthusiasm for seeing dad.

Which was weird because it was *dad* and he was back.

But he was back after walking out on us, back after more than a year of no communication. How were we supposed to act? I think we were all relieved he was alive, but I was sure there was no reason in the world that'd cover what he'd done.

Unless he'd been held hostage by terrorists all this time.

About as unlikely as mum pulling off a phoenix-from-the-ashes move. Wincing, I realised my gaze had been on the small vase on the writing desk. The desk had been one of the few furniture items to come to the States with us. It'd seemed a good place for her ashes, but meant that we kind of avoided that area of the lounge.

Except, when I glanced back, I noticed the desk was dust-free. Maybe Megan had done that.

She sat now on the couch, gaze on her hands squished between her knees. I couldn't even bring myself to quip she looked like she was outside the principal's office after doing something naughty. With her long blonde hair tied out of the way, I could see that she was chewing her lip.

Owen sat on the armchair pretending to read. I hadn't seen him turn a page in half an hour; no doubt the day of dad's disappearance was running through his head. I stared long enough to make him look up, but he didn't.

Andrew called my name from the kitchen, making us all jerk. 'Yeah?'

'Open one of the doors, will you? Let in some fresh air.'

I gave a nod and unlatched one of the French doors. Catching the fresh breeze rushing in, I realised how stuffy the room had been. I kind of expected Owen to push past me since he'd been acting like a claustrophobe all day, but when I glanced over my shoulder he was still on the chair and accepting a mug from Andrew. Megan took the other one, a smile lighting up her face briefly.

Regretting that I'd not wanted a drink, since at least they

had something occupy them, I came to sit on the other couch so we made a sort of circle. 'Why does this feel like a funeral?'

Megan spluttered in her drink, wiped her mouth. Owen just looked at me. Over his shoulder, Andrew's brows knitted just a bit as he came back with his own mug.

'Well, it does,' I said. 'It's weird, I feel… stuck. Like I'm on a conveyor belt and can't get off.'

'Me too,' Owen said, watching Andrew take a seat beside Megan.

I knew he worried about dad's reaction to Andrew, but we'd agreed to keep their relationship out of this first visit and just represent Andrew as guardian. That'd work as long as Owen could keep his worry hidden. Andrew, himself, looked like he'd put on a mask. No real chance that *he'd* slip.

Hauling in a long breath, I said, 'I feel guilty too, that I'm not looking forward to this.'

Andrew didn't comment and when I looked at my brother and sister I saw the same feeling in their gazes.

'He left us,' Megan whispered.

'He was gone before that,' Owen said, and I heard pain. Not so much over what *he'd* done to keep us afloat but that dad had only been a shadow those months before he walked out.

That Christmas really had been one to forget.

I cleared my throat, spouted a word of agreement.

Silence after that, and because we were so quiet we heard the vehicle pull into the drive. Megan leapt up, cup in hand. 'Back in a sec.'

She was gone down the hall before anyone could say or do anything about it. Owen and I stared guiltily at each other.

'I don't know how to do this,' he said with a croak.

'Me neither,' I told him.

Andrew rose, making us jump up too. 'You don't *have* to do this, if you don't want.'

Owen's smile was weak. 'Don't want,' he mumbled. 'But *need* to.'

His gaze came my way and I nodded. 'We… do it like we agreed. Pretend he's just back from a long holiday.'

It had seemed a good plan at the time, but now I wasn't sure we'd pull it off. I glanced at Andrew; he smiled encouragingly but, beyond that, I couldn't tell what he was thinking.

The doorbell made me and Owen jump.

'I'll get it,' Andrew said. 'Owen, go put the jug on again. Jamie, find Megan.'

His calm orders got us moving.

It was crazy how much dad hadn't changed. He must have, because we all had, but he didn't *look* any different. Even had the same stubble as in the portrait. He smiled and his brown eyes seemed to sparkle. He seemed genuinely pleased to see us, and he gave Andrew a decent handshake and greeting.

Andrew was polite back, but who knew where his thoughts really were?

Dad's genuine friendliness knocked a bit off our nerves, and Megan's eyes were bright when she stepped back from his hug. He held his hand out to me and I went to shake it, not overly resisting when he pulled me into his embrace.

'You've grown, Kid,' he murmured. 'Look at you.' He held me at arms' length. I mumbled something and smiled, found myself a little weirded out how strong his accent sounded. More American than I could ever remember.

Dad turned to Owen. 'Hey, Owen.'

'Hey, Dad.'

Owen sounded normal but he stiffened as dad moved toward him. His unease at people crowding his space or touching him stemmed from the brutal attack he'd suffered last year, and we usually managed to shield him from these situations.

Didn't know how to with dad, and I think Owen realised he couldn't not hug back. It was minimal though and I saw his fingers trembling as they pulled apart.

'Almost finished your schooling, huh? What're your plans?'

My brother went still, looked like he was struggling to breathe. Andrew shifted, mouth opening, then Owen said, 'I'm working, Dad, not studying.'

'Oh?'

Owen looked at me, letting me see the *what do I say?* panic in his eyes.

'Hey, Dad,' I said. 'Come sit outside, standing here's dumb.'

Dad gave a laugh. 'Sure, Jamie, lead the way. After you, Mr Gordon.'

'No, you go ahead,' Andrew said with a smile. 'I'll make some drinks. Coffee? Tea?'

'Owen knows what I like,' dad said, ruffling my brother's hair and then stepping away.

I guess he didn't see Owen's face or he'd have commented about how sick he suddenly looked.

'Go, Jamie,' Andrew said quietly. 'You too, sweetheart,' he added to Megan. 'We'll be right there.'

I grabbed Megan's wrist and tugged her after me, not wanting to give her the opportunity to bolt down the hall again.

Dad gazed about as he headed for the open door, but he wouldn't have seen anything new. I wondered what he thought when he saw that big family photo, if he even noticed he'd not seen his youngest children yet, or what he felt when he glanced at the writing desk.

Outside, instead of taking a seat at the table, he stood on the edge of the deck and drew in a long breath. 'That tree could do with a trim.'

Megan choked on a breath, and I didn't know what to say that wouldn't come out annoyed. I sat on the bench, watching him, and Megan dropped down beside me. Dad didn't turn to look at us until she asked how he'd been. He pivoted, head slightly cocked. 'Well, Megan, well.'

'That's good.'

I could feel her tension building, like she wanted to scream something and was desperately holding it back.

'So, Owen's working?' Dad glanced through the window into the lounge, brows creased.

'How's that surprising, Dad? You left us with—' I shifted sideways at the elbow in my side. Dared myself to continue but knew it best not to. Instead I said, 'He sucked at school anyway.' Shrugged.

Actually Owen hadn't but I was hoping a tiny speck of humour might—

Dad's face showed he didn't seem that thrilled, by me or Owen I wasn't sure.

Megan pulled her ponytail over her shoulder and started to braid it. 'He works with Andrew at his architecture firm. The rest of us are in school, doing really well too. Would you believe that Jamie's an honour's student this year?'

'Hey,' I grumbled.

Dad's brows inched up but he seemed to forget Owen after that, engaging us with school talk—academically and sportingly. Normal talk, so much so that it almost felt like a Saturday afternoon of old. Grief flushed through at how much I'd missed that. And yet I still preferred Andrew over dad right now, and that made me feel guilty because right here and now our dad was talking to us and it was like all those months hadn't gone by.

Dad didn't sit at the table until Andrew and Owen came out with a couple of trays. Cups, a coffee pot and a teapot, a jug of milk and a bowl of sugar. I swivelled around properly on the bench, making Megan do the same. Dad walked around to take the seat opposite me, watching as Owen made his coffee—milk, a teaspoon of sugar, the coffee. Stirred, then another teaspoon of sugar and stirred again.

I actually hated the fact that Owen remembered that *and* that he was doing it. Dad could have made his own drink!

Andrew sat on dad's side, meaning Owen sank beside Megan. I caught Andrew's gaze briefly and he seemed calm, but I kinda got the feeling that was over the seating arrangements. We three kids could easily leave the table if need be.

I was kinda worried that Andrew even *had* those thoughts, but I guess he'd listened to us enough over the past week to be on the wary side for this meeting and I, for one, appreciated his protectiveness.

'Thanks, Kid,' dad said as Owen shifted the cup across the table.

Owen didn't respond.

Turned out dad was the only one drinking coffee, so I moved the pot closer to him with the sugar. The rest of us didn't have sugar in our tea.

None of us seemed able to break the silence and then dad said, 'You kids look well. Megan, you've become a beautiful young woman.'

She started, red rushing up her face. Nothing came out when she opened her mouth.

'And you two.' Dad nodded at Owen then me. 'Handsome young men.'

Yeah, me and Owen couldn't speak either. What did you say to that kind of comment coming from a father who'd been gone for so long?

And then dad thanked Andrew—using 'Mr Gordon'—for looking after us, his children. Andrew cleared his throat. 'As I always will, Mr Tremayne. And it has been no chore.'

Owen's gaze was riveted to his mug but I knew he heard the faint edge in Andrew's tone as clearly as I did. I thought he'd say something or even that Andrew wasn't *his* guardian, but he remained silent.

'How long's my son been working for you?'

The question held curiosity but Owen jerked up, expression an indecipherable mix of weird. He opened his mouth, but Andrew said, 'Several months now. A damn good appointment on my part, as my colleagues tell me.'

They might, I had no idea, but I reckoned Andrew was working to diffuse the situation a little. He even managed a smile that didn't look put on. Owen's return smile seemed slightly embarrassed.

'Owen's always had a good level head on his shoulders,' dad said, looking across at him. 'So that may be true, Mr Gordon, but I'd have thought a finished education was a better step.'

'Yeah, probably,' Owen responded, 'but I don't regret

working instead of studying.'

How he said that and not a blast of other stuff, I don't know. I was fighting to keep my mouth shut, stunned at how dad didn't seem to realise *why* Owen was working instead of studying. Andrew sat stiff, probably made himself reach for the teapot to regain some normalcy. Owen picked up his own mug and drank, then held it out to be refilled too.

Between us Megan seemed to be breathing shallowly, and then she wiped at an eye. She didn't hide the fact her eyes were wet from dad, who'd looked her way.

'You okay, Megan?' His tone was soft.

I thought she might bluff, but she said, 'No' in a wavy voice. 'Dad, Owen didn't stay in school because of *you*, because you walked out on us. We didn't exactly have money for stuff.'

'Megan,' Owen warned.

'Well, it's true,' she said.

'Yeah, but—' He cut off; guess he didn't want a fight.

Megan knuckled her eyes, apologising at the table.

Dad didn't mention Owen or his education, simply said, 'I'm sorry about that.' Didn't go into any explanation of why or where, or even why he'd come back.

None of us asked, though we were dying to know. It was like there was some barrier on bringing that stuff up here and now.

Dad poured more coffee. My brother's eyes narrowed as he watched him stir in sugar. I was so sure he was about to burst or something, but he kept silent.

Until dad had taken his latest mouthful.

'What are your plans, Dad?'

'Pardon?'

'Plans,' Owen said. 'Are you back? Are you just visiting?

What do you want?'

Across from him, Andrew sat a little straighter but dad barely reacted, physically anyway. 'I'm back,' he said. 'Or, I will be. I've some things to sort out.'

'But not *here*, right?' I asked as Owen and Megan opened their mouths. 'I mean here at home.' Pointed into the table. 'You can't expect we're okay with that.'

Dad looked surprised by that comment.

'Come on, Dad,' I said. 'You walked out on us more than a year ago. Everything is different. *We're* different.' I thumbed between me and my sister and brother. 'We need some time to get used to this.' I glanced over at Andrew, who gave the barest nod. Most of his attention was on Owen, who sat hunched now, like he was readying himself to run.

Dad blinked and then sat back. 'I guess— Well, you're right, Jamie. We'll need to come at this slowly.' He smiled, dragging my memory to before mum died.

Megan pulled in a shaky breath.

Dad glanced at Andrew. 'There are definitely things we need to work out.'

'This is true,' Andrew agreed. 'And perhaps you'll come to dinner one night this coming week.'

Dad nodded. 'I'd appreciate seeing my other kids.'

So, he had realised Lisa and Matty weren't here. Wonder when it was that he'd twigged.

'Where are they, by the way? I'm surprised they're not here.'

'Prearranged museum visit,' Andrew responded. 'No matter how many times Matty's seen that sub, he treats every time like the first.'

'Sub?'

'At the MSI, Dad,' I said. 'There's a German U-boat there.

Matty's nuts about it.'

'Huh,' dad said, smiling. 'Kid still likes water stuff.'

Well, something remembered.

'They won't be home until later,' Owen spoke. 'He makes a whole day of it, including dinner.'

'They didn't go by themselves…'

'Of course not,' Owen said. 'Mr and Mrs Carter took them. Our neighbours, remember?' he added when dad looked blank.

'Oh… right.' After a moment dad said he'd enjoy doing dinner sometime soon.

Which at least seemed to mean he wouldn't try to stay tonight.

Everyone agreed, Megan trying out a smile even, and Tuesday night was chosen.

Then dad asked, off-hand, if Lisa and Matty had known about today's visit.

'They did,' Andrew told him with a nod. 'But since the tickets were pre-purchased we thought it best not to waste the Carters' time and money.'

Owen buried his face in his mug, so I reckoned he was fighting against spouting the truth—that the sub and dinner had more pull than dad.

'Ah, I see. Understandable.'

Dad seemed put out, but I wondered how he had thought today would go as if nothing was odd. As if he hadn't been gone all this time. Had he really thought we'd just be here with welcome arms because he was our *father*?

I snorted and yanked my cup of cool tea to my mouth.

'Well, I should go,' he said. 'Long list of things to start sorting.' He turned to Andrew who rose when he did. 'Thank you again for looking after my children, Mr Gordon.'

'It's been no problem,' Andrew said.

The handshake wasn't any longer than normal but it looked like they were testing each other.

Owen stood. 'Do you still like turkey, Dad?'

He and Andrew dropped hands, both turning to Owen which had probably been his ploy.

'I do, Owen, yes.'

'Cool, we'll try to find one for Tuesday.'

When he stepped out from the bench, turning his back, he missed dad's smile. Almost genuine, except I also saw the side glance at Andrew. I reckoned he was already thinking about severing the guardianship.

Megan got up, let dad hug her. I stayed seated, and he eventually just ruffled my hair.

'See you kids Tuesday.'

'Yeah,' I said.

'Bye,' Megan said, with a small smile.

Dad followed Owen into the house, Andrew walking after them. After a second Megan plonked back onto the bench. We didn't speak for a few minutes but as Owen stepped back onto the deck Megan said, 'I didn't enjoy that.'

Owen looked startled a second like he wasn't actually with us, and then shrugged. 'Went better than I thought.'

'You must have had low expectations,' I said, half serious, half joking.

He cleared his throat, looked up at the clouds—lines of them heading lake-wards. 'I thought he'd want to stay.'

'He does,' I said, making Owen look at me. 'You didn't get that? He wants back.'

'I meant tonight,' he mumbled.

'Yeah, well, reckon he realised that wasn't gonna happen. But I bet he's already thinking about how to cut Andrew's guardianship.'

'He can't do that,' Megan said beside me.

'He's our *dad*,' I responded with an edge.

'So?' Her edge was sharper than mine.

I changed the subject. 'Weird how he went on about your job, Owen.'

His smile was weak, but he looked appreciative as he said, 'Think Megan set him right on that.'

'Someone had to,' she said defensively. 'Why did you guys stay so silent?'

'No point in starting an argument, Sis,' I said. 'Dad doesn't seem to get what his leaving meant, or what his return means. I didn't think we should hammer *that* out first visit.' I looked at Owen. 'Right?'

He seemed to take an age to agree with me. Megan went stiff. 'Are you just gonna let him back in?'

'No,' Owen said, cold and definite. 'But we have to be sensible, Megan. If we…' He paused as Andrew joined us. 'Being all angry about things won't help. We can't give him the advantage.'

He looked at Andrew, but he stayed silent as if unsure what to say. Or, maybe he felt like he shouldn't get into this conversation because it was between us and about our dad. So I deliberately changed that. 'He's gonna try to break your guardianship.'

Andrew's brows came together, possibly because my words sent Megan inhaling a shocked breath. He didn't deny it though. 'Yes, I believe he will.'

'That's not fair!' Megan whispered. 'He's been gone *ages.*

How can he even think about that?'

'Because he is your parent,' Andrew said.

Owen squinted at him and I arched a brow. *Parent* seemed an odd word.

'Some parent,' I muttered.

'Fucking A,' Megan growled, shoved me hard when I nudged her for swearing.

As I saved myself from falling off the bench, she jumped up, told us we all sucked and launched into the house. Andrew looked after her but didn't move; Owen had a hand curved at his elbow. 'I should—'

'Leave her alone. That's what you should do.'

Andrew looked in two minds about listening to that advice, but I backed my brother. Megan needed time to sort through what was in her head. He squeezed Owen's hand then peeled his fingers off his arm. Shifting around to his original seat he asked how we were.

'Pissed,' I said.

'I don't know,' Owen said.

We looked at each other and he asked why I was pissed.

'How are you even asking me that?' I asked back. 'Aren't *you*? That was a ridiculous meeting and dad treated you like a little kid with that coffee.' I poked a finger at the coffee pot.

Owen looked surprised, glancing at Andrew as if for support but he didn't speak. My brother rubbed an eye. 'Well, of course I'm angry over how he seems to think nothing's wrong but I…' He sank to the bench. Looked into his mug then straightened. 'I don't know what to feel other than that. Except… I feel like I've been in a fight.'

He rubbed his eye again, then leaned his elbows on the table and set his face into his hands, obscuring himself from us.

'Yeah, well.' I glanced at Andrew. 'You break each other's bones?'

'Pardon?'

Owen didn't look up.

'With that handshake.'

Andrew grimaced, looked over his hand. 'Nothing broken. Just a little bit of power play, I suspect.'

'How are you so calm?'

'I'm not especially, Jamie.' He glanced at Owen as he lifted his head then looked back at me. 'But going off the deep end won't help anyone, and he may *be* your father but his return doesn't wipe a legal guardianship just like that. He'll need to go through appropriate channels and that will take time.'

'Would a judge back him?' Owen asked quietly.

'It's impossible to say,' Andrew replied.

'No way!' I said. 'Nobody would back him over you. Who'd be so… stupid to do that?'

'Nothing is set in stone, Jamie.'

'Are you sick of being our guardian?' That came out before I could stop it.

'What? No!'

'Well, I just— I don't—' I rose. 'Fuck it, I'm going over to Sean's.'

Andrew called my name.

'I'll be back for dinner,' I said but didn't look back. More fuck-it that my eyes were stinging.

Owen

I was pretty sure that, by eight o'clock, Matty had asked each of us separately what dad had looked like.

Didn't think he was trying to catch us out in what we told him, just that now the sub visit and dinner were over he'd turned his excitement to dad and kept wanting to hear about him.

It was wearing thin; I heard Megan growl she'd already told him twice and to go ask someone else. He asked Andrew.

'I can only tell you want I saw, Kiddo,' Andrew said, sounding apologetic. 'I can't really compare.'

'I know that,' Matty responded. 'But at least you won't tell me he still looks just like that.' He pointed at the family portrait.

That logic must have made sense in his brain.

Andrew humoured him and described dad. So well, in fact, that it was like he was describing him for a sketch artist, but Matty was lapping it up.

In the end, Jamie, who'd been listening to music while doing some homework, pulled out his earbuds and said, 'Matty, he really did look just like that portrait, even the bristles on his face.'

'But *we* look different.'

'Yeah, but we…' Jamie caught my gaze, clearly regretted interrupting. Probably also regretted coming home from his friend's place.

I just shrugged.

'Mathew,' Andrew said, recapturing our little brother's attention. 'Your dad does look like that portrait, but I'm sure he's changed too. However… if I was seeing that portrait just now, I'd recognise your father.'

'But it's been *ages*,' Matty said.

Jamie mouthed *Fucking A* at me. I told Matty that *we* were all still in our growing stage and that's why we looked different. He eyed me, doubtful.

'You're at least half a foot taller,' I told him. 'And look at Megan's hair; it's way longer now.' She'd had it in a neat cut just below her ears back then. Now it was below her shoulders.

'Amazingly though,' Jamie said, 'Owen's still as short.'

I frowned.

'Yeah,' Matty said with a grin.

I poked him with a toe. 'I'm still taller than you! Go pester someone else for a while.'

Matty just laughed and stayed sitting beside Andrew who was also smiling.

It was Lisa who dropped the serious question—at the table when Megan and I were trying to defeat her at Scrabble.

'Did dad ask about me and Matty?'

Megan and I went still, then looked at each other. She seemed as startled, and stuck, as I was. I cleared my throat. 'Yeah, Lis, of course.'

She cocked her head at me, swiped her hair back when it obscured her vision. Her hair had grown out a lot too. Last year, Megan had been cutting my hair—and my brothers'— but I realised she and Lisa hadn't been so diligent.

'We told him you'd gone to ensure Matty came home from the museum. Right, Megan?'

'Yep.'

'We probably shouldn't have gone,' Lisa said. 'Matty's seen that stupid boat a hundred times.'

'Couldn't really cancel, Lisa,' Megan murmured. 'Not when the Carters paid.'

Lisa nodded, then smiled. 'And dinner was really nice.' She

fiddled with a tile. 'Still wish I'd been here though.'

'Don't forget you'll see him on Tuesday,' I said. 'When he comes for dinner.'

Lisa perked up a bit. 'That'll be really cool. I can't wait to tell my friends.'

I forced myself to stay visibly relaxed. Megan caught my eye, gave a small shrug. We couldn't really tell Lisa and Matty to keep silent on dad's return, but I did worry a bit what Matty would tell his friends. Especially since he was capable of extending the facts.

Lisa wouldn't tell tales, at least, though it probably felt like a big one—a vanished father reappearing after so long.

'Did dad *really* sound American?' she asked as she placed her tiles on the board.

'He *is* American, remember,' I said, trying not to wince that she'd just boosted her score by a decent margin.

'Well, yeah, but… That's fifteen, by the way.' She grinned when I eyed her.

'Thank you, I spotted that quite well enough on my own.' I showed her that I'd updated her score correctly.

Megan laughed, then prompted Lisa to finish what she'd been going to say.

Our little sister cocked her head again. 'It's just… Jamie said he sounded really American. What does that mean?'

'Well, he's not had mum—*us* to weaken his accent,' I said with a swallow. 'And we… well, guess we're used to hearing ourselves and Andrew, and our friends. Lots of different accents.' I looked at Megan. 'Maybe it just sounded that way right then because no one else had the accent.'

Megan shrugged.

'Andrew's American though,' Lisa said.

'Nah uh, English,' I reminded her. 'Though… if he went home he'd probably sound American. Anyway, you can judge for yourself on Tuesday.'

Hoped I'd ended that conversation tidily, even as I felt muddled suddenly.

Dad's accent *had* been strong but I wondered if that was because we'd somehow forgotten he was actually American, not Kiwi, and so it had been a shock?

'Yeah,' I heard Lisa say and focused back on her. 'It'll be weird, but cool.'

Wasn't sure if she meant the accent or the visit, but dad didn't come up in conversation for the rest of the game.

Which *I* won, but didn't rib my little sister about.

[Three]

Owen

Andrew sent the kids down to the play-lot.

I'd never been so relieved to have them out of the house. Their incessant chatter about dad, getting in our way in the kitchen as we prepared dinner, had been sending my irritation levels to the point where I was about to burst.

'Thanks,' I breathed after we'd had pure silence for a minute.

Andrew squeezed my arm. After a moment he murmured, 'They're definitely excited.'

My sigh was long. 'Sure are.' I sent him a wry smile. 'Dad won't know what hit him.'

'I'm sure they'll work off some steam at the park.'

I shot Andrew an amused look and he chuckled. Lisa and Matty had boundless energy.

Energy that had been on show since they'd gotten home from school. Andrew and I had come home early to get dinner sorted, and the kids had been on the go over an hour already over what dad would be like, what they'd show him, what they'd ask.

Megan and Jamie were home too, but hadn't come out of their bedrooms. Funny how homework seemed a lesser evil this afternoon.

Putting down the knife, I wiped the back of my hand across my forehead and eyed the potatoes I'd been chopping. Then I pivoted to look over the rest of the dinner prep; other vegetables waited our attention but the two chickens were ready to be popped into the oven.

With another sigh, I said, 'Can't believe I spouted about turkey. In *April*. What a dick.'

We hadn't found a turkey, obviously, so had settled for chicken.

'Your father likes it, huh?' Andrew asked quietly.

'Well, he used to talk about turkey all the time,' I said. 'Even in New Zealand. Had it for Christmas once.' My brows scrunched a bit at that memory. 'He was more about Thanksgiving but that's not really a Kiwi thing, so they're not available then. Guess…' I shrugged. 'Guess I was thinking about the one we had after—' I cut off, lips pressed to a thin seam.

Andrew didn't push, but he probably knew I meant the Thanksgiving after mum had died.

I knuckled my eyes momentarily, didn't hesitate to slouch into his embrace when he stepped close. Out came a hiccup of laughter. 'Wasn't even that great a Thanksgiving.'

Andrew tightened his arms a little then murmured, 'I'm sure he won't mind chicken.'

I didn't respond but if he was looking down at me he'd at least see a ghost of a smile. I was so grateful he was here.

- # -

I don't quite know how I imagined the reunion would go, but Lisa and Matty jumped all over dad when he showed up, laughing and chatting at speed.

It hurt because of how he'd just left us, and hurt because Jamie, Megan and I didn't feel the same way about his return. But, since we couldn't begrudge their excitement, we let them greet dad as they wanted.

It didn't take long before the three of them pretty much forgot about the rest of us.

Andrew went back to the kitchen and I sat on one of the stools and watched him appearing busy but doing pretty much nothing. Megan vanished totally but Jamie sat on a stool beside me and we ended up playing Hangman on a scrap of paper.

Clearly on the same wavelength too since some of our words were *awkward*, *abandonment* and *clueless*, and neither of us barely had to draw a full stick man.

It'd probably have gone a lot smoother if we'd all met dad on Saturday, rather than pushing the kids off to the MSI. Dad would have had their distraction then, and not been so focused on me and my working for Andrew.

I didn't think he'd bring that up again, but I was still a little nervous. And at some point Andrew and I were gonna need to come clean about our relationship.

Tonight, though, we were going to do our best just to be friendly. That'd probably involve me just trying not to look his way. I knew that every time I did my appreciation for him was clear. Dad might take that as being for my job and for Andrew being guardian, but us being less close tonight would help prevent dad knowing more before we were ready.

Not that we wouldn't reveal— I let out a soft growl at how mixed up everything was.

I caught Andrew's raised brow. Before I could respond, Jamie said, 'He's just sore he's losing.' He tapped the paper with a finger.

'Dick,' I muttered under my breath, though I was grateful. I think he understood where my head space was and had been diverting Andrew from worrying about it.

Then we heard Matty say, 'What did you bring us, Dad?'

We both swivelled on our seats. Dad sat comfortably on a couch, with Lisa and Matty on either side. Matty was leaning forward, eager expression on his face.

Dad simply looked startled.

'Matty,' Jamie said, 'why do you think dad would bring you something?'

He looked over at us. 'Well, he's been away.'

As if absence equalled a holiday which equalled a right to presents.

'Yeah, but not on holiday,' Jamie said, a soft edge creeping into his voice.

'Anyway, haven't you got every toy on this planet?' I asked.

'No!' Matty spouted, and turned back to dad who'd barely moved during the conversation.

'Sorry, Kid,' he said, shaking his head. 'I didn't bring anything.'

Matty's bottom lip poked out.

'Uh, well, how about...' Dad fumbled in his pocket and pulled out a set of keys. He untangled a rectangular shape and held it out. 'Have this for now. I'll get you something else. You too, Sweetheart,' he said to Lisa, giving her a hug and a kiss.

She at least wasn't in the gift zone like Matty, who was eyeing the keyring. 'Alabama. Is that where you were, Dad?'

I felt myself freeze. Beside me, Jamie also went still. Dad had said absolutely nothing on Saturday about where he'd been. Would he—

'No,' he replied with a soft smile. 'That's just something I picked up on my travels. Trying to get one for each state or city I go to for work.'

'Are you still in that job you came here for?' Jamie asked, sounding careful about it.

Dad looked up at him, glanced at me. 'No. Haven't been for a while.'

Jamie gave one of those "oh, okay" nods, didn't ask just what job he had now. I tried to recall what plates I'd seen on the car he'd arrived in, but couldn't remember.

'Where *have* you been, Dad?' I asked. Tacked on, 'How many states have you collected?' as I pointed to the keyring Matty held. Had asked it to cover the fact I might have asked the *first* question a bit brusquely.

'Work's taken me over a pretty big chunk of the country.' He tapped the Alabama keyring, making it swing. 'I've got maybe twenty, twenty-five of these.'

I caught myself doing the same sort of nod Jamie had. Then I rephrased my first question. 'Where've you been living?'

Dad's gaze went to the keyring and then came back to me. 'St Louis mostly.'

'That's where the big arch thing is, right?' Jamie asked.

'The Gateway? Yes. Great views from the top.' Dad smiled at our little brother and sister. 'You'd both like it.'

Their faces lit up but as they were both starting questions, Andrew said, 'How about you kids go wash your hands? Dinner's not far away.'

I jerked, but mostly because Andrew had spoken from the hallway entry to the lounge. I hadn't heard him move out of the kitchen. As Lisa and Matty got up, Andrew told me and Jamie to tidy up too.

Jamie swallowed, cleared his throat, but shifted off the stool without speaking. He grabbed up the paper with our scribbles, screwed it up and tossed it at me. Walked off without watching me completely fumble the catch.

I picked up the crumpled ball, not daring to leave it on the ground in case dad got curious about it. As I straightened I caught dad directing Andrew a steady stare, one that came to me when I started to move.

Didn't think Andrew noticed though because he was inspecting the keyring Matty was showing him. He ruffled his hair. 'It'll look great hanging off your bag, Matty. Go put it there now before you lose it. And don't forget to wash your hands afterwards.'

Matty went off happily, leaving my partner, my father and me. I suddenly felt ridiculously awkward and blurted out, 'Sorry Matty asked about presents. He doesn't understand that you weren't on holiday.'

Dad stiffened, then chuckled. 'That kid hasn't changed. Still forthright.'

'And a chatterbox,' Andrew said with a smile. 'Owen, go wash your hands and hurry up the rest of the troops. Mr Tremayne, pick a seat at the table while you can.'

I half expected dad to refuse or something but he stepped forward and actually asked a food question. I took the opportunity to get myself away while not under scrutiny.

- # -

'What's with the missing tooth, Owen?'

So out of the blue, I only managed, 'Uh.'

Jamie and Megan went a little still, probably trying, like me, to beat back the memory of *how*. Opposite me, Andrew wore a neutral expression but I knew he was remembering too.

'Shouldn't you have sorted that, Mr Gordon?' dad asked, managed to sound curious above everything else.

Before Andrew could respond, I said, 'Why should he have, Dad? Andrew's my boss, not my guardian. And I'm an emancipated minor, he's not responsible for supporting me.'

Everyone was looking at me and, of course, back then I wasn't emancipated but I felt like I needed to defend Andrew. Even if he *had* actually paid for that dentist visit. I hoped he wouldn't refute me.

He smiled when I dared a glance his way. 'I offered, Mr Tremayne,' he said, 'but Owen refused.'

'And he reckoned gold teeth were tacky,' Matty piped up. 'So he didn't get one.'

'I believe it was Megan who said that.' I pointed my fork across the table at her. She told me to shut up.

Dad's brows curved up, and even Andrew looked a little surprised. I couldn't remember if I'd ever told him about *that* conversation. Didn't dare right now because Megan had a daggers look in her gaze. I grinned at her and went back to eating.

I continually forgot how I had one less tooth. Dad was the first to mention it in months.

After a moment he asked how it'd happened.

Don't know if anyone else heard the silent, '*Mr Gordon?*' on the end, like he was accusing Andrew of being directly involved. I tried not to react to that, almost jerking when Jamie said, 'I did it. Ages ago. I keep forgetting about it,' he added to me.

'Yeah, me too,' I responded.

'*You* did it?' Dad sounded genuinely surprised.

'Spur of the moment,' Jamie mumbled.

As dad seemed about to speak Andrew said, 'They had a brotherly argument. I'm sure they'll let you know about it later, so let's not bring it up over dinner.'

Jamie nudged my knee with his and my face heated. I liked Andrew stepping in here, even as I worried what dad would do. He seemed to be blowing hot and cold about Andrew, and all I could really think was how glad I was that he didn't know about *us* yet.

Definitely something to be avoided over dinner!

Dad shrugged, then started a conversation that at least didn't involve teeth. And which thankfully didn't involve my blurted-out legal status either.

Mid-way through dessert, around a mouthful of chocolate ice-cream, Matty said, 'We had hokey pokey the other day. Owen made it. It was the best, aye Lisa?'

Lisa enthusiastically agreed. I gave a soft snort. 'Half melted vanilla with honeycomb broken into it. Hardly the real stuff, Matty.'

'Yeah, but tasted like it,' he assured me. 'Did you know, Dad, they don't have hokey pokey ice cream here?'

Dad seemed to take a breath. 'I did know that, Mathew. One of the many things unique to New Zealand, I believe.'

His tone seemed a little off. Matty, of course, didn't notice, just launched into a list of things he missed. I felt a bit wooden over the conversation, but when Matty pestered for what I missed most, I responded easily enough. 'K-Bars.'

Andrew raised a brow. Matty beat me to the explanation, giving an enthusiastic description of the little candy bars. And then said, 'Orange is the best. No, blackberry. All of them.'

I was only half listening, like my sisters and Jamie, focusing back on my ice-cream. Most of the time, if we weren't the direct object of Matty's attention, we just tuned him out. Andrew asked what Matty's favourite candy was here, and Matty seamlessly swapped countries. Baby Ruth followed by Reece's Pieces.

I caught Andrew's gaze briefly, pretty sure he'd swapped the focus because of dad. Dad wasn't a Kiwi, and he'd been the one to shift us to America. Andrew was trying to find some "good" from us being here.

'Owen,' Jamie said out of the blue, startling me. 'Yours is that Laffy Taffy stuff, right?'

I eyed my brother a second, before managing, 'Yeah. The grape ones, then the apple.'

'Banana,' Megan commented. 'All the way.'

I pulled a face. 'Not on your life.'

Dad set his spoon down in his empty bowl. 'I seem to remember that sour candy was always your favourite, Owen.'

'Yep,' I said. 'Still is.' My heart was doing a weird jig thing, which was dumb because we'd spoken enough this evening I shouldn't be feeling nervy.

Maybe it was because he *remembered?*

Jamie

I cornered Owen when he went to his room to get a sweatshirt. We'd been sitting outside, but with the sun gone the air was chilly. He eyed me, but would have pushed right by if I'd not said, 'Have you told dad that you're gay?'

His mouth dropped open and then his brows came together. I totally expected him to do his usual 'I'm *not* gay' response but he simply said, 'No.' Then he cocked his head.

'Why are you asking?'

'Seriously? You guys might not be kissing but a blind man could read the signs.'

Owen frowned, looked mostly puzzled. I knew he was casting his mind over the evening and their interactions with dad. 'I don't think—'

I told him about the one-armed hug I'd seen on the lawn. 'Dad saw too.'

'What? But that…' He shook his head. 'Who'd get that…?' He closed his mouth.

'I haven't said anything, Owen,' I told him since he got a look in his eyes that said he was about to accuse me of doing so. 'I'm just saying that you guys either need to stay completely away from each other or confess.' I shrugged. 'And I mean confess before Matty does it for you. You know what he's like.'

Owen grimaced. 'Probably lucky he hasn't already done it. Bugger.'

That last was almost under his breath.

'Owen, dad's not homophobic.'

'Yeah, but… argh, I kinda don't want him to know.' He pushed his hands through his hair. 'As dumb as that is.'

Megan and I had agreed that we wouldn't let on anything until they were ready, but we'd not been explicit with Lisa and Matty. We probably didn't have to worry about Lisa, but asking Matty to keep quiet on something was like putting a light to a fuse. At some point, he'd reach ignition.

However, even though he knew how our little brother worked, Owen didn't look like he was going to march out to dad and spill the beans.

I cocked my head. 'You really want this news to be in

Matty's hands?'

Owen scowled and asked why I was pushing.

'Because *I* don't want to make a mistake, either, and let the cat out of the bag!' I told him, jabbing a finger, trying not to grin about it.

He looked like he was working out how to react, and then he sighed, scratched a brow. 'Darn it,' he muttered and walked away.

I didn't follow since I doubted he was going straight out now to do the reveal, just headed for my room to grab up a sweatshirt like he had.

- # -

We'd just finished our good-nights to dad, him with his arms still around Lisa and Matty in a dual hug, when Owen blurted, 'Dad, I'm gay. Andrew's my partner. We've been together for ages.'

Actually, it came out like this:

'DadimgayAndrewsmypartnerwevebeentogetherforages.'

I wondered, with how strong dad's accent was now, whether he even got half the words. Surprise spread over his face, with a touch of puzzlement.

Owen was going red, biting at his lip. Beside him, Andrew didn't seem surprised so maybe they'd had a brief chat or maybe he was just that good at keeping a neutral expression. Well, he'd had some experience since he'd gotten to know us. He gave a half smile when Owen glanced at him.

My brother swallowed and turned back to dad who hadn't said anything. His arms seemed a little bit tighter around Lisa and Matty though.

'That's… really why Andrew's not my guardian too. We're *partners.*'

'I see,' dad said.

Owen nodded.

The rest of us kind of just stood there. I'd reckoned dad wouldn't have some sort of homophobic reaction but he didn't look exactly thrilled either. Probably not surprising since he'd spent a lot of the evening giving off the vibe that he was thinking of ways to get Andrew out and get himself in. This reveal could jam a spanner in the works.

Andrew didn't speak, surprisingly, but I guess he'd decided to let Owen direct how this went. And, well, probably he was waiting to see how dad would react.

Dad squeezed my brother and sister and let them go, smiling, as he said, 'I thought there was something more.' He looked from Owen to Andrew to Owen again, then over to me and Megan. 'You guys all know?'

'Yeah, of course,' I said.

Megan nodded.

'They sleep in the same bed,' Matty said. 'It's great because Jamie sleeps in Owen's bed and I get my own room.'

I choked on a breath, caught Owen's gaze. His lips tweaked into a half wry smile; our blabbermouth brother at his best.

'Yeah, it's great alright,' I said, 'because I get a peaceful night's sleep. Can't hear your snoring from the other room.'

'I don't snore,' Matty groused.

'Get outta here,' I said, giving him a shove. 'You're like a jet engine.'

He went off in a huff, which had been my plan. Get him out of the way before he blurted about something else.

'Well, anyway,' dad said, a little stiffly. 'I better get going.

Thanks for the tasty dinner, kids, Mr Gordon.'

'It was good to see you, Dad,' Megan said, giving a tentative smile.

He gave her a genuine one back, hugged her when she went to him. Owen and I stayed where we were, but Andrew moved forward, offered his hand. Dad took it but I couldn't see any power play like the other day.

'You're welcome to come again,' Andrew said warmly.

'Oh, I will,' came the sure response.

With that dad turned to the door, Megan and Lisa following him outside to his car.

'Well,' I said, when we heard the engine catch, 'that was awkward.'

Owen pulled a face. 'Your bloody fault for freaking me out earlier. I didn't know how to bring it up and then he was leaving and...' He looked at Andrew. 'Sorry.'

Andrew flashed a smile. 'He was going to need to know sooner or later.' He reeled Owen in for a one-armed hug. 'Proud of you.'

Owen snorted. I expected, though, that he'd been a bundle of nerves about having to *tell* someone since he still hadn't really come around to thinking of himself as gay. Guess he'd realised the G-word was the only way he could describe his relationship to dad.

Our sisters came inside, Lisa hurrying toward the lounge, while Megan closed the door. When she turned to us she said, 'He seemed cool about that.'

Owen's smile was wry. 'Probably didn't know how to react. Bit of a facer for him, I guess.'

'More like he missed half your words first up,' I said. 'Did you even take a breath?'

'Shut up.'

Andrew gave my brother another squeeze. 'It'll be fine.'

Owen had a *guess we'll see* expression going on, but dad hadn't been angry or anything. Surprised, definitely, but not angry. And he hadn't tried to break Andrew's hand just now.

Owen

Dad showed up on Saturday for lunch with just us kids carrying a bag full of things for Lisa and Matty. A lot of it was branded St Louis but there were also a handful of keyrings from other states.

Beyond the phone call to organise the lunch, we'd not heard from him. I wondered if he'd hurriedly gone home so he could deliver on the gift promise.

In any case, the kids were delighted.

He'd brought us things too—a bag for Megan, a set of flash headphones for Jamie, and a University of Missouri sweatshirt for me. A subtle dig at my incomplete education, I was sure, but I thanked dad even so.

'You should go down for a visit, Owen,' he replied. 'They have a good bridging programme.'

'Ah, I'm… not—' I stopped myself before I could say I wasn't interested, instead said, 'It's not in my financial future.' Winced at how stupid that sounded, acknowledged Jamie's WTF brow with a grimace.

'Oh, that reminds me,' dad said, making me stiffen. 'What's with this emancipation thing you mentioned on Tuesday? When did that happen?'

'Happened while you were missing, Dad,' I answered immediately, though I wasn't liking this conversation happening with Matty right here (playing with the keyrings on the couch beside dad). 'Once I got a job with Andrew and could support myself.'

'Did I not need to be involved?' he asked casually, even as he was semi-focused on looking at a keyring Matty was pointing out.

After Tuesday, Andrew had had his lawyer confirm that my status held even with dad's return.

'No,' I said carefully. 'Court decision based on certain facts.'

I could tell I didn't say that right, but I was sure dad wouldn't be able to counter the emancipation even though it didn't wipe the fact I was still, in age, a minor. Though I wasn't under anyone's overarching control—parent or guardian—I couldn't vote or buy alcohol or cigarettes.

I wouldn't have full control over myself and everything I did until I turned eighteen, but being considered adult enough to have my own financial freedom and choice was liberating and satisfying.

Although I was worried how dad would take it all, I'd never regret going down that route the same time Andrew had become my brothers and sisters' guardian.

Dad gave a bit of a nod. 'How long have you been working for Mr Gordon?'

'Since about September,' I said, willing myself to endure such questions.

'And what is it that you do?'

A smile curved my lips. 'Lots of things.' I explained some of them and even if he didn't agree with anything he'd never be able to say I didn't enjoy my job.

'Dad, does it really matter what he does?' Jamie asked from the armchair.

Somehow he managed to make himself sound bored, like he was sick of listening to me go on about my job, but I was pretty sure he was asking to find out why dad was digging for such information.

Dad glanced at him, then up at me. He smiled. 'Just trying to understand how you've all been.'

'You could—'

'We've been fine, Dad,' I cut over Jamie. 'It was a bit tough early on before I got steady work, but we've been doing pretty fine.' I eyed my brother. *Go with that, Jamie, please.*

Jamie cocked his head. 'Yeah, nothing got repossessed.' He grinned up at me, making me straighten a little. 'Owen's not stingy with his wage. We didn't go without anything.'

Really, it was Andrew who wasn't stingy over fun things. My wage went on the necessities of life, like it always had.

'And how long has Mr Gordon been your guardian?'

'Since just before Christmas,' Jamie said.

'How'd it come about?'

'We asked him, Dad,' Jamie said. 'Me and Megan, anyway. And he said yes. Dad, he's been a great guardian.'

'And your brother's… partner.'

Jamie's gaze narrowed just a bit, and flicked my way. I didn't particularly like the tone dad had used but I said, 'Yes, my partner. They are two separate things, Dad.'

'I'm sure,' he responded, then glanced up as Megan came to us with an armful of stuff.

'You two,' she said to me and Jamie. 'Go set up the table.'

I found a tablecloth and plates in my arms before I could even speak, but I was glad to get out of dad's way for a while. I headed for the deck, hearing Megan say something about cutlery to Jamie and lemonade to dad.

As soon as Jamie came out to the deck, plonking cutlery down on the tablecloth I was still straightening, he said, 'Not sure I like his focus on you and Andrew.'

I glanced at him, then slid the plates into place. 'Hoping he's just trying to fill in the blanks,' I murmured, even as my gut was telling me his interest wasn't so simple and benign as all that.

Jamie sucked in his lips, cocked his head a second, and then gave each place setting a bunch of knives and forks.

'Anyway,' I mumbled, 'he can't change anything.' Not without a legal challenge, at least.

Jamie muttered something I didn't catch then said, 'Let's ask him some questions this time. This digging's gotta be a two-way street.'

I nodded, though I didn't know how we'd go about it. We'd already had the opportunity today to ask questions, but it was like our voices had some sort of block on them. Or maybe we didn't want to ask because we knew the answers would be acid in our wounds.

I reached over to straighten a fork, hoping to hide my grimace at that thought, but Jamie breathed out a long sigh and I heard him say, 'Yeah' as if he got exactly where my thoughts lay.

Food did its usual miracle of making everything outwardly look perfect, and this time there wasn't even the awkwardness present on Tuesday. We were simply five kids and their father having lunch, like it was a usual thing.

Long, long ago it had been.

Andrew still came up in conversation, but not as my boss or my partner. Dad even said several times he appreciated

Andrew's (Mr Gordon's) care for everyone.

Because of the relaxed atmosphere, I was a little concerned about Matty. The kid had a faulty filter switch sometimes and I worried he'd say something out of context as he chatted.

Didn't though, at least not in my hearing, just chatted about school and the neighbours and segued into the German submarine at the MSI. I suspected that once that tale was over, dad would do his best to never bring up anything that could lead around to it again.

I felt comfortable sharing a smile with him over Matty's non-stop chatter. He even chuckled when Megan laid down the law about no more sub talk.

'You're mean,' Matty told her.

'Nope,' she said. 'Just trying to save everyone's ears.'

Matty scowled at her and when she cupped a hand behind her ear and said, 'What? I can't hear you' he pouted and left the table.

'That kid's so enthusiastic,' dad said, sounding like it was a wonder.

'Wish he was that way about homework,' I commented.

Jamie snorted. 'Next time you're helping him, bring that boat into it. That'll get him going.'

'Yeah, nah.'

'Doesn't Mr Gordon help?'

'We're not totally useless without him, Dad,' Megan said, putting some amusement into it. 'Owen helps when he's home from work early and, despite being an *ass*, Jamie's not bad at it either.'

'It's torture,' Jamie complained.

Dad was swapping his attention between us, looking sort of puzzled. Maybe he could tell that had been Megan diverting attention off Andrew, I wasn't sure, but I decided a little clarification was needed.

'Dad, Andrew doesn't fully live here with us. He stays four nights a week and the other three he's at his place. We decided that a while back so we all had our space. It's working really good; he's not gotten sick of the kids yet.' I poked Lisa beside me and she whacked me with the back of her fork.

'Oi,' Megan said.

'And when he's not here, who is?'

'It's just us,' Jamie said. 'And we're perfectly fine. We've had a lot of prac—'

He cut off at my look, coughed as if he'd caught air. I didn't fill in for him, neither did Megan.

When he stopped coughing, he said, 'It's nice to be on our own sometimes, no adult harassing us about homework,' he added quickly as dad opened his mouth. 'Or cleanliness. Hang on—Owen harasses about homework, and Megan about cleanliness. I take back my comment.'

Megan muttered something under her breath, and I told Jamie he'd be on dishes duty later. He pulled a face, turned to dad. 'We're doing pretty nice, Dad. It's a sweet arrangement for everyone.'

Dad just nodded, but I thought maybe we'd kind of made a hash of things. Even though we'd been truthful.

We sat in silence a bit and then Lisa asked dad if he'd take her and Matty to the zoo tomorrow. We all turned to stare at her.

'Well, I'm sick of talking about homework on the weekend,' she said defensively.

I snorted and caught Megan grinning too.

'The weather's supposed to be nice tomorrow,' Lisa said,

turning back to dad. 'It'd be fun at the zoo.'

Dad looked a little puzzled.

'Lincoln Park Zoo, Dad,' Megan said. 'Down by the lake.'

'Oh… yes, I remember it,' he said with a nod. 'It's free, right?'

Megan nodded.

Thankfully it was, or the visits there would have broken the bank by now.

Dad smiled across at Lisa. 'That sounds like a fun trip, Lisa.'

'What trip?' piped up Matty, arriving on the deck.

'Big ears,' I heard Lisa mumble.

'Lincoln Park Zoo, Matty,' dad said, smiling. 'A trip there tomorrow—you, me and Lisa.'

Matty's pale blue eyes lit up and he swung an arm around dad's neck in a hug.

To avoid having to listen to the kids try to outdo each other on zoo talk, I got up and said I was going to parcel out dessert.

Dad said he'd help.

I caught Jamie's glance of surprise, but shrugged. Dad had probably remembered that his youngest son liked the zoo just as much as water stuff and wanted to avoid a pre-visit lecture. Couldn't fault that, and I was okay with us being alone a quarter-hour sorting dessert.

Except, within minutes, my nerves were pinging.

Trying not to let them get the better of me, I told dad that Megan had made the pavlova, the third one this week because she'd been nervous about *this* one.

'It looks perfect,' he said as he sliced through it.

'If it's anything like the last two, it'll taste perfect too,' I said with a smile.

After a couple of minutes working harmoniously getting

pav and ice cream into bowls, dad said, 'What's that man got over you, Owen?'

'What man?' I responded automatically, glancing at him.

'Mr Gordon,' dad said, setting the knife into the pav. 'What's he using to keep you pandering to him?'

I had to turn to him fully as if direct view would help my brain.

'Christ, Owen!' dad growled.

'What do you mean? I don't…' I sucked in a breath. 'Do you think he's *forcing* me?' My brows were up in surprise and shock.

'Isn't he?' dad asked.

'No!' I cried, taking a step back. 'Dad, why would you think he… That's ridiculous!'

He set the knife down on the bench. 'He's my age, Owen.'

'*So?*

'So, that's a bit disgusting, isn't it? He's old enough to be your father.'

Having never had any trouble with Andrew's age, I wasn't about to start now. I was going to say that but, instead, out came, 'Yeah, he's been like that to the others.'

Silence from dad. I happened to glance up across the room; Jamie was just entering the lounge. His head cocked as we caught gazes and then I turned back to dad, who wasn't looking so pleased. 'Sorry, Dad,' I said, 'but… it's true. It's not like *I* could really take that role.'

Dad's gaze dropped to the pavlova and then he shifted a slice onto one of the plates I'd already loaded with ice cream.

'And… I'm totally with Andrew. I love him, and there's nothing forced about it.'

Dad's jaw clenched.

'Man,' Jamie said, 'are you guys having a father/son sex talk?'

I choked on a breath and dad's eyes went wide a second. Then he sliced through the pav with extra force. 'Your brother's a lost cause, and *you* better not be doing anything.'

Jamie's expression bled regret about coming near us let alone speaking. I held back a snort of amusement by sheer will. I was pretty sure he and his girlfriend knew each other *quite* well. Jamie was a little red but dad had returned his attention to the pavlova so possibly didn't pick that up.

I pointed to the completed bowls. 'Take those out, Jamie. You go too, Dad, I'll finish the rest.'

Jamie moved quickly. Dad didn't. I felt myself go stiff, waiting for him to speak but he didn't say anything more about Andrew or his age or our relationship. He said, 'Pavlova was your mum's favourite dessert.'

A rush of grief whacked me so hard in the gut I almost had to gasp for breath. I forced myself to spoon out the last ice cream then take the container to the freezer.

When I turned back, dad was already on his way across the lounge, holding plates. My eyes stung a moment, but then I set the knife in the sink, put the remainder of the pav the fridge, and picked up the last two plates and spoons.

At least with them I couldn't just bolt off to my room. I was determined to last the visit anyway, wanting to report to Andrew when he came over later that everything had gone okay.

And, apart from that horrible conversation just now, it had. Though, I was beginning to wonder what dad had really asked for. *How* could he think that I was unwilling or being forced?

I had a sudden horror he might know something of my

past, but I was sure he'd have said something if he did.

Pasting a smile on my face, I stepped out onto the deck.

When dad headed to the front door late afternoon, I went with him, having this weird need to *see* him leave.

He hadn't brought up the age conversation again nor made any further comments about Andrew, but I was still feeling unsettled by the fact he had in the first place. I also kind of wanted him to leave on a good note, just to try and forestall him bringing it up again at some other time.

'The kids are really looking forward to tomorrow,' I said as I held the door open.

Dad smiled. 'I'm beginning to think I'll be exhausted before we get even half way around. That zoo hasn't grown since…' He cut off and I wondered if he was trying to remember the last time he'd been there.

'I don't think so,' I said, 'but there'll be things you've not seen. You'll know it like the back of your hand when you're done.'

He eyed me. 'You and the others are welcome to come, Owen.'

I shook my head. 'I want to… Any time away from the kids…' I forced my lips into a smile. I'd nearly said I want to spend time with Andrew, but bad topic just now. And the latter part was true too. Lisa and Matty seemed to feed off each other; they were exhausting!

Dad gave a nod, stepping out onto the porch. 'I guess Jamie and Megan *are* old enough to look out for themselves.'

'Pardon?' That came out mostly because it didn't really match the conversation thus far.

He looked over his shoulder at me. 'But Mr Gordon's

dubious relationship with you makes me wonder how safe my kids are.'

'No way!' I got out first, closing the door half on us. 'Don't make up stuff, Dad, that's a *really* bad idea. I'm with Andrew because I want to be, and him being gay does *not* make him a bad guardian. Please, don't be stupid about this.'

'Caring about my children is not stupid, Owen.'

I didn't know what to say, couldn't even make a retort about what he knew about caring given that he'd left us.

He smiled then and thanked me for lunch. 'I'll be here at ten tomorrow,' he said, turning away.

My stomach shifted uncomfortably and I still couldn't speak, just watched him walk to the blue car sitting on the drive.

Dad waggled fingers at me through the windscreen as he backed out, like all was perfectly okay, but no doubt he knew his words were driving knives into my veins.

It was good few minutes after I could no longer hear the car that I managed to pull myself together and go back inside. The thunk of the deadbolt soothed me somewhat and I knew I could keep my feelings hidden from my siblings.

- # -

A headache sent me to flake on my bed Sunday afternoon, but it seemed like I'd been there bare minutes before a small tap on my door jerked me out of a doze. 'Argh, wha-at?'

A universal word that also meant *come in* since that's what Lisa did. Her arrival forced me into a sit. 'Hey there, how was the zoo?'

She came up, chatting about various things but her actually

seeking me out wasn't that common so I knew she wanted to say something else.

Since she and Matty had just spent several hours with dad, I didn't want her to say it. I dreaded hearing that she wanted to live with him. In the end I said, 'What's up, Lis? Did you not enjoy the zoo, after all?'

'I liked the zoo,' she said a bit forcefully. 'But… dad…'

I held myself still so I didn't scare her. Inside I was all stiff.

'Dad said Andrew was filth,' she mumbled. 'And you too. I didn't like it.'

I was still now because I didn't know how to react. Dad had… *what?* He'd made those comments to me yesterday, but this— I rose, needed to…

… remember my little sister was with me, looking upset and puzzled.

'Dad's just a bit… frazzled at the moment, Lisa,' I said as calmly as I could. 'It's obviously hard, you know, coming back and finding us doing alright and really happy.'

'He doesn't like it,' she said.

'I know,' I told her with a sigh. 'But he—'

'He says it's safer if Matty and me live with him. I don't get why. It's not that bad here, is it?'

Though I was freaking out inside, I gave my sister a hug. 'It's not bad here at all,' I managed. 'And Andrew won't let anything happen to you, you know that.'

'I told dad that,' Lisa said, muffled, not pulling from my arms. 'That's when he said you guys were filth.'

'Just because I didn't shower this morning…'

Lisa shoved me, but she showed a bit of a smile.

'Lisa, don't believe everything he says, okay? He's still got things to sort out.'

She nodded, then told me she didn't want to live in St Louis anyway. 'All my friends are *here*. And Ginny's party is next week, I can't miss that.'

It was probably panic slip-sliding through my veins that had me say, 'Your teachers would never let you leave before the term ends, anyway. Think of all those tests they've got lined up for you.'

My sister screwed up her face. 'Maybe I *should* go live—'

'Come on,' I broke over top, while my inner voice told me what a dumb git I was. 'Let's go hear what tall tales Matty's telling.'

When she pulled another face, I nearly asked if dad had said the filth thing in front of him. Managed to force it back when I realised that asking might make her cotton on that the comment was more serious than I let on. She told me Matty hadn't shut up on the way home. 'You go listen, I'm gonna read in my room.'

I let her go, concerned but hoping she was okay, hoping that dad hadn't been explicit about being safe. I gritted my teeth, recalling what he'd said yesterday about the kids being safe around Andrew.

Because he was gay. Because of me.

I'd told Andrew about dad's words. He hadn't seemed too rattled, though had immediately started physically holding back. Difficult to do without being noticeable, more so when Matty was such a physical person himself.

I rubbed my brows; this recent thing with Lisa wasn't going to bring Andrew peace.

Not that he was getting any right now. Matty stood in front of him, giving the lowdown on the zoo like he'd had never been. Jamie and Megan were absent, probably gone the first moment Matty had opened his mouth.

'Owen!' Matty cried with joy, making Andrew twist.

His first expression was concern for me but when I smiled he mouthed *help me*. I came forward, perching on the couch arm. 'Matty, you know that Andrew's been to Lincoln Park several times.'

'Yeah, but not recently,' Matty told me. 'And there's lots of new stuff.' He turned back to Andrew and started in about meerkats and other cats.

'No wonder Lisa's in her room.'

Matty paid no attention to me.

I stayed, showing solidarity with Andrew, but also to *listen*. Except, Matty didn't mention filth or going to live with dad. Maybe he hadn't heard that or maybe the zoo and its occupants totally outranked it.

'How's the headache?'

I returned to reality, realising Matty was just stepping out onto the deck and Andrew had twisted on the couch to see me properly.

'Gone,' I said and smiled. 'Obviously couldn't beat Matty.'

Andrew chuckled. 'That kid's a born chatterbox, that's for sure. He'll be a great radio DJ one day.'

'Or tour guide,' I said.

Andrew smiled and squeezed my knee. After a moment he said softly, 'Something's up. Wasn't a nightmare, was it?'

I shook my head. 'It's nothing.'

'The kids got through today fine,' he murmured.

Obviously thought that was the thing, and I realised Lisa hadn't told him or even displayed her worry. 'Knew they would,' I managed, looking out through the door. Could just see Jamie standing on the lawn with his new headphones on.

Wondered if that was to avoid our little brother. I looked back at Andrew.

He sighed. 'I know it's a strange situation right now, but it'll get better.'

I sucked in my lips, hearing Lisa's words again.

'Okay,' he said. 'What is it?'

I revealed what Lisa had said. Andrew went rigid a second and then sagged. He didn't try to hide his anger or his concern. 'Poor kid. She and Matty don't deserve to be put on the spot like that. Is she okay?'

'I think so,' I said, 'though mostly because I don't think she understood what dad actually meant.'

'I'd like to believe your father would keep some decency around them, but...' He shook his head.

'Should we talk to them about it?' I asked.

Lisa and Matty were young but not stupid. And I wanted us to get in first in case dad got more open with his comments.

'Yes, I think we should, Owen,' Andrew agreed. 'But maybe in a day or two. I don't begrudge them wanting to see their dad so I'd rather not act like there's a hard line between us. And Matty enjoyed today obviously.'

'Yeah.'

'He didn't mention anything bad,' Andrew said quietly. 'I know you're wondering,' he added when I looked at him.

I gave a wry smile. 'Kinda think zoo stuff deletes everything else.'

Andrew gave a genuine grin.

[Four]

Jamie

This was absolutely surreal, our father driving me and Megan home from school and asking us how our day had been.

'Well, it was *school*, Dad,' I said.

'I thought your sister said you were on the Honour Roll.'

I glanced back at Megan as she sat behind him, and she pulled a bit of a face.

'Yeah,' I said, 'but it's still just school.'

Felt a bit annoyed now about letting her take the back seat, especially since she'd moved over behind dad. He'd barely be able to see her, and it wasn't like she was leaving space for Lisa and Matty. They were already at home. No, next door since Monday was one of the days Owen worked past the usual early finish.

Knowing it'd just be us and dad at home, if he came in, didn't make for an entirely fun thought. And an out-of-the-blue pick-up like this made me uneasy.

'So, what kind of car is this?'

Dad slid his gaze my way briefly. 'Just a run of the mill Nissan, Kid.'

I gave a nod, trying to hide my wince that he'd pronounced the car as *nee-sohn*, like most Americans actually, while to us it would always be *nis-san*.

'Are you learning to drive?' he asked.

'No.'

'Really?'

I looked at him, surprised he sounded so surprised. 'What

would I drive, Dad?'

He opened his mouth, probably to mention the Santa Fe in our garage, but said nothing and I didn't say that we'd never found its key. Shrugging, I said, 'I like walking anyway. Keeps me soccer fit.'

'You play?'

'Yeah.' Felt weird because I'd played back in New Zealand *and* here before he did a runner, and he'd been to several games.

'That's good to hear,' he said with a smile. 'I thought you might have had to stop.'

'Why would I have had to stop?'

I caught Megan's worried face but I didn't take it back.

'Well,' he said, head inclined briefly. 'I thought you might have had to go without some things while... I was away.'

I bit down to prevent, 'You mean, when you abandoned us?' He already knew we hadn't gone without anything, so I wasn't totally sure why he was asking here. I forced myself to shrug and say, 'We didn't. Did we, Megan?' I twisted to look back at her.

She swallowed but agreed, and said, 'All the bills were paid and everything.'

'Owen worked his—' I cut off. "Worked his arse off" probably wasn't a great thing to say even though it had kind of been true, even if dad had no idea about that. 'He was amazing, Dad.'

'How long's he been working for that man?'

'Andrew,' Megan piped up.

Dad didn't respond to the name reminder.

Despite him *also* knowing the duration, I said, 'For Andrew since September.' Then, totally getting the irony of saying it, I added Owen's old lie. 'Before that, Walgreens.'

Megan bit her lip, brows squeezing together.

'Some bills were a bit late early on,' I said, 'but nothing got repossessed or anything. Honestly, Dad, we owe Owen.'

Dad ran his tongue over his teeth.

'Better wage working for Andrew,' Megan said, 'and no uniform.' Her chuckle sounded a little wry. We had, of course, *never* seen a uniform.

'And how long have they been… together?'

'Uh,' escaped before I could stop it, because the question caught me off guard. I tried to remember if he'd asked Owen that already, or even Andrew. Couldn't remember and realised I wouldn't really get away with a response like, 'Why don't you ask Owen?' I shrugged. 'Since about November, I think. I can't recall. Megan?'

'Yeah, about then.'

I caught her smile, and grinned myself.

She leaned sideways a bit as if to see dad better (his brows were a little straight as he focused on the road). 'I never really pictured Owen for having a partner, you know. Yeah, that sounds mean,' she said when I arched a brow at her. 'But he's so happy with Andrew. It's great. He did so much for us, it's really nice to see him happy. He deserves it.'

'Hmm,' dad said.

Not sure what to make of that sound but fortunately the car pulled into our drive.

'Ah… you want to come in for a bit, Dad?' I managed. 'It is just me and Megan, though.'

'I don't like your brother with that man.'

Megan and I had both turned to our doors, but that made us stop.

'Dad,' I said, 'his name's Andrew, and Owen loves him.'

Dad's brows dipped low. 'It's filthy.'

'What?' Couldn't stop that coming out a yelp.

'Them together.'

'But… you didn't seem so…' Megan cut off like she didn't know how to say it. 'You've known over a week.'

'Didn't like it then either,' dad said quietly, 'but the kids were there.'

'They like Andrew,' I said, sharper than I probably should have.

'They'll have to learn not to,' he said. 'Since I'm back, his guardianship is no longer required.'

'It doesn't just stop because you're back,' I reminded him, refrained from saying that *his* track record of parental responsibility wasn't exactly hot.

Dad ran his tongue over his teeth. He glanced at me then over his shoulder at Megan. 'I'm your father and yet you seem to be hooked on that man. Why?'

'Why?' I echoed, puzzled.

Megan looked just as thrown, but she gave me a slight nod.

Hoping I'd read that gesture right, I said, 'Andrew's been an incredible guardian, Dad. The father we didn't have. Why are you surprised that we like him so much?'

His brows came down over his eyes. I sat stiff in my seat, waiting for his response, but he didn't give one. That made my nerves start to ping. Then he shrugged. 'He'll still be leaving. And he can take your brother with him. I don't want that sort of filth around my kids.'

'Owen's your kid too,' Megan said, and quickly hopped out of the car.

'No, he's not,' dad responded, but she didn't hear that.

'That's unfair, Dad,' I said, opening my own door. 'Owen *and* Andrew have been more like fathers to us than you have lately. So they're together? Being gay isn't illegal.'

Dad looked at me.

I said, 'Thanks for the ride' and jumped out, swinging the door closed hard. Felt dad's gaze all the way around the car and up the path. 'Hurry up and open the door,' I told Megan as if his gaze burned.

The car started before the door closed, but we heard it idle for a bit before eventually fading down the street. Once it did, I felt like I could breathe normally. 'Shit, I'll never complain about the school bus again.'

Megan grimaced. 'That was really… not fun.'

Andrew

'Who's that from?' Jamie asked.

'What?' Owen and I said in unison.

Jamie pointed at a green envelope on the bench, slightly under an AT&T bill. Owen picked it up. Turning it over, he seemed to jerk back a bit.

'It's for you,' he said, but didn't actually hold it out to me. Instead, he flipped it to face Jamie. 'Dad's handwriting, right?'

Jamie's brows came together as he leaned close, and Owen let him take the envelope. 'Don't know. Maybe.'

'Can *I* see it?' I asked, feeling a little taut. Not over them handling my mail but why I might be getting mail from their father.

Jamie handed me the envelope and I saw *Mr Gordon* scrawled across the front on an angle. No postage. Hand-delivered, which I was not comfortable with. Definitely less when Jamie said, 'He must have done that when he dropped us off.'

He took a breath about the same time Owen and I again went, 'What?' He swallowed, brows scrunching up. 'Me and Megan. He was waiting for us at school.'

Beside me, Owen went rigid, but before he could speak I told him to go and change.

'What? No, this—'

'I'm going to as well,' I said, starting to herd him. 'Jamie, find your sister and take a seat.'

'It was only a ride home,' Jamie said, but I could see it was more than that. His gaze kept going to the envelope I held.

'Just… do it, please, Jamie,' I said, then gave Owen a bit of a push to get him moving in front of me.

He went into his room without further resistance, and I headed for the other bedroom. I changed into jeans and t-shirt, but didn't feel relaxed because of the envelope. I opened it gingerly, but all it held was a ripped piece of notepaper. It carried one sentence only, and I screwed it up, anger rocketing through my veins along with a side of embarrassment.

I let out a soft swear. This unpleasant situation was turning worse. Glancing at the crumbled note then at the envelope on the bed, I realised Owen stood in the doorway. I couldn't call up a smile to reassure him; his brows were already tight. He asked what the note said.

'Nothing I want you to know about.'

That straightened him up and stepped him right into the room, pushing the door closed.

'Owen, I don't think—'

'Is he threatening you?'

'No, not—' I held my breath, let out a sigh. 'Promise me

you won't overreact. Your father's obviously got a lot going on right now.'

I couldn't credit that I was giving the man any sort of benefit of the doubt, but knew I was only doing it for Owen. His gaze slid from my face to my hand. He swallowed hard, like he was suddenly unsure, and then came forward. He held his hand out and after a few seconds I managed to let the wad of paper drop into his palm.

Owen looked at it for another couple of heartbeats, then slowly smoothed out the note. He clearly read it but I couldn't see any discernible reaction. That usually meant he didn't know *how* to react. Then he mumbled, 'You've got to be kidding.' Still didn't look up.

'Owen.'

He took a step back from me, but lifted his gaze; shock ruled. 'This is… is…' He shook his dark head. 'This is… *wrong!* That word was loaded with hurt and puzzlement.

'He did tell Lisa we were filth,' I murmured, in what was a poor attempt to try to explain Mr Tremayne's head space.

Owen's face crumpled for a second. 'Why would you remind me of that?' he rasped out. 'That's just—' He didn't finish, but I saw a flash of anger light his gaze as his chin tilted up. 'Yeah okay, he did, but this…' He held up the note. 'This is way worse, Andrew! *Paedophile?*

I reached for the note, seeing his hand trembling, but Owen took a few rapid steps beyond my reach.

'He called you a paedophile,' he croaked. 'That is *horrible* and. Not. True!' Then he said, 'Why are you just standing there?'

'Pardon?' I asked, honestly taken aback by the question.

'Why aren't you angry? Why aren't you on the phone to

Sergeant Morrison? Dad can't get away—' He started to turn.

I moved faster than I had in ages and got to the door before he did. He jerked back, fist closing around the paper. 'Owen, I'm angry,' I said quickly. 'I'm bloody furious, but it's just words on paper.'

Just words on paper obviously scrawled in a hurry going by the uneven nature of the ink and the hole stabbed through where the dot of the exclamation mark would normally be. Put in an envelope and left in the mailbox.

I hauled in a breath. Ink on paper that threatened my whole existence just by that one devastating word. 'Can I have it?'

Fingers fisted even tighter, then Owen held the paper out and I took it from him.

Get out of my house <u>PEDOPHILE</u>!

Capitals and underlined. The misspelling didn't make it any less vile.

'I'll talk to the sergeant, but I doubt he can do anything.'

'Dad thinks we're filth,' Owen said. 'And now that, and he's *already* made safety comments. *Why* can't Morrison do something? This stuff isn't fair, and it's wrong!'

'I know that,' I said 'Just… let's go hear what Jamie and Megan have to say about this ride.'

'I don't like that he showed up like that.'

'I'm not so comfortable myself,' I murmured, pocketing the note. 'But your father hasn't done anything untoward so we can't stop him seeing your siblings.'

Owen knew that as much as I did, though I was sure he viewed the note as a point of change. As I opened the door I quietly told him I didn't want Megan knowing what the note said. He nodded. I didn't want Jamie to know either, but he'd be harder to deflect.

Owen

Jamie probably didn't ask about the note because Megan was sitting on the armchair.

Andrew was relaxed and focused as he sat beside me, but I alternated between horrified and angry, with a bit of panic thrown in for good measure. I had to sit on my hands just so I didn't twist my fingers together.

'So,' Andrew said. 'Your dad gave you a ride home. That was nice.'

He even smiled a bit. I tried not to stare at him. Megan's lips curved up a little as she said, 'Yeah' in a puzzled voice.

'Wasn't actually,' Jamie muttered.

'Jamie, it wasn't…' Megan hunched up a shoulder, then looked at Andrew. 'It was weird. Normal, sort of. Almost like old times.' She almost looked guilty saying that.

'Did he come in?' Andrew asked.

She shook her head. 'We did ask, but he—'

'Didn't,' Jamie finished. 'He told us he didn't like you two together, that it was filthy.'

I stiffened but Andrew stayed totally still, just nodded.

Megan was staring down at her knees. 'He said he didn't say anything about it when you told him last week because Lisa and Matty were around, but he didn't… like it then either.'

I thought of the note in Andrew's pocket, tried to swallow back rising panic at what the words hinted at.

Andrew's jaw was taught, but then he shrugged. 'Well, as disappointing as that is, homophobia isn't illegal.'

'What?' Jamie cried. 'You're *accepting* what—'

'Jamie.'

My brother sat back scowling. 'You didn't see his face. *I* did. He wants you gone, wants Owen gone too.'

I jerked at that, somewhat surprised. Andrew's hand flattened on mine on my leg. I hadn't realised it'd escaped from under my butt and was picking at my jeans.

Megan drew in a breath. 'He said your guardianship isn't required, Andrew. Since he was back. I don't want him back, though.' She looked at Jamie this time and he nodded but held his silence. Looked like it took effort.

Just as Andrew started to respond, Megan spoke again, 'He asked what we'd gone without, even though he knows we didn't.' She frowned. 'It was like we didn't have that conversation on Saturday.'

'Dad seems unable to get his head around the fact that we weren't useless without him,' Jamie muttered.

'It is a lot for him to take in, I expect,' Andrew said.

'Did he tell you anything more about what he's been doing all this time?' I asked.

They both shook their heads. My sister's voice wobbled as she said, 'Why won't he?'

I reckoned it was because dad didn't realise that he should. And, well, we all seemed totally unable to confront him straight out about it.

Jamie chewed on his lip. 'He asked how long you'd been working for Andrew.'

That surprised me. 'He already… God, why's he so fixated on that?' I looked at Andrew but he just gave a slight shake of his head.

'I told him September and that, well, you'd been at Walgreens before then,' Jamie said. 'Seemed better to keep to that…' He trailed off but I heard 'lie' as plain as if he'd said it.

I winced, remembering all the anger that had caused, how Jamie had reacted when he'd first heard the truth. 'Yeah,' I got out, miraculously without a tremor. Beside me Andrew stayed quiet and I couldn't tell what he was thinking. I was afraid to look at him directly.

Megan then added that dad had also asked how long we'd been together as a couple. 'Jamie said November.'

Jamie squinted like he had something in his eye. 'I couldn't remember if you'd told him. Didn't think I should lie or anything.'

It's okay, Jamie,' Andrew said. 'That's all fine, and the truth is better.'

Jamie grimaced, locked gazes with me. Last year had been based on a lot of lies and secrets, which occasionally came back to niggle. But November was a truth and I'd been seventeen. Dad couldn't do anything about that.

Andrew brought us back to the car ride with, 'Did he raise his voice at all?'

Jamie shook his head. 'Didn't yell anything. Didn't actually seem *angry*.' He looked across at Megan.

'Yeah,' she said. 'Just… firm.' Her expression twisted. 'Like he was sure he'd get what he wanted. He didn't even seem to care when I said how happy you were, Owen.'

I ghosted a smile her way.

'But he did keep calling you "that man", Andrew,' Jamie said. 'How many times did we call him out on that, Megs?'

She scowled. 'A lot!'

I couldn't voice my appreciation of their support.

Jamie let out a noisy breath. 'I don't really think he wants us back. Like a family, I mean. He just seems really anti you guys.' He looked at me and Andrew. 'I think he's gonna use your relationship against you.'

'How?' I blurted. 'It's all legal. And Andrew's guardianship is all legal. That doesn't just dissolve because dad's back.'

'I told him that,' Jamie said. 'He said Andrew would still be leaving.'

'Do you think—' I cut off, remembering that we'd not revealed the note's message. Asking Andrew if he thought dad would somehow try to push that angle was a bad idea right here and now.

Andrew looked at me, revealing worry for a split second before reverting to basic concern.

Jamie cocked his head, then asked what the note had said.

Unsurprisingly, Megan leaned forward. 'What note?'

'Just something addressed to me, Megan,' Andrew said.

'From… dad?' she asked quietly.

'Yes, almost certainly.'

There was no "almost" about it, but I guessed Andrew was trying to shield her as long as possible. She didn't question what the note said, just got to her feet. 'I'm gonna get the kids.'

The way she moved made it clear she'd not have listened if one of us had tried to stop her.

Once the front door closed, Jamie said, 'What'd it say?'

'It was nothing,' I piped up before Andrew could speak.

'Yeah, right,' Jamie said. 'For a guy who kept secrets so bloody well, you suck at keeping your emotions hidden.'

'That is a very unpleasant thing to say.'

Jamie and I both looked at Andrew, because it had sounded so odd and stiff. I caught a slight tightening of his mouth but he didn't speak further. I shifted our clasp just a bit to give him a squeeze of appreciation, because Jamie's words *had* hurt and I was gladdened Andrew had spoken. Even if Jamie had been truthful.

And it wasn't surprising about my emotions right now. Seemed like every time I shoved one emotion back, another would leap out to claim its place.

'I'm not a child,' Jamie grouched.

Andrew sighed. 'Jamie, he simply wrote I should get out of his house.'

'This isn't his house! What else did he say?'

'Pardon?

'I'm not stupid, either,' my brother said. 'If that's all he wrote, then you'd let me see it.'

Which was true, in fact.

'Sorry, but I will not let you see the note.'

Jamie looked at me and I shook my head.

'Did he threaten you?' he asked after a moment.

'Not necessarily,' Andrew replied.

I hunched my shoulders. Not directly, but that word… Jamie looked like he was gearing up to push, but Andrew rose. 'Come on, you,' he said to me. 'Dinner duty calls.'

I let him pull me up and direct me away from Jamie who, when I glanced back from the kitchen, was still on the couch. He scowled when he caught my gaze, then reached for the TV remote.

Later that evening, I was snoozing on Andrew's shoulder when Jamie said, 'We didn't tell you earlier, Andrew, but dad asked why we were so hooked on you when *he* was our dad.'

He probably thought I was totally asleep, but if he'd really wanted me not to hear that he should have waited until Andrew was alone!

I pushed myself upright, getting hair out of my face. Jamie's scowl, like everything was my fault, startled me enough that I flinched when Andrew tugged my t-shirt straight. He instantly murmured an apology, making me spout, 'Not your fault.' I turned to my brother. 'What did you tell him?'

'Ah, just, you know… that Andrew was an incredible guardian.'

Andrew let out a soft breath. 'Thank you, Jamie.'

'Well, you are,' Jamie muttered, looking a little embarrassed. He gave a half shrug. 'Told him you were both more like fathers than he'd been lately.'

My mouth dropped open a second, before I managed a noisy swallow.

Jamie frowned. 'It's not that gobsmacking, Owen.'

I tilted my chin but didn't respond.

'That was nice of you to say, Jamie, thank you,' Andrew said, hand patting my knee. 'However…'

He didn't finish that, making me twist to look at him. Across from us, Jamie straightened. 'How*ever?*'

Andrew ran his tongue around his teeth, clearly in two minds about whether he should speak. He shifted position on the couch, almost like he was going to stand, and said, 'Jamie, I do very much appreciate your support, but I just wonder… Hmm, I don't believe your father does.'

'Of course not,' Jamie said. 'He doesn't want you here.'

I scowled at my brother. 'You don't have to *say* it.'

'Stick it,' Jamie told me. 'What do you mean, Andrew?'

'My official status has been something of a surprise to him,' Andrew said, getting to his feet.

I opened my mouth to say something or other but he gave a gentle shake of his head, making me suck my lips inward.

'I'm not sure *why*,' Andrew continued, 'but between it and you kids revealing how you coped after his disappearance, I believe he's feeling… unneeded.' He held up both palms—one toward me, the other toward Jamie as we opened our mouths.

Miracle palms because neither of us spoke.

Andrew gave an almost amused smile, but then he dropped his hands and said, 'I think he needs to know that he's been missed; that's why—'

'Missed like a fork in the eye,' Jamie spouted.

'Fucking A,' I said beneath my breath.

Jamie nodded at me. Then he asked Andrew why he was playing devil's advocate.

Andrew rubbed his neck. 'I'm not, especially. I just think that the more you tell him about how well you did, the more distant he'll become.'

'Which is what we want,' Jamie said.

'I don't mean—' Andrew broke off with a sigh. 'Look, just be circumspect when you talk with your father. He's made some serious mistakes, definitely. I'm not saying he hasn't, but he doesn't seem to see things the same way. Therefore, it'll be hard for him to understand why no one is overjoyed at his return. Hearing you say how well you did, how apparently non-missed he was, won't help his state of mind.' He looked down at me. 'Owen, you understand what I'm saying, don't you?'

Maybe he appealed to me because I was the eldest, I wasn't sure, but I nodded. Though, I would have nodded even if I didn't understand. He was trying to be fair and reasonable and I loved him for it. I got up and gave him a hug, making Jamie groan. Even though my brother was rolling his eyes, I knew he also understood.

Especially when he said, 'Bags not me having to tell dad we missed him.'

Andrew's breath lifted hair at my temple. When I glanced up at him, his lips curved into a small smile. Then I said, 'He probably won't believe me if I said it. We'll have to get Megan to do it.'

'Good plan,' Jamie said instantly.

'You don't actually have to say the word "missed".' Andrew sounded a little frustrated. 'Just that you thought about him now and then. Nice thoughts,' he added when Jamie opened his mouth.

Jamie pulled a face.

I didn't say that I, at least, had barely thought about dad at all, nice or otherwise.

- # -

Tuesday afternoon, I was sitting with Matty while he did his homework. Probably a dud helper given I'd left school half way through my junior year, but I wasn't actually paying him that much attention anyway, tracing knots in the dining table.

'Owen, if dad's back, why isn't he here?'

I jerked and straightened. Matty was looking at me across the table. 'Um,' I got out. 'What do you mean, here?'

'*Living* here,' Matty said. 'Why does he come around like he's just visiting?'

'Well, right now, he *is* just visiting.'

'So… he's not coming home?' Matty cocked his head, brows knitting over his pale eyes, obviously puzzled.

'I don't know, Matty,' I told him, even as I remembered

what Jamie had said last night about his and Megan's car-ride discussion with dad. 'He might come back, but not here.'

'Why not?'

'Because he's not—' I cut off. Drawing in a breath, I said, 'Matty, he's barely explained why he left, why he never contacted us. He doesn't... doesn't really feel like dad anymore.'

He looked at me a while, then down at his workbook. 'Yeah,' he said to the workbook, 'but... he *is* dad.'

'I know,' I told him, though didn't know how to explain things in a way he could really get it. So I said, 'Don't you like having Andrew here?'

Matty perked up on the bench. 'Yeah, of course.'

'Well, it's just... Matty, if dad came to live with us again then Andrew wouldn't be around so much. He wouldn't be your guardian anymore.'

Matty cocked his head.

'Understand?'

He eyed me with his pale blue eyes just like mum's. It was actually hard to not look away. His head cocked to the other side. 'You don't want dad here.'

I sat back, hands in my lap, and shook my head. 'No, I don't. He's taken too long to come back, yet thinks he can because he thinks nothing has changed.'

'Lots has changed,' Matty said.

His offended tone made me smile. He opened his mouth as if to begin a list of those things, but I got in first with, 'Anyway, there's still a lot of stuff to sort out about this.'

'I'd still get rides in Andrew's car, right? Even if he wasn't guardian.'

Unexpectedly, that made me laugh. Matty looked across at

me like I was making fun of him or something. I cleared my throat. 'I don't know, Matty. I'm not sure he'd come here much if he stopped being guardian.'

'But *you're* here, Owen,' he said with scrunched up puzzled brows. 'He'd come to see you.'

'Yeah,' I said, smiling at him. Though, if dad came back for good, I wasn't sure I could be in the same house with him. And I'd definitely not make Andrew come here to see me if I did have to stay. I let out a sigh. 'Dad... doesn't seem to like Andrew much.'

'But he's amazing!'

I let out a soft laugh, even as I said, 'That's partly why, I think. You know, like Andrew's been like a dad to you guys and so dad's feeling...' I couldn't find the right word. Jealous? Unneeded, like Andrew had said last night?

'Second best,' my brother announced.

'Ah, yeah.'

'But... he's still *dad*,' Matty said.

'I know, Matty. Anyway, it's all kind of complicated.'

My little brother shrugged and returned to his homework. After a second he muttered, 'Two dads are better than none.'

I chomped on my lip, staring, but he didn't look up.

[Five]

Owen

I wasn't comfortable with Sergeant Morrison phoning Andrew out of the blue. Definitely not in the middle of the day when we were at work and with Andrew looking grim as he talked. Not angry or overly upset, so I was pretty sure my brothers and sisters were okay.

That meant the topic was probably dad.

After my chat with Matty on Tuesday, I'd reported to the sergeant some of the things dad was saying about us, what he'd told my brothers and sisters.

Andrew had talked to his lawyer, I think, about that horrid note but it was me who'd told the sergeant about it. Mostly because it had just come out in my blurt of the stuff dad had been doing. The sergeant had said he'd talk to dad, but it seemed that calling people names and suggesting stupid things didn't carry enough whatever to prevent dad being able to call us or drop by.

I honestly struggled with dad being against me and Andrew. Though he'd told me our age difference was disgusting, his main dislike simply seemed to be us. Us together. Which hurt since dad had never displayed homophobia before. I couldn't recall him revealing it at any time, even when there'd been gay hate crimes on the news.

Part of the struggle was because of dad's change of tune. I knew now that he'd just hidden his dislike when he'd first heard, but to go from hiding that to telling my little sister that Andrew and I were filth and repeating it to Megan and Jamie was something my brain had difficulty reconciling. To be suddenly so mean about it, to write that horrible note to Andrew… How had he gotten to this point?

'What now?' I asked once Andrew had hung up.

He swiped his hair back. 'You and I have an appointment at the station this afternoon.'

'Why?'

'Your father wants to meet with you.'

I went rigid in my chair. 'Why?'

'I don't know, Owen,' Andrew sighed. 'Probably just wants a one-on-one.'

'Wait, without you? No way!'

Andrew inclined his head. 'I can't prevent it, I'm afraid. I'm not your guardian.'

I breathed out. Probably I could decline to meet dad, but… maybe this was him trying to be better and to clear the air, and the police station was neutral ground. I pulled a face. 'What time do we have to be there?'

'Three.'

Another facial twist. Two and a half hours to stew over it. I cussed, and then turned on a smile for Andrew because he hadn't really stopped looking grim. 'I'll be okay,' I told him. 'And I guess… Well, hopefully it's a good step.'

Andrew nodded, then changed the subject entirely, bringing my focus back to work.

- # -

The appointment wasn't just for me and dad to talk, but for Morrison to speak with Andrew and me too. Andrew revealed that as he drove. I just nodded.

Instead of having to wait in the reception we were shown to the sergeant's office straight away. My apprehension lessened when I saw dad wasn't there, but I still looked at Andrew, puzzled.

'Your father hasn't arrived yet,' the sergeant said.

'Oh.'

As we took seats at a small round table, he asked how things had been at home.

Andrew looked at me and I gave a half shrug. Given dad wasn't afraid of airing his opinions to my brothers and sisters, upsetting us all, I didn't think things were brilliant. However, since Tuesday night, when I'd called the sergeant to complain, it'd been pretty settled. Dad hadn't shown up again to give anyone a ride home.

'Megan said she had a blank call yesterday but… things seem okay.' Then added, with a sigh, 'Matty keeps asking when he's next coming over.' I wanted "next" to be "never" but had no idea how to make that a reality.

Sergeant Morrison nodded. When he didn't say anything I asked why dad wanted to speak with me. I'd had a couple of hours thinking on it and it really seemed weird given what he'd been saying.

'To clear the air, I believe.'

I looked at Andrew; he'd reverted to looking grim. 'He could try apologising to *you*,' I said, thinking of the note.

Andrew shook his head. 'I understand his anxiety.'

'I don't,' I said stubbornly. 'You're an awesome guardian, and *we've* done nothing wrong.' I turned back to the sergeant, about to say that I didn't want to meet with dad.

'Your partnership has a loophole,' the sergeant said.

'What?'

Andrew shifted in his chair. 'Pardon?'

Sergeant Morrison pursed his lips for a second and then said, 'I know you're of legal age for a sexual relationship, Owen, but being both your employer and your direct boss gives Mr Gordon a position of authority over you.'

After a second, I said, 'So?' I glanced between him and Andrew, who'd straightened in his seat and was slowly nodding. 'What's going on?' I asked. 'What're you nodding for?'

'You are aware of this factor, Mr Gordon?' the sergeant asked a little firmly.

'I'm am, yes,' Andrew said.

'*What* factor?' I asked.

Andrew looked at me. 'My being your boss makes our relationship a little less legal.'

'What? How?'

'It just… does,' Andrew said.

'A position of authority clouds the possibility of legal consent by the person under that authority,' Morrison said.

I looked at him, puzzled, and then… 'Wait, you think I'm being *forced* into this relationship?'

'I don't think that at all, Owen,' he said. 'Sit down.'

Took a few seconds for me to obey. I looked at Andrew. 'You knew about this?'

He nodded. 'I would never abuse that authority, Owen, but it…' He trailed off.

I'd never known the issue existed, and he'd never played the boss card. I turned back to the sergeant. 'What about *my* status?'

'Emancipation does not change your age, Owen,' he replied. 'You *are* still a minor.'

Which I knew, but I guess I didn't really get what this all meant.

'Your father has brought the illegality to my attention,' the sergeant said quietly, 'and I cannot just ignore it.'

'But, what…' I took a breath. '*Why?* Even if dad wouldn't accept I was willing, why would he go further with it?'

Andrew drew in a quiet breath. 'He's pushing a legal stance. Am I right, Sergeant?'

He nodded.

'A legal stance?' I queried. 'But *how?* I'm seventeen and I'm not under your guardianship.'

'No,' Andrew agreed. 'But you *are* my employee, Owen, and that makes being seventeen a problem.'

I felt totally insulted, grinding out that I was not a child.

'Owen,' Sergeant Morrison said, 'while you are seventeen and Mr Gordon's employee, you *are*. Though I know your relationship is fully consensual, your age and employment do make it illegal in the eyes of state law.'

'That's stupid.'

'It's there for protection,' Morrison told me.

I stared at him. Beside me Andrew said nothing, just looked pensive. I asked why dad had brought it up.

'To get us apart, Owen,' Andrew said softly.

I turned to him, hurt and puzzled. 'I know he doesn't like us together, but why would…' I sagged in my chair, unable to understand how simple homophobia led to me and Andrew sitting in front of Sergeant Morrison talking about some random tiny piece of law.

Andrew gave a weird smile. 'The only way he can break us up is to push your age. Go through legal channels.'

'Legal channels,' I whispered, stomach taking a drop as if it hit only now that there was something truly wrong with the equation. I looked across at Morrison. 'How can he do that?' I croaked out. 'He's not been *around*. Him poking his nose in isn't fair!' The sergeant opened his mouth but I got over him, to Andrew, 'I'm not letting you go.'

His smile was full of love. 'Same here.'

Morrison cleared his throat. 'Could I get some focus please?'

I shifted straight in my seat again, but I was beginning to boil with mutiny. If dad thought our meeting was going to be all nice and friendly, he was in for a surprise.

'I am not going to force the pair of you to dissolve your relationship,' Morrison said. He slanted a wry smile at me. 'I don't want *that* fight.'

My chin tilted up without my control.

'But your father's claim cannot be ignored either. It is rare this part of the law ever sees the light, but it is law. If we don't temper it, your father will have legal right to press charges.'

'What?' I gasped out.

Andrew was grim again.

'And *that* would likely lead to the dissolution of Mr Gordon's guardianship of your siblings.'

'But that's… dumb,' I said hollowly. 'I don't even think he wants custody again. He says he wants Andrew out, but he hasn't really said *he* wants *in*. Why would he bother doing all this? Does he think he hasn't done enough damage yet?'

I coughed to clear my throat. Andrew squeezed my knee. He didn't speak but I saw in his gaze that he'd fight tooth and nail for my siblings. I couldn't quite get my smile straight. The sergeant didn't respond to me. Maybe he didn't know just why dad was doing it either.

'Sergeant,' Andrew said quietly. 'You said the claim can't be ignored. What do you intend to do?'

Morrison seemed grateful that at least one of us was thinking. 'I'll be imposing a couple of restrictions,' he said. 'The first is that you will limit your time alone together.'

He paused here, gaze on me. Obviously waiting for my response, but I just looked at him, wondering how the hell anyone could actually police that. When I didn't respond, his gaze shifted back to Andrew. 'The second restriction, Mr Gordon, is that you don't spend the night at the Tremayne house.'

'Pardon?' Andrew got out, shifting in his chair.

'What?' I said. 'But…' I rubbed both brows. 'Andrew's their guardian, how—'

'And he will remain guardian, Owen,' Morrison spoke over me. 'That is what we're trying to protect here.'

I swallowed.

'Owen,' he said, 'it's your relationship—your *sexual* relationship—with Mr Gordon that's under the law's eye.' He looked pained having to say it. 'These two conditions are attempts to *restrict* that particular side. If the opportunities are removed, then the law is less likely to be broken.'

I sat silent.

'Do you understand?'

I mumbled I did. Felt massively embarrassed about it actually, but at least I held back saying we weren't rabbits. I looked at Andrew. 'What do you think?'

'I think the sergeant is trying to do his best for us, Owen,' he responded, 'and we need to agree.'

That left me feeling a little chastised, and I swallowed deeply.

'It's only a short while,' he said gently, giving my knee another squeeze. 'Until you turn eighteen.' He looked across at Morrison.

He nodded. 'When you turn eighteen, Owen, there is no law that can prevent your relationship or your working for Mr Gordon at the same time.'

I sucked in air. My birthday was almost two months away. Shit, it might as well have been years it suddenly felt that long, but I turned to Andrew and said, with more confidence than I felt, 'Okay, we can do this.'

'Yes,' he said. 'We can.'

But then I said, 'I work for you.'

A brow went up.

'I mean—*with* you, in your office.' I turned to the sergeant. 'It's just us there, won't…'

Morrison shook his head. 'The easiest way to nullify this law is to actually stop working for Mr Gordon, but I know that's not really going to suit you. I will not enforce an office separation either, but I suggest you keep to a professional relationship there.'

I sat back in my seat, nodding. Wasn't like we'd ever made love in the office anyway.

Morrison started to speak, and his phone rang. As he got up I twisted to Andrew. Despite what I'd said earlier, I whispered, '*Is* this gonna work?'

He let out a soft sigh. 'I hope so. We need to trust the sergeant.'

'Yeah,' I breathed, then realised Morrison had his eye on me as he set the phone down. 'Dad's here?'

'Yes, he's arrived.'

'I don't really want to speak with him,' I said, even as I

stood. What if he brought the law up? 'Does he know about these restrictions?'

'I have told him I'll act,' Morrison responded. 'But not *how*.'

'If he asks, can I say something?'

Morrison seemed to hesitate, but then agreed I could.

The knock on the door brought Andrew to his feet, shielding me, but it was just an officer bringing news that dad was in room three.

'Thanks, Simon,' Morrison said, and turned to me. 'Come on, Owen, I'll take you there. Mr Gordon, please remain here.'

Andrew nodded. He kissed my temple and sat down again.

My father was standing by one of the chairs, but he came forward as I entered with Sergeant Morrison. 'Hello, Owen.'

He said that with a smile so I forced back all I'd just learnt and smiled too. 'Hi, Dad, how's it going?'

As he answered, I obeyed Morrison's pointing-finger direction to the chair opposite dad. But when I realised the sergeant was shifting back toward the door I stopped. My mouth opened even as my brain was telling me there was nothing to be afraid of.

It was just me and dad.

He clearly hated Andrew.

'Sergeant,' I got out.

'I cannot stay, Owen,' he responded, 'but this room is monitored, like all our interview rooms. And Simon will be out in the hall if either of you need him.'

I forced a nod, while my father thanked the sergeant for his cooperation. Morrison's eyes narrowed momentarily; he said he'd return in half an hour and then the door clicked loudly closed. Since dad hadn't been violent, I guessed a police presence was unneeded and *I* obviously wasn't being treated as a kid here either. Found that a touch ironic, but knew I had to do my best to be an adult.

'You look spruced up,' dad said into the silence.

I turned to him. 'Work.'

'Oh… that's right.' He was smiling but it didn't seem to go far. 'What is it you do for Mr Gordon?'

I fought against speaking out of turn or saying something really, really stupid. 'I'm an assistant.' Though he already knew, I explained again what my duties were. As I did so, I relaxed; I liked talking about my work, and chatting was eating up the half hour.

Dad nodded along and smiled, even asked a question or two. So when he said, 'I don't want that boy-fucker around my kids' I was completely thrown.

Had to backtrack to find where that had come from, but it hadn't come from anywhere except the total blue. I couldn't even get out, 'What?'

He seemed to be waiting for my reaction but I didn't have anything together. His smile wasn't pleasant. 'Your sort foul the earth, Owen.'

Air wasn't reaching my lungs, so I forced in a deep breath. Dad opened his mouth but before he could let loose something else I said, hurt, 'What do you have against gay people, Dad?'

'One killed your mother.'

'*What?*

Dad smirked.

'What do you mean?' I got out, fingers gripping the table edge. 'It was a… car accident.'

'Yes, it was,' he said with a nod. 'Caused by a faggot texting his faggot boyfriend.'

I recoiled at the venom in his voice. Details of the accident had been kept from us bar that the other car had run a red light. Not speeding or anything like that, after all, but distraction.

'You… you're against Andrew and me because of *mum?* I couldn't get my head around it. I mean, I sort of could… but then he'd abandoned us and I hadn't been gay then and… 'It could have been anyone, Dad.'

'True, Owen,' he said. 'But that's not the only reason I think that you're filth.'

I sat like I'd been belted across the face, but still managed to get out, 'I'm not filth.'

Dad laughed, making me uncomfortable how genuine it sounded. 'You slept with men for money. Tell me how that's not filthy and disgusting?'

My heart missed beats all over the place. 'How do you know?' I asked hollowly. How would he *know* that?

Dad simply inclined his head.

I repeated the question in as stable a voice as I could manage.

'You think I'd come back without doing some checking?'

'I don't know,' I said. 'But… that's ages in the past. And I only did it because *you* weren't here for us and we needed money!'

'Don't pin your whoring ways on me, Kid.'

I leapt up, unable to stop myself. That he stayed smirking in his chair rattled me even more.

'Does Mr Gordon know you were a slut for others?'

I almost gagged. 'You can't… This…'

'Oh, he doesn't? Well, won't he be surprised?' dad said. 'Bet he'll run a mile when he finds out.' He shrugged. 'Works for me.'

'Why are you doing all this?' I rasped out, back-stepping. 'We've done *nothing wrong!*'

Dad scraped back his chair, making me flinch. 'Because I don't want you tainting my family any more, Owen, or that man in my house. Getting rid of both of you will make me a happy *father.*'

Tears stung as I looked at my dad standing there—so different from the one I'd known, different even to the one who'd come back only a few weeks ago. With a hand on the door handle, I said, 'You're no father. You won't get custody of them.'

'Yes, I will, Owen.'

He smiled and I had the door open and was out in the hall in an instant. Not to talk to the cop there, not even to head back to Morrison's office and Andrew, but to get out of the building into the fresh air. I gagged into some bushes, took off at a run when someone growled, 'Hey!'

My brain tried to insert some sense, like how I was making a spectacle of myself sprinting in work pants and shirt, but the need to outrun dad and his words and his smirk was stronger.

-# -

Sitting on the warm sand, arms around my knees, I wasn't wondering how dad knew about that long ago prostitution and what it meant, but what he'd said about mum. That it was a gay man texting his partner who'd caused the accident. How did dad know that? Did Sergeant Morrison? Was it even true?

And it couldn't have been why he'd deserted us that

January, four months after mum's death. He'd not said a word about it, not even in the couple of mentions of the other driver. It had always just been "the other driver". I couldn't recall if we'd even been told it'd been a guy.

How could that all cause dad's hate *now?*

I hugged my knees tighter and let grief seep out for a brief moment.

Around me guys and girls sunbathed and kids played in the shallow water along the shore. I was out of place in my work clothes but the soothing heat kept me seated until I finally realised Andrew wouldn't know where the hell I'd gone and he couldn't contact me. My phone was in my backpack in the car, along with my wallet.

I was gonna have a long walk home.

And some apologising to do, even though it had been quite a while since I'd done a bolt like this.

I sighed and rubbed my eyes, then rose and brushed sand off my pants.

Instead of walking through town, I headed down the lakefront trail. If Andrew was looking for me he'd drive by eventually because the lakefront remained a haunt of mine. Walking there kept me calm because of the distant views now and then of Andrew's building.

Shit, Dad knows.

I tried to keep that out as I walked but it wouldn't stay away. Did the sergeant know he knew? Was that part of the reason for the restrictions now? He'd not stopped the prostitution back then; could dad know that and be applying pressure? Would it add to dad's case?

We'd been open and honest when Andrew was made guardian, so I wasn't sure how it could, but I suddenly wasn't sure about much at all.

'It'll be fine when I hit eighteen,' I muttered to myself, eye on the hazy bulk of the miles-away John Hancock.

I hated that I hadn't known of that piece of legislation, though it wouldn't have stopped me. Was kinda flattered it hadn't stopped Andrew, but I was a bit annoyed he'd not revealed it. Though, he *had* looked startled earlier; maybe he'd forgotten.

I sighed. Man, my birthday was freaking ages away. Two months was a long time to be constantly apart at night, a long time to deal with dad if he kept up attacks like the one he'd just delivered.

I leaned on the rocks, gaze down the coast. Despite all that dad had said, I still didn't think he wanted custody of my brothers and sisters because he *wanted* to be a family again. So I was puzzled at why he seemed so against Andrew having guardianship, against the fact that someone really competent was looking out for everyone.

Maybe the driver who'd caused mum's accident *had* been gay, but why did dad feel so much hate that he was willing to hurt everyone to get Andrew out of our lives just because he was gay too? I swallowed; not out of *my* life. Just my brothers and sisters' lives. Seemed pretty clear that when Andrew went I'd be going with him, even if dad was trying to split us up.

I just didn't get it, and the words dad'd just used shouted in my head again, making me flinch. Jesus, even Jamie hadn't called me names like that at the height of his anger last year, and he'd been on fire a *lot*. I felt insulted and hurt, and angry too because it hadn't been like that.

Which was dumb, because it had.

When all was said and done, I'd been a whore.

Flinching from myself, I fought to keep all those memories back. They'd been locked away for months now, but… My next breath was ragged. Did dad know about—

An invisible fist to the stomach made me gag.

What if he knew about Jack Wheeler?

A horribly cold part of me said he didn't because what he'd just said at the police station was nothing to what he could have said about *that* man. Another part told me dad was just biding his time. Obviously wasn't going to spend it feeling any sorrow for what I'd gone through anyway.

I tried to be sensible that dad couldn't know that final stuff, just as he obviously didn't know about Andrew's specific involvement.

'Stop thinking,' I rasped out loud, forced myself to continue walking.

Except my brain hadn't finished dissecting dad's words and now it wouldn't get off Jack Wheeler. As I turned the corner onto the stretch of road that included the east entrance of Calvary Cemetery, I realised there *was* a way dad could know, or part know.

The insurance that had paid the big chunk of last year's medical costs.

Dad had never touched his bank account or the joint account, but he could still have been logging into other accounts. I'd opened the letter from the insurance company accepting the costs, but there'd been some on-line details. Though, to be honest, I couldn't figure out why dad might suddenly check out insurance.

A very nice black Mercedes came around the corner toward me. My heart thwacked at the sight and I almost got clipped by a car coming behind me as I hurried across the road.

Andrew was pulling into the cemetery entrance so I hoped he missed that bit. He jumped out and then just stood there, door open.

'I'm sorry.'

'Are you alright?' he returned.

I nodded. 'Physically, yeah.'

Andrew relaxed enough to close the door and say, 'Come on, let's walk.'

I moved beside him and he didn't flinch when I twined fingers with his, just squeezed back.

The late afternoon light caused the white tombs and markers to turn golden, the grass to seem even more bright green. We walked, silent, until we got to the Lynch monument. I loved the pointed-square layout with the mausoleum in the centre, double stone caskets in front and behind it, and single caskets in the points. Well, three points, the north-west corner remained empty.

Andrew and I perched against the angled stone wall surrounding the site where the kneeling angels overlooked the entrance.

'Are we alright like this?' Like being alone.

Andrew let out a noise that sat somewhere between amusement and anger, but responded with, 'I don't quite have the courage to make love in a cemetery.'

I looked at him, moving in closer. He slung an arm around my shoulder and hugged me to him. 'It's okay, Owen. It's okay.'

'Yeah,' I said, but didn't feel so confident all of a sudden. Not with dad's words yammering in my head. 'Sorry I ran. I should have come to you.'

'You haven't done that in a long time,' he said softly. 'Why did you? He didn't hurt you, did he?'

My shaking head wobbled his shoulder. 'He knows about… the prostitution. But not you because he… Well, he wondered if you knew I'd been… a slut for others.'

'What?' Andrew got out with a distinct chill.

'He reckons once you know, you'll run a mile.' I sniffed.

Andrew shifted, pushing me off him, holding me away with both hands. 'He said that to you?'

He looked as astounded as I'd felt when dad had spoken. I gave a jerky nod and repeated some of the conversation, though not that horrible B-word. Andrew's grip tightened but I didn't think he was aware of it. Definitely angry. 'I cannot believe Morrison left you alone with him.'

'I don't think…' I peeled one of his hands from my arm, making him drop the other with a murmured apology. 'I don't think Morrison thought that would happen.'

'Still, he can't have thought *nothing* would go on.'

I mumbled something about a rock and a hard place, then, 'Dad's definitely working to get you and me gone. Apart first, apparently, but gone.'

'I really cannot understand why, Owen.'

I whispered what dad said about the driver. Andrew's brows shot up. His lips parted but he didn't speak; clearly as stunned as I was.

'Gays never bothered him before,' I said.

'That's an incredibly weak reason to attack his own son.'

'I wasn't even gay back then,' I mumbled. Jeez, half the time I *still* didn't think of myself that way. Telling dad the other day had been the first time since Jamie had forced the words out of me months ago, and despite what anyone might think it had taken a lot of courage.

Andrew's arm came around me again. I felt drained, like my hard-won self-confidence was deserting me. 'Thanks for coming to find me.'

He kissed the top of my head, didn't speak. My indrawn breath wobbled all the way in and came out just as poor.

After a while I asked if he was staying over tonight.

Andrew stiffened a second and then said, 'Yes, but from tomorrow, no.'

'This is so dumb.'

'The sergeant's doing his best, Owen.'

'It's still dumb,' I said. 'How can you be a real guardian if you're not there at night at all?'

I rose, rubbing my pants in case the wall was dirty. Andrew looked sombre. My comment was probably dumb too since even now he only stayed over Thursday through Sunday nights. The others he was at home. It was a structure we'd put in place ages ago to give everyone space. Having the option completely stopped was what annoyed me. I kicked at a stray stone on the path. 'We don't even share a bed every time you stay,' I grumbled.

A smile flashed across Andrew's face and he got up. 'Come on, let's walk before I throw caution to the wind.'

I shoved him, making him chuckle.

'Do you know that Chicago's only female mayor is buried here?' Andrew asked after few steps.

I arched a brow. 'Is she? You better show me.'

Andrew snorted. I knew all about Jane Byrne because we'd already spent time wandering around this quiet and beautiful cemetery. Right now, though, I let Andrew lead me to her unassuming marker as if everything was all new. Like me, he probably just needed to be distracted for a while.

By the time we got home, Owen and I were both settled, as if the afternoon had simply been worked away in the office.

We'd agreed that revealing the station visit and restrictions could wait until tomorrow; a decision made more certain upon remembering that Jamie was out on a date with Sarah. There was *no* way we could speak to only part of the family.

When Owen brought plates to the table where I sat helping Lisa with some math problems, he gave me a tiny smile and I realised he had the same thoughts. One more night that we could spend normally was one more night to re-grow some confidence.

'You want us to pack up so you can set the table?' I asked.

'Uh, pack up so *you* can set it,' he said, tapping the plates then turning away.

'Well,' I said to Lisa, 'we've been told.'

She rolled her eyes, but started tidying away her school things.

- # -

It was just after midnight when I heard the soft creak of the bedroom door.

Owen had gone to bed in his own room. Although we didn't always sleep together, trying to be circumspect around the others, tonight's decision not to share had been a conscious one. Yet, before I'd fallen asleep, I'd spent a good hour telling myself *not* to go to him, that us staying apart after today and with that restriction coming in from tomorrow was best for both of us.

And, probably, I'd known at some point that Owen would come to me. I should have sent him back the moment I heard the door creak, but didn't. Just held myself still and quiet. He didn't speak either, as if he thought I was asleep. Obviously he didn't need anything other than to just be near. The far side of the bed shifted as he climbed in, and jiggled as he got himself sorted.

I bit my lip, trying to keep myself from turning and wrapping him tight in my arms.

Owen let out a soft sigh. One hand pressed against my back and I shifted, belying that I wasn't asleep. He whispered, 'Make love to me, Andrew.'

I was startled still a moment, then twisted to face him. 'Angel, I don't think—'

'I dreamed Jack Wheeler texted me. He was running a red light.'

That threw me so much I couldn't get my voice working.

'I need to you to get him out of my head,' Owen croaked.

'Whaat?'

'*Please.*'

Fingers twisted into my top as Owen shifted onto his side. I grasped one of his hands. 'Owen, I'm not...' Actually, I didn't know what to say. Hearing his words now took me back to the first time I'd made love to him after we'd re-met last year. He'd told me he wanted me to block out all the other men he'd slept with, especially Jack Wheeler with whom the sex had not been consensual.

I came back to the present when his fingers touched my chest and I realised he'd gotten some of the buttons undone. His breathing wasn't a whole lot steady, but I could hear that it wasn't desire making it that way.

'Hon, I don't think now's a good time,' I whispered, relieved my voice hadn't cracked.

'It could be the *last* time,' he rasped out. 'If dad… and J-Jack W-Whee— I need you to make them stop!'

He leaned forward, found my lips. I had no strength to resist; when he initiated something I was there with bells on, even in a situation like this. 'Oh, Owen,' I murmured and wrapped him in my arms, realising only now that he was naked.

Owen was still kissing me, fingers pointed into my back like he was afraid I'd suddenly pull away. My head was telling me I should, but nothing else about me was taking any notice. I kissed down Owen's throat, needing him as much as he needed me, listening to his breathing—hitching a bit, but panting too. One hand slid down his spine to cup a firm buttock, making him shift in against me, both of us clear about what the other needed.

Except, as I shifted a bit more comfortably, his breath gave a solid choke and then he was crying. Trying to stop himself, I could hear, but there was no way I could continue on that physical path now. I whispered his name, starting to pull back to give him his own space.

'Hold me tighter!' he ordered me, leading by example.

'Owen—'

'Just do it!' he cried angrily.

Seconds after that he was in full-blown tears, sobbing about his father and about Jack Wheeler. He barely ever mentioned that man, or the prostitution, so I understood that having it brought back to the present by his father today had become something he couldn't fight off.

I should have thought this might happen after hearing Owen talk at the cemetery. Should have started out the night in the same bed, taken care of him, shown that I was here when he needed me. All I could do now was hold tight and tell him things would work out. Tried to sound believable.

I'd understood and accepted Morrison's actions today but right now my own confidence was starting to eke out, and I had to keep that from Owen as much as possible. I bent my forehead against his soft hair, squeezed my eyes tight.

It took some time for Owen's breathing to settle and for him to relax into sleep. I didn't let him go, just hoped that my embrace would transmit safety to him even in his sleep.

Owen

I woke Saturday morning to find myself in bed solo, and it was after nine. Climbing into the pyjamas I'd dropped on the floor in the night, I felt embarrassed at how I'd been, insisting Andrew make love to me even as I was bawling about dad and Jack Wheeler. I held a hand to my head a second, but after a while relief that he'd held me all night flushed out that embarrassment.

Andrew was cooking bacon and eggs, even though there were already dirty plates on the table where Megan and Jamie sat. Jamie must have seen my glance because he said, 'The animals had to be fed first.'

Megan snorted, but sometimes it was just easier if Lisa and Matty were fed and sent on their way. It usually meant the rest of us could eat in peace.

Andrew glanced over his shoulder, turning fully when he spied me loitering at the end of the bench sorting out a cup of tea. 'Bacon and eggs?' he asked.

I shook my head. 'Not hungry.'

He paused just a moment, gaze flicking to my siblings before coming back to me. He didn't repeat the offer, just turned back to the stove. I took my cup to the couch, joining Matty and Lisa who were watching TV.

'I thought you didn't like X-Men,' Matty said.

I pulled an extra-disgusted face. 'Is that what's on?'

'Sssh,' Lisa cut in, 'I can't hear.'

'It's only an ad,' Matty said.

She gave him a look that warned him off, so he stuck out his tongue. Both of my brothers knew how to push buttons.

'Keep your hands to yourselves,' I told them before they could start.

Lisa huffed.

When the cartoon came back on I returned to the others. Andrew opened his mouth but I said, 'I'm sure' before he could ask.

'It's really good,' Megan said. 'Better than me.'

'That's not hard,' Jamie quipped. 'Oww,' he added, pulling a face at her.

I mumbled without thought, 'Better not get used to it.'

'Why?' Jamie asked, brows furrowing.

I straightened, realising what I'd said. Glancing at Andrew made the others look at him too.

'What's going on?' Jamie asked.

'Your brother and I met with Sergeant Morrison yesterday afternoon,' Andrew said.

Megan's eyes widened in surprise. I felt Jamie's gaze as he asked, with an edge, if it was planned.

'No, it wasn't planned,' Andrew said. 'At least not by us.'

'What was it about?' Megan asked.

'Why didn't you tell us last night?' Jamie's fingers tightened around the fork.

'Like we were gonna stay up til midnight to wait for you.' Actually, I had no idea when he'd gotten home.

Jamie opened his mouth but Megan got in first. 'Was it about dad?'

'Yeah,' I said. 'And some other things.'

This time it was Andrew who spoke before Jamie could. 'How about you finish your breakfasts, both of you? You,' he said to me, 'get dressed, and then we'll chat.'

I lingered over dressing, hoping to get a grip on my feelings before they gripped me.

Lingered longer than I thought since as I came out of my bedroom, Jamie stopped a few feet away. 'Oh good, you're still here.'

'What?'

'Just coming to check that you hadn't jumped out a window.'

'Don't be a dick, Jamie.' I brushed by him.

He made a sound but didn't spin me around to answer questions, just followed me out to the lounge, detoured to the kitchen when Andrew called his name. I spotted Megan, Lisa and Matty on the deck and headed toward them. I wasn't a whole bunch sure Lisa and Matty needed to hear all this stuff, but I didn't know how else we'd explain Andrew's complete absence at night.

As I stepped outside, I realised I didn't even know how tonight would go… how early Andrew would have to leave. Before dinner? God, that would be horrible. I glanced back to see him and Jamie heading for us, both carrying trays. A new pot of tea had obviously been made.

Andrew nodded over my shoulder. 'Under the tree.'

I turned and noticed a blanket had been set there and Lisa and Matty were already laying claim to half of it. Megan took a spot on the garden bench. I felt like I'd be on display if I sat there too, so I sat on the blanket, knocking knees with my little brother.

Andrew and Jamie arrived with the trays, and watching Andrew pour tea almost made my eyes sting. I loved the small gesture; it kind of reduced the stiffness in the atmosphere. Neither Megan nor Jamie were slow to take a cup, and I wasn't either. A cup in my hands meant I couldn't do a nervous fiddle with my jeans or the blanket or the grass. Lisa and Matty each had juice.

'So,' Jamie said, sitting beside Megan, 'this is nice and all but it's making me shit-nervous.'

'Jamie,' Megan hissed, jabbing him.

'Hey!' he exclaimed as he avoided hot drops of spilt tea.

She just stared pointedly. She was still on at us about swearing in front of Lisa and Matty.

'I bet you,' Jamie said, 'that when this conversation's over you won't remember what I said.'

'Let's not start a riot,' Andrew commented. He glanced at me. 'How do you want to do this?'

I recoiled for a second but then mumbled, 'Can you tell it?'

Guess that was somewhat cowardly because he would only be able to tell half of yesterday, and so I still had a chance to keep my chat with dad a secret. Except I also knew things would be worse if I did that. I squeezed my eyes shut a second, then looked back at him. 'I'll tell my bit, but can you start?'

Andrew nodded. He took a sip of tea, then set the cup on the nearest tray. 'Your brother and I went to see Sergeant Morrison yesterday afternoon, at his request.'

Jamie held his silence, even when Andrew glanced surprise his way.

'Morrison wanted a meeting because of something your father had brought up with him.'

'Dad?' Megan got out, a little hesitantly, brows knitting in puzzlement.

'Is he coming over again?' Matty asked.

My teeth jumped onto my tongue to cut back, 'I hope not.'

'We didn't talk about another visit right then, Matty,' Andrew said. 'But it's always an option.'

Matty smiled and started to babble about something he wanted to show dad. He cut off with a cry when Jamie pushed against his head with a foot. 'Shut it, Shrimp, there's more important stuff going on right now.'

'Jesus, Jamie, stop being—' I cut off as Megan's gaze sliced from him to me.

He wafted his foot my way but I was out of reach.

Andrew said, 'Jamie, you're right, there's a few important things to know, but please keep your body parts to yourself. Matty, you're always welcome to show your dad things when he comes over, but please just listen to me for now.'

My brothers both mumbled something. Andrew waited a second, glanced at me, and then came straight out with, 'Owen is technically underage for a... *our* relationship while he's also working for me, and your father has insisted Morrison do something about it.'

Silence after that and I was sorry to have made Andrew tell it, sorry that my younger siblings were hearing. I didn't think they'd understand and would only end up confused and hurt.

Megan pulled loose threads on her jeans. 'Are you going to be arrested?'

Andrew couldn't quite hide the jerk of shock at that really bald question. Jamie shifted straighter on the bench, suddenly totally serious.

'Andrew,' I rasped, 'did Morrison say that when I was—' I cut myself off.

'No,' he said. 'No one's being arrested. No one's being charged with anything.'

'But,' Megan began, 'if you're... if Owen's not...' She sounded as puzzled as she looked.

'So, what's Morrison doing then?' Jamie asked, sounding puzzled too.

My peripheral vision showed him looking at me but I refused to look his way.

'Sergeant Morrison has imposed two restrictions,' Andrew said, 'to keep us on the better side of the law.'

'Restrictions?' Jamie queried. 'Like what? You two don't come within ten feet of each other?'

'Something like that,' I told my cup.

'What?' he got out and I realised he'd been joking.

Andrew grimaced and said, 'Owen and I must limit our time alone together.'

Silence.

I glanced up; both Megan and Jamie looked like they didn't comprehend. Then Jamie said, 'That's dumb.'

'Yeah,' I agreed, even though I'd accepted the sergeant's reasoning.

'Mm.' Andrew looked at me briefly then back at Jamie and Megan. 'The other restriction affects you all. I cannot be in the house after eight at night.'

I shifted, realising that he and Morrison *had* obviously kept speaking while I was with dad. I couldn't believe how I'd not questioned him about that yesterday.

'What do you mean, not allowed in the house after eight?' Jamie asked slowly. 'That you won't be here overnight?'

'Exactly.'

'But… you're *supposed* to be here.'

When Jamie looked at me, I said, 'It's not like he stays every night anyway.'

'That's a fucking ridiculous restriction,' he responded.

Must also have been what Megan was thinking since she didn't tell him off for swearing. I looked at Lisa and Matty, wasn't really sure they were taking anything in. Matty was leaning back on his hands, looking up at the tree. Lisa was folding a fan out of the blanket edge.

Andrew looked like he wished we'd been able to reveal this another way. 'Jamie,' he spoke quietly, 'Sergeant Morrison is interpreting the law *for* us not against us.'

Jamie was blank.

'But you're our *guardian*,' Megan stated.

'Yes,' Andrew said, 'and that's not changing. It's just—'

He cut off when Megan jumped to her feet. 'This isn't *fair!* Your relationship was known when they made you guardian. What's the big deal *now*? Is it *just* because dad's back?'

'Yes,' I said before Andrew tried to answer. 'Dad wants us apart, and the law sides with him because I work for Andrew and I'm only seventeen. Morrison's got these restrictions to help us. They totally suck, but what choice do we have?'

'Megan,' Andrew said, 'the sergeant can't just ignore the law even if he knows everything is consensual between us.'

'But… you've been together for ages,' she said. 'Enforcing it now's stupid and unfair.'

Andrew did a sort of nod/head-shake and I realised he didn't know how to respond to help her understand. So I piped up with something totally stupid, 'Dad doesn't want Andrew anywhere near here.'

Megan looked at me. Andrew said my name quietly. I didn't look his way but at my sister. 'He doesn't want me here either. He's totally homophobic.' Had at least enough control to not blurt where that hate stemmed from. I hauled in a breath, then said, 'Dad's going for the loophole in the law because he knows he won't win otherwise.'

Megan sucked in a breath. 'Are you saying that he… wants *custody* again?'

'Fuck no,' Jamie stated.

Lisa stopped pleating the blanket. 'Custody? What's that mean?'

Alarm bells clanged in my head. Sure, we needed to come completely clean but not right here, not like this.

'It's a legal state, Honey,' Andrew said. 'Like guardianship.' He tried a smile. 'Nothing for you to worry about at the moment.' He looked up as Megan took a step back from us. 'Megan…'

'It's not happening,' she said. 'I don't care what he says or does, I don't want him back. He's changed and it's not nice! *He* is not nice!'

All we seemed able to do was stare as she took off for the house. Jamie caught my gaze and I saw shock, anger, and a little bit of admiration. I swallowed back the lump in my throat and started to stand, but Andrew held a hand up. 'I'll go.' His tone left no room for argument.

Owen watched Andrew hurry across the lawn and into the house. I cleared my throat and quietly suggested to Lisa and Matty they could take the trays inside. Was kind of surprised that they didn't even quibble about it. Owen caught my glance briefly. He didn't leave even though it was clear it'd soon just be him and me out here under the tree. He sucked in his lips, apparently absorbed in watching our little brother and sister move away.

'Well,' I said after a moment, 'this is all pretty shit.'

'That's only half of it.'

'What do you mean?' I asked. 'Oh man, don't tell me there's another restriction? I thought Andrew said only two.'

Owen drew in a long breath, shook his head. 'Dad said the driver who caused mum's accident was gay. That he was texting his partner when he ran the red light.'

'Oh shit,' I breathed, 'that… Hang on, when did he tell you that?'

My brother kept his gaze down, but his jaw was kind of clenched.

'Owen! *When* did dad tell you that?'

Not quite a bullet-point repeat, but close enough to get Owen lifting his head and shifting like he was going to stand. I slid off the bench and sat myself dead in front of him. Close enough to grab, if he did try to rise, and close enough that he couldn't ignore me.

He squeezed his eyes shut a moment, then looked back at me. 'Yesterday, at the station. He asked to talk to me.'

'*What?*

'Andrew said he couldn't stop it, I'm not under his care, you know.' Owen grimaced. 'Morrison thought he wanted to clear some things up, so he didn't prevent it either.'

'Why wasn't I included?' I growled. 'I'm not a child.'

'You should be grateful,' he said, sounding steely.

'What the fuck? Why should I—'

'He called me a slut and a whore.'

I knew my mouth hung open but for a moment I couldn't seem to get it closed. Then I had to cough to clear my throat. 'What?' I got out, sounding puzzled but unable to stop myself.

Owen sucked his lips over his teeth, then blew out a sigh. 'Dad said the accident is one of the reasons he doesn't like me and Andrew, and the prostitution's the other. When I asked how he knew about it he just said I should have known he'd do some digging before he came back. I don't know if that actually means he's *always* known, though.' He shrugged. 'Well, maybe those filth comments he's made relate to it.'

I watched my brother as he spoke. He seemed calm and his voice was even; surprising given the topic. 'Um, Owen—'

'He reckoned Andrew would run a mile when he found out I was a slut for others.'

Pretty good sentence to cut me off with, and to shut me up for a while.

Owen had a weird smile on his face. 'He obviously doesn't know Andrew's role in all that.'

I croaked out, 'Y-yeah' because I felt like I needed to say something.

'I don't remember him being homophobic after mum died,' he said softly.

'Me neither but, shit… hating you for all that stuff and because that driver was…' I shook my head. 'How does he know that? I didn't even know the driver was a *guy*.'

'I didn't either.'

'Doesn't matter anyway,' I told him, 'It's all just… wrong. He wants to break you guys up just because he hates gays?'

Owen smiled at me suddenly. I felt my lips curving out of reflex but I wasn't sure what his smile was for. I didn't think anything in this conversation was worth a smile. He looked down at his fingers picking at the blanket. 'Yeah,' he said with a nod, 'I think that's exactly why he's doing this.' After a second he looked up again, head slightly cocked. 'And being gay means Andrew's guardianship is rotten. Dad doesn't want him caring for you guys.'

My spine went stiff. 'Wait, is he accusing Andrew of—'

'No!' Owen cut me off. 'At least…'

'At least…' I prompted when the silence had lingered about thirty seconds.

He shook his head, which made me pretty sure he was hiding something.

'Did Andrew and dad talk?'

'Shit, no,' Owen said. Grimaced a whole bunch. 'It was just me and dad, not even a police officer. Treating me like an adult.'

His bitterness was loud and clear, and I understood why he felt it.

Owen shrugged. 'It was weird. The first half of the conversation was kind of normal. Well, me telling him *again* what work I did for Andrew. And then out of nowhere he said he wanted…' He pulled a face. 'Shit, Jamie, he called Andrew a…' Stopped again.

Since dad had called my brother a whore and a slut, my brain was running through other names in my head but if he didn't know Andrew's involvement in all that then—

'Boy-fucker.'

Didn't really come out with much sound, but I cringed like he'd shouted it for the whole neighbourhood to hear. He had a fist pressed against his mouth like he was stopping other words.

My hands were nowhere near my mouth so I couldn't stop, 'He said what?' in a stupid response.

Owen sagged. 'He said our sort foul the earth.'

Because the word coming out of my mouth was, 'What?' I pressed my hands tight to prevent it.

My brother rubbed his eyes. 'Kind of went south after that. That's when he mentioned mum, because I asked what he had against gay people.'

'Hey, you're doing pretty good with the G-word now.'

Oh, shit, what a stupid—Owen let out a chuckle.

'Sorry,' I muttered.

His lips curved in a brief smile, which relieved me and scared me at the same time.

'Does Andrew know about all this stuff? The name-calling?'

'Yeah,' Owen said. 'Well, what dad called me, anyway. I didn't... Couldn't tell him that other thing. That was just bloody horrible.'

'Did you tell the sergeant?'

Owen pulled a face. 'Didn't see him. I kinda...' He cleared his throat. 'Did my old usual,' he said with a wry tone. 'Andrew found me down at Calvary.'

I stared at him, mentally placing the police station and its proximity (or not!) to that old cemetery. Owen seemed to be waiting for my response, so I said, 'Lucky it wasn't raining yesterday.'

He rolled his eyes but nodded.

I didn't tell him that he needed to come clean about all the name-calling; pushing him to do anything usually just made him a clam.

We sat in silence for a while, listening to the breeze rustle the new leaves overhead. I was a bit surprised Andrew hadn't come back or even that Lisa and Matty hadn't; maybe we looked totally serious out here and they were avoiding us? Maybe Andrew was thinking a miracle was in play since Owen and I were talking (and keeping our fists to ourselves). I let out a long sigh. It'd been ages since I'd felt like I needed to thump my brother.

'Man, this whole thing sucks,' I said. 'Where's dad get off saying all that shit? It's not like he really wants us back.'

One of Owen's brows lifted up into his messy hair.

'Come on, you *know* that, Owen. Don't give me that look.'

The look turned into a nose-scrunching, lip-curling grimace.

'Wind'll change,' I muttered off to one side.

'He's still gonna go for custody,' Owen said, making me look at him again. 'I told him he wouldn't get it, he said he would.'

'No judge would dissolve Andrew's guardianship just because dad demands it,' I said sensibly.

'Yeah, but…' Owen tailed off.

I waited but he didn't speak again, and I didn't pester. Had this feeling there was more he wasn't telling me about yesterday but suddenly I didn't want to hear it just now.

'So, these restrictions then,' I said, making him stiffen just a bit. 'How long do we have to suffer them?'

Owen bit on his lip hard, then rubbed it and said, looking

like it took some effort, 'Until my birthday.'

'This all seems a weird thing to do,' I said.

'Yeah, but it's better than Sergeant Morrison straight out laying down the law. Andrew and I… Seventeen's legal, you know, except for…' He cut off, looking peeved and embarrassed. 'If I stopped working for Andrew, there'd be no problem. Well, aside from dad's homophobia, that is. He'd have nothing legal to back him. But I can't *not* work.'

'Yeah, I guess,' I heard myself say, trying to get my head around things.

'There's no "guess", Jamie,' he said. 'There's no way I want Andrew to have to fund us.'

'I'm working,' I reminded him.

He cocked his head. 'Sure.'

I scowled, but knew that had been stupid to say. My wage was nowhere near the fund-a-family-for-two-months level. I just… had to make a point. I didn't mention that he must have good savings that could help, and which would prevent Andrew having to shell out.

To be honest, having Owen at home 24/7 wasn't something I wanted, and I got the feeling that was *his* whole reason for not going down the stop-work track too.

'So, if the issue is that Andrew's your boss but you continue to work with him, what's actually changing? What was that other restriction again?'

'We can't be alone together. No,' he said with a head shake, 'we have to *limit* our time alone.'

I arched a brow. 'Don't you both work in the same office?'

'Yeah.'

'Then… what?'

'No sex at work.'

Owen said that looking me dead in the eye and I did my total best to hide sudden alarm. Can't have done a good job though because he smirked.

'That's gross,' I told him in the steadiest voice possible.

'It's not often I get one over you.'

'Yeah, well, you saying "sex" startled me.' Smiled that his grin got wider for a second. Owen was very easy to embarrass and now and then I enjoyed getting him that way. Realised I enjoyed him turning the tables just as much. I cocked my head. 'Have you ever—'

'No!' he cut over me with speed.

That made me chuckle.

He pulled a face. 'Definitely won't consider it now.'

Honestly, I couldn't picture my brother ever being so uninhibited that he'd get frisky in the office.

'Stop smiling,' he growled.

So I killed the mood with, 'Did dad give any more info about why he stayed away so long, why he decided now was a good time to come back?'

'Nope. He doesn't seem to think we warrant any of that stuff, though I didn't ask either.' Owen scratched his head. 'He just seemed focused on why he hates me and Andrew being together.' He looked up. 'I want to find out if that's true, if the driver was gay.'

'How would we find out?'

He shrugged. 'I'll start with Morrison.'

'Yeah, good plan,' I said, though wondered why he'd know or how he'd even find out. 'Hey, when am *I* going to get to chat with dad?'

Owen eyed me. 'When he next visits, I guess. You really want to?'

'Yeah,' I said. 'But *when?* I thought Andrew said nothing had been discussed.'

'Nothing was,' Owen said.

'So?'

'So, we'll obviously have to discuss it.' Owen's tone was a little on the side of stop-badgering-me-about-this-stupid-topic.

'Matty's not gonna get it,' I said, choosing to obey. 'Andrew not staying the night.'

Owen scowled. 'He doesn't stay—'

He cut off, probably because I jumped to my feet and walked out into the sunlight. I squinted a second at nothing in particular then spun about and came back to my brother, dropping to my knees. Owen reared back, but stayed on his butt. I swallowed hard, then said, 'We're all in this together, right, even Lisa and Matty. If dad wants something from us he's going to have to do some *real* explaining first. And I—'

I bounced up and walked away again, fingers fisted when I realised they were shaking. After hauling in a big breath, I rushed it out like someone had punched me in the gut.

After another deep breath, I turned. Owen was on his feet, looking unsettled. Hell, I felt unsettled all of a sudden, all that previous joking pushed aside by the recognition that our guardian was being prevented from being our guardian by a stupid father who—

'Okay… so, Owen, I'm with Megs. What dad's doing is completely unfair and I don't want him back any more than she does. If he ever bothers to ask what *we* want, he'll learn that. And he has no right to attack you and Andrew because…' I waved a hand. 'I consider Andrew to be more my dad than him.' I set a palm to my forehead, felt a little self-conscious over that but it was true. I liked Andrew way more than I'd realised. I did not want him out of my life. Out of *our* lives.

Owen cracked a smile. 'You've turned over a l-leaf.'

'Yeah, well, you deserve to be happy, Owen. If that's Andrew, then it's Andrew. Shit, don't look at me like I've spouted something foreign.'

'S-sorry.'

I sprang a hug on him, then stepped quickly back before either of us pushed the other away. Owen looked like he didn't quite know what to do. I grinned, then told him I was going to Sarah's.

'Andrew's doing a roast, don't forget.'

'Never,' I told him over my shoulder as I walked away.

Owen

Watching clouds calmed me like a good drug, so when Andrew came and sat on the bench I had myself together pretty good. After a short silence, still on my back, I said, 'Why eight o'clock?'

Andrew didn't miss a beat. 'Because that's the kids' bedtime. I'm hoping "good bye" won't be too dissimilar to "good night".'

I sat up, twisting to look at him. He tried out a smile but it didn't seem to reach me. 'I don't know how we're going to make them understand,' I said, thinking of Jamie's brief comment about Matty.

He let out a sigh. 'We'll figure something out.'

I shifted to the bench, left a gap between us. 'Did you have to sign something yesterday? Make things official?'

'I did, yes,' Andrew said.

'So… it's done then.'

'It's all done.' He drew in a long breath, let it out in a sigh. 'Owen, I agree with Morrison's restrictions. To keep you and your siblings safe, I'd agree to anything.'

'Please don't agree to stuff without speaking to me first,' I begged. 'You should have gone for nine. And what about your own safety? What's Morrison doing about that?'

Up until yesterday afternoon, dad had been just words. But yesterday… he'd really sounded like he could get physical. Except, Andrew didn't know the half of what dad had said and I wasn't sure I could tell him.

Andrew's gaze was somewhere on the grass. 'I don't feel unsafe, Owen.'

I sat silent, daring myself to ask if he meant that. He shuffled closer and put his arm around my shoulder, hugging me to his side.

'You know we shouldn't be doing this,' I told him.

'Don't fucking care.'

I had to straighten up to stare. He stared right back, but I wasn't challenging him. I sagged again, ran fingers down the top of his thigh because I couldn't sit still. 'I told Jamie about the no sex at work thing.'

'Ah,' Andrew said. 'That's… something.'

I pulled a face. 'I was explaining that restriction and how it related to us being in the office,' I said. 'Do you think it'll work?'

Andrew was silent.

'I mean the *restriction*,' I said after a second or two.

'Ah, well.' Andrew covered my fiddling hand. 'As long as you don't give me the come-on or anything, sure.'

'I'm serious,' I muttered, though couldn't blame him for that response since I wasn't explaining myself that well.

He squeezed my hand. 'I'm sure the threat of your father possibly dropping by will ensure its success, Owen.' He blew out a breath. 'I appreciate that Morrison didn't order me to fire you. That would, you realise, solve the entire legality issue.'

'Yeah, I know,' I said, wobbling his shoulder with my nod. 'But I can't not work, Andrew. Please don't fire me.'

'I won't, don't worry.'

We sat in silence after that.

Despite what I'd said to Jamie just before, it wasn't the money issue that really worried me about not working. It was the fact I wouldn't see Andrew during the day, the fact my whole comfortable routine would be tossed out the door. Sure, I'd see him at night but that wasn't the be-all and end-all to our relationship.

'Dad's timing totally sucks,' I mumbled. 'He was gone so long, why couldn't he have managed another two months?'

Andrew sighed.

More silence after that, and I should have kept it, but instead I said, 'Did you see dad after I left yesterday?' I'd told Jamie he hadn't but I didn't actually know.

'Nope.'

When he didn't say anything more, I wondered if I should push for a better answer. But just maybe he hadn't. Morrison had seemed keen to keep everyone apart, and maybe dad didn't even know that Andrew was there. I mumbled another apology for disappearing yesterday.

Andrew squeezed my hand again. 'You should tell the sergeant what your father said, Owen.'

'He called you a boy-fucker,' I blurted.

Andrew winced against me. 'Shit,' he breathed. 'That man…' He cut off like maybe he remembered that man was my stupid father. 'How… how did that come up in the conversation?'

I told him and he stayed silent, but his jaw was clenched and his arm got quite tight around my shoulder. Don't think he realised he was squeezing me so, and I didn't ask him to stop.

'Doesn't sound like he knows my involvement with your… stuff last year,' he said.

'No, he'd have been way worse if he did. And… I don't think he knows about the attack either.'

Andrew's gaze tilted my way.

'Well, he'd have said something,' I clarified. Though, momentarily, I thought he just might not care enough about it. 'God, I wish I knew how he found out. If he doesn't know about you and he doesn't know that last thing, how does he know about the rest? And how much *does* he know? Do you think Sergeant—' I cut myself off; that was too horrible a thought. There was no way Sergeant Morrison would have revealed all that stuff.

'Hmm,' was all Andrew said.

I shut up then, realising that running at the mouth wasn't helping him. I got the feeling he felt completely inadequate, and I *hated* that. 'Hey, thanks for going after Megan before. I'd have been useless. Is she okay?'

Andrew brushed through his hair. 'She's pretty upset, but I think she'll be okay. She went off to meet Alana.' His arm squeezed me a little. 'There's only so much I can help with, I'm afraid.'

I cleared a sudden onslaught of gravel from my throat. 'You do way m-more than enough.'

He let out a soft sound, then said, 'Your father has a hell of a lot to answer for.'

'Y-yeah, but we will get through this.' That came out a lot more certain than I actually felt. 'Jamie's on our side, you know.'

I think I heard a soft chuckle. 'I know, he told me.'

My eyes started to sting, so I pressed my face a little further into his shoulder to avoid him catching a glimpse.

'He's a great kid,' Andrew said. 'I'm so proud of the five of you.'

The sting got more serious but I held the tears back. Swallowed deeply to fight back any croak and then said, 'I'm proud of *you*. Me and four dependents. You didn't even bat an eyelid when I first told you about them.'

Andrew chuckled and ruffled my hair. 'I think that was because nothing else existed on the planet bar you.'

'I'm serious.'

'I know, Owen,' he responded. 'And I'll do everything I can for you kids.'

'Yeah, I know.'

We settled into a comfortable silence then, almost as if we had no worries.

I was half asleep when Andrew said, 'Come on, we better get inside before we get caught out here *alone*.'

I jabbed him in the side for breaking my peace, and then rose, pulling him up. He got a quick kiss on my forehead before I pushed him away with a half frown half smile and turned for the house.

Andrew was folding washing when I got home from seeing Sarah. I arched a brow at the domesticity and he murmured, 'Something I don't need to use my brain for.'

I looked at him just a bit closer but his smile didn't waiver. 'How's Sarah?'

'She's good,' I said. 'I didn't tell her anything.'

He paused in folding a towel. 'Jamie, you're welcome to tell her *every*thing. I won't stop you.'

'Yeah, but...' I shrugged. My girlfriend was already concerned about how dad had shown up out of the blue; no way I wanted to tell her this new stuff just yet. She had enough on her own plate anyway with her dancing. 'Where is everyone?'

It was just Andrew in the lounge. Probably because folding laundry was a pain in the butt and we all tried to avoid it.

'The kids are out there.' Andrew nodded toward the deck. 'Megan's still at Alana's and Owen, last I looked, is cleaning the bath.'

My brows jumped up and I turned away. What the hell had gone on to make Owen clean the bath? I was pretty sure this was like one of those once-in-a-blue-moon events. And, shit, he actually *was*—kneeling at the side, scrubbing the heck out of the bottom, teeth gritted.

He didn't notice me in the doorway until I flicked the light on and off, then he jerked sideways, swore when he caught his elbow on the raised edge. His teeth were in his lip as he rubbed the sore spot, clearly fighting against letting loose more language.

'How's it?' I asked.

'How the fuck do you think it is? I'm cleaning the fucking bath.'

'Ah, thought so,' I said.

Owen sat back on his heels, one hand on the edge to balance himself. The other wiped across his forehead, still holding the scrubbing brush. Despite feeling like I might wear the brush at some point I perched on the edge of the bath. 'How's it really?'

He let out a long sigh. 'Okay. I mean, things could be worse.'

'Yeah.'

He squinted up at me. He looked tired, but that could have been the energetic cleaning. Then he gave a half smile. 'We've cleaned this place top to bottom, trying to keep busy.'

I let one of my brows creep up and Owen's peeved expression showed he obviously knew where my thought process was going. Glancing down at the bath he asked if Megan was home.

'Andrew said she wasn't.'

'He wants us to have a chat tonight about a more serious meeting with dad,' he said.

I grimaced. If Megan knew that, then she'd stay overnight with Alana! She'd been really upset this morning. 'Hey, I could text that you're cleaning the bath. That'd bring her home in a flash.'

Owen let out a growl, trying to keep back a sort of grin. 'Get outta here before I foist the rest of this shitty job on you.'

Not something I needed to be told twice.

- # -

Megan did come home for dinner. Possibly because Andrew cooked a really good roast and she was a total carnivore.

Sitting at the table was the first time we'd been all together since this morning under the tree. Instead of a gloomy, stiff silence, we chatted and smiled as we ate. Strange how food always made us seem outwardly normal, but it meant that we had a stress-less dinner. I'd almost have thought the chat had been among some other family.

Looking at Lisa and Matty, I couldn't tell if they even remembered it, let alone understood anything. Would they get why Andrew wasn't staying the night like he usually did on Saturdays? I glanced over at Owen; how was *he* going to be? He sat opposite me, trying not to yawn, arched a brow when he spotted me staring. I just shrugged.

We'd just finished our ice cream when Andrew brought it up—us kids having an official meeting with dad. 'One evening is best, when all of you are home.'

Owen straightened. 'I'm not agreeing to any meeting if you won't be here.'

'I don't like that idea either,' Megan said beside him.

Andrew sighed. 'I don't actually like it myself, but my presence could make things worse. I don't want to make this harder for you guys. Owen,' he added with another sigh, 'please don't get that look on your face. You know it's best.'

Owen's look was straight out stubborn refusal, and since he'd been cleaning the bath I reckoned he was practically breathing that feeling right now. 'You not being here is exactly what dad wants.' He stabbed a finger into the table.

'Yes, I know,' Andrew responded. 'That's why I've suggested it. The restrictions are in his favour, I know that too, but if we play our side fairly then I'm sure things will go more smoothly.'

'You mean,' I said, 'that if we kowtow to his demands we might get out of this without losing you.'

Andrew closed his eyes a second, but he didn't deny what I'd said. Across from me, Owen was scowling. I didn't back down. Andrew and I were singing from the same song sheet, I was sure.

'So,' Megan broke the silence, 'we have to meet dad alone?'

'No, Hon,' Andrew said. 'A police officer will be present.'

Megan gaped. 'What?'

Owen ran his tongue over his teeth but I couldn't tell if he'd known about that already. I turned to Andrew. 'Will it be Sergeant Morrison?'

'I don't expect so,' Andrew said, 'but there will be someone. The sergeant agreed to that request.'

'You requested it?' It was a dumb question but I was startled.

'Of course, Jamie.'

He didn't explain how that was an "of course" thing, and it made me wonder again whether something had happened yesterday that he and Owen hadn't revealed. Especially since both of them had said there *hadn't* been discussion about a meeting. My brother's brows seemed to come together a bit tighter.

'Will the policeman have a gun?'

Trust Matty to ask.

'No way!' Megan delivered in such a tone that nobody was going to correct her.

Though, honestly, why would a gun be needed? It was just… 'Did he hit you or something?' I asked Owen.

'What? When?'

'Dad. Yesterday. Ring a bell?'

Megan twisted on her seat. 'You saw dad yesterday? At… the police station?'

Owen leaned back a little. 'Yeah, but—'

'Why didn't you say anything about it?' she cut him off, then turned to Andrew. 'Were *you* there?'

'Andrew wasn't with me when I talked with dad,' Owen said, like he wanted to forestall her getting angry at Andrew. 'He asked to speak with me, to clear the air a bit.'

The teeth grinding belonged to Andrew, who made his face blank when he noticed my gaze.

'Clear the air?' Megan asked. 'So, *why* have we got those restrictions then?'

'That was a different thing,' Andrew said quietly.

Megan picked up her spoon, clenched it tight then set it down again. Guess she realised that throwing it was a bad idea. 'Why am I only hearing about this one-on-one *now?*'

Owen winced, mumbled an apology. Then he gave an incredibly brief run-down of the conversation he and dad had had, brief because of Lisa and Matty.

No mention of the name-calling, no mention of what dad had against gay people.

I was sure Owen knew he'd have to come clean on that to Megan at some point, but I backed that he didn't want to say it in front of the others. Dad had already said some things to us about what he thought of Owen and Andrew, but at the moment Lisa and Matty weren't getting the *real* picture.

'So,' I said, after a bit of a silence, 'this meeting. You're our guardian, Andrew. I get that you want to keep things even, but you should be at it. Don't you have the right to be?'

'I do, Jamie,' he replied, 'and I want to be present, I just think… Look, your father's got some issues and my presence won't help them. I don't want him to react to me. I don't want *you* guys to do that either.'

'What?' I asked.

Andrew rubbed a brow. 'I don't want you to say or do things just because I'm there, because you feel you have to.'

I glanced across at Owen as he rose from the table and headed into the lounge without a word.

Andrew sighed but he didn't try to get past me to go after him. He looked at me and then around at the others. 'Do you understand what I'm saying?'

Since Megan had the same expression that I felt was on my face, I knew she did, but Lisa and Matty looked kind of blank. Lisa shook her head. 'No. Are you saying dad's coming to live here?'

Megan choked on a breath, and I held mine.

'No, Sweetheart,' Andrew said in a gentle voice. 'That's not what I'm saying. I just—'

I should have stayed to help him out but I scooted off the bench and joined Owen. The way he was glaring at the portrait I knew he'd heard Lisa's question.

'We ought to take it down,' he said after a second.

'You know, I always thought this would be the first of many. Like we'd get others done at important times, even with our own kids.'

Owen looked at me like I'd not spoken in English. I pulled a face but I actually *had* thought that, though… no kids from *him*. His brows furrowed. After a moment he asked if I wanted it to stay up.

'I don't know,' I said. 'It hurts, looking at it, but it's a good one of us, you know? And… mum.' I swallowed back the lump.

Even though she hadn't wanted to move here, she'd done her best to get us settled in and to act like everything was okay. She'd even had the fence put up out front and the letterbox stationed there, just because it'd been like that at home. Her smile made lots of things okay, and it still sort of did.

Owen had his head cocked. He didn't speak about mum, just said we'd leave it for now.

'Yeah, good.'

When he glanced at me, I forced out a smile. He didn't smile back, then his gaze shifted slightly and he walked back to the others. I stared up at the portrait, trying not to see dad, trying not to see that even back then I looked quite a bit like him.

Scratching my ear, I turned away.

Andrew leaving at eight wasn't the big drama I'd imagined it would be.

Maybe the novelty of having him leave us on a weekend night numbed the reason behind it, but we all went about saying 'Good night' and 'See you tomorrow' like it was just one of the usual days he didn't stay.

And once he'd gone, it was just another evening—the kids playing a board game at the table, us watching TV.

Owen's brows were more bunched up than usual, though. He hadn't known, until the table-talk, that Andrew had actually been in contact with the sergeant today, but I didn't think he was miffed at him. More so at dad.

I really wanted to talk about the gay driver thing, but Owen still hadn't revealed it to Megan. I guess he had to get it sorted in his head first because, after her reaction this morning, who knew how she'd take that news? And it was definitely something not to be told to Lisa and Matty straight away.

[Six]

Owen

It was crazy, but when the tenth of May was chosen for Dad's serious visit with us no one had twigged that date was already taken.

Megan's fifteenth birthday.

We didn't catch the unpleasant clash until the night before. Andrew tried to say it should be rearranged, but Megan had just shrugged. We'd still be able to go out for dinner, as planned, and that would make everything all okay.

God, my sister was amazing.

In any case, her birthday started off good. We went out for breakfast and did the gift-giving then.

Deteriorated just a bit when Andrew stood firm and said nobody was missing school (or work), but at least everyone would stay occupied with routine things.

And, after school, Megan went off with her friends for a while. The rest of us spent most of that free time in Barnes and Noble, spoiling Lisa and Matty. Probably wasn't the best thing to do, but they couldn't quite get why dad visiting needed a cop. They didn't know about the wider name-calling or dad's focus on safety and no one had the stomach to truly explain.

Buying happiness wasn't brilliant but for a while at least I think Lisa and Matty forgot what was coming.

I wished I could, but the names dad had called me and Andrew kept going around in my head. What if he used them in front of Lisa and Matty? I wasn't confident that having a police officer with us would stop dad getting vocal. After all, he'd had no problem telling Jamie and Megan he thought me and Andrew were filth. Hell, he'd even told Lisa that. And she was only twelve.

Though I appreciated that an officer would be present, I was still a bit edgy. Because… as horrible as the name-calling was, did it *justify* a police presence? I wouldn't cross Andrew over his insistence nor query that Sergeant Morrison had apparently quickly agreed, but I couldn't help wondering if Andrew and dad had clashed somewhere or sometime that I didn't know about.

I tried to tell myself Andrew was simply being protective and that I was worrying needlessly.

Maybe this would just be a father and his kids talking.

Maybe dad would just be… dad.

About forty minutes before dad was due to arrive, we were tidying the house. Domesticity seemed to keep us all in control of ourselves. Lisa and Matty hadn't even argued about tidying up their bedrooms, not that I expected dad would go down there.

Megan and I were organising the lounge, when she suddenly said, 'Should we take the picture down?'

I turned to look up at the portrait, trying not to wince at all of us smiling there like nothing was wrong. I had to make a conscious effort not to crush the cushion I held. 'What do *you* think?'

'I think we should.' She bit on her lip, grimacing. 'I really don't want dad here, Owen, not any more. If it's gone, maybe he'll get that.'

My chest felt tight at her words. I looked over to Jamie,

who'd been clearing the bench. 'What d'you think, Jamie?'

'Take it down,' he responded without hesitation.

I nodded, glanced back at Megan briefly. Her eyes were a bit shiny but she nodded too. I stepped forward and carefully hefted the large portrait from its hooks, biting back an apology to mum.

'I'll take it,' Megan whispered.

I gave it to her and she turned, heading out of the lounge. Jamie glanced over his shoulder, through to the entry way. Megan was obviously taking the portrait to the garage. When my brother turned back and caught my gaze, I was sure I saw a flash of guilt. I swallowed, felt guilt myself but towards mum not dad. I heard a soft breath near me and turned to see Andrew stopping by the couch, his gaze dropping from the empty wall to me.

'We thought…' I shrugged and tossed the cushion toward the closest couch.

'I support you.'

I flashed him a grateful smile then turned back to my tidying.

I was trying to decide how close the chair for the police officer should be to the rest of us when Andrew told me it was time he left. I held back a curse about it, just nodded and moved with him to the door.

Even though he'd be back later so we could go to dinner, I said, 'I wish I could go with you.'

'Oh man, so do I,' Jamie said, coming up beside me.

Andrew smiled at us but I could see concern in his eyes. He sounded confident, though, when he said, 'Everything will be fine. The officer will keep things under control.'

Jamie cocked his head. 'He better.'

'Jamie,' Andrew said, 'please don't—'

He cut off, gaze passing over us. Megan had herded Lisa and Matty into the entry way, and they'd stopped as if a fence blocked them. Andrew moved to them, speaking quietly so that Jamie and I didn't hear. Lisa smiled momentarily though and Matty stuck his tongue out, so it can't have been too horrendous. Andrew ruffled his hair, then kissed Megan's cheek. Her eyes seemed a little watery but her smile was strong enough. She encouraged the kids into the lounge out of view and Andrew came back to us.

'I'm counting on you two,' he said. 'I know this is an odd situation but you need to remain calm for their sake.' He gave a nod toward the lounge.

'Yeah, we know,' Jamie said.

I nodded, but I was beginning to feel decidedly un-calm.

Andrew glanced between us, and then opened the front door. 'I'll be back at six.'

Only a bit over an hour away, and he'd planned to just sit in a cafe in town rather than go home, but for a second that all seemed about as far away as my birthday. I forced myself to smile and say that we'd see him at six, and then Andrew stepped outside.

The sound of the deadbolt locking home caused a weird shard of grief to stab me.

As I turned to Jamie, he said, 'I'm going… to wash my face' and hurried toward the hall before I could speak.

I didn't follow to see if he was actually washing his face, instead moved to the lounge where Matty and my sisters were all perched on the same couch, Megan in the middle. They kind of looked like they were on a judging panel. 'Um, anyone want a drink?' I thumbed at the kitchen.

For a second Megan's expression was *what the fuck?* then she jumped up. 'Good idea, I'll make us all a hot chocolate.'

I didn't stop her, though *I'd* been intending to distract myself with the drinks. Instead, I found myself left with Lisa and Matty and since I couldn't walk away, I sat down. 'What sort of thing are you going to eat tonight?'

Incredibly out of the blue, and weird, but we were going to a buffet restaurant and food usually got at least Matty talking. Thankfully it did this time too, and soon he was prattling on with Lisa adding her dining plans now and then.

Jamie joined us. 'Andrew is not going to let you just have dessert,' he told Matty.

'Yeah, he will,' Matty said. 'He told me I could.'

Jamie pulled a face at me, and I shrugged. All-you-could-eat dessert was no different to him and me buying all sorts of stuff for them today. Lisa said Matty would get fat like Augustus Gloop, but very little put our youngest brother off food so he didn't look like he cared.

Megan came to us with a tray of hot chocolates. We were *all* gonna end up like that kid in Willy Wonka.

With a milky moustache, Lisa asked what time dad was coming. I glanced down at my watch. 'In about fifteen minutes.'

'What about the policeman?'

'Pretty soon.' He was supposed to arrive before dad did. Well, at least before dad's *planned* arrival time.

Lisa gave a sort of nod and then Matty asked why a cop was coming and why Andrew wasn't staying.

Megan and Jamie turned to me; I became fascinated with my half-drunk drink. Megan spoke before Jamie could. 'Andrew didn't think staying was right,' she said. 'And a police officer is coming to the meeting just to make sure it all goes smoothly.'

'But it's *dad*,' Matty said.

'Yes, it's dad,' she said, with a little hitch. 'But he left us, Matty, and it's not… We're not…' She looked at Jamie and me.

'Dad's been pretty rude and angry to Andrew and Owen,' Jamie said before I even got my mouth half open. 'Even though Andrew's not here, he could still be rude to Owen. The cop will prevent that.'

I wasn't sure I liked Jamie's tone, sort of like he was a hundred percent ready to get into the fray even if the cop was doing his job. Instead of warning him, I looked at Matty, tried out a smile. 'He's here to stop us being rude, too. We're still trying to get answers. It won't happen if we're all grouchy or yelly.'

'Dad won't hit you, Owen. I know he won't.'

My lungs squeezed air out and for a second refused to let any back in. How had Matty got *hit* out of the conversation? Reflex had me trying to smile, to agree with him, but when I looked up at Jamie and Megan their expressions displayed concern. I swallowed, then blurted, 'This is all my fault. If I hadn't—'

'If *dad* hadn't left in the first place,' Jamie cut me off. 'Owen, all this is his fault, not yours. It's him coming back after all this time and expecting us to be okay with it that's the problem. It's his jealousy that we're perfectly fine without him that's the problem.'

'But—'

'No buts,' he said with a growl. 'It's not your fault!'

His angry expression challenged me to refute his words but

I didn't have the strength. Wouldn't have got far anyway because the doorbell suddenly went. We all jerked to attention. My heart thudded painfully as I got up. 'Everybody ready?'

Rhetorical because I didn't wait for an answer.

The man on the porch was in full uniform. He introduced himself as Officer Ben McCorkindale and showed me his ID. 'You're Owen, I presume?'

'Yes,' I croaked. I pulled the door open wider so he could enter, noting that the car on the drive appeared mostly unmarked. Hopefully that meant our neighbours would notice nothing odd.

As he stepped in, looking around the entrance space, he asked if dad was here yet.

'No.' Even if he had arrived early, we wouldn't have let him in.

The officer nodded. 'Alright, that's good.'

I shut the door then led the way to the lounge. Jamie and Megan were on their feet, Jamie with his eyes slightly narrowed. 'Um… this is Officer McCorkindale.' I cleared my throat, waved a hand toward my siblings. 'Jamie and Megan, and Lisa and Matty on the couch.'

Jamie just gave a stiff nod, but Megan greeted him by name and he smiled and said we could call him Ben. For some reason Jamie's gaze came to me, and I blurted out if the officer wanted a drink while we waited for dad.

'No, I'm fine, Owen,' he responded.

'Okay then, um, take a seat.'

He sat in the chair. Megan plonked herself down beside Jamie, so I sat with Lisa and Matty. They were openly staring but none of us warned them off doing so. My heart hadn't really settled from the rough beat that had started when the doorbell rang and I felt sick with nerves. Jamie drew breath between his teeth but didn't speak.

I didn't want to speak but the silence was shredding my nerves, so I forced out, 'Uh, you know what this is about, don't you Mr… Officer?' My face heated at the title hash.

'Just call me Ben,' he said, smiling. 'And yes, Sergeant Morrison gave me a full briefing.'

'Oh,' I got out. 'Good.' Wondered how just how full a "full briefing" really was.

- # -

Dad stopped just behind the single chair and smiled. 'Hi, everyone. How're you all doing?'

Though my focus was on him I saw Jamie's gaze swivel my way. I didn't look at him but I was probably thinking the same—that dad was acting like he hadn't just been let into the house by a uniformed police officer, who stood within reaching distance. His smile seemed genuine.

My gut knotted even though I was thinking this was just what we needed right now—a sort of nothingness so that we could start again. To help with that, I indicated the chair. 'Hi, Dad, take a seat.'

I felt Jamie's gaze more keenly for a moment, but we *had* to try. That was the plan we'd come up with—try to be friendly, try to stay calm.

As dad moved to the chair, Megan asked if he wanted a drink.

'No, I'm fine, thanks Megan,' he responded with a smile.
'Ok-kay.'

Jamie glanced at her as she sank back against the couch. He sat right on the edge, like he was seconds from standing.

No birthday comment from dad, and I had to bite my tongue not to speak about it; it'd probably hurt Megan more than help.

Officer McCorkindale cleared his throat. 'This meeting is for you all to participate in a family discussion in comfortable surroundings.' His smile was a little tense. I dropped my gaze to the coffee table since both dad and Jamie looked at me. 'Apart from ensuring that everyone gets the chance to speak in safety, I won't be taking part. However, please do let me know if I can be of assistance.'

Megan was nodding. I flinched when I felt my t-shirt tug; Lisa taking a fistful of it, face pale. I smiled as confidently as I could at her and didn't dislodge her hand.

'Thank you, Officer,' dad was saying, 'but I'm sure you won't be required.'

Jamie coughed, as if choking back words, earning a bit of brow furrow from dad.

Aside from trying to be relaxed and friendly, we'd also agreed to stick to some questions we still wanted answers to, try to get more clarification around why dad had been away for so long. And what his plans *really* were. I hoped he'd give such good explanations that we'd all become comfortable with him back in our lives.

Yet, dad's gaze on me gave off the vibe that things wouldn't go quite so smooth. Before I could stop myself, I mumbled, 'This isn't about me.'

Dad crossed one leg over the other and said, 'What was that, Tramp?'

Couldn't stop the flinch, but I think the look on my face

prevented Jamie speaking. His mouth stayed open a second, before closing, jaw tight.

'Dad, *please*, this meeting isn't about what I did last year.' Proud of myself that I hadn't emphasised the big time gap. 'These guys deserve answers about why you left and were gone so long without contact.'

'Fucking A,' Jamie said. 'We want to know where you've been. You said St Louis, but was that *all* the time? And what *are* your plans? Andrew's guardianship doesn't dissolve just because you're back, Dad, you know that. You've got months to make up for. You need to—'

'I don't *need* to do anything, Jamie,' dad cut him off. 'And I don't see your guardian here now.' He made a show of looking around.

'You know why that is,' I said steadily.

Dad smirked at me, but his attention was taken by Megan when she asked *why* he'd come back.

'Because I've sorted myself out,' he said. 'I know that leaving was a terrible choice, but I couldn't cope anymore.'

'Dad,' Jamie said, 'we were five kids! How the fuck did you think *we* would?'

'You appear to have managed very well,' came the even response. 'As you've told me several times, in fact. Didn't lack anything.' Dad's gaze locked me in place. 'Customer every night was it, Owen?'

My chin came up, jaw tight. 'I did what I did to keep us alive.'

Dad snorted.

'You left five kids alone, Dad, all under seventeen.' I rose. 'We'd only just lost mum and then we lost you too. We had no idea what was going on and it wasn't like any of us had a job. You don't have *any* right to scoff at what I did.' I dragged in a breath, indicated my siblings all sitting stiff and silent. 'At least I d-didn't ditch them.' I shifted on my feet.

That appeared to be the signal to get Jamie upright too. 'Dad, this isn't about Owen,' he said. 'He did what he did, blah blah. Where were *you* when we needed you? Did you stop to think how we would manage, where we'd get money from, what we'd do if one of us got sick? Why did you never contact us, even to let us know that you were alive?'

'I wasn't in the right head space for contact,' dad said, stiffly. 'Your mum's death hit me hard. I felt so guilty forcing her here, thinking that if I hadn't done so then she wouldn't have been in that accident.' He drew in a breath. 'I had to stay away until I was sure I could cope.'

My throat was tight with grief over mum, and I could see my brothers and sisters were upset too but I also got that Jamie and Megan were angry or insulted, definitely puzzled. Grief does weird things, for sure, but abandoning your kids? For taking *more* than a year to get back in contact?

'We needed you, Dad,' Megan croaked out. 'At least… at least to know you were *alive*.'

'I'm sorry, Megan.'

She shook her head, but she did it long enough that it didn't seem to be a non-acceptance of his apology.

Jamie glanced sideways at me, as if to check about what we did next. I really didn't know but at least dad seemed to have gone away from being nasty about me. Except, he must have seen my flicker of relief because he suddenly said, looking at Megan and Jamie, 'Did Owen tell you where that money was coming from? How he earned it?'

They both looked puzzled, and then Megan said, 'Yes.'

'And you were okay with it?'

My sister and brother remained silent, as if they weren't sure how to respond. Officer McCorkindale shifted on the dining chair but he didn't speak.

Dad pursed his lips, a brow slightly raised, and then he shook his head. 'You kids clearly have no clue.'

'What?' Jamie got out on a croak, looked at me but I had no idea where this was going either.

Dad came straight out and asked if they knew what happened when two guys had sex.

'What?' Megan squeaked.

Jamie looked too stunned to speak.

'Dad,' I began, 'this has—'

'Shut it, Fag.'

My mouth hung open, and horror tried to crawl out. The names I'd heard in that meeting started crowding the side-lines in my head, getting louder and louder. Oh God, *please*, don't start that here. 'Please, don't—'

'Your opinion means nothing, you disgusting little whore,' he cut over me.

'Stop it, Dad!' Jamie growled. 'What he did's way in the past.'

'How so?' dad challenged. 'He and that man—'

'Andrew is my *partner*,' I got out around the spike in my throat. Edged just a little more into the open.

'I don't care what you call him, Owen,' dad told me, and turned back to my brothers and sisters as if I was some bug he'd just swatted away. 'Do you kids not understand what he's been doing? Is that why you support him, because you don't know?'

'We're not fuck-wits,' Jamie said.

'Oh?'

A chill dripped down my spine; Jamie'd responded honestly but I got the feeling he'd played into dad's hands.

Dad said, 'Because you've seen?'

Jamie blinked. 'What?'

'You know what goes on because you've seen?' Dad asked.

Jamie just stared.

'Do they do it in front of you? Do they involve you?'

'No!' I cried. 'Dad, you're—'

'Mr Tremayne,' Officer McCorkindale said. 'I don't see how this relates to the discussion.'

Dad held his hands up, smiled. 'This is between me and my children, Officer. I'm sure you acknowledge I have the right to ensure their safety.'

'Fuck off, Dad,' Jamie spat, looking angry and disgusted. Then, probably because I just stood there, he growled at me to defend myself. Megan rose beside him, took his arm as he started to take a step.

Dad laughed. 'Owen's a gross little buggerer. There's only one defence for *that.*'

'What is wrong with you, Dad?' I said. 'How do you not get that you can't just come back like nothing's changed? You think mum might not have died if we'd not come here, but we did come and she did die, and you left *your kids* all alone! You really couldn't suck it up and contact us at least once?' I took a breath to get my voice down from angry heights. 'There's no way that what I did is *worse* than you running out on us. A *father* wouldn't do that, and I hope you *do* feel guilty about mum. I hope it haunts you because of what you put us through.'

A threatening scowl colonised dad's face. I just stood

straighter, ground out, 'And saying all this stuff in front of Lisa and Matty just proves you're a shit father. *No* one is involved in anything that Andrew and I do. You're sick in the head and depraved thinking that!'

'Who's depraved, Owen?' dad asked.

'*You are!*' Megan screeched, making us all jump. She jabbed a finger my way. 'We're not here to discuss his and Andrew's relationship. This is about *you*, Dad, and us. If you're not going to talk about you and us, then just… l-leave.'

Jamie went to put an arm around her and she shoved him away. She was upset, sure, but also really, really angry. Jamie glanced at me but I couldn't speak, couldn't even warn Megan that she was just lining herself up in dad's gaze.

Except, she didn't seem to be. Dad's gaze was on me. 'Nice job of turning my kids against me, Owen.'

'Don't insult my brothers and sisters,' I got out. 'They can form their own opinions.'

'Fucking *A*,' Megan growled, though her breath hitched and she wiped at her eyes.

Jamie was sucking in his lips.

Into that speck of silence, Matty shouted, 'I hate you, Dad' and dashed out of the lounge. We all stood in shock a second, as if we'd forgotten about him and Lisa on the couch. I croaked out his name and started to go after him.

Dad grabbed my arm and swung a fist. Stars exploded in my vision and pain radiated from my face. I got out a croak or cry or something, struggled to stay upright. Dad actually helped with that because he didn't let me go, but then he spun me around against the armchair and twisted my arm up my back. 'You aren't fit to be a Tremayne,' he snarled in my ear.

The chair jabbed my ribs and dad's harsh breathing lifted

my hair. I felt his nails dig into my wrist, and… was he tugging on my jeans? I was screaming to be let go before common sense could tell me I *wasn't* back in Jack Wheeler's house.

Megan and Jamie were shouting and then I leaned against the chair on my own. No pressure over me, no nails in my arm. Dad was swearing but Officer McCorkindale had a pretty good hold on him as he dragged him away from me, speaking over top of him. Arresting him, I think. I pushed back from the chair and stumbled, vision swimming. Shock and pain had me in a panic, and… a fork lay under the chair. Heh, wonder how long—

'Owen.'

'Don't touch me!' I shrieked at Megan, making her jump back. I scrambled up myself, reeling until the grip on the chair steadied me.

My sister's eyes shone and beyond her Jamie looked blank, like he couldn't gather any one emotion to the front. The officer had dad in a shoulder lock, but that didn't stop him mouthing off. 'When I get that criminal out of this house, you'll be going too, you little slut.'

'Y-you, you—' The right side of my face reverberated harder than my heart was beating. I really felt like throwing up and was only just stopping myself from stumbling from the room. I wanted to stay, to prove that I was strong against dad. I heard Jamie tell Megan to get Lisa out of here. She didn't need to be told twice.

'Make it easier for them, Owen,' dad said and I looked at him. 'Tell that paedophile to disappear.'

'No,' I whispered. 'Dad, it's not—'

'Then you better warn him to watch his back.'

'Mr Tremayne, threatening someone is an offence,' Officer

McCorkindale said. 'You are damaging any case you might have against Mr Gordon, any case you might have to get your children back.'

'He has *no* case,' Jamie spat. 'We don't want him back. Andrew's our father.'

'He fucks your brother,' dad said. 'That man isn't—'

'I'm not listening to this,' I blurted and turned on my heel.

Jamie yelled my name, and I might have managed to stop myself if dad hadn't shouted, 'Get your ass back here, I haven't said you can go.'

Like I was listening to *him!*

Andrew

My cell phone went on the passenger seat just as I was turning into the long road that led to Owen's street. I'd been intending to stay in the cafe until it was time to get back to the kids, but my nerves had been too tight to sit about in public, so I was driving back to park close by. Sitting in the car, listening to the radio, was at least out of public view. The phone ringing gave me enough of a shock that I let out a loud curse, and almost over-corrected the turn.

I hurriedly parked at the side of the road and reached for the phone, heart missing when I saw who was calling. 'Uh, hi Jamie, what—'

'DadhitOwentheofficerhas—'

'Kid, slow down! I can't understand you.' Had I just heard that Owen had been *hit?*

Jamie took a deep breath. 'S-sorry,' he said. 'It's just—Shit, Andrew, dad was saying stupid shitandhehitOwenMatty—'

'Jamie!' I cut over sharply. 'Please! Take a *breath.*'

His panic was ramping up my own. My heart thrashed in my chest now and when I realised I'd unclicked my seatbelt I froze. No way I could rush—

'Sorry, sorry, I'm good.' He sounded muffled, like he was trying not to be overheard.

'Are you safe?' I demanded.

'What? Yeah, we're... The officer's arrested dad.'

I was speechless a second. What had... 'Is Owen *hurt?*'

'Yeah, sort of, not... He ran out.' Jamie got in another breath. 'Dad hit him and he ran.' A big breath. 'Can you look out for him? You were staying around close by, right?'

'Yes,' I said, trying to stay in control myself. 'I'll look for him. Are the others okay?'

'Matty won't come out of his room, but we're okay. Just... It was... anyway—'

He kept talking, sped up again, but I didn't hear it because I happened to look up. Stumbling down the pavement on the other side of the road was Owen. I choked on my breath momentarily.

'Jamie,' I croaked. 'The officer's still with you, right?'

'Yes.'

'And you *are* safe?'

'Yeah.'

'Has Sergeant Morrison been contacted?'

'I don't know. Dad's been... Well, the officer's been kind of busy. Should I—'

'No, no, I'll do it.'

'T-thanks.'

Jamie actually ended the call before I could speak again. I tossed the phone to the seat and jumped out of the car. 'Owen.'

Across the road, Owen jerked and looked about. When I called again, crossing the road, he spotted me and stopped dead.

I slowed my approach, though I wanted to rush, because he looked like he'd bolt at the drop of a hat. His eyes were huge with pupil, and an angry mark bloomed over his cheek. I swallowed down my rage that his father had caused the damage and just waited, wanting it to be Owen's choice to close the gap between us.

We stared at each other a moment, then Owen said, 'I found a f-fork under the chair.'

Totally thrown, I looked at his hands but though fisted they weren't clutching anything.

I caught movement, prepared myself to run after him, but he was coming to me; stood toe to toe and gripped my shirt hard, face against my chest. He wasn't crying, too much shock, I think, and I could feel him trembling even without holding him.

I was in shock too, but I let us stand like that on a public street for ten minutes before I encouraged him over to my car.

'Don't take me home,' he whispered.

'I'm not,' I said. 'We're going to a clinic.'

I caught his brows rising as I executed the U-turn. 'I want your face checked.'

'It's not that b-bad.'

'You can't see it, Owen, it is that bad.'

He gave a sort of shrug.

Barely spoke at the emergency clinic except for a few essential answers, including that he'd tripped and hit his face on the outside table. I let him go with that lie for now, trying to keep back my growing rage at the truth. While he had a few minutes alone with the doctor I texted Jamie to let him know I had his brother, and then phoned the sergeant and told him I'd be showing up very soon.

I didn't tell Owen we were going to the station so he tensed like a spring when we pulled into the parking lot, but he didn't balk me. I stayed close, not because I was afraid he'd try a runner but because he was shaking and I wanted to be able to catch him should he collapse.

The sergeant's door was closed. Since he was expecting us I rapped a knuckle on it and opened it, pulling Owen with me into the room.

Morrison was on the phone. He looked up, annoyed, but that expression turned to shock when I shifted Owen and his bruised face into view. 'Uh Bernie, I need to go.'

As soon as the phone clicked into its holder, I said, 'Here's what a badly bruised cheek delivered by a father looks like.' I hadn't meant to start like that, but my anger pushed all other emotion aside.

Morrison swore, unbidden going by his expression, and rose. Owen hunched a little closer to me. He swayed a bit and I encouraged him to the chair just behind him. The sergeant handed me a folded blanket, which I flapped open and swung around Owen's shoulders, guiding his hands so he was gripping the material himself. Then I turned back to the sergeant.

'What are you going to do about this?' I ground out. 'Mr Tremayne assaulted Owen *in front of a cop*, in front of all of his children!'

Behind me came a small whimper, and I tried again to rein back my anger but I was speaking through clenched teeth now. 'I agree that the kids and their father should talk, and that it's best without my presence, but that man has lost the plot! Assaulting his *own child?* Sergeant—'

'I don't want to be here.'

The tiny voice replaced my anger with sadness. Tears stood in Owen's eyes as he looked up at me. I dropped to my knees and gently drew him into my arms, careful to ensure his head came to my left shoulder, protecting his injured face. I felt him trying to hold control but then I heard, 'He had my arm… arm… t-twisted l-like W-Wheeler. Over the ch-chair.' He choked on a sob, fingers gripping into my shirt.

Now I understood Owen's horror. It wasn't so much that his dad had hit him, but that the man had done something that had linked him to a terrifying action from Owen's past. I twisted to look up at the sergeant. 'I don't want that man anywhere near my kids.'

'He *is* their father.'

'Look at what he did! He almost broke one of his children's cheekbones,' I returned. 'And I'm sure you haven't forgotten Jack Wheeler.'

I took a moment after that, hearing Owen's half cry and feeling him trembling against me, hating myself for even mentioning the name out loud. But Sergeant Morrison straightened, maybe now realised the situation was more serious than first thought.

I continued, in any case, needing to get my point across. 'Jamie's panic was clear, Sergeant, when he phoned me, and I didn't think he even knew what that state was.' Winced a little, since that sounded poor, but I realised it was Jamie's panic that had really driven up mine. Anger was that kid's usual emotion in anything, but this time— 'Have you been in contact with your man there? Is Mr Tremayne out of the house?'

'I've been in contact,' Morrison said, with a short nod. 'And no, Mr Tremayne has not left.'

'*Why not?*

'He has been arrested, and matters are calm there now.'

I breathed out. Arrested…

'That's because I'm not there,' came a mumble. Owen pushed off my shoulder, looked worse now with red-rimmed eyes.

'Angel, it's not—'

'It's because I'm not there,' he said over me with some force.

I eased away from him, took the spare chair.

'What do you mean, Owen?' Sergeant Morrison asked, leaning against his desk.

Owen put a hand to his cheek briefly. 'The first few minutes were… okay, but then… It was just like when I met with him here. He ranted on about the stuff I did last year, right in front of everyone. Lisa and Matty…' He scrunched up his brows. 'Matty yelled he hated dad and ran to his room.' He looked at the sergeant standing grimly. 'Are they okay? Did the officer…?' He trailed off, and his glance at me showed guilt. 'I ran,' he whispered, eyes filling.

An old habit that had made another reappearance. 'It's okay, Owen,' I said softly.

'It's not,' he croaked back. 'I didn't even want to be there *at all*. I'm such a coward.'

He got to his feet as if he was about to run a second time, but turned to me. I drew him into my embrace, half entangled in the blanket. I looked at Morrison over him, brow arched.

'Ben hasn't reported any further issues,' Morrison said.

'Because I *left*,' we heard Owen mutter.

I understood why he felt this way. My experience of Mr Tremayne and hearing Megan and Jamie relate pieces of the various visits had me think the same; that his agenda was really just to get me out of their lives. He was using Owen's age—and now obviously his past—to do it. Not that he seemed to actually care about his son's welfare, since many of his words had indicated Owen would go when I did.

On top of everything else my young man had been through, this treatment had to hurt even if he didn't *want* his father around. Being a pawn in Tremayne's machinations wasn't doing much for his mental health. He had become so much stronger and confident in himself over the past months that regression would be a heart-breaking thing to allow to happen.

I asked if I could take Owen home. Sergeant Morrison shook his head. I stiffened and Owen pulled back, obviously feeling it. 'I want to go.'

'And you will,' Morrison told him. 'But I'll take you.'

'I don't—'

Morrison cut me off with, 'Mr Tremayne is still at the house, Mr Gordon.'

'Then get him out of it,' I growled.

He didn't respond to that. Holding my breath, I willed my anger back along with the sudden sense of helplessness. Owen tweaked my sleeve. 'We'll see you later anyway.'

I had momentarily forgotten that we were going to dinner. Shit—Megan. I looked at Owen. 'Did your dad remember Megan's birthday?'

Owen's eyes went wide a second and then he shook his

head, lips pressed. 'At least… at least not that I heard.'

I blew out a breath. Christ, I should have tried harder to get this meeting shifted. That poor girl…

Then Sergeant Morrison said, quietly, 'It would be best if you didn't see the kids tonight, Mr Gordon.'

'*What?*'

Owen's mouth dropped but he didn't speak.

'In this circumstance,' the sergeant said with a taut voice, 'we should let matters ease a little.'

'My time is not up,' I heard myself say with the same sort of tautness. Our restaurant plans were definitely done with but it wasn't yet eight o'clock.

'I am aware of that, but I appeal to your common sense.'

I didn't know how to respond to that.

'What do you mean?' Owen asked. 'We're supposed to be going to dinner.' He shifted to spy the clock on the back wall, mouth dropping a little as he saw it was nearing quarter past seven. He looked at me.

I just looked back, feeling like my rights were being stripped. I turned to Morrison. 'They need an adult with them tonight, Sergeant.'

'I agree,' he said. 'So Officer McCorkindale will stay.'

'What?' Owen got out. 'But… what?'

I let out a long sigh, pressed hands to my forehead. 'I believe the good sergeant is worried about how you kids will be—having dealt with your father and then having me back and then leaving again. And you, Angel…' I murmured. 'You probably shouldn't be on your feet much longer.'

'I feel okay.'

He didn't look okay, and adrenalin and the initial pain relief would fade. I hated it but clearly the evening's plans were cancelled.

Owen took a step back, shaking his head. 'This isn't fair.'

'Owen.'

'This. Isn't. Fair.'

I kept my hands to myself. His anger was now first and foremost.

'Dad can't do this!' Owen cried at Sergeant Morrison. 'We were all trying… and he…' He took a deep breath, attempting control. 'He made my little brother and sister c-cry.'

'What are you going to do,' I asked the sergeant in a soft voice, 'to ensure this doesn't happen again?' Soft, but I knew he heard my anger.

'Mr Tremayne *has* been arrested. He'll be charged with assault.'

'*And?*

Sergeant Morrison's brows came together. 'Mr Gordon, we must follow—'

'Oh, don't give me that,' I broke over him. 'Owen and I have been following *your* rules, doing everything right, and yet it seems to me that Tremayne has had no limits placed upon him!'

'Andrew,' Owen said softly, and I saw his worry.

'I'm sorry, Owen,' I said, 'but I want the good sergeant to reassure me that this sort of thing won't happen again.' I turned back to Morrison. 'You are penalising me and the kids, while that man can come and go as he pleases, and assault his children at the same time. How can you let him be in the house after what he did to Owen or what he said in front of the younger two?'

Sergeant Morrison stood silent. I guessed he faced angry people every day in his line of work and I was just another to be dealt with, but I would ensure my voice was heard and that he understood the situation. For that reason, I wasn't about to offer an apology. Into the tense silence Owen whispered that he didn't feel well.

'Oh, Owen,' I croaked. 'I'm so sorry.' Tears stood in his beautiful eyes, and my heart squeezed tight. I turned to the sergeant. 'I don't want that man near my kids after tonight.'

Morrison went stiff, but I saw a half nod. I knew, for Owen's sake right now, I had to accept that and stop pushing. I turned back to Owen, brushed some hair off his forehead, tried a smile. 'The sergeant will take you home, Owen, and I want you to go to bed when you get there. Take some of those pills if you need. We'll sort out another date for a better dinner.'

As I talked, I was herding him from the office, Sergeant Morrison following quietly.

'I'll come over early tomorrow, alright?'

'Yeah.'

Owen's voice had no tone; he was drained. I knew that when all his senses kicked back in he was going to be hurt and resentful about the situation. I just hoped he'd be okay without me tonight.

If all had gone well with this meeting, and the dinner, then me not being there the night would have been like any other. Owen hated it but he was coping. *Tonight* though… with his cheek, his father's words, his siblings, the abandoned dinner…

I understood Morrison's reasoning behind me not showing up but I couldn't help feeling my absence would make everything worse, not better.

At my car, I kissed Owen's unblemished cheek but he

didn't speak or otherwise react. In fact, he'd gone pretty blank. I remembered this from other bad situations; a sort of coping mechanism for him, but one that scared me. Except, I couldn't do anything to help this time.

Sergeant Morrison and I shook hands. He agreed to keep me updated, and then I forced myself into my car.

As I drove away out came a long line of swear words that had been building. I felt no better about anything when I ran out of breath.

I didn't do the thing I most wanted to do—go to Owen's house and show that man my fists. And then take the kids away. There was no way I could ever act like that, even in their defence, not with my guardianship in such precarious balance.

Owen

As Sergeant Morrison drove, I felt compelled to apologise for stuffing up the meeting.

He darted me a glance. 'I cannot see how you are at fault, Owen.' He let out a sigh. 'Like Mr Gordon, I really did think everything would go fine with my officer there.'

'I don't think dad cared at all. And even without Andrew he still had me to go at.' I let out a long sigh, rubbed my tight cheek. It didn't really ache because of the drugs but I rubbed like it did anyway. 'Megan shouted, you know,' I said after a bit. 'More impressive than Jamie.' Couldn't believe that amused me.

There was a long silence, but I wasn't surprised. What *could* the sergeant say to that?

After a moment he said my name. I didn't turn from the window, so he just continued, 'Your father *will* be formally charged with assault. He may have a legal case regarding your relationship, but he won't get away with assault.'

'He won't care,' I mumbled at the window.

Morrison growled that he *would*. I guessed he meant that a charge would dent his chances of getting Andrew's guardianship annulled. That was good, but I still thought dad would just carry on anyway. He hadn't cared about violence tonight in front of a police officer.

The rest of the journey was in silence.

As we pulled into the drive I noticed dad's car on the road. Still here, of course, but it surprised me now. I hadn't obviously been taking a lot of notice when I'd rushed from the house earlier. Would they just let dad drive off?

We were halfway to the front door when it opened. I let out a startled cry as Sergeant Morrison took my arm and shifted me to the other side of him, putting himself between me and dad. My heart hammered at the sudden move, but missed a beat when I caught dad's gaze. He opened his mouth and Sergeant Morrison said, 'Ben, put him in my car. He'll be coming to the station with me.'

The officer said something but my ears were only on dad telling me I was a good-for-nothing faggot.

'Mr Tremayne,' the sergeant growled, 'that is enough.'

Dad sneered.

'Better a faggot than a father who hits his kids.'

Even the sergeant swung his glance to me. I felt a bit of shock myself that I'd spoken, but I raised my chin and stepped up beside Morrison who stiffened in alert. But then I realised something—dad stood there in handcuffs—and I could only stare rather than continue speaking.

They jingled as the officer encouraged dad to start walking.

I flinched when Sergeant Morrison pulled me back again but I didn't try to break free.

'At the station, Mr Tremayne,' Morrison said, 'you will be formally charged with assault. I will also be initiating a restraining order preventing you from being on this property or approaching your children without permission.'

'I am their *father*,' dad growled.

'That doesn't give you the right to hit me, Dad,' I said. 'Or scare the others. If you think—'

'Owen,' the sergeant said in a stern voice, making me subside. 'Mr Tremayne, the order will also forbid you to approach Mr Gordon.'

'That man,' dad spat. 'He's a bloody—'

'Your case grows thinner with every word out of your mouth,' Morrison told him. 'Any assault on Mr Gordon will nullify it. And any further assault on your children will see you do jail time. Is that clear?'

I went still. Jail? Part of me was suddenly all for that, but… *jail?* That threat would only—Yes, dad had an expression on his face that made my insides tighten. When it came my way I involuntarily stepped back, almost tripped on the first porch step.

'Get yourself inside, Owen,' the sergeant told me. 'I'll be in shortly.'

'The kids are out on the deck,' the officer said. 'They'll be happy to see you.' He almost smiled, but then dad opened his mouth and he went back into cop mode and hustled dad away.

When I just stood there, Sergeant Morrison said, sternly, 'Go on.'

Since I got the feeling he'd have helped me along if I'd continued just standing there I went, heart thudding harder as

I stepped inside and the door closed behind me.

There was no sound of anything, and as I slowly walked around toward the lounge I saw the officer was right. My brothers and sisters were outside and the French doors were closed. I wondered if they'd been out there since I'd bolted—a sort of safety measure while the officer dealt with dad.

Megan spotted me first. She jumped up but it was Matty who came flying in and grabbed me around the waist, knocking me back a step. I didn't shove him away, just held him as tightly, swallowing hard as the others came in. Jamie looked utterly furious.

God, I shouldn't have run. How weak was that, leaving them all here?

I opened my mouth and Megan said, shakily, 'Are you okay?'

'Y-yeah.'

'Your cheek…' She trailed off, glanced back at Jamie as he let out a feral sound.

'It's not broken,' I managed. 'Just… ugly.' I had a bottle of painkillers in my pocket for when the first round of drugs wore off, but for now I felt okay. 'How… how are you guys?'

Given that Matty was squeezing me hard, obviously not brilliant. Megan glanced back at Jamie; he scowled at her, turned it to me so I had a feeling something had gone on. 'What?' I asked.

'Jamie tried to hit dad.'

That was Lisa who'd been hanging back by the door. My brother hissed her name, though without menace. When he looked back at me he was still angry but I could see a sort of embarrassment too.

'What did you do?' I asked.

Jamie rubbed his hands over his hair. 'It was just… he was spouting such shit, I couldn't…' He turned his head briefly, jaw clenched. 'Even after he was in cuffs, he just wouldn't shut up. Guess…' He let out a sigh. 'I saw red.'

I could only stand and stare at him, then apologise to my little brother when he let out a whimper and I realised I'd been squeezing him extra hard. I unravelled him from me, and he went to sit by Megan who'd collapsed to the couch.

'I didn't actually touch him,' Jamie said. 'Ben… kept me back.'

I was pretty sure Megan mouthed *headlock*, but because the front door opened my focus turned that way. In my side vision I saw Megan pop onto her feet, pulling Matty up and telling him and Lisa to get outside. I glanced that way briefly, noting that they obeyed her, and then it was just us three watching Sergeant Morrison come into the lounge.

The sergeant opened his mouth, but my brother and sister both spoke:

Jamie: 'Where's dad?'

Megan: 'Where's Andrew?'

Jamie turned to look at her, and then they both looked at me as if only now realising I'd come in alone. I swallowed.

'Your father is safely in my car, Jamie,' the sergeant said. 'I will be taking him to the station shortly. And I have asked Mr Gordon to stay away for the rest of tonight.'

'Why?' my brother demanded.

'I thought the situation was rough enough without you having to cope with his return and then departure tonight.'

'Shouldn't *we* be the ones deciding that?' Jamie asked, thumbing between us.

'Andrew agreed,' I mumbled.

Jamie scowled.

'But, dinner,' Megan suddenly said. 'It's my—' She cut off, pressed a hand over her mouth.

Guilt shot through me, somehow allowing pain to eke out around the drugs. 'I n-need to lie down,' I whispered.

I was done with standing upright, and being around people. Guilt, pain, grief, shock, horror—I needed to be on my own for a bit, so I turned and headed for my room without waiting for any sort of response.

Jamie

Watching Owen walk stiffly away made me wonder if something else had gone on that we didn't know about. I turned back to Sergeant Morrison. 'What's up?'

He looked at me in total surprise. 'Pardon?'

'With Owen, with dad, with… everything.'

Now Megan was looking at me, brows bunched in puzzlement.

'Andrew texted he was going to take Owen to see you,' I said. 'What happened?'

'Just that, Jamie,' the sergeant said. 'From what Mr Gordon said, your brother's cheek is badly bruised not broken. We talked for a while and then Mr Gordon agreed to stay away, and I brought Owen here.'

I gave a stiff nod.

'And as well as the assault charge against your father,' he continued, 'he will also have a restraining order placed upon him.'

'Does Owen know that?' I asked.

The sergeant nodded. 'And it will protect Mr Gordon also.'

I felt my brows go up at that because I hadn't really thought of danger to Andrew.

Dad had only mouthed off about Owen's prostitution; for some reason he seemed to think that was great ammo to get everyone against Owen. We'd told him otherwise before the officer had ordered us all to get outside. I scratched my head, hoping suddenly that Ben hadn't told Morrison about my own little attempted thing.

Megan got my attention by speaking my name. I turned to her. 'What?'

'Go sit with Owen for a bit.'

'What? Why?'

'Because it's a good idea,' she said, firmly. 'Right, Sergeant Morrison?'

The sergeant suppressed most of his surprise at being brought into the conversation. 'Sure, Megan.' He even managed a smile. 'I expect your brother would appreciate some company right now.'

I pulled a face, managing to stop myself saying that the appreciated company was Andrew not me, and left the lounge.

Owen lay on his back, looking at a white pill container. His expression was just a little weird, so I whisked the container from his hand, made a show of looking it over and reading the instructions. He didn't speak. 'Need any?'

He shook his head. 'I'm just tired. Later though.'

I set the container on the drawers across the room, then sat on the computer chair, spun around on it for a second.

'Jamie, you don't have to stay.'

'Megan's orders,' I said, giving a tiny smile. Then that

wiped. 'Dad scared you, didn't he? Not the cheek, but with the chair/arm thing.'

Owen jerked, startled.

I pulled a bit of a face; probably could have led that in a whole bunch better but it had suddenly come back to me. His next expression made me think he was going to deny it, but I'd been there and I'd *seen*. However, he pushed up onto a hip and nodded. 'Yeah. It was…' He let out a breath. 'Jack Wheeler did the same thing.'

I stiffened, making him look at me rather than at the bed cover. He did a weird, jerky head shake. 'I was instantly back *there*, Jamie,' he whispered, 'and I… I just had to get out, away from dad and his words.'

Despite what I felt about Owen and his tendency to run rather than face up to things, I backed him. I'd have run too, if I'd been the subject of that abuse and that outpouring of horrible words.

Both those things, and seeing how frazzled Owen was, had ramped up my own feelings. I remembered my call to Andrew. He'd had to tell me several times to take a breath and calm down, that he couldn't understand me. When I'd managed to communicate properly he'd been really concerned. God, I could only imagine what he was like now, being made to stay away.

Owen drew in a ragged breath, drawing my focus. He probably should have been horizontal but I refrained from telling him that. As if he sensed I was thinking it, he said, 'Did the officer put you in a headlock?'

'What?' I yelped.

'Megan mouthed it,' he said, 'when we were talking before. Did he?'

'No!' I scratched my cheek. 'Well, almost.'

'Fuck, Jamie, that was stupid.'

Instead of retorting angrily, defensively or rudely like the Jamie of last year would have, all I did was snort.

My brother looked surprised momentarily.

'Well... he freaked Matty out, he freaked *you* out. What else could I do?' I held a hand up when he opened his mouth. 'Rhetorical question, so shut it.' I gave him a second or two to respond but he did shut his mouth. 'I really just saw red. Dad didn't seem *any* kind of sorry, Owen, even after Ben had cuffed him. Man, he was spouting some shit.'

The non-purple side of my brother's face pulled up in a grimace. Then his head inclined just a little. 'You went after dad when he was already cuffed?'

'Ah...' I cleared my throat. 'I didn't actually touch him, you know, but... yeah, he was already cuffed. He was so smug, like everything was going his way. He told us about the driver. Mum's accident,' I added when he looked blank.

'Oh.'

Suddenly Owen looked devastated and I hurriedly said, 'I don't know if they really heard though cos it was amongst other stuff he was ranting.'

Owen squinted at me but I reckoned I spoke true about that. Dad really had been vomiting up words.

'Anyway...' I forced out a smile. 'Ben made us all get outside and we couldn't hear him through the door after that. Then Megan made Lisa and Matty recite all the states in reverse order.'

When Owen raised a brow, I said, 'Yeah, absolute torture.' But it had taken the kids' minds off dad for a while.

My brother gave a glimpse of a smile. 'Guess you got Matty

out of his room, then?'

I nodded, didn't say that it had taken decent encouragement and that he'd really only come out once Andrew had texted that he had Owen. 'You know,' I muttered, 'he was the last one I expected to shout at dad.'

'Yeah,' Owen said on a crooked breath.

I waited, but he said nothing more and I didn't want to go there either just now, so I said, without a great deal of thought, 'Man, your cheek's something else, Owen. Can't believe it's not broken.'

My brother sucked in his lips, lifted a hand as if to touch then dropped it.

The bruise had nothing on the black eye from Jack Wheeler's horrible assault last year, but if Owen had managed to catch himself in a mirror I doubted he'd be comfortable with the colouring or how it'd bring back memories.

I wondered if he'd mentioned to Sergeant Morrison what dad had done and how it had momentarily linked up with last year's really unpleasant events.

Running my fingers through my hair, I said softly, 'Dad seems to have dug himself a hole with all this, Owen.'

'Yeah,' he agreed, then said Andrew had been really angry at the station.

'He should be,' I replied. 'Dad's not playing fair. You guys have been doing everything by the book, and *he* seems to think biological right will get him everything. If Andrew's guardianship somehow does get cut, I'm not going with dad. None of us will.'

I relished Owen's small smile of gratitude.

'Hey,' I said, 'why don't you get into bed properly? Let me put you to sleep with some chat about this stupid essay I have to write.'

Owen looked startled a second then nodded.

I should have told him outright that I really just wanted to stay in his company a while, but couldn't quite bring myself to say it.

Andrew

Once home I swallowed back enough bourbon that I wouldn't have been able to drive without recrimination if I got pulled over. Stupid of me, but I was also sure that if I *did* turn up at Owen's place, Sergeant Morrison would force me away anyway, probably with some handcuffs.

I eyed the bottle on the bench but turned away from it. Drinking out of fear and anger was a terrible reason. So not a good role model for…

Who was I kidding?

Suddenly I was no one's, and my heart ached with it. Ached that Tremayne hadn't chosen to be sensible. I went for the bottle and swigged straight from it.

Realising my hand shook, I carefully set the bottle down and walked away again. Throwing it in frustration would only make me irrational like their father.

Father.

I sucked in a breath, pinched my nose. That man surely had to have wiped that tag tonight. Violence against his child? Coming on the heels of abandonment? He wasn't a fit parent!

Pacing my lounge end to end, I felt insulted and well pissed at the situation. At the fact that simply because Owen was my employee it meant our relationship was illegal. We were following the restrictions Morrison had set in place and yet

Tremayne, who wasn't following any sensible form of anything, continued to have access to his kids no matter what.

Owen had been drifting into a dark space where bad memories lurked ever since his father had returned, and I felt both helpless and furious over my inability to prevent it.

Instead of heading for the bottle again, I dug out some old track-pants, changed clothes, and went down to the gym. I really wanted to hit something. Instead I got on a treadmill and ran the anger out.

Well, ran the breath out anyway.

Back in the apartment, showered and dressed, I felt in control. Enough so that when Megan texted *We're okay here. Officer is staying night* I was able to respond with *Ta for letting me know hon. I'll see you all tomorrow* without so much as a heart elevation.

I wanted to phone to apologise for her ruined birthday dinner, but realised that hearing my voice would probably be as difficult as my presence would have been.

I wasn't at all surprised her father had had no idea of the date. I leaned back on the couch, rubbing my brow. If he continued to be so aggressive then I was absolutely going to refuse to stay away from the house, even it was my presence that drove him.

Owen was mature beyond his seventeen years, as was Jamie, but both kids had a mountain of baggage. It wasn't right or fair that they should be on their own at night now, being the adults, trying to keep the younger ones calm. No doubt Megan was helping too, but she was still so young herself.

God… fifteen today… Not a birthday she would want to remember.

I drew in a breath.

Sergeant Morrison phoned as I was designing prison cells. My earlier anger resurfaced, but I held it just below lip level. Managed, 'What can I do for you, Sergeant?' in a calm manner. I didn't ask if he was still at the kids' house.

'I have started the process to impose a restraining order on Mr Tremayne,' he responded. 'He will not be allowed on the property or near the children without permission.'

I drew in a breath. 'I'm pleased to hear it.' As pleased as I was, I didn't prevent my stiffness. Owen's fear and shock and Jamie's panic were still topping my memories, and it was about time the sergeant understood the situation.

'You will be protected under the same order, Mr Gordon.'

I stared a moment at my graphite creations, surprised, before saying, 'I appreciate that, Sergeant, thank you.' Even though Owen had reported his father's animosity mostly involved me, I hadn't *really* thought of my safety being compromised. At least, not until this evening. 'Does Owen know about this order?'

'Yes. As does Mr Tremayne.'

'And where is that man tonight?'

'He is not at the house, Mr Gordon,' the sergeant reported evenly. 'Officer McCorkindale remains there with the children.'

That reassured me only a little. 'Alright.'

After a short moment, as if he was giving me time to add to my response, he told me he'd bring a copy of the order to the house tomorrow. 'I presume you will be there.'

'Of course.'

'Good. I'll come about ten, and I want to take statements

from Owen, Jamie and Megan while I'm there.'

My stomach dropped a little, but I didn't speak; Morrison obviously was taking this seriously. I asked if they knew about that.

'No,' he responded. 'They already have enough on their plate tonight.'

A small acknowledgement of how badly things had gone. 'Yes, they do,' I agreed, and managed to keep my tone even.

Soon after that, the call ended. I felt drained. A restraining order against a father... No matter what I thought of him—and very little of it was positive—I knew such a thing would be tough on the man. Yet, he'd brought it upon himself, and I could only hope the kids weren't feeling guilty about it.

Though, knowing the older three, they would because of Lisa and Matty, because they didn't really understand what was going on with their father. I doubted they'd get why an order was in place and what it meant.

Tomorrow I'd find out just how they really were, try to alleviate their worries, even as I wanted to talk with the police officer about extra security around the house.

[Seven]

Andrew

Arriving at Owen's house in the morning, the car already in the drive (unmarked bar an official police department sign across the top of the back window) gave me some relief. Not relief that the neighbours would be wondering what the hell was going on, but relief that the sergeant *was* taking this incident seriously.

I had to press the doorbell since the chain was in place. A man in uniform opened the door via the chain, and I introduced myself. He might have asked for ID but I heard Matty call my name behind him.

In the house, door re-locked, I got down on a knee to hug the boy. He was half dressed—jeans and a pyjama top. 'You plan on going to school like that?'

'Ha, maybe,' he said, looking down at himself. 'It's a pretty cool top.'

Dark blue with stars. Missing the bottom button.

'Mm. How about you go find a t-shirt?'

Matty went off easily enough and I straightened. The officer remained close. 'How was the night?' I asked quietly, unsure if anyone else was up and about. I couldn't hear anything from the kitchen though that didn't mean it was empty.

'Quiet,' the man responded. 'Outside and in.'

I nodded, relieved, though I expected the older kids had kept to themselves a fair bit. And Owen… I let out a sigh. Probably he'd crashed at some point, but I hoped he'd managed a decent sleep in spite of everything. I stopped myself rushing down to see him, instead headed into the kitchen. I'd had breakfast but I wanted to see if anyone loitered at the table.

No one did. I didn't think any of them would have gone off to school already, and in fact I planned on keeping Jamie and Megan at home. Sergeant Morrison was due at ten, in any case, to take statements, but I thought a day at home together was a good idea.

I wondered about Lisa and Matty, though; perhaps school would take *their* minds off things. I'd make that decision once I'd seen them all this morning.

Megan appeared first, though talking over her shoulder to Lisa. She froze a second when she saw me and then was in my arms. I hugged her tight, whispered how was she.

I heard a mumbled, 'Okay' and then she pulled back, wiping her glistening eyes. 'It was horrible, Andrew. I don't want him here again. He's crazy.' Her breath hitched.

'Sergeant Morrison told me about the restraining order,' I said. 'That's a good start.' Though I didn't really believe their father would honour it. 'Is the rest of the gang awake? Shall I make some breakfast?'

She eyed the clock.

'No school today, Honey,' I murmured. 'I want you all with me, and the sergeant's coming over later this morning.'

Megan swallowed, brown eyes filling even as she gave a jerky nod. 'I didn't want…' Her smile was thin. Then she seemed to realise Officer McCorkindale sat at the table, reading part of a newspaper. She asked if he wanted anything and I left her to it, heading down the hall.

Matty met me half way there, properly attired, and I told

him to go set the table. He went on his way without argument. Someone was in the shower, Lisa maybe. Owen's door was closed so I knew it wasn't him. A little down the hall, the boys' door was open and light shone into the passage. I leaned in. Jamie lay on his back, arm over his eyes. Couldn't tell if he was asleep or just shading his eyes.

Knocking lightly on the door got, 'I'm not going to school' in response. A smile curved my lips. 'My thought too,' I said. 'But breakfast will be on the table in half an hour.'

The arm didn't move.

I turned away, stopping when my name aired. Jamie was now sitting up, hair spiked. I raised my brows.

'Um, don't know if Owen told you but dad...' He trailed off, pulled a face as he rubbed a hand over his head. 'He had Owen over the chair, arm up his back. Owen said it was... like...' Jamie glanced up at me, a little unsure. 'I didn't hear him in the night but I know that...' He trailed off for the third time, looking upset and uncomfortable.

'He did tell me,' I said quietly, relieved that they'd obviously talked. I thought that might help them both. 'How are *you*?'

'Yeah, okay.'

Like his brother, getting feelings from Jamie was as easy as extracting blood from a stone. I waited though, in case he continued.

Jamie pulled a face and told me he'd gone after his father. 'Well, no, I tried but the officer... He...' Another pulled expression.

I stayed quiet, didn't feel I had the right to rebuke him.

'I was so angry,' he said, looking up. 'Dad just focused on you and Owen. We kept trying to steer him back but... He made Matty run from the room and then what he did to

Owen, I just… Yeah.' Jamie sighed, watched his fingers creasing the covers in his lap. 'It was just… I don't want him here again. It was horrible, Andrew, really… He was…' The kid shook his head, clearly unable to articulate everything he felt.

I held my breath, stomach turning at how affected everyone was. I hoped the sergeant realised this when he arrived later so that his restraining order would be binding.

'Is the cop still here?'

'Huh? Oh… yes, he is. He'll probably stay until Sergeant Morrison arrives.'

'He's coming back?' Jamie looked a little more alert.

I nodded. 'He wants statements, and I want to talk to him about better security.'

'But won't a—' Jamie let out a breath, didn't finish where he was going with that. He flung back the covers and I turned away.

I stopped outside Owen's door. Should I check on him or let him sleep? As I was reaching for the door handle, it turned and the door swung inward. Owen let out a yelp, then, 'Jeez, don't scare me like that.'

Before I could comment, he took hold of my arm and tugged. I let him get me into his half-light room—one curtain had been opened—shifting slightly as the door clicked, and then he was leaning against me, fingers gripped into the back of my jersey. His breathing was unsteady, and with his head turned so his right cheek wasn't against my shoulder I could see the bruising and the graze all too easily.

My teeth ground, which I forced to stop when I felt Owen go still. Then he pulled back. 'Kiss me,' he croaked out.

'Owen, your cheek…' I raised a hand, but he grabbed it and

pushed it down.

'I'm not asking you to kiss my cheek,' he said, gaze steely.

He needed physical comfort. If the household hadn't been so alert, I'd have taken him to the bed and driven all thoughts from his head. As it was, the kiss nearly made me do so.

I expected Owen's face was stiff and sore, but he kissed, mouth open, like it didn't bother him. I reacted the same, pretended nothing was wrong for his sake. As he stretched up, his pyjama top lifted and I let my hand slide a little so I could touch fingers to his warm skin. I felt his immediate reaction, but sheer will power kept me on the straight and narrow.

He broke off the kiss when I inadvertently stroked my thumb down that bruised cheek, making him wince.

'Oh Owen, I'm sorry.'

He took that hand and squeezed it. 'It's n-nothing,' he whispered. Then he eyed me. 'It's casual day at work?'

For a second I had no idea how to respond, and then I shook my head. 'No work today. No school either. Morrison will be here at ten to take statements.'

Owen let out a soft sigh but nodded. Then he pushed fingers through his hair, offered up a sliver of a smile. 'He's organising a restraining order against dad. It's going to protect you too.'

'I know,' I said softly. 'He told me last night.'

Owen nodded, one of those overly long ones, but he had a semi-smile on his face. And then he said, 'Maybe we can go out for dinner tonight?'

'Pardon?'

'Megan's birthday.'

'Oh… yes.' I was surprised suddenly that Megan hadn't said

something just now. 'I should apologise for—'

'No.' Owen took my arm as I half turned. 'None of this is your fault.'

He had that steely look back; his "I'm not going to listen to anything you say about it" expression. I made myself nod, then forced a smile. 'I'm going to cook up breakfast. I expect you dressed and ready to eat in twenty minutes.'

I *didn't* expect him to say, 'Easier to eat if I'm undressed.'

I stared. He grinned.

'Jesus,' I got out and left his bedroom, able to let a silly— and slightly wobbly—grin cross my face out of sight.

Owen

Sergeant Morrison arrived in full uniform and armed, which made us wary. Well, not Matty. His eyes went wide. 'Wow! Is that real?'

Even as he reached out, Andrew hustled him backward and the sergeant put a guarding hand on the black gun, even though it was latched in a case. 'It is, Mathew.'

I could see Andrew wasn't comfortable with the weapon being in the house, but I thought it was probably more because of Matty's curiosity than anything. Before my little brother could spout something else, we all seemed to notice the woman standing behind the sergeant. She'd been talking quietly with Officer McCorkindale.

'This is Grace Johansen,' Morrison said, and I remembered her from ages ago at the hospital; the one failed time that they'd tried to get me to talk about how I felt about the assault.

I put a further step between me and the psychologist, making Jamie stiffen. Megan looked at me, puzzled, and then at Andrew, whose jaw seemed taut. He greeted the lady pleasantly though.

'We don't need a shrink,' Jamie said.

Sergeant Morrison was super impressive at hiding his eye-roll. 'Grace is here for your young brother and sister, Jamie. They witnessed violence yesterday from their father, and she will be able to help them express what they feel about it.'

Jamie's lips pressed tightly together. So did Megan's. At least I stopped myself from saying that Matty had in fact *missed* dad going at me.

Andrew was thanking the sergeant and the psychologist, and trying to get us all away from the door.

Eventually, she and Officer McCorkindale sat with Lisa and Matty at the picnic table. The kids liked the officer so that was probably a good ploy, even without the game that materialised on the table along with some pens and paper. They didn't appear at all fussed.

I looked at Jamie; he seemed as thrown as I felt, and defensive, as if waiting for the sergeant to toss a curve ball about counselling at *us*.

He didn't.

Instead, he sat the four of us at the kitchen table; me and Andrew opposite Megan and Jamie, himself taking the one real chair. A large tan envelope sat on the table, unopened, alongside a black notebook. He didn't mention the envelope (I presumed it was the restraining order) but asked us how the night had gone.

Jamie spoke first. 'Better if our guardian had been here.'

I frowned at him.

'You think that too,' he ground out.

I tried to hide the flinch, and turned from Andrew's pained

expression. I looked at Morrison. 'It was okay.'

His gaze flickered briefly to my bruised cheek. Before he could say anything Jamie asked why we weren't doing the statement thing at the station. 'Is it still legit if it's here?'

One of the sergeant's brows rose, and then he said, 'It's legit anywhere I am to take it.' He *almost* seemed amused, but then he sobered. 'Your father is currently still at the station.'

We all focused fully on him. None of us—not even Andrew, going by his expression—had realised dad had spent the night there. Across from me, Megan's eyes were wide with shock. His car had been towed last night but we hadn't even thought about *him* in relation to that.

'As slight as the risk is,' Sergeant Morrison continued, 'I didn't want any chance that you and your father would see each other.'

He said that to me and out came, totally without control, 'Why would you care?' I clapped a hand over my mouth, horrified, and hoped beyond—no, everyone was looking at me. Shit, I had spoken out loud.

'Owen,' Andrew said, 'that was unfair.' He sounded shocked, and a bit appalled.

I couldn't look at him for shame. 'I know,' I croaked and turned to the sergeant. 'I'm sorry,' I rasped. 'I didn't mean it.' Crap, in that moment I *had* meant it, and I knew he knew.

Sergeant Morrison reacted in a way none of us could have expected. He chuckled. The sound sat me stiff on the bench. Jamie looked like he expected him to pull the gun. Megan was just pale. I still couldn't look at Andrew but I knew he was alert beside me.

'Owen, I know you've always hated my rules and lectures,' the sergeant said, 'but everything I've done and am doing is to help you, and your brothers and sisters. *And* Mr Gordon.'

A lump of embarrassment was wedged in my throat.

He tapped the large envelope, and all humour was gone when he said, 'Your father is not a happy man. I didn't want any chance your paths could cross at the station this morning.'

I felt justifiably rebuked, and couldn't look up.

'The gesture is very much appreciated,' Andrew said. 'Isn't it, Owen?'

His tone was encouraging *and* pointed, and I knew I'd let him down with that dumb, non-thought-out comment. I felt my nose start to tingle; stupid tears weren't far away. I hated upsetting Andrew. I nodded at my hands.

Sergeant Morrison suddenly jerked and let out a half expletive/half yelp.

Megan was going fire-engine red. 'I'm sorry, I'm sorry, Sergeant. I meant to kick *Owen*.'

'What?' I croaked.

'Pardon?' The sergeant sounded confused.

'I meant to kick you!' Megan cried across the table at me. 'Sergeant Morrison is doing everything he can for us, for *you*, and all you can do is *nod?* Show some gratitude!' She was on her feet now. The rest of us were frozen, then Jamie reached to take her arm. She moved out of the way, stepping over the bench. 'And thanks for ruining my birthday!'

She fled, and we were so quiet we heard the door slamming down the hall.

Morrison coughed. 'What was that about?'

'It was Megan's birthday yesterday,' Jamie said slowly. 'We were supposed to do dinner. Didn't quite...' He shrugged.

'I ruined it,' I said softly, staring at a knot in the wood.

'You did not,' Jamie said.

'Owen, you didn't.' Andrew stopped reaching when I flinched from him.

'You heard her.' I swallowed hard. 'It's true. It was *her* day, but it became all about me and this stupid—' I waved a hand at my cheek.

'I hardly think she—' Morrison cut off as I leapt up and shouted, 'It's *my* fault!'

My sudden move had him spring upright, Andrew and Jamie following not far behind.

'Owen, Angel,' Andrew cajoled. 'No one's blaming you.'

'And we'll have another dinner,' Jamie said. 'A better one.'

'It doesn't matter,' I mumbled. 'Her real one was ruined.' No one stopped me as I left the kitchen and went down the hall.

The door to mum and dad's old room was closed. Ordinarily I might have backed off but I'd hurt my sister and needed to apologise. I knocked on the door. 'Megan, can I come in?'

I heard her yell, 'Go away.' I held my breath a moment, paused, but then pushed the door open. 'Megan, I'm really sorry, I—'

'I hate you. *Go. Away!*' screamed at me through the gap, accompanied by a flung pillow.

I jumped back, pulling the door closed. My heart slammed against my ribs, sick that Megan was so upset.

A noise had me turn; Sergeant Morrison stood just down the hall. My face flamed that he'd heard what she'd yelled but, over that, I suddenly felt afraid and cornered; the sergeant was an imposing bulk there in the hall, with the gun at his hip.

Behind him Andrew looked concerned. 'Sergeant, please move out of the way. You're only making matters worse.'

'I'm not doing anything,' Morrison replied, puzzled.

'Don't question me,' Andrew said. 'Just give Owen space.' He looked at me, smiled. 'Angel, you're safe, no-one's going to hurt you.'

A frown started on the sergeant's face at that.

I *knew* I was safe, but I didn't move. Not until the sergeant gave a sort of shrug and turned, heading back toward the lounge.

'Come on,' Andrew said to me. 'Give her some time.'

He held his hand out and I started forward. As upset as I was, he spoke reason; Megan needed time to calm down before she and I could talk. *I* needed a new brain because, as soon as I saw Sergeant Morrison with his arms folded, embarrassment bled through me and I rushed out the front door.

Exiting the house wasn't bright; the door dead-bolted behind me, locking me out. I thought about going down to the play-lot but my face ached, and the sight of the crowded drive struck me immobile.

Officer McCorkindale's car was mostly unmarked, sitting on the far side of the drive, half unseen because of Andrew's black Merc parked beside it. I hugged my ribs and eyed Sergeant Morrison's vehicle. No doubt about *his*; it had all the bells and whistles a police car should have, and it was blocking Andrew's.

I felt sick at the sight, even as I also felt relieved. Sergeant Morrison *had* been doing what he could to protect us, and I'd been a shit in not giving him an inch. Megan was right to yell about it.

The door unlatched behind me and I half turned, straightened when I saw the sergeant. He looked surprised to see me there. He pulled the door closed and stepped off the porch. 'Can we talk?'

'I'm not getting in there.' I nodded at his car. *One* of those chats was enough to last a lifetime.

'I won't make you,' he said a little tightly. 'As long as you promise not to run.'

He got no promise, but I shifted to lean against the Mercedes. Sergeant Morrison came closer; blocking my path to the road, I noticed. After a moment he apologised for making me uncomfortable in the hall.

'It's okay,' I mumbled.

'Does it relate to your father or to Jack Wheeler?'

I squeezed my ribs. Sergeant Morrison held his silence; clearly he awaited an answer. I glanced up at him, let him hear the hurt as I asked if it mattered who.

'I guess not,' he answered slowly, 'but I'm concerned. You've had so many bad experiences, Owen, I'm worried they'll start getting the better of you.'

I frowned down at the driveway. 'If that was going to happen, it already would have. Sergeant, I'm not nuts or anything.' I shifted onto a hip to face him more directly, as if that gave me control of this conversation, and said, 'You know that.'

The sergeant let out a short snap of breath. 'I *know* that you're stubborn, Owen,' he said, 'and argumentative and occasionally obstructive.' He held up a hand as I opened my mouth to protest. 'But, I also know that you're dedicated to your family and to Mr Gordon, that you defend what you believe, and that you're courageous. But these things don't prevent me being worried.'

My chin lifted a little. 'I only reacted like that before because

I was upset over Megan.'

He gave a tight smile. 'Don't worry, I won't make you talk to Grace. You do, however, need to keep talking to *me*.'

He meant right here, right now. Maybe Andrew wouldn't let me back in the house anyway until I'd talked. I scowled momentarily at the front door, and then rubbed my face. That made the sergeant ask how my cheek was.

The concern with the undertone of anger shouldn't have startled me, but it was a couple of seconds before I could mutter that it was a bit stiff but okay.

'Kid,' he said with a sigh, running a hand over the silver trim on the backseat window.

'It *is* okay.'

His eyes rolled and I realised that wasn't what the 'Kid' was for. I straightened, hand on the wing mirror. Except, before I could say anything, I spotted the couple coming down the pavement, the guy getting his arm yanked out by a dog straining on a leash. Going still made the sergeant turn, hand on the leather latch that held his gun safe. I choked on a breath, but then Morrison was saying, 'Good morning, nice day for a walk.'

'Yeah, it is,' the man said, but he and the woman picked up their pace a bit.

I wanted to die of embarrassment and horror. The police car was one thing, but having a fully uniformed officer, with a gun, in full view talking to me was something else. And with my bruised face too… I groaned.

Morrison eyed me. 'You know them, Owen?'

'Not really. They're a couple doors down, I think.'

He didn't suggest we continue our talk inside. Instead he just turned fully back to me and said, 'I will do everything I can to make sure this doesn't happen again.' He nodded at me, at my face.

'I don't think he meant to,' I said. 'Just… got me because I was going by him.' I nearly rubbed at my wrist that dad had grabbed. I had a bruise on one side that I'd managed to keep hidden thus far, and wanted to keep it so. Then I mumbled that dad had told me to tell Andrew to watch his back. I looked up, watched the sergeant's brows knit. 'It's me and Andrew dad's all weird at, not the others. It's never been the others.' I touched my cheek briefly. 'I don't even think it's really my age. He just doesn't like gay people.'

Sergeant Morrison's gaze seemed to really focus for a while, but when he spoke it was only to suggest we go inside.

Andrew let us in when the sergeant rang the doorbell, and I immediately caved against him. He squeezed arms around me but didn't speak.

'Mr Gordon, I think it might be best if we leave the statements until tomorrow.'

'Tomorrow?' Andrew said, surprise clear. I was sure he was looking down at me but I kept my gaze averted.

'Today *would* be best,' the sergeant said, 'but I doubt that tomorrow will have diluted anything. The kids, and you, yes, need a moment to regroup.'

I twisted in Andrew's embrace so I could eye the sergeant. He actually looked pretty stern. I wasn't going to argue about putting things off.

Andrew shifted me around so I was only under one arm, the other stretched toward Morrison. 'I appreciate that, Sergeant,' he said. 'Thank you.'

As they shook hands, Jamie came into the foyer. 'What's up?'

The sergeant told him he was going to defer receiving our statements until tomorrow, then turned back to Andrew. 'Let me run over the Order with you, Mr Gordon, before I go.'

I wasn't sure if the startled jerk was mine or Andrew's but for the moment I'd forgotten about the restraining order, that envelope on the table.

'Sure,' Andrew said, and disengaged from me.

As Andrew led Morrison back into the kitchen, Jamie started to speak but cut off when Matty came bounding up crowing that he'd beaten a policeman and a doctor in Snap. Jamie bit his lip, ruffling his little brother's hair. 'Bet you can't beat me, Shrimp,' he challenged and next thing I was standing alone by the front door.

When I moved, I saw them getting out onto the porch, the officer smiling at something Matty was saying. Lisa and the psychologist seemed to be taking turns at drawing. In any case, my kid brother and sister seemed pretty okay, releasing some of my worry.

Then I glanced down the hall. That bedroom door was still closed but all of a sudden I needed to lie down. My cheek ached and so did my head.

I would apologise to Megan, but wanted a clear head first. Because if she was still inclined to yell I'd cope with it better.

- # -

A bang shattered my sleep.

I sat bolt upright, heart crashing against my ribs, one hand over my mouth since the ache pounding in my cheek made my stomach queasy. A second bang sounded, followed by a scream that sent the hairs upright on both arms. I leapt from the bed, running for the lounge.

My father's laugh was the soundtrack as I skidded to a disbelieving halt at the edge of the lounge. Jamie and Megan were frozen against the TV, eyes wide. I couldn't see my little brother and sister, but blood had splattered up the wall by the open French doors.

Andrew knelt there, clutching at his shoulder. 'Owen,' he gasped, 'stay back.'

Standing between me and Andrew, Dad swung around and I saw the gun. 'The little fag *finally* shows his face. Go to your lover, Owen. Can't you see he needs help?'

'What have you done, dad?' I cried. 'Are you crazy?'

He jerked the gun at me. 'Move!'

I did, stumbling in my panic so that I had to scurry to Andrew on my hands and knees. 'Are you okay?' I rasped, hands on him as he started to lean over.

He didn't answer, lips pressed tight, pain making his face white. I shrieked at dad to leave as I struggled to keep Andrew upright.

'Not until my business is finished,' dad said, making a show of checking bullets or something. Whatever he was doing made my stomach drop and I had to force myself to breathe. Dad cocked his head. 'I told you to warn the boy-fucker to watch his back, didn't I?'

I held my breath. God, I *had* done that, hadn't I? Shit, maybe I hadn't, maybe this was all— I twisted to see my siblings. 'Call the sergeant!' Repeated it because the first version barely had any sound.

Jamie opened his mouth, but it was Megan who said, 'He shot the phone.' She waved an arm that way without looking.

'*What?*' I knelt higher so I could see above the couch. There on the wall was the phone, broken in half, part dangling. 'No, no.' I gulped in air, shifted on my knees to prevent Andrew's sagging weight toppling me. My brother and sister still stood rooted to the spot, horror and total disbelief on their faces.

Where were Lisa and Matty?

'Go get help,' I cried. 'He won't hurt you. *Go!* I screamed in panic when they continued to be statues. '*Fucking go!*

Megan dashed out of the lounge. Jamie croaked her name and went after her and that let me focus a little better now they were gone. I turned back to dad.

He shrugged. 'You're right, Slut, my business isn't with my son and daughter. It's with you and the paedophile.'

'*Don't call him that!* I jumped to my feet in front of Andrew.

Andrew let out a cry—fear and pain. 'Owen, save yourself, not... not m-me.'

'Don't say stupid shit!' I cried at him, trying to keep my fear from showing as tears. I swung back to dad. 'Dad, come on, you know this is wrong. You're going to get in serious trouble here. If Andrew dies—'

'Too right he's going to die,' dad said over top of me. 'He's not going anywhere near my kids again.'

'They want Andrew here, Dad,' I responded on a half breath. 'He's not hurting them, *you're* doing that.' I held my hands out, slowly stepping forward. 'Come on, stop this.'

The shot nearly blasted my ears, and I cowered, eyes squeezed shut. Andrew cried out and I swung to see blood spurting from his thigh. Oh fuck, in walking forward I'd stopped shielding him!

'Dad, stop!' I yelled, stumbling back to Andrew. 'Stop it, *leave us alone*!' I pressed on Andrew's thigh, trying to hold back the blood, trying to remember to breathe myself so I didn't pass out over him in my fear.

'Owen,' Andrew said, a hand reaching for my face. 'I love you.'

I froze, staring, feeling the stickiness where his hand curved to my bruised cheek. He was horribly white and I barely felt his breath even though we were so close. He hoisted himself up, grimacing, and clasped both sides of my face. His grasp made pain radiate through my face but I couldn't pull away. His lips were cold against mine.

Grabbing his wrists, I held him upright as I pulled back, shaking my head, tears blinding me. 'No, *no*, don't you d-dare leave me.' I shook him.

His blue eyes were incredibly dark. 'Save yourself,' he mouthed.

'No! I *won't* leave you.' I tried to get an arm around him. 'Come on, I'll hold you. G-get up.'

Andrew had no coordination and I heard his pain as he breathed, but I kept trying. Until I realised dad was standing over us, smiling. 'Regret your life, Boy-fucker?' he asked coldly.

'*I hate you*,' I screamed at him, hand out as if I could shield myself and Andrew. 'Leave us alone. *Please*. He's never hurt anyone!'

'He certainly won't after this.' Dad pulled the trigger.

Screams ripped up my throat. Hands grabbed at me and I fought to get free, shrieking for Andrew.

'Owen, I'm *here!*'

My eyes flashed open, finding him right in front of me and Megan and Jamie by the door, staring. My cheek thudded in time with my heart. 'Where's dad?' I cried, trying to see beyond them, fighting Andrew as he tried to keep me still. 'He was shooting. You—' I focused on Andrew's shoulder, and then touched his thigh. 'You're not bleeding,' I croaked, and looked up at him.

Andrew looked afraid but certainly not in pain. I felt his breath on my face, his strong grip on my shoulders, and realised the trembling this time was mine and that I was actually sitting on my bed. I glanced over at my brother and sister, both wide-eyed, Megan with her hands pressed over her mouth.

'It was… a d-dream?' I rasped out.

Before anyone could answer, relief rammed me so hard I threw up on my lap. That made Andrew cry out in surprise, but before he could get me up and moving to the bathroom I was bawling. From dry to hysterical in seconds, fingers gripped into his shirt so tight I heard the material rip.

Andrew held me against him, one hand curved around the back of my head. 'It's okay, it's okay.'

It wasn't at all. I was too afraid to let him go in case I was dreaming this and what I thought I'd dreamed was actually real.

Andrew kept murmuring, didn't push me back, and held me even tighter when I sobbed out what I'd dreamed. I felt him turn his head. 'Megan,' he said. 'Get some clothes for you and Lisa. Jamie, get some for Matty and yourself. We're not staying here.'

'But…' Jamie began.

'Morrison was releasing your father this afternoon. We're not staying here tonight.' Andrew rubbed a hand against my back. 'Go,' he told my brother and sister.

I heard them leave and Andrew began to shift me back from him, murmuring that I was safe. I clung on a moment and then sat back, noticing the rent in his shirt. I looked up at him, hand over my mouth. His own eyes shone. 'I won't let him harm you again, Owen.'

'I'm not worried about *me*,' I sniffed, and then reared back when I caught the pungent smell of—Oh heck, I'd… I shoved a hand over my mouth and scrambled off the bed, this time making it to the bathroom.

Andrew came with me, somehow managed to calm me enough to strip the grotty sweatshirt. My jeans weren't in good shape either. 'Wait here,' he told me and left.

I did, but I was standing in just underwear and t-shirt when he came back. He made a soft sound in his throat when he saw me. I took the clean jeans and dressed, whispering that he needed to change his shirt.

He plucked at the hole I'd made. 'Brush your teeth,' he said with a bit of a croak. 'Freshen up a bit.' When I nodded, he turned away.

When we all gathered at the front door not long afterwards, Megan had a white-knuckle grip on her backpack. I took a moment to realise that I hadn't yet apologised to her. I opened my mouth now, but nothing came out.

Lisa and Matty were more unsure than they'd been all day, and I couldn't apologise to them either. And, in fact, I had to turn away from Jamie because he just kept looking at me and I had nothing left to give, already feeling guilty that I'd caused this to happen.

Andrew did a quick move around the house, ensuring the doors and windows were all closed and locked, before herding us out to his car.

How odd it was going to look, going from a crowded drive to an empty one.

Jamie

Owen was ballsy when he was sick. No, wussy when sick, ballsy when hurt. It was like he hated anyone seeing him as a victim or something.

Or maybe he was just stupid.

Anyway, he was arguing with Andrew about going to lie down. Half his face was several shades of black and purple, the rest grey, and he looked like he was going to puke any second, yet he was insisting he was fine.

'Owen, *please.*'

My brother shook his head and happened to meet my gaze. He didn't say anything and the expression didn't change but I had a flash of insight. He didn't want to be alone. Man, why couldn't he just *say* that?

'I'll sit with you a bit,' I said.

'No, I—'

'I wanna talk anyway,' I cut over him, pretty much walked directly at him so he was forced to step back. 'Come on.'

Owen stopped arguing, and I heard relief behind me when Andrew said, 'Thanks, Jamie.'

'Yeah,' I got out and headed down the hall to the bedroom, shutting the door after us.

Moving over to the window, I peered down at the street busy with people out doing their daily whatever. I'd forgotten it was a weekday. I glanced over my shoulder; Owen had given in and was on the bed, sitting up against pillows. He had a hand over his mouth.

'You gonna puke?'

He shook his head.

I sat on the opposite edge of the bed. 'Shit, Owen, you *really* dreamed dad was shooting Andrew?'

He looked at me. It was a dumb sort of question because I'd heard him blab it out and I'd heard the screaming. Really, really horrible screaming.

'Yeah,' he breathed. 'I don't know why but… Jamie, it was so, so real.' He smoothed his hair back and I saw the hand shaking.

'Dad's being a right dick,' I said, 'but he'd never do anything like that. That's crazy.'

Owen swallowed.

And just maybe we were both thinking that dad *might* do something like that. Except… 'There's a restraining order against him now.'

'That'll only make him angrier.'

'But that's *his* fault,' I said.

Owen shook his head, but didn't speak.

I traced the squares on the bed cover, jerked when he said, 'How am I going to make it up to Megan?'

For a second I didn't understand but then re-heard her anger from this morning, Owen's own reaction. 'You don't have to, Owen. You didn't ruin her birthday.'

'You heard her.'

'Everyone heard her,' I responded, wryly. 'And she *was* upset, sure, but you didn't know dad would beat you or make Matty run off or *you* run off.' I frowned. 'Well…' I shut up when his brows bunched. 'Look,' I carried on after a second, 'we'll do dinner some other time, when you're less like a grape. And maybe we could get a few extra presents.'

'There was a necklace she liked.'

'What?' I sat up straighter, staring across at my brother.

'She mentioned it last week.'

'And you'd recognise it?' I asked sceptically.

'Lisa would. She was with us.' Owen was seemingly not embarrassed to reveal that he'd been around jewellery shops.

I inclined my head. 'Okay. Okay, that sounds good. How about you get that and I chat to Andrew about the dinner?'

Owen looked across at me, sucking in his lips. 'Yeah,' he said. 'Thanks.'

'No prob.'

He looked about to speak again, but silence held.

'Did you happen to bring that pill bottle?' I asked.

Owen shrugged so I suspected not. 'Let me go check with Andrew.' I got off the bed. 'Won't be long.'

He nodded this time.

Out in the large front part of the apartment, Andrew hovered in the kitchen. My brother and sisters were sorting out Scrabble.

'That's *my* version,' Andrew said, obviously realising I'd wondered at the fact we'd managed to pack a game.

'Oh, thought that was… Anyway, you packed those painkillers of Owen's, right?'

Andrew looked down the hall.

'He's okay, just… wired and flat at the same time. I bet his face hurts like hell.'

Andrew let out a sigh. 'I'm sure I grabbed them.' He moved around to the dining table and looked in a bag. I watched how his lips pressed tight; obviously massively concerned but trying to hide it. He pulled out a small white container and set it on the bench top. 'Here you go.'

'Um, why don't you take them to him?'

Andrew looked at me, sort of surprised. A hand ran back through his hair, and the grip that closed around the container was tight.

He got some water and went past me down the hall saying he'd order pizzas for dinner. Dinner? We had at least three *hours* yet before dinner. Jesus, they wouldn't… I put my hands over my ears ridiculously, but then shifted into the lounge, dropping to my knees at the board game.

'How is he?' Megan asked quietly.

'Shattered,' I said.

'It's my fault.'

'What? No.'

'If I hadn't yelled like that he wouldn't be so stressed,' Megan said on a whisper. 'He wouldn't have—'

'Megs, don't be dumb.'

She held her breath a moment then turned away from me, making the effort to smile and get Lisa and Matty into the gaming spirit.

They hadn't really been told why we'd suddenly decamped from our place, but both of them liked Andrew's apartment so being here wasn't a hard sell. Though… I did wonder what we'd do about sleeping arrangements. So far as I knew, there was only the couch here in the lounge and the one bed.

And right now… I bit back a grin.

Except, barely ten minutes later Andrew came and sat on the couch. He looked as shattered as Owen. 'He's asleep,' he said. 'Hopefully peacefully this time.' Gave a small smile. 'I promised to wake him for pizza.'

'That's just a waste of pizza,' I commented.

He pulled a face.

'Andrew,' Matty piped up, 'are you going to play?'

'No, Kiddo,' he responded. 'You and Lisa are demons at this game. You can pick on your siblings for once.'

That made Lisa and Matty crow at us. Megan talked up her own chances, but I was watching Andrew. Though he was still smiling I didn't think he was a hundred percent with us.

It can't have been easy, dealing with everything from yesterday and then Owen screaming and hearing what he'd been dreaming. But at least the restraining order covered him too. Except… if he wasn't with us at nights then who was really going to stop dad if he tried something? Maybe the order *would*, though I felt a bit like Owen—that dad's main reaction would be anger. I reckoned bringing us here showed that Andrew didn't hold a serious amount of faith either.

Lisa told me it was my turn, so I made myself join in.

Maybe ten minutes later Andrew, still on the couch, said to let him know if we wanted something to drink. Lisa asked about juice, Matty added his voice. Andrew smiled at them. 'I'm sure I have juice.'

As he started to lean forward to rise, I breathed, 'Megs, can you do it?'

She looked at me, puzzled, then understood why I'd asked. She jumped up. 'Sit, Andrew, I can sort something. Water's fine.'

'Are you sure? I—'

'Yep, sure,' she said and headed for the kitchen.

Andrew sat for a second on the edge of the couch before leaning back, giving a weak smile when he caught my gaze. I rose and took a seat beside him.

'How're you doing, Jamie?'

'Better than you, I think.'

He let out a sigh. 'Thought I was hiding it.'

'Heh, I'm a pro,' I said. 'Long experience.'

Andrew pulled a face, and then shifted a little straighter.

'He just didn't want to be alone, you know,' I said softly. 'That's why he was being stupid.'

'I know,' Andrew said. 'Not the stupid part,' he added evenly when I managed a smile. 'I just… oh well, hopefully he'll manage a couple hours' sleep now.'

'You didn't leave the pills with him, right?' I remembered the weird look on Owen's face last night.

Andrew dug into his pocket and pulled out the container. I took it from him, rolling it along my leg.

We both watched, attention taken a moment by Megan bringing the kids their drinks. Then I said, 'That dream, no, absolute nightmare's scared you, hasn't it?'

Andrew held my gaze a long moment. 'Yes,' he said. 'But mostly because of Owen's reaction.' He swallowed. 'Has he ever woken so freaked like that?'

I paused a moment. 'Um, I kinda never…' I inclined my head. Last year, I'd heard Owen cry out a lot but never went to investigate or even see if he was alright those times before I knew the reasons.

My throat constricted and in a half voice I told Andrew I'd only ever once witnessed a bad dream in action. When Megan begged me to wake Owen I had in the end because he had himself twisted in the bed covers, making things worse. Owen'd woken with me clamping both wrists, half lying on him to stop him flailing about. He hadn't tried to punch me, just started crying, and I'd lain there holding him.

'When was that?' Andrew got out in a croak.

I read Owen's name on the side of the container. 'A while back. I don't remember exactly.'

He nodded and I was glad he wasn't going to push.

'You're gonna have a restless night, I think,' I murmured.

Andrew's brows went up and then he realised what I meant. 'Ah, I thought actually that you and your brothers could share the bed. The chair in the study folds out and I've a camp stretcher; the girls can use those.' He patted the couch. 'Me on this.'

I raised a brow. 'You really think Owen's gonna agree with that?'

Andrew rubbed a hand over his head. 'At some point I have to phone the sergeant. They're the sleeping arrangements I'm going with.'

He knew as well as I did those arrangements *weren't* how we'd be spending the night. I cocked my head. 'Did you really think dad might come to the house or were you just unsettled by Owen?'

'Both, Jamie,' he said. 'I would like to believe your father has sense in him somewhere, but until that house gets better security I really don't want you kids in it, especially not alone. And Owen…' He blew out a breath. 'I've a feeling that if I left you all there he'd just bolt from it out of sheer panic. I don't want any of you feeling afraid there.'

I didn't think Lisa and Matty felt like that, but I understood his reasoning.

'And, dammit, you're my kids and I want you with me!'

His voice broke on that and for a second his breathing wasn't even. All I could say was that we wouldn't go with dad.

Andrew forced a smile, gave my knee a squeeze, then hauled himself upright. 'I better go make that phone call. It's a bit early to order, but why don't you find out what pizzas are wanted?'

He waited until I nodded, and then headed away, to the study I presumed.

For a moment I just sat on the couch and kinda stared at nothing. It was scary knowing that Andrew was scared. Which was stupid since he wasn't stone, and Owen *had* dreamed dad was shooting him.

'Shit,' I breathed, and thought back to that night last year when I'd woken Owen; a week or so after he'd gotten out of hospital. Obviously he'd not told Andrew about it. I'd thought then that it had been bad, but that nightmare actually had nothing on the one from today. The screaming had brought Megan running from the bedroom, and the hair had been up on my arms. Owen's terror, the look in his eyes, the panic in his voice… Chills had vibrated up and down my spine.

Actually, it was no surprise Andrew had brought us all here—an immediate safe place. I glanced toward the hall, wondering what he was telling Sergeant Morrison. Shit, what if *he* said we couldn't stay here? What if he sent us home, had a cop stay again instead of letting Andrew be with us?

I swallowed, felt a weird smile on my face. The sergeant would have to physically drag Owen out, probably get scars from it. I'd back my brother because I didn't want to be home tonight either.

Happened to look up then and catch Megan's serious gaze, so I made an effort to be with my brother and sisters. 'What's everyone want on the pizzas? Andrew said to make a list.'

My little brother existed for food and nothing else, I swear. He went straight on topic, rattling off toppings.

'Whoa, man, slow down.' I scrambled to dig my phone from a pocket so I could take notes.

'Oh hell, Owen, put your makeup on before coming out and scaring us.'

I stopped still, made myself focus. Everyone was looking at me, Jamie grinning, Andrew concerned but also a little amused. I raised a hand to my hair.

Megan jumped up. 'I'll help.'

That got a snort from Jamie and next thing my sister was hustling me to the bedroom just like Jamie had done earlier. I didn't feel completely tuned into what was happening but clearly there was nothing I could do about it.

The bedroom door clicked closed and I blurted, 'Megan, I'm so sorry about last night, I didn't—'

I cut off with a squawk as she sprang forward and hugged me, spouting her own apology. I wasn't up to responding verbally. Not when she was crying, and all I could remember was her explosion at the table this morning.

Megan let me go after a minute or two and sat on the end of the bed. She wiped her eyes and gave a half smile. I drew a breath, said quietly that she didn't need to say sorry. 'Morrison's doing his best and you were right to call me out.'

She bit her lip. 'Yeah, but…' She shrugged. 'Shouldn't have done it like that. I guess…' I think I heard, 'Easy target' and didn't feel angry. Even if she was apologising and feeling bad, she'd felt all that truthfully this morning and I couldn't fault her.

Glancing across the room at the pale stone of the condo over the road, I said, 'We should have changed the date. It was stupid not doing that.'

Out the corner of my eye, Megan shook her head. 'It only

sucked at the end. I way overreacted about it.'

I didn't agree but kept silent. When I turned, she rose, saying, 'How's your face?' as if she wanted to get away from talking about her.

'Comes and goes,' I said about the pain in my cheek. At the moment that ache was minimal, it was the headache that I wanted relief from.

Megan nodded then softly said she'd heard me from mum and dad's room. 'It was... terrible.' She breathed that out almost like it wasn't what she'd meant to say.

'Sorry.'

'No, don't... I didn't say that to...' Her brows bunched a bit. She didn't speak again, as if not sure what to say, and then she looked about. I couldn't recall if she'd ever really looked in here before and I strove to stay relaxed should she comment. She drew in a long breath and said, 'Dad said it was a gay driver who caused mum's accident.'

I started at the topic, gulped in air and said, 'Yeah.'

She eyed me. 'He told you when you had that meeting with him, didn't he?'

I nodded. I didn't apologise for not revealing it the other week, just held my tongue.

My sister eyed me a little longer, then glanced around the room, before announcing to the carpet, 'I think it's why dad's so stupid about you and Andrew.'

'I think so too,' I said softly, wishing she'd get off the subject.

'It's dumb.'

'Mm.'

Megan cocked her head when I didn't respond further, but she didn't carry on herself either. Instead, she flicked a hand at the rumpled bedding. 'I think you need more sleep. You don't look so hot.'

'Thought you were going to help with that.'

Even though her eyes sparkled a bit, Megan stuck her tongue out at me. Somehow that prompted me to say we'd have another birthday dinner for her, a far better one.

'We're having pizza tonight. That's better than anything.' She lit up with a sudden smile. 'Jamie reckons it'll be wasted on you, but I'll wake you when it comes anyway.'

'He's such a—' Cut myself off, shrugged. 'You don't need to wake me, I'm not gonna sleep. I spied Scrabble just now, right?'

'Yeah, but—'

'Set up a new game,' I said over her. 'I'll be out in a moment.'

Megan hesitated, then nodded.

I smiled but the one she returned didn't seem that willing. I probably could have done with more sleep, but more than that I needed to be around people.

Once she left, I spent a few minutes in the bathroom freshening up. Couldn't do anything to sort out my discoloured face, though at least the swelling had gone. Rubbing my eyes had made them red, so I'd honestly garnered Jamie's earlier remark. At least a comb got my hair tidy.

A knock on the open door startled me but it was just Andrew. 'Should you be on your feet?'

'Yeah, or I'm never sleeping tonight.' I came to him. 'I *am* okay.'

He brushed fingers through my hair.

'Hey! I just tidied that.'

Andrew pulled me against him and I heard his breath hitch.

My fingers twisted into his top as I breathed in the faint cologne I loved so much. He felt guilty for what had happened and nothing I could say would relieve him. I'd tried earlier before the drugs had sent me to sleep.

I hated that he felt that guilt, hated knowing that every time he saw the bruise he'd feel it.

I whispered that I loved him.

Andrew's sigh was ragged. He released me and stepped back. 'Love you too,' he murmured.

I gave a small smile. 'I think me and Megan are sorted.'

He rubbed up my arm. 'Good to hear, Angel.'

'And she said we were having pizza?'

'We are,' he responded. 'I hope you like what Matty likes. He's owning the planning.'

Like he did every time we had pizza. Asking him to choose toppings was ridiculous. 'At least we're not making them,' I said. 'That's even worse.'

Andrew arched a brow.

'*Don't* suggest it,' I warned him. 'Not today anyway.'

That seemed to intrigue him more but thankfully he didn't announce a change of plans when we got out to the lounge.

Matty and Lisa were flipping tiles upside down to ready the game. My brother pointed to the side opposite him and told me to take it.

'Okay.'

Andrew rubbed a hand up my back. 'I'll make you a cup of tea.'

I nodded with a smile and headed for my brother and sisters. Jamie sat on the couch, headphones on. He nodded at me, gave a quick grin. I managed a jerky nod in return then sat. Neither Matty nor Lisa made a comment about my face.

I'd worried they'd heard me screaming but Andrew had said they'd been outside playing. My little brother and sister hadn't known anything until they'd been hustled through the house and out to the car. I cleared my throat. 'So, what type of pizzas are we getting?'

Megan groaned, Lisa actually punched my arm, and our little brother launched in like I knew he would.

'Um,' I said when he finally stopped. 'Just how many pizzas do you think we're getting? That's enough toppings for ten.'

'Don't be dumb, Owen. They'll all be mixed up.'

I glanced sideways at Lisa and she grinned. Matty scowled but Megan told him to start the game and his attention shifted to his tiles.

'We're getting four,' she said to me. 'And I'm sure they'll hate us because two are deep-dish, two are not, but all will be half and half.'

'But still a better dinner?' I asked quietly.

Megan smiled. 'Yep.'

- # -

The clock on my side of the room glowed 12:03 when I got carefully out of bed. I hadn't dreamed because, apart from when I'd gone to bed at nine, I hadn't really slept.

Not *all* of that was because of Matty's snoring, but once I'd heard him I couldn't block him. He wasn't overly loud but the inconsistency was hard to tune out. On the other side of him Jamie slept, obviously having developed some blocking mechanism.

I made my way out to the kitchen, thinking that a cup of tea might settle me down. Just as I was reaching for the light

I remembered that Andrew slept on the couch. No way I wanted to wake him. I hesitated on the cool linoleum floor, not sure what to do. Being out here with Andrew was now suddenly a very strong desire, but I—

'Owen?'

I jerked, managing to get a hand over my mouth to block the cry but unable to prevent the several rapid steps backward into the kitchen, heart thwacking. Andrew stood darkly in the hallway.

'What are you doing up?' he asked softly.

I nearly asked him the same thing but probably he'd just been in the bathroom. 'Couldn't sleep,' I said. 'I thought… cup of tea…'

He let out a sigh that seemed to cover everything but said, 'Sounds a good idea. I'll make us one. Go turn on that lamp by the couch so we've got some light.'

Relieved he wasn't just encouraging me back to bed, I went carefully in the required direction and fumbled around the tall lamp for the switch. Turned it quickly to the dimmest setting when it came on bright, startling me into a cry.

When I went back to sit on one of the breakfast bar stools, watching Andrew, a flash of déjà vu poked at my gut. He glanced at me as I sucked in a breath but before he could question how I was, I waved a hand at the couch and asked if he was okay sleeping on it.

He glanced that way then went back to tea making. 'Yes, sleeping okay. It's actually pretty comfortable.'

'That's good.' I hated to think he was getting no sleep just so the rest of us could.

We took the tea to the couch. It wasn't cold in the lounge, but Andrew ensured one of the blankets was wrapped around me. As he settled beside me he asked if I'd managed any sleep before now.

'A bit. Not for a while. Matty… I don't hear him from my room but he *is* really loud.'

'Is Jamie awake too?'

'Not that I know,' I said. 'Guess he's had to put up with Matty long enough he's used to him.'

Andrew scratched his face and I heard the soft scrape of bristles. It was all I could do not to shift closer to him. I was actually intending to go back to the bedroom, to get through this night like an adult. But that soft sound, his breathing, even the movement as he lifted the cup to his lips… It was possible the couch and I were stuck together now, and my brothers could spread out in the bed.

Andrew was talking about Matty, how he wasn't sure if kids snoring was usual.

'I don't think he did it back in New Zealand,' I said. 'Though… I was sharing with Jamie then so…'

'I might get him in to see a breathing specialist.'

I nearly spilt my tea I shifted to eye him that fast.

'Just a check-up, Owen,' he said quickly, 'nothing serious, obviously.'

His gaze flicked briefly to my cheek and I held my tongue, didn't want doctor visits to turn my way.

'When all this is over,' Andrew said after a moment, 'we really need to look at sleeping arrangements at home. Jamie really should have his own space now. Megan too.'

'Yeah,' I said, even though the existing number of bedrooms weren't enough to make such changes. I ran my hand back through my hair. 'Seems odd that mum and dad didn't get a house with more bedrooms.' I remembered that mum had insisted I needed my own room but maybe they'd just thought that Jamie and Megan were still both young enough to still be able to share with Matty and Lisa.

Maybe a bigger house had been the plan after we'd settled into our new environment.

I tried to keep my breathing normal, didn't need grief to flare up now and worry Andrew.

Andrew didn't respond to what I'd said about the house, verbally anyway. His free hand settled on my thigh. Even through a thick blanket I was sure I could feel the heat. I held my breath, willing another type of heat to stay back.

'The sergeant's asked me to drop by the station tomorrow on our way home.'

That other heat vanished. 'Are you in trouble with us here?'

'No,' Andrew responded. 'He saw sense about that. He still needs to talk to you, Megan and Jamie. Particularly Jamie.'

I looked at him. 'Jamie? Why?'

'Because of his actions yesterday.'

'You mean… about him reacting to dad?'

Andrew looked down at me. 'He told you?'

'Well, bits of it,' I said. 'I wish he hadn't—gone after dad, I mean, but I…' I cocked my head. 'I'm kinda grateful, you know.'

Andrew's brows went up but I didn't try to explain that response. I think it was simply because Jamie *hadn't* aligned himself with dad. Letting out a soft sigh, Andrew said, 'Your brother's a good kid.'

He squeezed my leg when I rolled my eyes, but he spoke true. Despite the niggling and the occasional sly comments, it wasn't half bad having Jamie as a brother. Though I wished he and the others didn't have to deal with all of dad's crap.

'It's not fair, all this stuff,' I said. 'And pissy that my emancipation didn't fix things.'

'Well,' Andrew said after a moment. 'You aren't legally under anyone's control. You're a minor, sure, but your father has no parental control over you, Owen, as he would if you didn't have the emancipation.'

A bolt of fear zapped through me as I thought what a stroke of luck it was that we'd gone down that route. And I was relieved that Andrew had been checking out what my status contained; if there'd been a loophole in there, like with that law, he and his lawyer would have found it.

Andrew shifted his arm around my shoulder and I sagged against him.

We drank the rest of our tea in silence, me dragging it out so I could stay as long as possible right where I was. Where I should be allowed to be without recrimination.

I woke horizontal, tucked up on the couch with my head on Andrew's lap. The lamp was still on and when I shifted enough to see Andrew, he was asleep too, head back, breathing softly.

Though I was warm and comfortable, I doubted he was even if he slept. I carefully pushed off his lap and then woke him. He eyed me kneeling there so close, clearly not sure for a second what was going on. Then he croaked, 'So, this is why I was having a good dream.'

That made me flush, which made him smile like everything was alright.

'You should lie down properly,' I said, trying to keep my purpose on the straight and narrow. 'Or you'll be so stiff later.'

Andrew flexed and then rubbed his neck. But instead of shifting he asked if I'd gotten more sleep.

I nodded. 'Good sleep too, but I want us *both* to be comfortable.'

I climbed off the couch, dragging the blanket with me. That seemed to make Andrew fully aware of his surroundings. He got up and reorganised the rest of the bedding.

'You're joining me, right?'

'Yes.'

'Good.' He took the blanket from me and set it over the couch, then got on, shifting onto his side.

That gave me plenty room to get in beside him, immediately feeling heat where we touched. Andrew settled the bedding over us, then wriggled an arm under my back to curve around me rather than curl up in a cramp between us.

'Your cheek's okay?' he asked softly.

'Yeah.' It was stiff but not really sore.

'Okay.'

Andrew twisted and managed to flick off the lamp, plunging us into darkness until we adjusted to see the various glowing buttons on the TV and the microwave. I turned further onto my side to give him a bit more room, then slid my hands to press against his chest.

It was only just a week since we'd been this way at night but that gap felt like the Grand Canyon, and the days until my birthday like the other side of the world. I bit my lip to keep my breathing steady, biting harder when his hand slipped over my waist, nicking skin, and settled at my lower back so I was fully within his embrace.

Andrew's breathing was steady, *really* steady like he was putting some effort into it. I smiled. No way we could get too intimate here but it was nice realising he probably wouldn't deny me if I asked. Was comforting knowing that his feelings for me weren't being diluted by dad.

I grimaced; didn't want to think about him here.

Andrew whispered he loved me, pressing his lips against my forehead.

'Love you more,' I managed back without a tremor.

- # -

Being at the police station for the third time in just over a week made me feel like it was becoming another home, and I didn't like it.

Liked it even less that I was there with my brothers and sisters. Jamie had been here ages ago with me when we'd first talked to the police about dad's disappearance, but first time for the little ones and for Megan. She didn't look around the private waiting room we were taken to, just fixated on getting Lisa and Matty starting a game of Chinese Checkers.

I sat next to Andrew with my arms folded so I didn't fiddle. I knew this room was because of Lisa and Matty but I wasn't that comfortable with it, still freaking out a bit that Andrew could find himself arrested. Well, he could out in public too, but this room just gave me more quiet to listen to my stupid thoughts.

'Must feel like home for you,' Jamie commented.

'Don't start,' Andrew told him.

I didn't even look up to see how Jamie responded to that, but he didn't speak again.

Lisa and Matty, as they played, got chattier but the rest of us were pretty subdued.

It was maybe fifteen minutes before Sergeant Morrison showed up. We all responded to his greeting fairly easily, all of us on our feet but the kids, but I definitely wasn't the only one on edge that he didn't come alone.

Two uniformed officers accompanied him. He introduced them quickly as Simone James and Damien Cook, and explained they'd be taking Megan and Jamie's statements.

Megan looked at Andrew, eyes wide. 'Are you allowed...?' She gulped a swallow, looked down at her fingers.

'Mr Gordon is welcome to accompany you, Megan,' the sergeant said, even gave a little smile when she looked up at him.

She gave a rapid nod. Beside me I heard Andrew let out a quiet breath. He glanced at Jamie who shrugged and said he'd be fine. Got a little tense, though, when it became clear the sergeant would be going with him.

I remembered Andrew saying that the sergeant wanted to talk to him over his actions on Thursday. I kind of felt sorry for him, but also not because what he'd done was dumb. I appreciated his thoughts and feelings, but it was still dumb.

Andrew broke into my thoughts asking if I'd be okay here with the kids. I started, having not realised until then that'd be the case.

'Ah, yeah, sure.' I glanced over at the kids; they'd stared when everyone showed up but were now refocused on their game. 'They're occupied.' I could sit down and relax.

Or freak out how my older brother and sister were doing, or whether Andrew was being arrested without my knowledge.

I forced myself to smile, then went forward to give Megan a quick hug. 'Just tell it like it was, Megs,' I said softly. 'That's all you need to do.'

She swallowed hard, but nodded and looked a little calmer.

I didn't say the same thing to Jamie, but I knew he wouldn't embellish. Just as he wouldn't hold back telling his side. Everything dad had said about me he'd reveal in his statement. He gave me a nod and then turned to follow the police officer out of the room.

When they'd all gone, I turned to Lisa and Matty, needing to engage them in some talk since the room suddenly felt ridiculously huge. All I did was ask them which one was better at Chinese Checkers, but it started off quite an argument.

Didn't seem that long before the door opened and Sergeant Morrison stepped in. I had to look at my watch, sure that it'd only been ten minutes or so since he'd left.

'Jamie's still with my officer,' he told me. 'I was only there to talk to him about his actions.'

'He had the right to be angry,' I said.

'Certainly,' Sergeant Morrison responded, heading for the small table and chairs. 'But he needs to think before he acts. Come, take a seat.'

I noticed he had his black notebook and guessed it was my turn to give my version of events—a more coherent version than I'd babbled on Thursday. I glanced at my siblings, now arguing whether a particular move had been legal or not. Possibly they hadn't even realised the sergeant was here. I wished I could tune out like they did. Since I couldn't, I walked across the room and sat.

Morrison's gaze was on my face and I had to really fight against covering the bruise from his view, though part of me was *let him see what dad did*.

He asked how I was feeling this morning. I knew I probably didn't look a million dollars but I wasn't up to telling him how I *really* felt. 'Not bad. The pain pills are really good.'

His expression was impressively neutral so I couldn't tell how he was reacting to that. The pain pills *were* good, so that hadn't been a lie.

'Tell me about this dream you had.'

I recoiled, hands curled against my chest. A posture I couldn't change even though I tried. '*Why?*'

'To understand why Mr Gordon chose to move you all to his apartment.'

The tone was steady and firm.

'Because he cares for us,' I responded. 'Because dad did this in front of a cop.' I poked at my face. 'Because…' I sagged; no use getting upset with the sergeant. I drew in a long breath. I didn't want to relate what I'd dreamed but if it helped the sergeant accept Andrew's decision then I needed to.

Opposite me, Sergeant Morrison sat quietly. He hadn't even reacted to my first response.

'I dreamed dad shot Andrew,' I said, voice low though Lisa and Matty weren't paying us any attention.

The sergeant cocked his head just a little, perhaps surprised. As I revealed the dream more fully he didn't try to hide his concern. Didn't interrupt at any time either, not even when I came to the end and told how I'd reacted upon waking.

'Andrew said you were letting dad out, I think he was afraid he'd come to the house.' I leaned forward in my chair. 'He only did what a good guardian would do.'

'Owen,' the sergeant said, 'I am not going to penalise Mr Gordon. I understand his reasons.'

I went stiff a second, then nodded. 'I didn't dream last night, not even Thursday. I think yesterday was just…' I shrugged. 'You showing up with the shrink and Megan doing…' Another shrug. 'Everything just got to me.'

'Have you had this type of dream before?'

I don't know why the question shocked me, but I blurted, 'Shit, no!' before I could stop myself. 'Um, well, never a shooting dream.'

He cocked his head and I mumbled that sometimes Jack Wheeler disrupted my sleep.

'Kid, I wish you'd—' He cut himself off, obviously realising that pushing counselling just wasn't ever going to work.

I'd been through stuff first hand; I didn't need to do a second-hand telling to someone who'd just ask how it made me feel. I couldn't actually believe I'd even just revealed that about my abuser. To get totally away from counselling I asked if I was still supposed to be giving a statement.

The sergeant went still for a moment, probably suppressing frustration, then nodded. He glanced sideways but the game still held my siblings' fascination. 'They're definitely kids who can amuse themselves,' he commented softly.

'Just competitive,' I said, feeling proud of them suddenly. 'They don't get half of what's happening but it all seems to glide over them anyway. Give them a game or food and…' I snapped my fingers.

Morrison looked at me. 'Grace reported no concerns over them, which is comforting.'

I nodded to that. 'They didn't hear me yesterday, thankfully. They were outside. Megan heard me from mum and dad's room though.' I frowned at myself. I wanted away from the dream, not towards it!

Sergeant Morrison looked a whole bunch grim for a moment, then tapped his pencil on the notebook before opening it to a clean page. 'Tell me about your father's visit.'

So I did, putting aside all of my emotion, until I realised

that Megan would be telling the same stuff, recalling what dad had said, and Andrew was with her.

'Owen?' the sergeant prompted.

I looked at him, whispered Andrew's name.

He glanced over his shoulder, then back at me, head cocked.

'He...' I swallowed. 'We didn't talk about it yesterday. What he heard on Thursday *here*—and bits and pieces—that's all he knows... knew... But Megan...' Shut up to try to get myself into order.

Sergeant Morrison sat silent, but he seemed alert.

'Sorry,' I got out. 'I just... Dad said horrible things. Some about what *I* did and some about Andrew.' I cringed. 'He's gonna hear Megan tell it; that's not...' It wasn't fair to hear about it that way, even if he had some basic knowledge of what he *would* hear. I held my breath, trying not to picture his reaction, trying not to "hear" Megan recall the words, trying not to picture him listening to Megan or watching her as she did so.

I pressed a hand over my mouth, struggling to get all that out of my head. Doing my best to beat back the fear that Andrew would become overwhelmed with it all and decide to leave.

'Owen.'

Said in such an authoritative tone that my head cleared and I said, 'Yes, Sergeant?' pretty much instantly.

A brow flicked up, but then he said, 'Can you please finish telling what happened?'

For a moment I thought that was cruel, cutting over my concern for Andrew, but he was right—I did need to finish what I was doing. And Andrew would... Well, anything he felt at hearing how the meeting went he'd hide, just to keep Megan calm.

I pushed my focus onto giving the rest of my version of events as clearly as possible, right up to meeting Andrew on the street and telling the doctor at the clinic that I'd tripped and hit the picnic table.

Sergeant Morrison had been writing things down but I suddenly realised it was mostly a bunch of lines and squiggles. When he caught me looking he said, 'Shorthand. Incredibly valuable skill.'

I just kind of stared a moment. He turned the notebook around, and after a second I could see there was a pattern to everything. 'Heh,' I got out and sat back, feeling a bit embarrassed.

'The statement will be typed up and given back to you to check and sign off.'

I nodded.

As he closed the notebook he asked in an incredibly casual tone, 'How much does Mr Gordon know about your job last year?'

I nearly went, 'What job?' it was such an odd question, but then I sat stiff on my chair. 'Why?'

'You were concerned about what he'd hear during Megan's statement,' he said. 'Would he hear things he didn't know?'

I swallowed back a rock. 'No,' I got out. 'It wasn't… I was just worried about him hearing that dad had said that stuff in front of everyone.' My heart was picking up a solid beat now as I worried where the sergeant was going with this.

He simply repeated his first question. So I asked why he was asking. He gave me this look that said my reactions were telling him all he needed to know, but he answered me.

'Because even though you seem to have buried everything and are functioning, it's all still sitting below the surface. Yesterday's dream is a manifestation of that.'

'What? No!' I said. 'I'd have dreamed of Ja—' Frowned when he raised a brow.

'The point I want to make, Owen, is that if Mr Gordon doesn't know much about your past, he won't have the full tool set to help you when things get unmanageable.'

I was sure he could see I didn't quite get what he was talking about a tool set for. I raised my chin. 'Andrew helps me by just being with me.'

The sergeant drew in a breath. 'Look, I know I won't prevail on you to talk to someone professional, but I do really recommend you talk to Mr Gordon. With this current situation, he needs more than ever to know your back story.'

I sat looking at him, thinking there was no way in hell I wanted to tell my partner about sleeping with other men. I was sure, too, that Andrew wouldn't want to hear it! But… a tiny part of me got what the sergeant was saying. I didn't think the prostitution affected me, but maybe it did in certain ways or at certain times that I wasn't aware of. And, if Andrew knew all that had happened, perhaps he'd be able to counter things before they could break the surface.

Aside from that dream where Jack Wheeler had texted me while running a red light, I had had a couple of other related dreams recently. One where I'd been offered money, one where I'd been in bed with someone random. Neither had really startled me awake, but it had been some time since that sort of thing had made it into my dreams.

Maybe all this stuff with dad and his name-calling was unlocking the past's door?

God, I didn't want Andrew to hear about that stuff!

I rubbed my cheek.

Sergeant Morrison sat silently opposite me but when I chanced a glance at him, his attention was across the room. Actually, at my little brother who was heading for us. I straightened in my chair.

'How're you doing, Mathew?' the sergeant asked.

'I want to be a cop when I grow up,' Matty said in answer.

Bless my brother for completely taking Sergeant Morrison's attention.

I stayed in the chair, listening to them talk, and accepted that Morrison really had been doing all he could for us. Right from the very start. And I hadn't given the respect that was due, or the gratitude. He could have kept Andrew from me a long time ago but he hadn't, and now he was riding a fine line for us, interpreting the law for us, doing what he could to keep me and Andrew together and to keep him with us as a family.

'Sergeant Morrison.'

Honestly, he looked as startled as me. 'Yes, Owen?'

'I'm sorry for everything we've put you through, me especially. And I *am* grateful for what you're doing.'

He sat, silent for a moment like he had to translate what I'd said. Then he gave a stiff nod. 'Thank you, Owen.'

'Um, what you said just now about… what Andrew doesn't know. Do you…' I paused, drawing up all the courage I had. 'I can't *tell* him, but do you think writing…' I couldn't finish, definitely not with Matty still standing there.

Sergeant Morrison looked about as serious as I'd ever seen him, gruff and concerned all in one. 'Whichever way you find comfortable, Owen,' he said quietly.

My head jerked all over the place in a nod. For some dumb

reason I could feel tears building at the back of my eyes. Not at all helped when Matty flung his arms around me in a tight hug. 'You're the best brother!'

I was too choked up to react, even when he added, 'Jamie's pretty cool too and he's a good singer, but you're older so you're still the best.'

Sometimes I wondered if Matty had a screw loose, but I let out a croaky chuckle and hugged him tight. As he pulled back he challenged me to Chinese Checkers.

'Uh.' I glanced at the sergeant who smiled and said, 'Be my guest.'

'Do you want to play too?' Matty asked him. 'You can be on Lisa's side.'

Maybe my apology had weakened the sergeant or maybe he just couldn't deny my little brother, but next thing I knew I was playing Chinese Checkers against a police sergeant like it was natural.

Jamie

I felt caged. I liked Andrew's apartment a lot but it was way too small for six of us to relax in, especially with Owen hogging the bedroom for a nap and Andrew working in his study. He didn't have the door closed but clearly he was also taking a moment. Possibly regretting the Sergeant's generous suggestion that we remain at the apartment for another night.

Biting my lip, I turned back to the window. Guess the sergeant had realised that being at the station this morning was a bit of an ordeal for us. Owen too, even though it must be like another home for him, since he'd told the man about his nightmare. Anyway, Andrew had graciously accepted the suggestion and we'd all been relieved.

Problem was, it'd only been two hours since then and I was ready to climb the walls.

Partly because I didn't have an outside to easily go to. I could clap my headphones on but unless I took over the bathroom I'd still be aware of my sisters and brother. But that wasn't the only thing driving me to walk up and down at the window. Beyond being able to drown out and ignore everyone, I needed to sing out loud.

Each time I glanced at the TV cabinet the niggle got stronger.

In there was a karaoke machine. Andrew had revealed he had one when I'd met with him back while I was looking after the house finances and we'd gotten off-topic. Far enough off for me to mention I was secretly doing Show Choir this semester and I'd be in the class concert at the end of the year. I couldn't recall what had led me to spill that secret, but he'd kept it for me. My brothers and sisters had no idea about the class or the concert.

Every glance at the cabinet edged me closer into coming clean. But I couldn't blurt it because that'd mean I'd have to tell Owen that I'd been *here* a couple of times over the last month to practise. Even if Sarah had been with me, he was still odd about things like that, like he didn't quite trust me to be nice.

I regretted not taking the machine home like Andrew had offered or even keeping it with Sarah.

More fool me now as I pressed my hands against my forehead, grimacing at the view. My secret had *nothing* on those Owen had kept but I was really on edge about revealing it. Which was dumb because I wanted them all to come to the concert on the final day of school.

I took a breath and headed for the study. One knock on the open door and then I was in and closing it behind me.

'Jamie,' Andrew said. 'What's up?'

'I need to sing.'

'Pardon?' He sat straighter in the chair.

I babbled about liking the apartment but feeling caged and the karaoke machine was right there and— I got hold of my tongue, almost literally. Andrew's brows were dipped together in concern.

'Sorry,' I got out. 'Maybe I should just go for a walk.'

'You're welcome to do that, Jamie,' he said. 'I'll give you my access card.'

I pulled a face. 'I'd rather sing.'

Andrew didn't show any surprise, and I was grateful he'd never treated me like a bit of a freak. Or a cliché—a sports' playing singer. How often was that a teen-movie theme? I let out a long sigh.

'Well,' he said. 'How about I do that grocery run, take Matty and the girls?' He got up.

'You don't have to do it *now*,' I said quickly.

Andrew smiled. 'I'm done with work. Fresh air will do me good too.'

'Owen?'

'I'm not waking him,' Andrew said. 'You're going to have to be careful about the sound.'

I shrugged.

'Maybe, if he wakes, you can talk to him about it?'

'No way!'

'I doubt he'll laugh, Jamie,' he said.

'It's not that,' I responded. More likely he'd be angry, and I didn't fancy being called a secret-keeping hypocrite.

'Well, if you want to keep it to yourself, keep the sound down.' Andrew gave a smile. 'He knows that machine's there; just thinks it's broken.'

'He knows?' I asked. 'What? When?'

His smile broadened, became slightly wry. 'You think he doesn't know every inch of this place? When he discovered it, I told him it was broken.'

'Why? You *can* sing, right?' I said. 'I mean, that's why you've got it, isn't it? Why tell him it was broken? He's actually not horrendous himself, he'd probably—' I cut off. No need to lead Andrew to suggest I really ought to tell Owen so we could sing together or something.

Andrew scratched his jaw. 'Just other things on my mind that night. And he's never asked again.'

Put my hand over my mouth to cover a grin even though Andrew's gaze was steady like what he'd said and what I was thinking *were* two different things. He cleared his throat. 'In any case, if you want to keep your secret, keep the sound down.'

'I will,' I said, nodding. I didn't need to do a full version of the song anyway, just sing it once or twice to relax the caginess. I'd be quick, too, and Owen would never know.

'Okay, then.'

Out in the lounge, Andrew announced his plans and my sisters and brother didn't put up any argument about going with him. Megan looked a whole bunch relieved actually, but she managed a serious tone when she told me not to pester Owen.

'No intention of it.'

She eyed me, but even if he was awake down in the

bedroom I wouldn't go near. Didn't want him to ask what the sergeant had said this morning, something I hadn't even told Andrew.

'We'll be an hour or two at the most,' Andrew said.

I nodded. 'Thanks,' I murmured as he turned away.

He lifted a hand but didn't look back.

First thing I did when the door closed and silence fell was draw in a huge breath and let it out long and noisily. Wandering back to the window, I turned my back on it and eyed the lounge—pretty spacious when no one else was in it.

I glanced toward the hall, but I knew Andrew had kept the bedroom door shut after his quick check on my brother. So, even if he was awake I doubted he'd hear the music.

For about ten minutes I didn't move toward the cabinet, funnily enough just relishing the silence.

Except, when this morning at the station began to repeat, I started digging out the karaoke machine and setting it up.

I didn't need the words on the TV as prompts so I ended up closing my eyes, going through the performance in my head. Sarah would be dancing as I sang. So far we'd been alright as a team, and I was really enjoying doing something like this with her, glad she would be able to show off her talents. If I sucked, I knew *she* wouldn't. She wasn't in Show Choir, so her involvement was extra special.

For a moment I struggled to keep singing and not just imagine her dancing. Had to stop in the end because I suddenly wanted to see her more than sing, and that was something I couldn't do right now.

In the end, I packed away the gear—Owen none the wiser—and phoned Sarah, let her know we were at Andrew's again tonight. I didn't tell her about this morning; we just chatted about random stuff and then the two dress rehearsals coming up. She ribbed me about how I was going to need to iron the white shirt I had to wear, something I wasn't quite skilled at, and I countered that I was sure she'd be able to give me lessons.

When the call ended, I was more relaxed than the singing had made me.

Which was just as well because, as I was getting into the kitchen to get a glass of water, Owen showed up, looking mussed.

'Are you even awake?' I asked.

He palmed his eyes. 'Of course.' He didn't really look it as he shifted into the lounge. 'Where is everyone?'

'Grocery shopping.'

'Ah.'

When Owen's gaze came back to me, I told him Andrew'd volunteered me to babysit. He got a peeved look on his face, then came back to the kitchen.

I shifted around to the bar stools and sat while he made a cup of tea. He definitely knew his way around this kitchen. I dialled back as much of the smile as I could, recalling Andrew's earlier comment, and asked how he was feeling.

'Drained,' he said. 'Probably shouldn't have slept so long.' Pushing his fingers through his hair didn't make his hair any tidier.

'And your face?'

'Still got it.'

I rolled my eyes at the response but didn't push. He was obviously done with being asked and I knew by experience that if I did push then he'd retaliate with a question or comment about something *I* didn't want to talk about.

When Owen had made his tea he took it around to the window, gaze downward and then left toward Navy Pier. I swivelled on the stool to watch him, couldn't read the expression. He let out a soft breath, lips half curved, and sipped at his drink.

That unsettled me just a bit, like I was witnessing some weird intimate moment. I choked on a breath of laughter, got off the stool as he raised a brow at me.

'Nothing,' I said, which made the brow get a bit even.

But he turned away without speaking, looking towards the Pier again.

I came up beside him. 'We should go on the Wheel while we're here.'

'Nope.'

'You're weird, you know,' I said. 'It's a sixty-plus floor drop'—pointed—'yet, you're standing here like it's nothing. That Wheel's tiny compared.'

'Don't care,' Owen said, then glanced at me. 'We *should* go there though, do something fun.' His voice dropped a little on that last word.

I slung my arm around his shoulder. 'Hey, we had a fun family outing this morning.'

Not my best blurt, but Owen just stood there, unresponsive. Wincing internally, I waited. Didn't apologise since I doubted that'd cover my mistake.

'Well,' he said, clearing his throat. 'I did get to play Chinese Checkers against Sergeant Morrison. Not something I expected.'

My arm dropped because we shifted and turned more fully toward each other at the same time. Owen had a half smile on his face, which hit me more than the comment did. My brother had been through so much last year and now he was dealing with more shit. The bruise seemed darker right now. How he wasn't a raving mess I didn't know.

'You're amazing, you know that?'

'What?' he croaked, stepping back.

Even though heat rushed up my face, I said, 'I'm not taking it back. You are, Owen, and I don't let you know it enough.'

'Ok-kay.'

I didn't try to hug him, thinking I'd probably end up wearing what was left of his tea. Praise rattled him, obviously.

'Who won?'

Owen looked at me.

'The game.' I recalled Matty crowing but I wanted to keep Owen talking.

He smiled. 'Me and Matty. Felt kinda good,' he said, wryly.

I bet it did. Having been on the receiving end of the chat this morning, I was beginning to understand Owen's feelings toward the sergeant. He was on our side, yes, but he was a cop too. He had a job to do, the law to uphold, people to protect. He did it gruffly, but… he also did it fairly. I shouldn't have gone after dad like I had and I deserved to be reprimanded about it.

'Hey,' Owen said softly. 'Has Megan said much?'

'About her statement?' I shook my head.

'Andrew told me she was really calm.'

'Yeah, she looked it,' I said, remembering when they'd come back to the waiting room. Megan had been kind of pale but her chin was up and she'd engaged with us fairly easily. I cocked my head. 'You think she's hiding stuff?'

'Don't know,' he responded. 'I just… Yesterday when she yelled… Up to *that* point she'd been all calm then too.'

'She's not gonna try to kick you again, Owen.'

'It's not that,' he said with a frown. 'I just… You know how the psychologist talked with Lisa and Matty, maybe she…' He cut off as I took a step back. Then he scowled. 'I'm not suggesting *you*, Jamie.'

'Good,' I told him, 'cos I don't need a shrink.'

He ran his tongue over his teeth a second, making me more rigid, then said, 'Maybe Megs would benefit talking to her— or someone, at least.'

'Maybe,' I said, but I wasn't going to put up my hand to make the suggestion. Then I sighed and said the sergeant had told me counselling was available any time I needed it.

Owen sucked in his lips. 'Yeah.'

Wasn't quite sure what that related to, though I guessed that word had come up in his conversation too.

Owen drank the rest of his tea and then sank to his butt, sitting cross-legged. I stood for a second, unsure if that was a signal for me to leave him alone. Then he glanced up. 'I'm dreaming more and more about last year.'

I croaked out something, then got down beside him. 'Wheeler?' I asked hesitantly.

'Sometimes.' He inclined his head. 'Actually, just once recently. Not… the attack but texting me as he ran a red light.' He grimaced. 'Last week after I met with dad.'

'Ouch,' I breathed out.

Owen's face screwed up briefly. 'Mostly it's just random things. But sometimes the… men… involved. It's a bit unsettling.'

'Have you always dreamed…?'

He shook his head, then offered up a weird smile. 'The more I fell in love with Andrew, the closer he got to you guys, all that stuff faded.'

'Magic man,' I muttered.

A full smile washed my brother's face a second and he breathed out, 'Yeah.'

We sat in silence a short while, Owen fiddling with the cup, and then he said, 'Dad's bringing all this stuff back, with his words, and I don't...' He leaned over his knees. Without straightening he said, 'I'm scared I'll end up dreaming about the attack. What dad did on Thursday brought—' His shoulders hunched.

'You didn't dream that night?' I rasped out.

He shook his head. 'Good drugs. But it's like I'm on tenterhooks, waiting. Just now I... I dreamed I was in Uptown.'

When I looked puzzled he whispered that's where he'd met Jack Wheeler.

'You need to tell Andrew,' I said, lump in my throat.

'I *can't*,' Owen responded. 'He's already worried not being with us at night. I can't tell him and worry him more.'

'You can't leave him in the dark, Owen,' I said, wondering at how I sounded so normal saying that when I actually felt a bit panicked.

He jerked, making me spout, 'What?'

'Just...' He shook his head, then grimaced. 'Sorry for babbling. Not fair laying it on you either.'

'I'm your brother,' I said, though it felt sort of hollow.

Owen wrinkled his nose.

'Hey,' I said after a second. 'If there's any night you feel...' I shrugged, didn't exactly know what to say there. 'Come and wake me. Or... maybe we can do a bed swap. Matty in your room and you sharing with me.'

I couldn't fault Owen staring at me. Part of me had been saying *no, no, no* even as I'd been speaking, but I shut that part down. He was obviously feeling alone without Andrew and bad that the rest of us were affected. I needed to stand up and remind him that we were still a family and that we knew how to act like it.

Owen looked embarrassed and puzzled and upset and amused all in one. Then he said, 'You just want to get away from the snoring.'

Took a second for me to let out laughter. I shoved him.

He stopped himself toppling over. 'Once I heard him last night, I just couldn't block him out.'

'Ah ha,' I said. '*That's* why you weren't there this morning.'

'Of course.'

I laughed again and got up. 'I think Andrew intends to get an air bed.'

Owen looked up at me but didn't react to that or my grin. He just turned back to the window, lips pressed into a smile.

I waited but he said nothing more and I realised our little brotherly bonding session was over. Something of a miracle we'd had it but it made me feel good. Not about dad chipping away at Owen's confidence and calm but that he'd revealed that stuff to me.

Remembering Andrew's concern yesterday as we'd chatted about the dream, I wondered if I should let him know that was possibly the tip of an iceberg. Though, I didn't want to worry him any more than Owen did. Yet I also didn't want to witness another dream on that scale.

'Hey, now you're awake, you mind if I go for a walk?'

Owen jerked, twisting, then got up. For a second I worried he'd say he'd join me but he said, 'No, why should I?' And then, 'I'll give you my access card.'

He left the lounge and I looked about for my shoes and sunglasses.

When he brought the card back I tucked it in a back pocket. 'I'll probably just go around the block.'

Owen shrugged like he didn't care, and didn't even watch as I left. A grin split my face as I headed for the lifts. Brotherly moment definitely over!

[*Eight*]

Owen

I wasn't really a plane geek but sitting lakeside watching them come overhead on their way into O'Hare gave me a feeling of peace.

At Margate, near the end of the outer drive, Andrew and I sat under the middle flightpath. Overhead came a Qatar jet, easily identifiable because the belly spelt it out. Good way to advertise. As I leaned back, tracking it out of sight, I thought about the direct flights to/from New Zealand that were starting at the end of the year. It'd be cool to see the first one come in, the koru on the tail that I couldn't actually recall the detail of. I let out a sigh, really wanting to be on a flight *out*.

'Bored?' Andrew murmured beside me.

'Nope.'

I knew he was looking at me but I didn't turn from tracking planes. Then I did turn. 'Are you?'

We'd been here maybe forty-five minutes already, having left work to get some real time to ourselves.

Though we were alone in the office it wasn't like before the restriction. Andrew was a lot more formal, even when he didn't have meetings. And he seemed to have a lot more of those. Must have been tiring, but even so there were some days when I almost had to drag him to eat at the break-out space instead of at his desk.

We could have gone to his apartment today, but it wasn't actually naked intimacy I craved. I just wanted to be with him, on our own terms, in a quiet space. I wanted to be in public with my partner. Internal eye roll at that since we were not exactly *open* in public. I rubbed my brow, trying to get all that jumble out of my head, and glanced down at the art pad Andrew held. He'd been drawing columns.

Since he hadn't answered my question I asked again if he was bored.

'Not at all, Owen,' he said with a smile. He turned the pad so I could see properly. 'Measure up?'

I flushed. We'd been talking in the office about ancient architecture and the number of columns on buildings around the city. He'd never been called upon to design anything with columns but he reckoned he could. So while I'd been reading and then quickly diverted skyward, he'd been putting his pen where his mouth was.

Taking the book off him, I gave the drawings a good stare, but there was no way I could say he'd drawn crap. There weren't even any scribbled out lines. 'You're not half bad,' I told him.

Andrew laughed out loud and I soaked it up. Hearing him laugh that way was rare these days.

He held out the pen. 'Going to try?'

'No way,' I said, pushing his hand away. 'I know my limits.'

He took back the pad, eyeing the columns with a smile. As he flipped to a new page he asked, 'How's the book?'

'Good.' It was closed, on its spine, between my feet. I grinned at him and leaned back on my hands, searching for jets.

I don't think I dozed off but I jumped when Andrew said, 'Wow, that's a threatening sky.'

'What?'

He pointed across the lake at a bleak scene: black formless

clouds like a huge wall. 'We should probably get moving.'

A British Airways with its bright tail came overhead.

'Nah, wind's not changed yet,' I said. 'Anyway, I don't care if I get wet.'

Andrew arched a brow and I just shrugged at him. I knew he wouldn't hustle me home until he really had to. Reality waited at home and he could probably tell I wanted to meet it as late as possible today.

We were going to watch Megan compete in her final badminton games and dad would be there. And then we'd all be going out to dinner afterwards.

I knuckled an eye. Last Friday Andrew had taken us to his place out of massive concern, tonight—a week later—we were going to be a weird family as if all that stuff hadn't happened. 'I wish you hadn't agreed to tonight.' I straightened when Andrew went still. 'Sorry, that was unfair. I just…' I shook my head.

'I know it's not going to be an easy few hours,' he said, 'but there wasn't much I could really do.'

I leaned against him briefly.

When dad had found out about the evening, Megan had made the suggestion that he join us. I reckoned she'd felt she had to since dad had given her a belated birthday present— mum's diamond engagement ring. What else could she have done?

Sergeant Morrison probably had something to do with the situation too. We'd not heard from dad since that upsetting night, then on Wednesday the sergeant had dropped by to say dad had asked to see us. He wanted to apologise. Everyone had looked at me, maybe thinking I'd do a, 'No way in hell!' response, but I'd said, 'Good, that's the least he can do.'

So, Sergeant Morrison had brought him around last night and he'd apologised for forgetting and then ruining Megan's birthday, for upsetting everyone, and for what he'd done to me. He didn't say he'd spoken wrong just said he acted in a blind spot and should have had better control.

I'd thanked him automatically, though when he'd smiled I'd had to get a hand over my mouth to keep back the gag.

Dad had mentioned making things up to us with dinner and it had been Lisa who'd said we'd already had plans for Friday.

Out came those plans and then Megan invited dad along. Guess she couldn't have done much else, and she kept looking at the ring on her finger.

Andrew didn't deny her but he'd made it clear that he'd still be joining us. Sergeant Morrison had stated that dad would meet us at the school; he obviously wasn't going to let dad have us on our own yet.

Gazing at an insect crawling near my shoe, I leaned into Andrew. 'I really don't want to go tonight.'

He hugged me, didn't tell me I didn't *have* to go. I kind of did. It was Megan's night, and we were going to support *her*.

Jamie was coming, but not with us. He'd been the angry one yesterday, but Andrew had shut him down before he got too vocal. So he'd ended up a bit pissed at Andrew too—one of the reasons I was dragging out our time *here*. He was getting to school with his friends and sitting with them too, but he *was* going to join us for dinner. *Fun times ahead*, I thought.

'It'll be okay, Owen,' Andrew murmured. 'It's a school gym, after all.'

'Yeah,' I mumbled, then bent to pick up my book when I accidentally stepped on it. Glancing across the lake, the sky seemed darker. Threatening, Andrew had called it earlier. I hoped it wasn't an omen for tonight. *School gym*, I thought sternly to myself. Dad wouldn't go all weird in public, surely.

Hearing the soft roar of a jet, I looked about for it—there, off to the left, heading out over the lake. About then I felt the breeze on my face and noticed the lake seemed a little rough. 'Guess we ought to get going,' I said, with a groan.

'What about this "I don't care if I get wet" stance?'

When I scowled at him, he smiled and patted my knee. 'Come on, Gorgeous.'

'You know how to say all the right things,' I said, making him laugh out loud again.

Jamie

Though I heard the front door unlocking, I didn't stop myself saying, 'Megs, if you didn't want him to come, why did you ask him?'

'What else could I have done, Jamie?' Megan cried. 'He gave me mum's *ring.*'

'And that makes up for everything?' That was cruel but I was angry over this thing too and couldn't make myself stop.

Tears built in my sister's eyes and she was rubbing her finger, but she wasn't wearing the ring.

'What's up?' Andrew said softly as he came into the lounge.

I looked at him, then twisted as Owen moved into view in the kitchen. We caught gazes just a second and then I turned back to Andrew. 'Why can't you *do* something?'

His brows went up. 'Pardon?'

'Megan doesn't want dad there tonight.'

Andrew looked at her. 'Hon?'

'I d-don't,' she said, sniffing. 'I was okay yesterday but…'

It had been stewing in her head all day, enough that she reckoned she'd totally flunked one of her tests.

'It was all okay,' she mumbled, 'when he gave me the ring, but now… I know he apologised and all that but I don't… I don't want him to think everything's *good*.'

'Has he contacted you?' Andrew asked carefully. 'Since yesterday?'

Megan looked surprised a second. 'No, nothing. That's not why I've changed my mind.'

Andrew looked at me and I said, 'Me either, but you still need to do something.'

He rubbed his brow. 'I'm not sure I can, Jamie.'

'Why not?' I asked. 'You're our legal guardian.'

'Yes,' he said, 'but—'

'But what?' I cried. 'But. *What?*

After a breath, Andrew said, 'But I'm afraid to push because I don't want to lose any of you.'

Megan and I stared.

'You're my kids by signed agreement only,' Andrew said. 'Your father has blood right. There's only so much I can do before I step over some damn line. And I don't want to risk it, Jamie. I'm *sorry*, but I won't. Risk. It.' He turned and strode from the lounge.

Guilt tried to hammer down all my other feelings as Owen hissed my name then went after Andrew, but I was hurt myself. Couldn't anyone see that? Didn't I have a right to question things? Was I the only one who thought an apology did *not* make up for what dad had done last week?

A sniff made me turn. Megan was getting to her feet, eyes brimming again. I thought she was gonna abandon me too but she gave me a hug. I swallowed down a stinking large rock.

'I *know* he's stuck, Megs,' I rasped out, 'but… I want him to stand up for us more clearly.'

'He's doing his best,' she replied. 'I understand there's… Well, that he can't out and out refuse stuff. Definitely not after last week.'

'That's why he *should*,' I cried. 'Jesus, dad almost broke Owen's face, scared the shit out of the rest of us. He should refuse to let dad be here at all!'

'I don't think he can,' Megan mumbled. 'It's like he said, and I think Sergeant Morrison would say he couldn't refuse.'

My scowl dug deep into my brow. '*He* should refuse dad too.'

Everyone should, including *us*. If we didn't want dad here—and we didn't—then we needed to make it clear. Show that we wanted to be with Andrew. 'I hate this,' I said.

'You hate everything,' Megan told me, called up a sliver of a smile. She put her hands briefly to her face. 'Let's just…' She sighed. 'Let's just get through tonight. Matty's excited dad will be there.'

'Wish that kid could read the vibe better,' I grumbled.

Matty went through stages of being unsure and then totally cool. He'd spun that roundabout yesterday. Fairly quickly too, which made me wonder about what other things dad might be saying behind the scenes when he had time alone with the kids, even just out in the garden. Lisa had taken a bit more convincing about dad, but by the time he went last night Matty was back on board. Guess he'd totally forgotten his own performance last week.

I sighed and looked at my sister. 'You gonna be okay?'

She gave a half shrug. 'Least I'll know what to blame if I don't win,' she said wryly.

I managed half a smile, then said, 'I'm gonna go for a walk or something.' Knew I should find Andrew and apologise but I needed to settle down first.

At the park at the end of the next street I sat texting Sean to confirm tonight's stuff.

Coulda done it at home, but I needed space from a place that more and more lately hadn't felt like home. Somehow, dad's arrival was taking that from me, as if the time spent there without him was disappearing. Had had some shit times I'd welcome disappearing, but also some better times I didn't want to lose.

The house we'd had back in New Zealand popped up, which was weird since it belonged to the way distant past now. Yet, I could still walk it in my head and remember things. Remember sharing a room with Owen.

My lips curved.

But then my eyes started to sting, so I focused back on my phone.

Seconds later a large drop hit the ground near me. I jumped first, laughed second, and when I saw how black overhead was I took off for home.

There I found Owen sitting with Lisa and Matty at the table, trying to keep their focus on homework. Getting blood out of a stone was easier than getting them to do any schoolwork on the weekends, and there'd be no time after the badminton tonight. We were supposed to be getting dinner out.

With dad.

I felt my face twist up.

'Smell a fart?' Matty asked.

'That's gross,' Lisa said.

'Hey, focus,' Owen growled, directing me a peeved scowl like it was all my fault.

I didn't answer Matty, just headed out of the kitchen. Andrew wasn't in the lounge. Nor was Megan. A tour of the bedrooms revealed that we'd lost two people, and then I realised I'd not seen the Merc in the drive. Back in the kitchen, I leaned against the bench. 'Has Andrew taken Megs to school?'

'Yeah,' Owen said, not looking up from pointing out something to Lisa who sat beside him.

After a second, I said, 'I know he can't work magic, Owen.'

'No point in saying it to me,' he responded. 'Check again, Lis, you're a number out.'

Owen clearly wasn't gonna give me the time of day until I apologised to Andrew. I shrugged and walked off. Outside, rain bucketed down and thunder rumbled like a long growl.

#-#-#

'Gotta say, Jamie,' Sean spouted suddenly. 'This is the weirdest dynamic yet.'

'What?'

He nodded across the courts. 'Your family.'

On his other side, I caught Lincoln mouthing *Fucking A*. I was surprised to find myself not pissed at them, but looked across and admitted, 'Yeah. Why do you think I'm *here?*'

The line-up went dad, Matty, Lisa, Andrew, Owen.

My brother was not having the time of his life, barely smiling, hardly reacting even when Matty and Lisa jumped up cheering when Megan had been introduced. Andrew seemed both alert and wary, but not overly stiff, and dad sat at the other end like nothing was odd. I felt a wry smile show up; looking at them, one might think that dad and Andrew were the couple.

Maybe that was why Owen sat so rigid.

'So, your dad's back for good?' Sean asked. 'I didn't think…' His shoulders lifted. 'Well, didn't expect to see him here with the… rest.'

He meant alongside Andrew and Owen.

'It's a freakin novel,' I groaned. 'Not telling it right now.'

I hadn't yet apologised to Andrew, hadn't actually seen him face to face to do so though I could have phoned. Then I said, 'Megan suggested Dad come tonight. Think she feels she owes him or something.'

Her turnaround this afternoon hadn't actually been surprising, but she was doing her best right now to act like nothing was wrong and she'd greeted dad with a smile and hug. She sat on the side-line, almost directly below them, tightening her shoelaces. Her first game was up shortly.

'Harsh,' Lincoln said.

'Harsh what?'

'That she's in this position. Can't be easy.'

'It's fucking not,' I said, swallowed when they both looked at me. Coughed to clear my throat but they knew how things had been the last couple of weeks. I didn't speak further just texted my brother *Hows the execution?*

Owen jerked in his seat and dug out his phone. He probably hadn't realised how loud his posture was. He didn't look up to scan the crowd, which kind of impressed me. He said something to Andrew, who nodded, and then rose and made his way along the seats to an aisle.

'Back in a minute,' I said to the guys.

'Bring me a soda,' Lincoln said by way of response.

Sean shoved him for me, then added his own order. I flipped them both a finger and left.

Owen was probably in the toilets or something, needing space to vent in private. Except, I actually found him standing at the soda vendor.

Handy.

His brows went low when he saw me, but he smiled and thanked the canteen lady when he took his drink. He didn't head back into the gym, just stood off to one side. When I joined him, like I'd been invited, he said, 'You could make an effort.'

'Much more fun watching.' I'd join them all for dinner, that was enough. 'So…'

'It's hell, Jamie. Hell.' No humour. 'I hate it.'

'Come sit with us a while.'

'I can't leave Andrew alone,' he growled.

I very nearly spouted about Andrew being fine there with the other father, but didn't want my relationship with Owen to die in a school hallway. I also nearly sucked one of the straws to take a moment before remembering neither were my drinks. Then I swallowed some coke anyway. Nothing like sugar fizz to regain energy. 'I better get these to the guys.'

Owen eyed the straw I'd sucked, but when he spoke it was just, 'Yeah.'

'I *will* be at dinner,' I told him.

Owen just shrugged and walked off.

Great, still not happy with me. But we were *all* stuck in a tight spot; it wasn't only him and I wished he could see that just once.

Unable to sleep, even though Matty wasn't making a racket tonight, I finally grabbed up my phone and went out to the dark lounge.

I texted *I'm sorry* to Andrew without much thought to the time—11:23, it turned out—then sat there. Not waiting for his reply, just needing to sort myself out.

Much of this evening's atmosphere was my fault, right from dad's apology actually. I'd expected Owen to be the sour one with that, but it had been me reacting angrily. The apology had felt so weak.

Grimaced, since mine just now to Andrew was probably the same.

When I used my head properly I understood he was bound in what he could do, knew he worried about his status. But I kinda didn't get that part given how dad had been acting; in a guardianship battle, surely no one would pick dad?

There was something more to it, I was sure, that stopped Andrew from straight out refusing to let dad see us. More than just those restrictions he and Owen were following. I didn't have the courage to dig though. Didn't think Andrew would tell me, and Owen had spent a lot of the evening acting like I didn't exist.

I let out a growl, then jerked as my phone beeped beside me. My heart suddenly dive-bombed my ribs and it took at least a minute before I could see what had come through.

Jamie.

That's what Andrew had replied and, weirdly, I read it like a resigned sigh—probably just like he'd felt. For a moment I felt rebellious, but then had to wipe my eyes. Face heated though no one was here to see me.

And then I let the tears out a bit more. This was such a shitty situation and I was angry at myself for making it worse. Recalled dad sitting opposite Andrew at the restaurant and saying…

'My son doesn't seem happy with you, Mr Gordon.'

'He's not, particularly,' Andrew replied calmly.

Next to him Owen put extra effort into chewing, but the comment had been about me not him.

'Oh?' Dad asked, straightening and glancing at me.

Andrew took a sip of water. 'Mm, he's upset I'm not doing something he wants.'

Dad cocked his head, eyes narrowing just a bit. He turned to me but Lisa, on my left, asked a question and I bent my focus fully on her.

There'd been a few other comments, but at least no out and out yelling or anything.

Even so, not a dinner I ever wanted to repeat. And there was no way in hell now that I'd tell my brothers and sisters about next week's concert. I did *not* want dad there and I was afraid that if I told everyone about it then it'd get back to him at some point and I'd be forced to offer an invite.

Nope, better to leave it to Andrew to spontaneously take them out and surprise them. I pulled a face; there'd be fall-out, no doubt, but I preferred that over dad.

I realised suddenly that I had another message: *Call me if you need.*

A minute or so ago. Did he mean now?

I choked up again briefly and then growled at myself to stop being stupid. I meant to go back to bed but next thing a phone was ringing in my ear and then Andrew said, 'Jamie.'

'You said to call,' I began in defence.

'Yes, I did,' he agreed. 'Is your brother asleep?'

'I'm in the lounge,' I told him. 'I couldn't sleep. I acted like a fucking dick today. Sorry. I didn't think what it would do.'

A bit of silence after that.

Then a half breath sounded in my ear and Andrew said, wryly, 'I doubt dinner would have been fun even without that.'

'Dad niggled,' I said. 'That wasn't fair.' I knew it was me who'd given him the ammo, but it still wasn't fair. 'He should have focused on Megan.'

'It wasn't all doom and gloom.'

'I hate you doing that,' I grumbled. 'Trying to insist there's good in this.'

He drew breath but I got out another apology before he could speak. 'I just… I hate that you have to walk this stupid line and he can do whatever.'

'I appreciate your feelings, Jamie, and I'm sorry that I can't do more.'

I sighed. 'I get why. Don't like it but I get it.' I leaned back on the couch, feet hooking up on the coffee table. And then I heard myself telling him about the concert plan—how I definitely wanted it kept a secret. 'I don't want dad there, he'll just kill…' I trailed off.

'I back you,' Andrew said. 'And, don't worry, I'll get everyone there. It'll be fine.'

I smiled into the dark, though nerves picked at me a second. 'Thanks,' I mumbled. 'And… for now. I feel dumb talking but… thanks.'

'Kid, it's no problem. Even if I can't be with you all the time, I'm still contactable.'

'I appreciate it,' I said. 'But you won't tell—'

'This is just between us.'

'Ah, good.'

'But please do remind your sister she can contact me too,' Andrew said.

'Na uh, she'll only whine to you about me and Owen.'

I was sure I caught a slight chuckle.

'And he's okay, by the way,' I said. 'Grumped his way to bed not long after you left. We didn't face off.' I made that sound light, but I *had* sort of expected something.

Andrew was silent.

I shook my head at myself. Dumb thing to say given mine and Owen's track record. 'Don't worry, I'll apologise to him.'

'Mm mm.'

'Anyway,' I said. 'I better go.'

'Okay, and don't forget I won't be around until noon.'

'Oh right, yeah, no problem.'

'Good night, Jamie.'

'Good ni—Andrew?''

Yes?'

I bit my lip a second. 'Thank you. I mean it.'

'Any time, Jamie,' he said quietly.

I nodded, then got out a whispered, 'Bye' and hung up, swallowing hard.

For all my anger about him not being hard-nosed against dad, I admired him for it, for being the far better man, for having *our* interests at heart. God… for letting me talk in the middle of the night!

My snort of laughter had a bit of a sob sound mixed in, so

I leapt up off the couch and returned to my bed. Matty was sleeping peacefully tonight so I hoped I'd drop off quickly now that I'd released my guilty conscience.

DIGGING DEEP

[Nine]

Owen

For someone who kept saying he wanted back in, Dad kept irregular contact with us. Not that me, Megan and Jamie minded that he didn't seem to want to seek permission to visit. But the lack of even a phone call was distinctly nerve wracking given the last couple of weeks.

Andrew, himself, seemed relaxed but we were home early every day of the final week of school. Wasn't quite sure what impact that had on his work, but I appreciated his company and I knew the kids did too. Leaving at eight still fluctuated on a varying scale of okay-to-hard, but the extra hours in the afternoon helped.

Especially since he also took on the role of tutor for anyone needing last minute encouragement or help for tests that seemed to be running every day.

I had never regretted working instead of studying, and as I watched my brothers and sisters stressing over final assignments and tests I definitely didn't regret that choice. I helped where I could but mostly just sat and watched Andrew doing magnificent work with my siblings.

On Friday, I sat at the big flat table in the office putting together a 3-D model of a studio apartment. It was one of several being created for display for a new building. It constantly amazed me that physical models were still made when it must have been so much easier to do a digital one, but I never complained about the work. I enjoyed seeing something arise out of mere card and paste. Wondered if it was because I'd liked playing with Lego as a kid.

Andrew sat opposite, cutting up the designs that we were using to make the models. He'd had a three-hour meeting this morning so I guessed he wanted something sort of mindless now so he could recover. Anyway, I liked watching him do the basic stuff.

'You're making me self-conscious, you know.'

I grinned as he glanced across at me, hadn't realised I'd been out and out staring for a while. 'You should be used to me staring by now.'

He snorted. 'Sure, but not when I'm busy cutting around tiny shapes and trying not to make mistakes.'

'Pfft.'

He didn't show me anything he'd cut and I was pretty sure he hadn't made any mistakes. I just lowered my head and refocused on my work. His soft chuckle was the best sound in the world.

After a while Andrew asked if I'd had any thoughts on what I wanted to do when we went to Madison on Monday.

I snorted. 'You think we've got time to see things *we* want? Matty's pretty much organised the whole day.'

Andrew smiled, but it was true. Ever since the plan had been hatched to get out of town for Memorial Day, Matty had been treating it like his own personal tour.

We'd decided Madison over other places because it was close enough to drive but far away enough to feel like a real day out, and it had a free zoo. That had gotten the Matty tick of approval, but the city had a lot of other interesting places to visit too like the State Capitol and the Olbrich Botanical Gardens. Megan had looked up the latter and said it had the only Thai pavilion in the US so she was quite intrigued about that.

As I screwed the cap on the glue I said, 'I'm quite looking forward to seeing the Capitol and all the classical architecture.'

Andrew grinned at me. 'You're turning out to be quite an architecture enthusiast.'

I stuck my tongue out.

'Tell me something, though,' he said. 'Matty said he wanted to find New Zealand's stone there. I have no idea what he meant.'

I'd heard him say it too. 'I think he's remembering something from home,' I said. 'There's a memorial in Wellington that has different stones in it. I think some of them are from sites soldiers had fought, but I can't remember. Anyway, I think he thinks the Capitol has a display like that, which includes one from home.'

Andrew cocked his head. 'Sounds fascinating, though I'm not sure why a US capitol building would carry stone from New Zealand.'

I blew out a breath. 'I doubt it does, but I'm not gonna tell Matty that. He's really excited.'

A brow arched. 'So… you're going to let him search for something that doesn't exist?'

I cleared my throat. 'Yep.' It was better sometimes to let Matty do his own thing than tell him straight out that something wasn't going to work. Fall-out afterwards was better than a tantrum beforehand.

'Well, okay,' Andrew said, sounding a mix of amused and sceptical.

'What do *you* want to see?' I asked.

'Nothing specific,' he replied. 'Just looking forward to the whole day.'

We held each other's gaze for a moment, and then he smiled. 'I'm drawn by the Capitol too.'

I let out a laugh. 'I'd be horrified if you weren't.'

We talked a little more about what to see and do before starting to pack up. We were leaving work even earlier today so we could pick Lisa and Matty up from their early finish at school. Even though it was a Friday we'd decided that Mrs Carter could have a day off from the usual Friday ice-creams. I suspected she didn't mind much, probably knew that today, being the last day of school, the kids would be hyped up even before they got sugar in them. Not that they were going to get it today; we were heading out to dinner instead. Megan was joining us but Jamie had chosen to attend Sarah's end-of-year dance show.

A decision I understood, even if tonight's dinner wasn't going to be a replica of last Friday's.

Dad wasn't coming, and no one had ventured to suggest inviting him. Not even Matty. He hadn't mentioned dad much over the last few days, but then again his focus was really taken with Monday's trip. It was probably a miracle that he hadn't asked if dad could come along on that, but once he'd learned about the zoo and decided that the Capitol would have a stone from New Zealand that was about all that was in his brain. It'd been hard to get him to remember school this week!

As crazy as I knew Monday would be, I was really looking forward to it; the six of us together as a family, enjoying new sights and not having to worry about anything.

- # -

I guess none of us had realised just how far Matty's obsession with the black Mercedes went, until Andrew showed up on Memorial Day without it.

Since there was no really safe way the six of us could fit in the Merc on a five-hour round-trip to Madison, Wisconsin, Andrew had rented a seven-seater. Megan thought it was a great idea.

Matty though… He burst into tears, stomped his foot and refused to budge from the front porch.

Didn't help that the rest of us laughed.

'Doesn't *our* car have seven seats?' Lisa asked me.

'Well, yeah, but we've got no keys for it. You going to push us?'

She gave me "the look".

'Guess that's a no,' I said with a grin, as Andrew got down on his knees, trying to get Matty smiling.

'Just give up, man,' Jamie said as he headed back inside. 'Nothing beats the Merc.'

Andrew rolled his eyes, but kept trying.

I followed Jamie inside, and Megan came after us, giving final orders about checking we had all the right stuff for the day as well as directing Lisa and me to hurry up with the breakfast dishes. We'd been half way through them when Andrew had arrived.

'Slave driver,' Lisa muttered, sharing a grin with me.

Once finished, I headed to my bedroom to make the important decision of should I take a sweatshirt or just a coat for over my t-shirt? The weather lately had been half sun, half rain, and apparently the same up in Madison.

'Well,' Andrew said behind me, making me turn. 'I had to promise I'd teach him how to drive the Merc.'

'What?' I yelped.

'I didn't say right now,' he said with a grin.

'He'll badger you,' I told him. 'Bad promise to make, Andrew.'

'Heh, I also said he could sit up front with me.'

I pulled a face. He ruffled my hair, looked a lot like he was trying not to grin.

'Another bad promise,' I told him, ducking away. 'You'll understand that pretty quickly.'

He huffed out a laugh, but he'd not really had to deal with Matty in the front passenger seat much. And the drive to Madison was two and a half hours. He was so gonna regret it.

For myself, it'd been some time since I'd been in a back seat, and I couldn't recall I'd even actually sat in the back, back seat of our old car. But here I was today, feeling like I'd almost have to shout if I wanted to talk with Andrew.

Matty had come out all smiles and was poking bits and pieces in front of him, lifting flaps and saying what they were—drink holders, phone holders, charger…

I decided that the very back seat wasn't too bad after all. With Megan and Lisa directly behind him and Andrew, they kinda blocked my little brother's babble from reaching me at full sound. I chuckled to myself.

Jamie arched a brow beside me, but he already had headphones on. I turned to gaze out my window.

I was a little surprised he'd chosen to come today, instead of staying home alone in relative peace and quiet. Maybe he was worried dad would do an appearing act because we hadn't actually seen him since we'd had dinner after Megan's badminton. That was all good, but it felt like we were on tenterhooks, just waiting for him to show up. That was partly why we were totally getting out of state today.

Possibly Jamie was just trying to forget he and Sarah had become stars on Friday. His rendition of *Total Eclipse of the Heart*, with Sarah dancing, had gotten everyone on their feet clapping and cheering.

We didn't know anything about Jamie singing in the Show Choir or the concert until we'd got to the school Friday night, confused as all heck since we thought we were going to dinner, and he'd met us there and given us entry tickets.

Hadn't known Andrew's sneaky involvement until then either.

Funniest thing of all was, I hadn't been angry about the secret-keeping. Couldn't be, anyway, when Jamie had revealed he hadn't wanted the risk that Lisa or Matty would let it slip to dad and then we'd have to invite him along. Guess the badminton/dinner experience had put him off.

And Andrew had already promised he'd sing something for me on the not-broken-after-all karaoke machine.

Dad was none the wiser about today either, but I doubted anyone felt guilty about that. Getting completely out of town was going to be therapeutic for all of us. Well, maybe not for Andrew who probably already regretted giving Matty the front passenger seat.

'You know that grinning to yourself makes you look crazy.'

I produced a middle finger for Jamie, who'd flipped one of his headphones back, but couldn't get the grin to leave. Just to rile him a bit I asked how many "likes" he had now. He scowled, let out a groan.

'Over ten thousand,' Megan piped up.

'What?' Jamie yelped.

He reached for her phone, growling why she even had the YouTube video playing. 'Holy shit,' he said after a second. 'This is *crazy!*

'Nah, it's not,' I told him. 'You were really good. So was Sarah.'

'Yeah, but… Shit, I'm gonna *kill* Sean for this.'

Sean had posted it to the high school's channel and his own.

'You could ask him to take it down, you know,' Megan reminded him.

Jamie didn't respond, but his face was getting hot. I leaned over and saw that he was scrolling through the comments.

'Good thing school's over, huh?' I said, catching Megan's eye.

She grinned back.

Matty piped up that he wanted to see and Megan reached for her phone.

'Please don't, Megs,' Jamie mumbled.

She held still a moment then told Matty she needed to save the battery for taking photos of our trip. 'We'll get it on the computer when we get home.'

Jamie rolled his eyes, put his headphones back up, and I wondered if he was listening to himself or some other song he was gonna sing. He'd already admitted he'd continue Show Choir in his senior year.

I watched him for a bit, wondering how dad would react when he found out about the concert and those thousands of likes on the web.

Maybe he wouldn't, maybe he'd prefer a singing son to a gay one.

I frowned. Time to cut dad from my thoughts!

Sitting on the steps of the Capitol with Owen was the most peaceful part of the day thus far.

It was only our second stop on the Madison tour but the morning been spent visiting Henry Vilas zoo. As expected, Matty had been totally thrilled with it, and we'd toured around the large park at least three times. Somehow each time he found something that he'd missed on a previous loop. If nothing else, the kid was going to sleep soundly tonight with all the exercise and fresh air.

Owen and I had walked around inside the Capitol, looking over the beautiful classical architecture, but when he'd suggested we go sit in the relative peace of outside, I didn't disagree. The rest of the troops were still in the building. At least, I hoped Jamie and Megan hadn't abandoned the kids for their own sanity. I seemed concreted to my step, so I couldn't go and check.

'Your job for the rest of the afternoon, Owen, is to figure out how to swap car seats with Matty.'

Owen gave a loud snort, covered his mouth. 'I told you,' he said, waggling a finger. 'You made that mess yourself, you fix it.'

'Pfft.'

He grinned. 'I'm finding it quite nice in the back seat. Don't think I'm willing to swap.'

'What do I have to promise you?'

Owen tweaked his jeans straight over his shoes, funny curve to his lips as he gazed down the steps. When he tilted his head to gaze back at me, that smile seemed positively devilish. I arched a brow. He straightened up with a shrug.

'Don't know. I'll think about it and let you know.'

I let out a soft laugh and his devil's grin turned shy.

The moment was broken with chatter and we twisted to see Lisa and Matty jumping down the steps toward us, the older two following behind.

'Was beginning to think you'd gotten stuck in a toilet or something,' Owen commented.

Matty shoved him with a foot. Lisa hit him with the brochure she carried.

'We were trying to find New Zealand's stone,' Matty announced.

When he'd heard that the Capitol had stones from around the world, he hadn't investigated as to what that actually meant. The building *did* have foreign stone, sure, but it wasn't because of a geological display. The international flavour came from the various coloured marbles incorporated in the pillars and walls and floors.

Megan and Jamie both looked a little peeved, so I was extra impressed they'd kept up the ruse. I owed them for not bailing like we had.

Still, as I rose, I asked Matty if he had found the stone.

He pouted. 'No.'

'Well, that's tough,' I said. 'You didn't think to ask—'

'No!' Jamie and Megan said together.

I strove not to let my amusement show. They were such good kids amusing the littlies like they had, but obviously they'd reached their limit. Owen pressed his lips together and turned away, but I saw the grin break free. Matty had his head cocked as if thinking.

I squeezed his shoulder. 'Bet all that hunting's made you hungry. How about we find somewhere to have lunch?'

'Heck yeah,' Matty said. 'I'm starving.'

The kid was always starving, but it was nice that even here in Madison food worked like a charm in directing his attention. Megan let out a relieved sigh while Jamie just rolled his eyes. Owen, on the other hand, had turned into the devil. 'What countries *did* you find, Matty?'

'Owen!' Jamie hissed.

Owen's brows went up in mock innocence, but he took Matty's hand, swinging it, as he walked his brother down the steps away from us, engaging in chat about stones and countries and other facts the youngster had learned.

I chuckled, even when Jamie said, 'He's on Matty duty the rest of the day!'

'Hell, yeah,' Megan said.

They were both grinning but I had a feeling Owen would outsmart them over it.

- # -

Jamie tilted his head back, gazing up at the magnificent details in the ceiling of the Thai pavilion. I wasn't sure, though, that he was actually seeing them.

'You okay?' I asked.

He jerked, looked at me. 'Yeah. Why?'

'Mm, you just seem preoccupied.'

He stilled, then straightened, rubbing his neck. 'Just… this singing thing. I never expected…' He graded his fingers through his hair. 'I mean, it's cool and all that. Way cool even, but dad—' He cut off, walked out to the edge of the pavilion.

I stayed in the shade, but followed his gaze. Lisa and Matty were walking around the main pool while Megan snapped photos of the view across the creek. Where had Owen got to? I straightened up then remembered Jamie. Owen could look after himself, had probably gone to find a restroom or something.

'What about your father, Jamie?' I asked softly.

He turned, half grimace on his face. 'Just wondering if not telling him was a good idea. I really hate the thought of him finding out via YouTube.'

'Your friend could take the video down.'

'Ah, it's not *that*, so much, but…' Jamie came back into the shade beside me. 'It's the not telling part. I didn't want him to come along, not after last week, but I kinda…' He pressed a hand over his mouth a moment. 'Shit,' he mumbled, 'I feel guilty about it.'

I found myself nodding, but didn't actually know what to say. I certainly couldn't feel anger at Jamie. No matter that their father had moments of utter craziness, he was still their father and that was a hook in skin that couldn't be removed.

Jamie looked at me, brows up.

'*I* can't tell you that you should or shouldn't feel guilty, Jamie,' I said. 'But you made that decision based on *your* feelings, and the evening went amazingly well. Just stick with that, maybe?'

His brows came together, nose scrunched up like that wasn't what he wanted to hear. Then he let out a noisy sigh. 'Yeah.' After a moment he added, 'Don't know how he'd find it anyway.'

'And, if he does, then deal with it then,' I said. 'There's no way he could be upset, Jamie, you were really great. I'm so proud of you.'

Even in the shade of the pavilion I could see his blush. But my praise wasn't misdirected. The kid had talent.

A series of loud sneezes made us jerk alert. Jamie glanced over his shoulder. 'Heh,' he said. 'That foghorn's ours.'

That made me turn; Owen had his nose in a tissue as he came up the path behind us. 'What?' he got out when he looked up.

'You okay?' I asked.

He sniffed and shoved the tissue in a pocket. 'Yeah, just something here's set me off, that's all.'

[Ten]

Owen

Clogged up with a bug, I opened the door on Wednesday without thinking about using the chain. My brain clicked in once it was half open but I wasn't quick enough to stop dad shoving his foot against it and pushing it wide, making me stumble back.

'Dad, what… *Dad!*' I cried that, going after him as he stalked into the lounge, growling, 'Where's that paedo?' His fists bunched as he turned to look at me. 'Where is he?'

'At work, of course. I'm the only one here, Dad, don't—' I yelped and staggered back from the slap across my face.

'Keep out of my face, you little fag,' he growled and headed down the hall.

'You can't be here!' I yelled, coughing after it. 'Dad, you're breaking the rules!'

He came stalking toward me, lips curling as I took a step back. 'This is my house, not his. Tell him to get out.'

'No! Dad, Andrew's not—'

His hand raised and I shrank back, making him laugh. 'You're a coward, Owen, and a disgusting little slut.' He looked like he smelled something off.

I hauled in a breath and straightened. 'I'm not,' I told him. 'Get out of here before I call the cops.'

He took a step toward me but I stood firm this time. When he laughed, my chin went up. 'Dad, get out.'

'I'm not your father,' he spat.

My mouth dropped open, but I couldn't find the voice to

say, 'What?'

'You're not my kid,' he told me, lips pulling apart in a sneer. 'That's why I'm happy to kick you out, Owen.'

'No,' I breathed. 'That's not—'

'*All* true,' he cut over me. 'I *adopted* you.'

I looked at him, heart pounding, stomach queasy. *Was* it true? He almost seemed amused with how this was obviously affecting me. I swallowed hard, wanted to blow my nose but couldn't afford to take my attention off him. I got my chin up again. 'You still don't control me. Get out.' I pointed at the front door, which was still open.

Dad shrugged and started to move. Then he swung back, caught me across the face with a hard backhand and I never sat so suddenly, fighting the urge to faint *and* throw up. Dad squatted. His fingers gripped my jaw and wrenched my head around to meet his cold gaze. He held something up in front of me—an envelope, I think. 'Give this to the boy-fucker.'

I started to speak, but tightening fingers made me yelp in pain instead.

'Make sure he gets it, Owen.'

He forced my head up and down like I was agreeing to his order. Then he let me go and I nearly fell backward, hadn't realised he'd had me lifted a bit. He held the envelope out and I gingerly took it.

Dad rose and I scrambled backward out of his way in case he tried to kick me, getting up using the armchair as a support. 'You're… breaking the rules being here.'

'You let me in,' he responded, then nodded at my hand. 'Make sure the paedophile gets that.'

'He's not a paedophile!' I shouted.

Dad laughed.

'Why do you care anyway? If I'm not your son, why are you doing this to us? To me?'

'Because you turned my kids against me, Owen,' he replied.

'What? No…' Pressed my hand to my mouth as I tried to swallow back the need to cough.

'They keep telling me how amazing you were, how you kept everyone afloat. It's always Owen this, Owen that.'

'Why are you against that?' I asked, hurt. '*Some*one had to, Dad, it—'

'*Don't* call me that,' he yelled.

I cringed back, took a moment before I could straighten and face him again. 'I looked after my brothers and sisters,' I said, 'because you ran out on them. If they are against you, that's not *my* fault.'

'Yeah, it is, you and that paedo—'

'*Andrew is not a paedophile!* I tossed the envelope at him, but it just spun about and fell to the floor. 'Get out of this house! Get out of—' I cut off dead, spying Jamie looking white in the foyer between dad and the door.

'What's…?' He didn't finish.

'Just a difference of opinion, Jamie,' Dad said and smiled at him.

'I don't— You shouldn't be here, Dad,' Jamie said, gaze flicking between him and me.

I had no idea what he'd actually heard but he could obviously tell what kind of visit this had been. I dropped to my knees, no longer able to fight the cough.

'I'm going,' Dad said. 'We'll chat another time.' He nodded at the envelope on the carpet. 'That letter's for your guardian.'

He spoke like the word was poison. While Jamie turned to see what he meant and I scrambled to grab the envelope, Dad banged the door closed after him. Jamie jerked, swung that way then back to me. 'What the fuck was that all about?' he rasped out. 'Why was he here? What did he—?' And then an impressive amount of swearing and staring.

For some reason I'd looked under the chair to see if the fork was still there from the other week. It was, so I'd grabbed it and gotten back to my feet. Wasn't sure if it was the piece of cutlery or my face that had set him off. 'I noticed it the other day,' I muttered, lifting the fork.

Jamie's mouth opened, then closed. His gaze went to my white-knuckle grip on the utensil, then came back to my face as he made a harsh swallowing sound. 'Dad… hit you again?'

'He's not my dad,' I responded.

'Jesus, Owen, you… Sit down,' he said. 'You're white as fuck.'

Since I just stood there, clutching the envelope in one hand and the fork in the other, Jamie had to physically move me around to the couch. I sat. He didn't try to take either item from me, just made a messy attempt at getting his backpack off, swearing as it caught on something, and dug around inside it for his phone.

I thought he was ringing Andrew, except he demanded to speak to Sergeant Morrison.

'No, Jamie,' I croaked.

'Shut it,' he cried at me and then started blasting the phone and, presumably, the sergeant with fast-paced anger and panic. Even in my shocked condition I knew he wasn't making sense.

Jamie let out a growl, then sucked in a breath like he wanted all the air in the room. 'Okay,' he said. 'Sorry. Dad was here. He and Owen were yelling. Owen's face is… ugly. Bruised.

He doesn't look with it… Andrew's at work. *Owen?*

I looked up at the growl.

'Right? Andrew's at work?'

'Yeah.'

'Yes,' he told the phone. 'At work. Should I… Okay. Lisa and Matty? No, not here at the moment. They're doing some summer school stuff this week. No, he doesn't… I don't think.' He looked back at me. 'We didn't tell dad about the school stuff, right?'

'Don't think so.'

Jamie fed that back.

I put the fork on the coffee table and got up, needing the toilet.

'Owen, don't… Shit. I've gotta go, Sergeant. Owen, wait, you're—'

Jamie didn't let up, but I didn't hear him talking anymore to Morrison. 'How'd he get in? How long was he here before I got home? Why'd he hit you?'

He didn't seem to care that I was chucking up in the toilet, head thumping as much from my bug as from this latest horror.

'What's with that envelope?' he asked just as I realised I still held it and tucked it into a jeans pocket. 'Owen!'

'I'm busy, Jamie,' I growled.

My brother didn't respond but I caught movement at the corner of my eye; him sitting on the edge of the bath.

When I sat back, feeling exhausted, I rested an arm over my eyes and tried to drag in a breath that didn't rattle in some way. Water ran, and then Jamie said, 'Here, put this on your face.'

I lifted my arm; he held out a facecloth. I took it and held it gingerly against my left cheek. 'I'm sick of people hitting me.'

Jamie let out a soft curse as he returned to the edge of the bath.

I grimaced, hadn't meant to speak. Except then I said, 'Dad came—heh, apparently he's *not* my dad.' I looked at the wet cloth a second before putting it back against my cheek. I looked at Jamie. 'He said he adopted me.'

'No way!'

I let out a half laugh, shrugged. 'I don't know what—'

I cut off when Jamie suddenly sat straighter, frowning. His head cocked a little. 'Just remembered something,' he said with a bit of a croak. 'Back when he gave me and Megan that ride home. He said you weren't his kid.'

'What?' I asked, stomach dropping. I still couldn't really believe this, but...

'He said he wanted you and Andrew away from his kids and Megan said *you* were his kid too, but he...' Jamie drew in a short breath. 'He said you weren't. I thought he was just being shitty.'

'Why didn't you say something?'

'Because I *thought* he was just being shitty,' Jamie repeated with an edge. He looked around the bathroom.

'He seemed... serious, Jamie.' I struggled onto my feet and flushed the toilet, then re-wet the cloth in the sink. I had a bruise across my cheek, and a couple of finger marks either side of my jaw. Andrew was gonna freak when he saw me. I put a hand over my mouth, managed to keep the lone sob muted.

Jamie stood and came to my side. 'We've got bruise cream somewhere,' he mumbled.

Yeah, left over from the last time I had a purple face. No, probably from the time *before* the last time. I watched him dig about in the top drawer, then took the tube when he handed it to me.

As I smeared stuff gently over the worst area, he said, 'I don't know where he gets off calling Andrew a pae—'

'*Don't!*'

He looked sombre, said, 'You know that no one would listen to that.'

'Doesn't matter,' I said. 'It's damaging anyway.'

'What? How?'

'It just… Jamie, it's a vile word. Imagine if it was made *public*. Even if it's untrue, what do you think it'd do to Andrew's business, his reputation? I think he's worried shitless, but he won't talk to me about it.' Dragging in a steadying breath, I screwed the cap back on the tube and set it on the vanity, mumbling, 'Dad hates me because I kept us afloat.'

'What?'

I told him what he'd said. Jamie stared, brows raised in puzzlement. 'He's doing all this because he's *jealous*? Are you fucking serious?'

I gave a helpless shrug. 'That and he's anti-gay. I'm like a double-whammy. Triple if I'm not his kid. Funny as hell, huh?'

'You need to go lie down,' Jamie said.

'No.'

'I'll sit with you.'

'No.'

Jamie eyed me.

He didn't stop me leaving the bathroom or heading for the lounge rather than my room, but he didn't plonk himself beside me on the couch. He went into the kitchen, came back with water and drugs. I mumbled my thanks and swallowed back the pills.

Jamie had obviously decided to sit with me wherever I was because now he dropped to the other couch.

We sat in silence maybe ten minutes before I asked what Sergeant Morrison had said. Jamie choked on a breath like he'd forgotten I was there and then gave a one-shoulder shrug. 'He might come around this evening.'

I sighed. 'He wants to talk to me then?'

Probably deserved the brow arch, though Jamie simply muttered, 'Guess so.'

'Mm.' This was going to be just one more thing to upset Andrew, and then I remembered the envelope in my pocket. I'd have retrieved it but didn't want to remind Jamie of its presence.

'How'd dad get in?'

'Huh? Oh…' I closed my eyes a second. 'I opened the door.'

'What?' he cried. 'Owen, you know—'

'I didn't think,' I cut over him. 'My brain… all foggy.' I regretted the hell out of that moment of stupidity. 'And then he wouldn't go. He was looking for Andrew.'

'Why'd he think *he'd* be here? It's daylight in a working week.'

My face worked itself into a grimace, and relief had me press a hand over my mouth. Andrew *had* been with me this morning, keeping me company a few hours in my clogged-up, sickly state. Thank *God* he'd had a meeting this afternoon he couldn't cancel, or he'd have been here when…

I let out a half breath. If he'd been here, he wouldn't have opened the door. Shit, I was so stupid for not thinking things through when I'd heard the doorbell.

Jamie

Owen flicked on the garage light and I went forward to pull the sheet off the big portrait.

Then we just looked at it. In the artificial light you couldn't really see how blue-green Owen's eyes were, but they still looked different from those of us who were brown and the two who were light blue.

Christ, it hurt to look at; not just the eyes, but the whole happiness going on with all of us. Grief thickened in my chest and hooked into my throat like I was growing some massive strep infection.

Beside me, Owen coughed into his sleeve. He was in a mental flap, I knew, though dad can't have been telling the truth about his parentage. He must have said it simply in attack. I'd heard Owen yelling back at him, was kind of amazed over that since he'd finally told me what I'd missed up until that point. Reckoned him still standing up to dad had made dad attack harder.

Saying Owen wasn't his son was fucking low, though.

'What if it *is* true, Jamie? What does that mean?'

I took his arm and forced him out of the garage. 'Doesn't mean anything.' I didn't let him go as I headed for the lounge, amazed that he wasn't yanking out of my grip. I kinda shoved him at one couch and as he collapsed onto it I took the other. 'You're still our shitty but awesome brother.'

His lips tweaked a little upwards. Then he said, 'What about everything else? Me being here? Andrew's guardianship?'

'Andrew's our guardian, not yours,' I said. 'Your parentage has nothing to do with that. How could it? And what do you mean about you being here? What should change because of that?'

'I just mean... me,' he said.

'*What* about you, Owen?'

'Well... what ties do I have to—'

'Oh shit, no, don't be so stupid.'

His eyes went wide with surprise. Man, they could be *green* sometimes.

'Owen!' I said with some force. 'I get you're all shocked and stuff, but thinking you've got no ties here because dad might not be your dad is fucking stupid.'

He opened his mouth like he was actually going to argue but I got in first. 'Even if you're not dad's kid, you're *mum's*, and she's *my* mum and everyone else's too. And this was her home too so you've got that tie.'

I actually couldn't believe I was even saying this stuff. Especially since the more I listened to Owen being stupid the more I was sure dad had said it to unsettle him. Even if I'd heard him say that thing when he'd given me and Megan a ride home from school. Even if it seemed a really strange thing to attack someone with.

Because... surely it didn't change anything.

- # -

Just like Owen used an open book to look like he was busy and shouldn't be pestered, I put headphones on. This time without sound because it wasn't music I needed; just some semi-peace from Lisa and Matty who were with me in the lounge trying to out-do each other with tales of their day.

Megan had dragged Owen off to our parents' room, last I looked, to hunt down old photographs. Didn't think they'd find proof one way or other about Owen's parentage, but it gave Megan something to do other than freak out that dad had shown up, raving, and hit Owen again.

The doorbell cut into my muted world but I didn't stir until Lisa jumped up. Then I leapt up myself, hooking my headphones around my neck. 'No, Lis, I'll get it.' I thought it'd be Andrew, but just in case it was dad I didn't want her anywhere near the door.

It was Andrew and he was just calling, 'Hello?' through the gap.

'Hold on a sec,' I told him and pushed the door closed. Once de-chained, I opened it again. 'Hey.'

'Hey, Jamie,' he responded. 'How was your day?'

'Yeah, good.'

Must have been something in my tone because he stopped and looked at me while I closed the door and carefully slid the chain home. 'What's up?' he asked.

'Um.' I scratched my ear. 'Dad dropped by. Said Owen was adopted.'

'*What?*

He glanced about like he'd see evidence of the visit, then looked back at me because I was just standing there. 'He's not here…'

'No, no,' I said quickly, 'but…' Wow, my ear was way scratchy tonight. 'You're not gonna be happy when… He's in mum's room with Megan.'

Andrew's gaze stayed on me as if he was computing how to put all that together, but he didn't ask for clarification. He just dropped his satchel by the door and headed for the hall, halted after two steps because Owen was just coming out of it and he held a photograph. He stopped when he saw us.

Silence for a second or two, then Andrew rasped in a breath like he was trying to stay calm. 'Your father did that?' Came out soft but his anger was loud anyway.

Owen put a hand up like he could hide the marks, but gave a half nod.

'Owen! Why'd you let him in? That was a stupid thing to do!'

'I was sick,' my brother responded, frowning. 'I opened the door without thinking. He pushed past before I could stop him.'

Andrew made an indecipherable noise, then drew Owen out into better light. My brother stood with his jaw clenched, shied back when Andrew lifted a hand. 'It's nothing, Andrew,' he managed without a tremor. 'Doesn't hurt or anything.'

'Your father hitting you is not nothing.' Andrew sounded like he was barely holding onto his temper. He took a breath and a step back, eyed me still hanging around. A shift of his gaze showed him the kids who'd settled down to watch TV and weren't even looking our way.

I could see he wanted to talk about this visit but wasn't sure if he should push the kids to go outside for a bit. Owen coughed, making us both jump but it turned Andrew's attention. 'You should be in bed.'

My brother shook his head. 'Nah, I feel a lot better than this morning.' His smile even looked real. Except then he said, 'Dad didn't stay long but he was looking for you. He called you those usual names, and gave me—' He cut off, looked down at the photograph a moment. 'Anyway, when I told him to go, he told me he wasn't my dad, that he'd adopted me. This seems to prove it. Me and Megan don't know who the man is.'

His voice shivered on the last words and he held out the photo. I crowded up beside Andrew as he took it.

Mum was instantly recognisable, even so much younger, with the smile like in the family portrait. The guy beside her had wavy dark hair and blue-green eyes, and was smiling just as much as mum. He had one tanned arm around her shoulders, the other held a onesie-clad baby with the same hair and eye colour as he had.

'Wow,' I said, unable to say anything articulate because this was mum and Owen but not dad.

'Turn it over,' Owen whispered.

Andrew did so and we saw writing: *Plimmerton Beach Nov 2000.*

My breath whistled out. 'Shit.' That beach was only a few minutes from our old house.

'They look really happy.' Owen made a sound that could have been a cough, could have been a sob.

'Are there other pictures?' Andrew asked softly, giving me the photo when I held my hand out.

'Some,' Owen said. 'Of him and mum, but the rest are of us when it's mum and dad.'

'Could just be a friend,' I made myself say, still unable to believe this twist.

'Just a friend holding mum's baby?' Owen asked. '*Me?*'

'Yeah, why not?' I asked, a bit steely. 'It's not like last century, you know.'

Andrew rolled his eyes. 'Wasn't uncommon last century, either,' he said wryly, which made me redden a bit.

'Megan's looking for birth certificates and passports for proof,' Owen said. 'But I… Actually, I don't know what to think.'

'How about you lie down?'

'No.'

Said with all the stubbornness my brother had, and he had a lot of it.

Andrew pursed his lips but didn't push. Instead he asked if Owen had called the cops about the visit. 'Did he take anything?'

'No,' Owen said. 'He just stalked down the hall looking for you. When I told him you weren't here and he was breaking the rules, he hit me. A backhand.'

My brother carried on about the father/adoption bits, either not noticing or possibly just ignoring how angry Andrew was getting. I could understand the anger; he must feel helpless in these situations. Though… I also knew some of his annoyance was at Owen for opening the front door. Sick or not, he should have had more sense!

Owen didn't mention the envelope that was probably still in a pocket. But he did say that I'd called Sergeant Morrison.

Andrew's brows went up. 'You were here?'

'No,' I said. 'Well, not all of it. I got home just at the last bit, heard the shouting from the drive. I reckon dad brought up the adoption thing just to rattle Owen because he was giving as good as he got.'

Andrew's brows dipped low so I refrained from openly stating I was proud of Owen for standing up to dad like he had.

'Don't think it was just to rattle,' Owen mumbled, looking at the photo in my hand.

I ignored that and said, 'I didn't see dad throwing his fists about, but I called Sergeant Morrison once dad was gone.'

Andrew sucked on his lips like he was counting to ten or something then asked if the sergeant had come around or sent someone.

'No,' I said. 'But he said he might come this evening.'

'Might?' Andrew growled.

'Probably wanted to wait until *you* were here,' I said, trying to diffuse the situation a little.

Andrew drew breath, let it out without a sound. 'Okay,' he said softly, looked at Owen. 'Do you think you need to see a doctor?'

Owen shook his head.

The marks at his jaw were faint; Andrew might not have really noticed them. The bruising over his left cheek would probably be gone by the weekend, not that a short bruise duration would appease Andrew.

'Okay,' he repeated, giving a sort of nod. He glanced down at the photo, then over his shoulder. He'd left the satchel by the door and now he turned to get it.

Owen caught my gaze a moment, then turned after Andrew, saying, 'There's something else.'

I saw him reaching to a back pocket and took myself into the lounge, suddenly not wanting to be at the reveal of that part of dad's visit.

Owen

Andrew eyed the envelope I held out with total reluctance. I understood that, remembering the first one.

'He told me several times to make sure you got it,' I

mumbled, wishing I'd just ripped it up.

He didn't look any less reluctant but he took it from me. I thought he was just going to pocket it, but he drew in a breath, called up whatever to make his face a mask, and tore the envelope open.

Since I was watching closely, I saw the shock widen his pupils, the way his jaw went stiff. 'What's it say?' I whispered.

Andrew shook his head, but I knew that didn't stand for "nothing". He shifted the paper back into the envelope. Seeing his fingers shaking made me really worried. 'Is it like the—'

'I need to make a phone call,' he said abruptly, and turned away.

'Not dad,' I said, horrified at the thought.

'No!'

He headed for the door, envelope crunched in his hand, making me voice his name in surprise.

'I'm just going to the car,' he said.

'You're… leaving?'

'*No*,' he growled.

I stepped back, startled.

'Owen, please,' he said with some effort. 'Don't ask me about this. I'll be back shortly.'

'But, what—'

I reached out stupidly like I thought somehow he'd just give me the envelope. He fended me off fairly strongly, letting out a sharp, 'No!' at the same time. I curved my hands to my chest. Andrew swallowed audibly, seemed distressed, but he opened the door and went outside without another word.

I just stood there, looking at the chain swinging beside the door, feeling frightened. Not because Andrew had shoved me, but because whatever it was that dad had written had really rattled him. And he was furious. I hadn't seen such visible anger since dad had hit me. I swallowed—the *first* time he'd hit me. Bit at my lip; he hadn't exactly been *non*-angry when he first got a glimpse of my face twenty minutes ago.

Dad had been insistent about the note, and I dreaded knowing what it contained. A threat? A promise? Blackmail? Something violent?

And who was Andrew ringing? His lawyer? Sergeant Morrison? Wasn't *he* supposed to be coming around at some point?

I pressed a hand over my mouth, realised I was shaking. Andrew's reaction made me wish even harder that I'd gotten rid of the envelope as soon as dad had left.

'Where's Andrew?'

I jumped and swung about. Jamie's brows were up. 'Has he gone again? I thought—'

'He's making a phone call.'

'What? Outside?' Jamie cocked his head. 'Shit… the note. What did it say?'

'I don't know,' I rasped out. 'He wouldn't let me see. He's upset and furious, Jamie. Whatever it is…' I got in a stable breath. 'Whatever it says, it's *not* good.'

Jamie mostly looked puzzled, like he couldn't imagine what could be written to get Andrew even more angry. My imagination was running total riot with possibilities.

When the door opened a few minutes later, we were still standing there.

Andrew stopped when he saw us, then closed the door and came up to me. Concern was now his main emotion. 'Owen,' he said, 'I… need to go.'

'What?' I squawked out. 'Why would…? It's the note, isn't it? What—' I cut off. After a second, I said softly, 'It's hours til eight.'

Andrew glanced at Jamie then brought his attention back to me. 'I know,' he said, 'and it's not just the note.' He coughed to clear the croak from his voice. 'I'm too angry, I need some space. And I pushed you before, that was unforg—' He put a hand to his face.

'That was nothing,' I said hoarsely. 'I was a dick, shouldn't have—'

Andrew drew me to him and kissed my temple. When he let me go, he squeezed my arm briefly. 'I hate leaving,' he said, 'especially with…' He gently touched my face, expression flicking between concern and anger. 'But I… I need to be on my own right now.'

'Is everything okay?' Jamie asked slowly.

Andrew forced a smile. 'It will be, Jamie.' He looked down at me. 'I'm sorry, Owen.'

'Hey,' I managed, 'it's okay. I'm over chicken too.' We were having it for dinner again.

His crack of laughter sounded a bit like a sob, but his smile was more natural.

'I'll get the train in tomorrow,' I told him. 'So, sleep in.'

Andrew didn't argue about that or suggest I stay home again so I knew how upset he was. I leaned up and kissed his cheek. 'Love you.'

'Love you back,' he said roughly.

'Oh man,' Jamie groaned and turned.

'Jamie,' Andrew said. 'Walk me out to my car.'

'What?' he yelped.

I eyed Andrew, feeling put out, and then made myself smile

to show I wasn't bothered. I didn't *really* think that he'd tell Jamie what that note had said.

Andrew ruffled my hair. 'See you tomorrow.'

'Yep.'

I turned away, not watching them step out the door.

- # -

Even if Thursday wasn't already one of my "be home early" days I'd have been home early. As the day had worn on, with Andrew present but distant and refusing to tell me anything about the note or who he'd called last night, the bug I'd stayed home for yesterday reasserted itself.

Andrew would have driven me home but I had an uncharacteristic want to be without him for a bit, so I'd gotten a cab. That silly want made me feel even sicker, and I sat at the kitchen bench counting down flips of the carving knife on my wrist. The cool smooth metal seemed to make me feel better, at least made me feel like I was in control of something.

Though maybe I wasn't all that in control since I'd also had to do this in the middle of the night. And, right now, I had to restart the counting several times because my thoughts kept returning to Andrew's anger.

What the hell had that note said?

Why was he hiding it from me?

I let out a sigh and set the knife on the bench, wished Andrew'd talk to me. I tried to tell myself I'd ask him direct tonight when he got here, but I had this weird feeling that might push him away and, out of anything that could come from this horrible situation, I was most terrified of Andrew leaving me. Terrified that he might decide that walking away was the best thing to do, or that he'd walk away because he wanted to, because I wasn't worth the stress.

Thoughts like that grew painful spikes in my chest.

As I reached for the knife again, the phone started to ring. I choked on a sharp breath and had to scramble to stay upright on the stool, heart thumping. Drawing in a long breath, I got off the stool to grab the phone.

'Hello, Tremayne household.'

A moment of silence that no one spoke to break.

'Hello?'

Which was dumb, because I knew who it was and picking up the phone had been stupid!

'Stop doing this, Dad,' I cried into the silence. 'It's not fair!'

I slammed the phone down, angry at myself. Not for the shouting, but for answering in the first place. We'd been getting blank calls for weeks. Sometimes we heard breathing or swallowing, but no one ever spoke. We knew it was dad, anyway, because they always picked up in frequency after a visit or something. Which was why I should have known not to pick up; yesterday was still bloody raw.

Except, sometimes we'd get normal calls from him as if the other sort didn't exist, and so most of us were still answering.

The phone started to ring again and, without thinking, I grabbed up the knife and swung it. It sliced the cord with such ease that I dropped the knife on the bench and stepped back, stomach twisting as the two cord ends swung gently.

I backed away, blinking the sheen out of my eyes, and then rushed to throw up.

Jamie arrived home barely minutes after I'd recovered my control, put the knife away, and settled on the couch to watch some mindless TV.

'Don't know why you bother with these hours if L and M aren't actually here,' he said as he flopped onto the other couch.

'Peace and quiet,' I returned pointedly.

He snorted, looked about to say something else and then went still, gaze focused. He leaned forward as if to stand. 'What happened to the phone?'

'Dad rang.'

Jamie's gaze shifted to me. 'What?'

'Dad rang.'

'Yeah, I got— *Why* is the cord cut?' He jumped up and headed for the phone, inspecting the cord ends. Then he bent over and when he straightened he held a small length of cord. His brows dipped together and, as he twirled the cord between his fingers, he glanced back at me. 'How'd you cut it?'

Instead of waiting for me to say something, he dropped the bit on the bench and moved around into the kitchen and seemed to look in the sink. No idea what he thought he'd find there.

I rose and went to the phone. Dead, of course, but couldn't stop myself testing it anyway.

Next thing Jamie was grabbing my arm and yanking up the sleeve.

'Fuck off,' I told him, pushing him back.

He clung on even though I still held the phone. 'You used the carving knife, didn't you?' he said with a growl.

'This *hurts*,' was how I replied, trying to disengage his fingers.

'Tell. Me.'

'What the fuck are you so angry about?'

'You used the carving knife, didn't you?' he responded.

'Yeah,' I said. 'Not like scissors would've worked.'

Jamie let me go and stepped back and I turned to set the phone on its hook, then rubbed the red mark at my wrist. We had a staring match, until I had to pull a tissue to wipe my running nose.

Jamie poked his tongue into his cheek. 'What did dad say?'

'Nothing,' I got out. 'Another nothing call.'

Didn't ask how I knew it was dad. We *all* knew.

'I yelled,' I admitted with a sigh. 'Angry. *Really* angry, that's why… just.' I shut up since I wasn't making any sense, glanced at the piece of cord on the bench. 'It was dumb.'

Jamie's smile was kind of grim. 'We always wanted a cordless.'

I looked up; he shrugged and walked away as if he hadn't recently been so in my face.

Rocks tumbled jaggedly down my throat as I swallowed. Even though *I* thought my dark moments were just between me and myself, perhaps he… But how could he think that? I hadn't… I glanced over my shoulder. Shit, I *had* just sliced a phone cord!

Hands pressed to my face, I had a short battle with myself, then trailed my brother to his room. He didn't tell me to go away, just kept looking for something in the dresser drawer. I sat on Matty's bed and admitted softly that I had moments.

Jamie's gaze flickered my way and I knew I was lucky not to get a comment. He didn't speak, just turned back to the drawer. I sat and waited and eventually he asked why I couldn't just say something.

'Why couldn't you have asked?' I responded.

Jamie turned to me. 'Were you thinking about killing

yourself?'

Hearing it direct sat me still. Jamie was still himself. I heaved in a deep breath but said nothing. He sank onto his bed opposite me, shocked even though he'd obviously been wondering.

'Not really,' I said into the silence.

'But… you had the carving knife out,' Jamie said. '*Don't* tell me it was just to cut the bloody phone cord.'

I shut my mouth.

'Does Andrew know?'

'What?' I yelped. 'No!'

Jamie shifted.

'Don't you *dare* saying anything to him, Jamie.'

'Are you kidding me?'

'Look, it… I don't…' I broke off with a growl. 'I'm not suicidal, I just… sometimes things get overwhelming. When I've got the… knife there'—I lay fingers over my wrist—'it kinda calms me.'

Jamie stared.

'I can't explain it,' I said. 'But… I don't know, it makes me… okay. I don't want to kill myself.' I told him how the day had gone. It probably just made me seem crazier. 'Jamie, please don't tell Andrew. I'm *okay* mostly, I would never…' I trailed off.

Jamie fidgeted with the seam on his jeans. 'I saw you last night.'

Automatically my mouth was open to respond, 'Saw what?' but he was looking at me and I knew exactly what he meant. We stared at each other for ages and eventually I managed, 'Why didn't you say something?'

'I c-couldn't.' He coughed. 'I wanted to but I couldn't.'

'Did Andrew tell you to watch me?'

Jamie frowned. 'No, he didn't. Not in the middle of the night, anyway. And I don't know why you're getting all in *my* face; wasn't me flipping a blade on my wrist.'

I rose.

'Sorry, sorry,' Jamie said, latching onto my arm. 'Owen, stay. *Please.*'

I hesitated a second then sunk back to Matty's bed. 'Yesterday shook me more than I thought.' I acknowledged his expression with a wry smile because I'd been openly rattled. 'And Andrew's reaction to whatever that note was about, his leaving.' I sighed. 'It didn't all hit until night.'

'Then you went—' Jamie shut up, appearing to realise I *didn't* need to be told what I'd gone and done. Then he swallowed. 'I heard you counting.'

I bit my lip. 'Yeah.'

'What for?' he asked.

If he'd been watching a while, then he probably knew exactly what for. I said, 'It's a challenge.'

His eyes narrowed in puzzlement.

'To see how long it takes me to feel in control and put the knife away,' I said. 'I count down from a hundred.'

'I heard forty,' he said with a bit of a catch.

'Yeah,' I said with a half nod.

'Have... have you been lower?'

'Yes.'

Jamie didn't ask how low, or even when, and I was glad. It kind of felt good to be talking but I also didn't want to. I leaned forward a bit. 'Jamie, please don't tell Andrew any of this. It's just my way of coping right now.'

He eyed me for a long time. I sat and waited, just hoped

he'd back me. Andrew would blame himself for the knife if he knew about it.

'I won't tell,' he said. 'As long as you promise to talk to *me*.'

I sagged, throat blocked with relief. When I didn't say anything he didn't try to make me promise. He just changed the subject, saying that we'd at least have some peace from the phone tonight. Then he pulled a weird smile. 'I'm scared as shit over you, Owen, but… Man, I wish I'd seen you swing at the cord.' He bit his lip, tried to scowl.

'Cut like butter,' I muttered.

We both burst out laughing, couldn't stop even though there was nothing funny about it.

Andrew

It took an hour after Owen left for me to gather a sense of calm, unsettled as I was over how the day had gone (mostly my fault) and Owen refusing to let me drive him home. I hated to think what reception I'd get tonight, if he wasn't all choked up in bed with the return of that cold.

Ah, but whatever reception I got, it'd be my fault.

Except there was no way I was ever going to reveal what that note had contained.

No words, just a drawing.

Without any words, either on the paper or the envelope, my lawyer had advised there was little I could really do about using it against Tremayne.

Apparently a crude drawing of— My teeth ground, forcing me to take a deep breath. Apparently a drawing of me and a guillotine, where it wasn't my head being separated from my body, wasn't enough of a threat to allow me to bring charges of my own against a man whom, in my book, was becoming more and more deranged.

Because the man hadn't *written* on it, it was just a drawing.

A drawing that had stoked my anger to such levels last night that I couldn't be around Owen and the kids. Not without it spilling out to them, and I still felt guilty at shoving Owen in that anger.

I pressed my hands to my face, trying to ignore the bourbon calling from the cabinet behind me. Owen hadn't been worried about that shove then, but I hated to think that his earlier refusal to let me drive him home was part caused by that moment.

I could show him the drawing, it would certainly explain everything, but that was the last thing I wanted to do. He'd told me he'd wanted to toss the envelope out and no doubt he already regretted not doing so. Knowing what was in the envelope would upset him even further.

Drawing in a breath through my nose, I got myself calm enough to shut down my computer. Owen had told me that Sergeant Morrison had dropped by for a brief visit after I left but reported there were no changes to the restraining order against his father. So, now I was going to add my voice. I picked up the phone.

Perhaps the man had been waiting for my call because he seemed to sound weary when he asked what he could do for me.

'Prevent Tremayne from being on the property without an escort.'

'Mr Gordon, I—'

'Sergeant, *I* am following all the rules you've laid down for me, and so is Owen, and yet nothing is in place to protect the kids from their father. That restraining order is not restraining him.'

'They shouldn't open the door if they're worried.'

'They're kids! They open the door. And the man's their *father*. There's still a stu—' I pinched the bridge of my nose. 'Look, there's still a level of trust in him being their father, but the man takes advantage. If I can't be there, then I want your assurances that he won't be either!'

Silence on the other end.

'That is what that order contains, isn't it? A statement that he can't be on the property without permission. Did you *give* him permission to show up yesterday? Do you know he hit Owen twice? Do you know he told Owen that he was adopted?'

I caught my breath. I hadn't meant to let that out, and probably Owen hadn't revealed that particular thing to the sergeant last night.

More silence and then, 'Mr Gordon, I don't have the spare resources to monitor Mr Tremayne twenty-four-seven. I am sorry about that, but Owen and his siblings need to take some responsibility themselves. They know their father comes and goes in his mood.'

He kept talking but I suddenly had to put the phone on the desk and take a serious moment.

I understood where the sergeant was coming from, I did, but my young man was frazzled and sick and I was afraid he was getting to the stage of just not being able to cope anymore. A very mature almost-eighteen, but how much longer would he last before he was just a young kid with too much going on? And Jamie and Megan… and the littlies…

I held the phone back to my ear; the call was still live but the sergeant had stopped speaking. 'I'm sorry, Sergeant, I didn't hear half of that. I need to go and be with my kids.'

I hung up like a child having a tantrum, then forced myself into another half hour's work just to settle myself down. I still had Megan to pick up and I didn't want her to get any sense that something wasn't right.

Jamie

The lock tumbling heralded Andrew and Megan's arrival home, but I was too focused on my dinner prep to go greet them.

Megan must have gone to her room but Andrew walked through to the lounge, barely starting a greeting to Lisa and Matty before Matty jumped up from the couch. 'Andrew! Andrew, look, we've got a cordless phone.'

I winced as he rushed around the couch, holding out the phone. Andrew took it, automatically, I think, and his gaze zeroed all but instantly on Owen, who sat outside at the table.

Andrew's expression didn't exactly show pleasure, but then he smiled down at Matty, handing the phone back. 'Be better if it worked, Matty,' he said, ruffling his hair. 'What say we find a new one this weekend?'

Matty's agreement shone all over his face. I felt my eyes start to roll so I turned my attention to the pasta pot, taking it to drain in the sink. After flushing the spirals several times with cool water, I dumped them in the big serving bowl to cool down further. Andrew was standing at the bench and I wished I could keep on ignoring him, but knew I couldn't.

I turned back to the chopping board to cut up the cherry tomatoes, saying, 'It'll be just you and Matty looking for a phone, you know that.'

A brief smile flashed but he didn't speak.

Uncomfortably aware of the knife in my hand—at least not the carving knife—I said, 'I know nothing.' Focused on gathering the tomatoes into a bowl. Fuck. Shoulda stayed quiet!

'Just answer me this,' Andrew murmured.

I looked up, seeing how concerned he was. I suddenly really wanted to tell him what had happened, but wanted to keep Owen's confidence more.

'Is he hurt?'

I drew breath. 'Not physically.'

'Okay,' Andrew said on a sigh.

He didn't say anything more. Unexpectedly, he didn't cross outside to Owen, just headed out of the lounge in the other direction. I stared that way then jumped as Megan came into the kitchen behind me and asked if I needed help.

'Of course not,' I told her. 'I'm a top chef.'

'Perfect! Gets me off dinner duty forever.'

She grinned as she walked away, lost the grin pretty quickly when Matty excitedly told her about the phone. She said some stuff and hurried back to me—or to that side of the bench, eyeing the phone base on the wall with the cord hanging. 'What happened?' she whispered. 'Where's—' She spun about, stopped when she obviously located Owen.

'Why do you think Owen did it?'

Megan spun back. 'You?' came out in such a surprised tone that I frowned. 'You didn't,' she said matter-of-factly.

It was depressing that both Andrew and Megan had instantly pegged Owen for the destruction.

'Why?' she asked.

'Blank calls,' I said. 'Obviously got sick of them.'

'He could have just disconnected it,' Megan said.

'Not the same satisfaction, Sis,' I mumbled. 'Anyway, can you get L and M doing the table? I'm almost done here.'

Megan looked like she'd stay, but we really couldn't just have a conversation about this ourselves. I turned back to the pasta and heard her start to give orders.

Through the noise that ensued I looked across the lounge, but Owen wasn't outside. He might have been wandering in the garden, but I hoped that he'd actually come inside and was talking with Andrew since *he* hadn't returned.

Fifteen minutes later I yelled down the hall that dinner was ready, and was just stepping back into the kitchen when I heard a door open.

Owen's eyes were red but he otherwise seemed okay, and he took part in dinner like nothing was wrong. On the outside nothing was, but inside… Andrew maintained an air of concern, which worried me, though it all could have been because of the tomato half that Lisa's mistimed fork jab sent his way. On the other hand, that made Owen smile properly and warn Matty because *he* had a look in his eyes like he might start something.

My memory went back months ago to the food fight the night I'd dragged the truth from Owen about him and Andrew. I breathed out, crazily wished for my brother to be like that again—fire instead of ash. These days he was much too quiet. Didn't even rise to half of my quips.

I shovelled in food to take my mind off that, because there were bad moments back then too, and remembering them could still easily take me to an angry place. 'So, how was badminton, Megan?' I blurted.

She looked like I had two heads, and even Owen eyed me, but I was sure I recalled her saying…

'Yeah, good,' she responded, sounding a bit puzzled. 'How was work?'

Walgreens, somewhat ironically. Hadn't gone down totally well when I'd told Owen that at least one Tremayne should work there, but he was over it now. And I got staff discount so that helped. 'Same old, same old,' I muttered, wished I'd just kept my mouth shut.

Then Lisa asked me about book discounts, and things got a little less awkward.

- # -

Owen had had some pretty good meltdowns last year but none of them—to my knowledge—had ever been towards Andrew. I couldn't even think of a time when he'd really raised his voice at him.

He was now, and all because Andrew had said he was going to stay the night. I couldn't fault Andrew on that at all because of yesterday, and I guessed Owen had told him about the knife thing and he was concerned how *tonight* might go.

Except, my brother wasn't having a bar of it. 'You *can't* stay!' he cried for about the fourth time. 'It breaks the restriction, Andrew. That'll give dad power, I—'

'Owen, he won't know I'm here,' Andrew said. 'And we're not alone so we're not breaking *that* restriction.'

Nope, not alone. Both Megan and I were witnessing the drama. Mercifully, Lisa was missing it, having decided to have a bath, and Matty had taken himself outside. I think he remembered the shouting that night of Megan's birthday.

'Come on, Angel,' Andrew said, somehow still calm. God, he had mad skills when dealing with my brother and his roller coaster emotions.

'No!' Owen shouted. 'He'll *know*! He'll take it to Morrison and you—' He cut off dead, hands dropping to his sides.

We all went tense.

'You want an excuse to leave. You don't want me anymore.'

'What?' Andrew gaped. 'No—'

He looked completely lost for words. Couldn't blame him. My brother had lost the plot!

Andrew seemed unable to do anything, so I did. I grabbed Owen and shook him. Hard. And it was all I could do to not slap him. 'Stop it!' I shouted right in his face. 'Stop being so fucking stupid. This isn't all about *you*, Owen! *I* want Andrew to stay. I heard the shouting yesterday; it was fucking horrible, and I watched you laying that *knife on your wrist!*

'Jamie—' Andrew began.

'And Megan's been hunting down stupid bloody photos and birth certificates. *We're* affected too! Andrew's our *guardian*. He should be here for *us! Don't be selfish!*

I shook Owen with pretty much every word, unable to stop myself even though his teeth clacked with the violence of it. I felt Andrew's hands on me but I think I might have snarled at him because I didn't feel his grip any longer.

Owen's face contorted and I knew he'd bitten his tongue. I tightened my hold as he started to pull back. His gaze was weird—wide, fixed—and I wasn't sure if he was seeing me, let alone whether he'd heard me.

I took a breath. 'Look, do you think dad cares about the rules? Don't you fucking *dare* say "yes",' I growled when he opened his mouth. 'If he did, you wouldn't have an ugly face and we wouldn't be having this stupid battle. He came here yesterday without notice, without permission. That's *his* restriction and he. Broke. It.'

'Jamie, I'm not—'

'Someone's gotta make him see this,' I hissed at Andrew, still not letting my brother go.

I heard a cough and turned back. Owen hadn't said anything during my rant, hadn't tried to get out of my grip, or even have a go at me. For some reason, the bruise over his cheek suddenly made me grip him harder. *'Please,'* I rasped, dragging in a breath.

Owen's blue-green gaze flicked to me, no longer blank, but full of hurt and anger. I felt his arms tense under my hands and I let him go; the non-noticing rag doll was starting to breathe fire.

Still, I lifted my chin and held his gaze, challenging. 'You turning eighteen is not a silver bullet,' I said. 'We've known that for ages. Dad's using your age against you but he's not gonna stop even when you turn eighteen. You know that. *Owen!* You. Know. That.'

Bulleted out because he stood there shaking his head. I back-stepped because any second now I was gonna start shaking him again.

Owen lifted a hand to his cheek and then dragged both hands back through his hair. He glanced at Andrew and I glanced that way too; man, he was so concerned but he didn't move. Maybe scared Owen would start yelling again, maybe scared I'd start shaking him instead.

Biting my lip, I glanced back at Megan; she was full of shock and horror, eyes shimmering. She caught my gaze; upset, too, at my actions.

Owen let out a long sigh. 'I hate this.'

'So do we,' I insisted. 'That means Andrew should stay tonight; we *all* need him here, Owen.'

My brother looked at me and I could have sworn a sort of pink was changing his face—embarrassment rather than the angry red of earlier. He mumbled an apology, directed at all of us. 'I know dad won't stop but…' He rubbed his brows. 'I just don't want him to get the upper hand.' He pulled face, squinted at Andrew.

Andrew stepped forward now and enveloped him in a hug, and I got the feeling we'd have another night without our guardian. I felt myself sag, and then Megan whispered in my ear, 'What was that about a knife?'

I jerked, startled. 'What?'

'You said—'

'Ssh,' I whispered, taking her arm and pulling her away from Andrew and Owen.

She didn't argue but I knew she'd not back down about getting some answers. Shit, I *had* blurted about the knife in my rant, had been trying to get Owen to see he wasn't the only one affected by everything, but that was news to Megan. And now I was going to have to tell her. I looked over my shoulder. Andrew was kissing the top of Owen's head and then my brother nodded and headed out of the lounge.

Andrew glanced at me, but said nothing. He was angry at me, probably, but *some*one had had to get Owen back to his senses. Obviously there were softer options but subtle didn't always work with my brother. I croaked out an apology.

He shook his head, but gave a half smile. Maybe deep down he was grateful I'd had the balls to get in Owen's face and end the meltdown.

'Jamie.'

I'd forgotten I had Megan's wrist clamped. I let her go, apologising.

'Just tell me what you meant about a knife.'

Before I could speak, Andrew said, 'I think that's something best kept for another time.'

Megan frowned. 'I don't like being kept in the dark.'

'I know, Hon, and I'm sorry,' he said, 'but that story needs a calmer space for telling. Definitely not tonight.' His gaze flicked my way; yep, anger there at me.

I didn't tell him that I reckoned Owen hadn't even heard half of what I'd been saying, just dropped my gaze, knowing that most of what I'd said had been stupid to let out. Apparently I could rival Owen for meltdowns. 'He gone to bed?' I asked after a moment.

'No, to get some shoes.'

Not an expected answer at all. Megan looked just as thrown.

'We're going to walk down to that play-lot and back,' Andrew said. 'Get some fresh air. I won't be staying the night.'

I breathed out, but held my tongue against my annoyance and against saying a walk with just the two of them would crack one of the restrictions. The way Andrew's jaw went taut, I guessed he got where my thoughts lay. I turned away, headed outside to find my little brother.

Owen

Jamie shaking the hell out of me hadn't done much for my cold or the sore spots on my face, but the fresh air as Andrew and I walked slowly down the street seemed to douse some of the headache.

'I know I'm two-faced,' I muttered. 'Freaking out earlier and then doing this.' I flicked my hand out to encompass him and me and no one else. 'But I'm all out of caring.'

Andrew gave me a quick squeeze.

I understood why Andrew wanted to stay and I understood why Jamie and the others needed him to stay, but so openly breaking the restrictions Morrison had imposed felt too dangerous. Even if Andrew was right that dad couldn't know if he stayed the night or not. No one had reported strange men or cars loitering in the street and, as far as we knew, dad hadn't even re-introduced himself to Mr and Mrs Carter.

'You know I *do* want you to stay, right?' I murmured after we'd gone half the street in silence.

'Of course, Owen.'

I gave a jerky nod. 'I just… God, Jamie was right to yell all that stuff, but I can't just stop with that feeling. And I know it's selfish and all that.'

'Jamie could have done it softer,' Andrew said, voice a little edged. 'And I… I'm sorry I didn't stop him.'

I gave a rueful smile. 'He'd have just started shaking you.'

'He didn't hurt you with all that?'

I shook my head. I'd bitten my tongue but that was my own fault for being such a dick that Jamie'd had to act. Probably I was lucky he'd not done it ages ago because it wasn't like I'd only just gotten all dumb about these restrictions.

Sliding my hand into Andrew's as we walked made me the biggest hypocrite about, but his fingers tightened around mine instantly and I didn't regret it for a second.

'I keep forgetting that it's not just you and me in this,' I said as we crossed the road and headed through the gate into the play-lot.

'So do I, sometimes,' Andrew replied, as he gazed up at the little tower fort. He let out a long sigh then bent a smile down at me. 'Remember the last time you and I were here?'

I felt a flush heat my face. 'Yeah,' I said. 'It was after another meltdown.'

He started and I realised he hadn't been meaning the *reason* for why he'd found me in the tower on that grey, drizzling day. Then he said he didn't remember that confrontation with Jamie being a meltdown. He smiled, but sounded slightly frustrated when he added, 'You and your brother.'

'Yeah,' I said with a sigh. '*You* need to shake the pair of us now and then, you know.'

'Wouldn't dare,' he murmured, walking away from me to take a better look up at the tower.

I shifted to one of the wooden seats, wondering if he was remembering that night or the whole day. The day I'd picked my rapist from a line-up, the day my blood had been taken to test it for HIV and Hepatitis, the day I'd told Jamie and Megan all about it then run away afterward.

Andrew had found me here in the little building getting wet, and had taken me to his apartment rather than just drop me off at home. He'd dealt calmly all day with my weird stuff and dealt just as calmly all night with perhaps even weirder stuff. And his presence had given me the best night's sleep, even with a brewing cold, that I'd had in ages.

'Please stay tonight,' I whispered out.

Andrew didn't hear that, of course; in any case, he was mostly obscured around the other side. I couldn't bring myself to repeat it louder.

When he came back and joined me on the seat, I gave him

a tiny smile. 'You saved my life that day,' I murmured.

He slung an arm around my shoulder. 'I always will, Owen,' he said just as softly.

We sat in silence for a bit, me fighting to keep from coughing. I didn't want him to hustle me back to the house. I was gonna have to give my brothers and sisters a huge apology and I needed time to get my words in order. Thinking of them brought me a fresh round of guilt too, because they were suffering just as much. I drew in a breath and said, 'This whole not staying the night thing is because of me, right?'

Andrew raised a brow.

'I mean… it's that whole "limit the temptation" thing.'

'Ah… yes,' Andrew said. 'Though I'm not sure why you're bringing it up.'

'It's just… What if I stayed at your apartment for a few days and you stayed at home with the others?'

Andrew straightened on the bench, arm sliding from my shoulders. He looked kind of shocked.

'I feel guilty,' I whispered.

'So do I,' he responded, 'but I—'

'I'd be safe in your apartment,' I cut over him. 'You know that.'

He sat silent, but surely he couldn't refute that.

When he opened his mouth, I got in first with, 'I just don't want you to fire me, and I know that's the only other thing that'll sort all this. Legally, anyway,' I added.

Jamie was right, dad wasn't gonna stop being a dick, but he wouldn't be able to do anything legal against me and Andrew and his guardianship if I didn't work for Andrew.

'I can't be at home, Andrew, either alone or with the others, just waiting for dad to show up. I can't put on a brave face for them anymore. I'm exhausted doing it, trying to pretend it's not as bad as it is.' I let out my breath, feeling like I'd been stripped of everything. 'I'm not… not strong anymore.'

'Oh Owen,' Andrew whispered. 'You are. Even back at the house just now… that was strong.'

I couldn't see how he could say that but I forced my lips into a smile because he looked concerned.

'Hon, it's a tough, tough situation,' he said, 'but I'm so proud of how you've been. Just like you were last year.'

'I think you're talking about someone else,' I mumbled.

He let out a soft breath. 'Come on, we better get back.'

'This sucks.'

'Definitely,' Andrew agreed.

Down the road I said I was sorry for accusing him of wanting an excuse to leave.

'I've already forgotten about it, Angel.'

I cocked my head. 'Well, I'm sorry anyway. It was dumb and mean.' It had come out without any sort of constraint in my freak-out about the restrictions because I was afraid that one day he *would* just give up and leave. I scratched my head like I'd find a switch there to flick and be normal again.

Andrew snagged an arm around me briefly and as he was dropping it I noticed him glancing at his watch. Except I couldn't ask about the time because the cough that had stayed back until now escaped. Andrew went into protective mode and hustled me into the house and to my room, though honestly it was just an annoying cough.

But next thing I was in pyjamas, sitting up in bed, holding a cup of hot water with honey and lemon in it. Andrew sat on the side of the bed, eyeing me like he was trying to decide if he should get me off to a doctor.

'It was just all that yelling and then walking,' I rasped out.

'Hmm,' he said. 'You're not coming in tomorrow.'

'No way, I'm not that—'

'You are that sick, Owen,' he cut over me. 'God, I shouldn't have let you come in today.' He pushed hair off his forehead. 'Definitely not after…' He stopped speaking.

'Hey,' I said softly after a moment, wanting to change the subject, 'tell me again what presentations you're going to next week.'

Andrew's brows went up a second and then he let out a half laugh. 'Forgot about that briefly.'

Attendance at the conference in New York had been planned before dad had even shown up. Andrew'd be away from Tuesday night to about midday on Saturday.

'I'm thinking I might cancel.'

'No, don't do that,' I responded automatically. 'That'd be dumb, Andrew.'

His brows went up and then he squeezed my knee. He didn't tell me about the presentations but he didn't say he was cancelling either. He rose.

'That time, huh?' I asked with a sigh.

'Almost, yes.'

'I wish I had your faith that dad *wouldn't* know,' I said. 'I know it's killing the others as much as us.'

'Angel, don't stress about it,' he told me gently. 'You're not going to get better if you do.'

I felt my brows try to come together in a frown at that response.

Andrew had a tiny smile on his face. 'No work tomorrow, okay? And Jamie said he'll be home.'

'Neat,' I muttered.

'He'll keep to himself,' Andrew said, 'as long as you keep to yourself.'

I bristled but he was smiling a bit broader now. I told him to go away. Instead he leaned down and kissed the top of my head. 'I'll see you after work, but ring me if you like, let me know how you're doing.'

I nodded, but as he turned away I closed my eyes so I couldn't see him leave.

[Eleven]

Jamie

When I opened the door on the chain on Friday I had a weird feeling that not going to the movies with Sean and Lincoln had been a dumb decision.

Not that it had been a *hard* decision, since I pretty much had the house to myself and I'd appreciated playing computer games without interruption. Owen hadn't once shown himself out of his room—which was all good, since I didn't want his bugs or any sort of face-off that could pick up where last night had ended between us.

Except, now I was staring through the gap at a pretty lady holding a kid in her arms. 'Hang on,' I said as she opened her mouth, and closed the door so I could release the chain.

When I opened the door again, she smiled, untangling little fingers from her hair. 'Hi, I'm looking for my husband, Chris Tremayne. Is he here?'

'I'm sorry but—' Stopped when my brain realised what she'd said.

Ridiculously, I stared extra hard but, of course, this woman wasn't mum. Hair too dark for one thing. American accent for— I shook my head. Mum was *dead*; it didn't matter the difference in sight or sound.

She raised her brows. 'I'm sorry, I should introduce—'

'Hold that thought.'

I pretty much slammed the door in her face and took off for my brother's room. 'Owen!' I shoved open his door and hit the light switch with a fist, making him cry out, then swear.

'Yeah, yeah. Get your ass up. There's a lady at the door. She has a kid. She's looking for dad.'

Owen stayed curled on his side. 'Go away, Jamie.'

'You're not getting it!' I yanked the bed covers off him, ignoring his snarl. 'She said she was looking for her *husband*.'

'So?' he grumbled. 'Wrong house.'

'Owen! She said dad's *name*. She's here looking for him. *She has a kid*.' I hugged myself just to keep from taking a fistful of his PJ top and hauling him out of bed.

Owen stared at me from beneath pissed-off brows, then sat up on a hip. 'What?'

'Fuck, listen to me!' I yelled, making him rear back. I rattled off what the lady had said. 'She's still out there. You have to do something.'

He coughed into his sleeve. 'I'm sick, Jamie.'

'And I think dad's *wife* is on our doorstep.'

Owen coughed again, reached for a tissue and I realised half the box seemed screwed up on the floor near my feet. I back stepped. 'Please, just come. I don't know what to do. Do we invite her in?'

Owen straightened at that. *Finally*, something to make him act. He grumbled as he got out of bed, but dragged a sweatshirt over his head.

'Um, maybe jeans?'

'No.'

He didn't even finger his hair into less of a mess. Since I was making him do this I guessed I shouldn't push. I followed him back to the door, where, through the speckled side glass, we could see the woman was still there.

Owen looked at me. 'Dad's *wife*?' he asked, now sounding all strange.

'She said "husband" so I'm guessing *yes*.'

He blew out a breath.

Shit, had I done something extra stupid here? Owen was pale, definitely not well. Wasn't like I couldn't really have handled this on my own.

Owen reached for the deadbolt. As the door came open we heard the lady speaking. '—went to check something. I'm Melissa Tremayne.'

Shit, who…?

'Our aunt?' Megan asked.

Owen and I looked at each other and then crowded on the doorstep, making the lady turn to face us. Megan stood halfway between her and the drive, Alana beside her.

'Oh,' the lady—Melissa Tremayne—said. She looked a little surprised by Owen but he *was* standing here in pyjamas and looking as sick as he probably felt. The child was on his feet at her side, clinging to her jeans. 'I'm sorry,' she said. 'I'm only just realising this is a surprise for you. You *are* Chris' children, right?'

She looked at us then at the girls, gaze focusing on Alana. Alana cocked her head. 'I'm not.'

Megan glanced at her, then cocked her head the same way. 'Sorry… *who* are you?' She'd clearly remembered that dad didn't have a sister named Melissa. Dad didn't have *any* sisters.

'I'm Chris' wife. We've been married a little over a year.'

She must have realised by our silence and stares that this was *complete* news to us. She faltered, then said softly, 'Did… he not tell you?'

'No,' Owen responded, short and sharp. His gaze was on the little dark-haired kid.

'Oh, that man! I *told* him to be upfront when he saw you.'

'I'm sorry, Mrs—' Owen stopped like he couldn't say it. 'But, dad's not staying here with us. He's in a hotel. I can't remember which one.' He put a hand over his mouth to cough. 'I thi—' Another cough made me and the lady give him some space. He straightened up. 'I think you need to leave.'

The woman went from looking concerned to startled. 'But didn't—'

'Dad isn't welcome here,' I said quickly. 'Seems there's a *lot* he hasn't told *you*. Please… leave.'

A slight flush rose up her neck, and she bent to pick up the child who immediately cried to be put down. 'Hush, Sammy.'

Beside me Owen flinched and I was sure he was thinking my thoughts—that this kid was dad's.

'I'm sorry,' she said. 'I had hoped things would be okay. I'd looked forward to meeting you all. This seems a lovely neighbourhood for kids to grow up in.'

My brother went stiff, but didn't speak. I managed, 'Yeah, it is.'

'Well, I'd better go, if Chris isn't here.' She smiled tentatively. 'Hopefully I'll see you all again soon on better footing. Hope *you* feel better soon,' she added softly to Owen.

'Uh… th-thanks,' he rasped out.

As Mrs Tr— Nope, I couldn't do it either. As the lady moved down the path to the drive, Megan and Alana stepped onto the grass to let her go by. Megan's face was quite a mask, then she said, 'He's a cutie pie. How old is he?'

'Sixteen months,' came the answer. 'And cutie pie only when he's quiet.' Amusement in the tone.

'Is he walking?'

I had no idea why Megan was asking this stuff.

'A little, not on his own though. But we don't think that's too far off.'

Megan actually walked with her to a small, red car out on the street, Alana just stood on the grass stunned. I realised Owen wasn't beside me anymore.

I wanted to make sure the lady left, but I needed to check that Owen hadn't collapsed somewhere. He was sitting in the lounge. Hadn't gained any colour and when his gaze came to me I saw nothing but shock.

Then the front door slammed and Megan, followed by Alana, came hurrying in. 'Dad's *wife?*' she cried.

'Apparently so,' I said.

'But… *what?*'

'Why are you so shocked?' I asked. 'You seemed to get on like a house on fire.'

'I was trying to get answers,' she rasped out. 'Did you hear how old that boy was?'

Owen sat stiff, so he'd obviously not left before that.

'Sixteen months,' I said. 'And, yeah, Megs, we can calculate.'

It put a birth-date about January, right around the time dad had run out on us.

I swallowed.

'It might not be dad,' Owen said tonelessly.

'Oh, come off it! That kid had dad all over him.'

He looked up at me. I knew none of us wanted to believe it but I reckoned the evidence was pretty much in our faces.

'So…' Megan got out. 'He left us because…' She glanced at Alana, who stepped up and gave her a hug.

'He *left* us,' I said, 'because he met someone else—Melissa—and had a child with her.'

'Before mum,' Owen croaked out.

'What?'

'*Before* mum,' he repeated. 'Long before, if he was born in January.'

I got what he was saying. Nine months for a pregnancy. That meant—

Megan choked on a sob and ran out of the lounge, Alana after her.

'Shit,' I breathed, sinking to the chair.

Owen looked at me, eyes still full of shock. 'He brought us all here and then cheated on mum.' He dragged in a breath that sounded like it was running over a cattle stop. 'And when that kid was born, dad left *us*.'

We stared at each other, and eventually I said, 'So... his grief had nothing to do with it?'

Owen didn't speak, just rose.

'Where are you going?'

'Bed,' he said.

'But—'

'B-*bed*.' He shoved a hand over his mouth.

I followed him because I didn't want to be alone. Owen didn't stop me, but didn't exactly acknowledge me either. Not until I said, 'We need to tell Andrew.'

'What can he do about it, Jamie? Leave him *alone*.'

I rocked back on the computer chair. 'What... I...'

Owen seemed to pull himself together. 'We'll tell him when he gets home. It's pointless ringing now and worrying him. Now, go away. I want to sleep.'

He closed his eyes, but he probably knew I stayed right where I was.

Owen

I should have talked with Jamie.

I should have checked on Megan.

Instead, I slept the rest of the afternoon. And when I woke I kept to my room, needing to digest this thing on my own.

If that kid was dad's, then he *had* cheated on mum. He'd said that he left out of guilt at forcing us here when we didn't want to come, at thinking mum might have not died if we hadn't, but he'd been having an *affair* all that time. Had he known about the pregnancy? Was *that* why he'd left us?

And had the woman—Melissa, wasn't it?—known dad was married with five kids when she'd hooked up with him? If so, then… she'd also know that mum had died. And yet… she was obviously still with dad.

Married.

Through the ache in my head I recalled her face at the door but couldn't settle on if she was mum's age or younger. She'd simply been a woman with a kid and she'd sounded American, not necessarily old or young. She'd had brown hair tucked behind her ears, and was wearing jeans and sneakers and a flower-printed top.

Just kind of regular.

And surprised, too, at hearing what we said. Dad can't have told her much—or, at least, not how nasty things had become. I touched my cheek but I had only the faintest mark now.

Melissa had seemed almost like she was springing a surprise visit, so maybe she hadn't been with dad all this time. I guessed that made sort of sense, that he'd come back and sort some things before bringing his… Shit, his *other* family.

I choked on air. Did that make her our *stepmother?* I took

317

two rapid swallows from my water glass, heart galloping. Had dad been meaning to move them all in with us? Was that why he wanted Andrew gone? Because he was taking up space needed…

I held my breath, squeezed my eyes shut to try and block these crazy thoughts. Crazier that I pinned my hope on the fact dad just wanted Andrew out because he was gay, and me out for the same reason.

Lying back, hand on my forehead, I felt water trickling down to my ear. I angrily brushed it away and forced my recall back to Melissa standing on the porch with the child in her arms. My breath squeaked out; the kid had dad's hair. Mine, Jamie and Lisa's hair. No… apparently *not* mine. With my jaw clenched, I mind-erased the kid so I could "see" Melissa without distraction.

She'd expected us to know about her, but she hadn't shown up to be nasty. That much I knew. So I guessed she had no idea about these last few weeks and how dad was actually a monster rather than a father. I wondered if she even knew about Andrew, though if she didn't then she was probably wondering what was taking so long to get us all together. What had dad been telling her, and what had he not told us?

Shit, had mum known about her?

For a little while my breathing was hard to control.

Why hadn't dad mentioned Melissa and the child in one of his visits? Had he been testing the waters, seeing how things lay before revealing them? Had he turned mean and nasty because it became clear that he *wasn't* going to be just moving in like nothing had happened?

Maybe he did carry some homophobic feelings, but I reckoned they'd only sharpened because we weren't doing what he wanted. And he'd gotten so uptight about all that, that he'd strayed from the original plan and so Melissa had shown up.

My head hurt trying to unravel it all so I rolled onto my side and curled up, trying not to think. I had my own issues, I didn't need to find myself worrying about her and that child.

Shit, dad had a *child*.

I swallowed a jagged lump, then reached for tissues to hold against my running nose.

Andrew

I was surprised to get in the house without needing the chain to be released. More surprised to not be greeted in some way by a call or a flying body. Silence was out of the ordinary.

'Anybody home?' I called, nerves tightening as much as my fingers did on my keys.

'Andrew!'

Next thing Megan was flying into my arms, sobbing noisily. I held her tight, unable momentarily to get my voice working to ask what was wrong.

Surely it wasn't her father? I'd seen no sign of a visitor on the street. If he was in the house, I'd know by now. Yet, my heart kept up a monster beat in my chest.

'Hon, what's up?' I asked.

Megan responded but it was too muffled and then I stopped in full surprise. I'd been shuffling us toward the lounge, and now I spied Jamie on one couch with Sarah beside him. Alana looked at me from the other. 'Uh, hi girls.'

They both greeted me and smiled. Neither seemed scared but having both of them here and Megan sniffing and wiping her eyes did not relax me. I gave the room a quick glance. No Lisa and Matty, and no Owen.

My stomach dropped like a sky diver and I turned to Jamie as he rose and said, 'He's in bed, still blocked up. Dad has a new wife.'

I looked from Jamie, whose expression was anger over dull shock, to Megan who was nodding but also full of shock.

'He has another son,' she whispered. 'Not even two.'

'A...' My mind blocked. 'How...' I rubbed my forehead, drew in a long breath. 'Okay, someone please tell me what I'm missing here.'

Jamie opened his mouth but Megan said, 'Go check on Owen. I know you want to. I'll make us all a drink. Alana? Sarah?'

Both girls immediately popped onto their feet and followed Megan into the kitchen, leaving me standing startled and Jamie shoving his hands into his pockets. I swallowed and managed to ask where Lisa and Matty where.

'Next door, as usual.'

Oh, right, it was Friday. Mrs Carter had been pleased to continue the Friday afternoon ice-creams even with school finished. I looked at my watch.

Jamie pulled a face. 'We kind of asked Mrs Carter to have them stay for dinner.'

'I see,' I heard myself respond. 'So... they don't know?'

'No.'

'Okay.' I thought that was a good idea. As I turned away, knowing Jamie would follow, I asked if Owen knew.

'Them being next door for dinner, no. The wife, yeah.' That came out on a long breath.

I stopped outside Owen's closed door and looked at his

brother. He smiled but he looked discomfited.

'Did your father show up also?'

He shook his dark head. 'No, just… Ha, her name's Melissa. She actually seemed quite nice. Thought dad would be here.' He shrugged. 'Thought *we'd* know about her.'

'And he wasn't anywhere around?'

'Not that we could tell,' Jamie said. 'She had a small, red car, nothing like what he's been using.'

I nodded. 'Okay. Did she come in at all?'

'No.' One side of his mouth turned up. 'Owen told her to leave. I think she did to avoid his bugs.' He touched the door briefly. 'He's been sleeping since she left.'

I didn't ask how long ago that was or why I hadn't been called, just gave another nod.

Jamie left me and I hesitated a second. If Owen was still sick I should let him sleep. But, after yesterday, I had an overwhelming need to see him even if he was asleep. I tapped a heads' up on the door and opened it enough to poke my head through the gap.

Owen wasn't asleep; he sat up against pillows, half lit by the night light. Tissues littered the carpet. He turned his head and for a moment I wasn't sure he recognised me. Then his breath sucked in and he said, 'Hi' in a weak voice.

'Can I come in?'

A smile beamed out. 'Yeah.'

As I did so he told me to turn on the light, but even while I did that he dragged the closest curtain back.

My young man didn't present a particularly stunning sight. His nose was red, crusty and sore looking, his eyes were without their usual brightness, and his top lip was puffy and red. And it looked like every hair on his head had decided to do its own thing.

Though he was a mess I still perched on the side of the bed and kissed him. He pushed back after a second, wiped his nose. 'You'll get my bugs,' he said, sounding all blocked.

I smiled; even though he said that he looked satisfied, and his other hand still gripped my sleeve.

I held out the tissue box and he swiped out two and blew his nose. He groaned as he did so. 'It's so sore,' he said, dropping the tissues in his lap.

'You're giving Rudolph a run for his money,' I murmured.

Owen stuck his tongue out. 'I do actually feel better, but my nose just…' He lifted one of the tissues and held it there.

'Jamie says you've slept much of the afternoon.'

He nodded, eyeing me. 'You know, obviously.'

'Well, not much,' I said. 'Just the fact your father appears to have another family.'

I watched Owen carefully but he just sighed and said, 'Yeah.' No anger, no upset.

Perhaps he wasn't feeling either thing, though it was more likely the cold was dulling them. He looked worse than he had earlier in the week when he'd first come down with the bug. He gave a long sniff.

'Think you could manage a shower?' I asked. 'That might help clear your head a bit.'

He cocked his head.

I waggled a finger. 'I cannot join you,' I told him, making him stick his tongue out again. 'We have guests—Alana and Sarah.'

'Oh… Alana's still here? Megan must—' He shook his head. 'What *is* the time?' He angled his gaze to my wrist. 'Six?' he got out with some surprise.

'You knew Alana was here?'

'Yeah, she and Megan came home while the lady was here. She was really upset. Megan, I mean.' He pushed fingers through his hair while he spoke. 'I'm glad Alana stayed. I… I just came in here. I was too… knackered.' He eyed me. 'Is Megs okay?'

'She's making everyone drinks,' I said.

'Oh,' he said. 'Not really then. She does that, you know, when she's upset or needs to keep busy.'

There *had* been a lot of glassware on the coffee table. My tongue pressed to my teeth a moment then I looked back at Owen as he said, 'Sarah's here too?'

I nodded.

'Hmm,' he said.

I waited but that's all he said. I tapped his knee. 'How about that shower?'

'Yeah, sounds good,' he said. 'I was gonna get up anyway, I'm a bit hungry.' He shoved me when I exaggerated my surprise. 'Go away.'

I chuckled and rose. 'The kids are dining next door so we— What?'

He'd looked startled a second, then flushed. 'I kinda forgot about them. Do they know?'

'Jamie told me they don't,' I said. 'And they're next door to give us time to talk.'

Owen pulled a face. 'The Carters deserve gold medals.'

'Joan told me she loves having them around. Apparently they keep her young.'

He rolled his eyes.

'Fifteen minutes, okay?'

'For what?'

'Shower,' I said.

'Oh, right.' He glanced up. 'And what if I take longer?'

I snorted. 'I'll send Jamie to turn the water cold.'

'You're no fun, you know that?'

I leaned down, cupped his nape, and kissed him, pressing his mouth open. Fingers curved into my clothing. Then I heard a ratcheting breath and pulled back. Owen pressed a hand over his mouth, coughing. Dragging in air he said, 'Blocked nose, can't breathe kissing like that.' He didn't look upset, just promised me something better tomorrow.

I chuckled, heart feeling steadier now. 'I'll see you shortly.'

He nodded, grabbed up a tissue.

Closing the door behind me, I leaned against it for a moment's calm. No need to give Jamie any ammo for sly comments. Definitely not tonight.

Returning to the lounge, I noticed the French doors had been opened and that Jamie and Sarah were sitting out on the step. Jamie had his arm around her shoulder, tangled in her long hair.

'I made you a coke float, Andrew.'

I brought my gaze to Megan. She and Alana each sat on a couch and the table now only had their glasses and mine. Mine, with a puddle around it, sat on a tray.

'It overflowed a bit, sorry.'

'Ah, no problem.' I moved to the single chair. I couldn't remember the last time I'd had a drink made with soda and ice cream but the sugar hit seemed a good idea. 'Thanks,' I said, reaching for the glass.

'We'll need to get more coke,' she said, watching me.

'Just add it to the list,' I said, 'and we'll get it tomorrow.' We'd planned a major grocery trip. With Megan nodding, I looked across at Alana. 'How've you been, Alana? Enjoying the first week of holidays?'

She smiled. 'Yeah. Not having to deal with Mrs Sanders first period is amazing.'

She caught Megan's gaze and they both grinned. After that they started reminiscing about classes and friends and other students. Since there was laughter and smiling, I didn't mind becoming a third wheel. I stayed in my chair with my sugary drink and watched their animated conversation, thanking heaven that Megan had such a good friend.

While I was drying glasses, Jamie and Sarah wandered up to the bench.

'Do you need help with anything?' Sarah asked. 'Jamie's got free time.'

'Hey,' he got out, shifting back from her elbow.

I smiled. 'No, I'm all good, Sarah, thanks.' Since they stayed at the bench, I asked how she'd been doing with all the limelight from last week's performance.

A blush made her blue eyes brighter. Then her lower lip pouted out. 'I'm all forgotten about. Just a dancer.'

'You were superb,' I told her.

'Thanks,' she said with a grin. Then she added, shyly, 'I've been offered a late audition for one of Joffrey's summer intensive programmes.'

'That's wonderful news, Sarah. Congratulations.'

Jamie nudged her. 'You know he has no idea who they are, right?'

She flushed.

'I can still give my congrats without knowing,' I told him, then looked at Sarah. 'I'm sure it's an amazing opportunity,

Sarah.'

Her face went redder. 'I'm so excited.'

'And here's me, the forgotten singer,' Jamie said, giving a loud sigh. 'I've not been offered anything.'

Sarah snorted. 'I've read those YouTube comments. You've been offered *lots* of things.' She grinned, told Jamie to hush when he tried to play down the comments. 'Apparently, you're quite a babe.'

'A babe?' sounded behind me. 'When did that happen?'

Owen stepped up to the bench, clothed, wet hair slicked back. He looked a lot brighter, though he had tissues tucked in one hand and his nose remained Rudolph-esque.

'Well,' Jamie said, 'whenever it did, *you* clearly missed out.'

'Works for me,' Owen said. 'I've seen some of those comments. I'm quite happy with my lot.' He elbowed me.

'Rat bag,' I murmured, but enjoyed the to and fro between the brothers. Definitely enjoyed the smile Owen flashed my way before he greeted Sarah. Obviously hadn't seen her yet today.

'Hey, how're you feeling?'

'Yeah, better,' he said with a smile. Noticed that, out of her sight, he tucked the tissues into a pocket. He turned toward the fridge. 'What're we having for dinner?'

Jamie and I exchanged a look, trying to keep surprise hidden. Owen had told me earlier that he was a bit hungry, but to see him looking in the fridge and actually asking about dinner—well, lately, that'd been a rare event.

'Thought we'd get take-out,' I said, encouraging him away from the fridge. 'Go sit down and relax. Outside.' I pointed. 'The fresh air'll do you good.'

He looked a second like I'd suggested something mean, but

then he shrugged and went. I heard him briefly speak with Megan and then he was outside sitting himself at the table. Jamie followed him out, but Sarah stayed at the bench.

'Everything okay?' I asked her.

She nodded. 'Just giving them some space.'

I glanced up—the boys *were* talking, though Owen had a tissue pressed to his nose so it could all have been Jamie joking. I wondered if outside wasn't such a good place after all, but the evening was still warm and no breeze wafted.

'Jamie told me that when the lady introduced herself, he'd briefly thought she was his mum.' Sarah darted a glance at me before watching her finger follow a pattern in the bench top.

'Did you see her?' I asked softly.

She shook her head. 'I wasn't there, it's just what he said.'

'Probably shock.'

Sarah gave a tiny smile. 'Yeah, since he also said the lady looked nothing like her.'

'She didn't,' we heard Megan say, as she and Alana came to the bench. 'Total opposite of mum—dark hair, brown eyes, and American. Pretty. Ah, not that—' She glanced over her shoulder but the family portrait remained under a sheet in the garage. She choked on a breath.

Alana slung an arm around her shoulder. 'Your mum was gorgeous, like you.'

Megan's eyes glittered, but she smiled.

'Alana's so right,' Sarah added.

Megan wrinkled her nose, obviously trying to keep the tears in her eyes from spilling. 'Th-thanks.' She looked over at me as she wiped an eye. 'Can we not talk about it for a while? You said… take-out?'

'Yes, I did,' I agreed with a nod, happy to change the

subject. 'How about you ladies decide what we'll have?'

Pizza was our usual, but we'd accumulated a number of other take-out menus. Megan retrieved them from under the notepad and the girls gathered around.

- # -

Although my conscience told me that today's events meant there was even more reason to stay the night, I said I wouldn't. Owen looked too exhausted to re-enact last night, but everyone was on edge and I didn't want to start something that could easily turn nuclear. In any case, the kids were home and still unaware and that meant the rest of us treaded carefully.

Jamie rolled his eyes when I said it was time for me to go home. Owen was probably too sick to turn pink but he looked embarrassed. I gave him a squeeze then headed for the door, Megan accompanying me.

'Hon, you sure you didn't want to stay with Alana tonight?'

Megan gave a lopsided smile, shaking her head. 'Yeah. I feel… well, like I just need to be here, even if only half of us know.'

I gave her a hug. 'You'll be alright?' If she asked me to stay, I probably would. Nuclear fall-out would just have to be cleaned up later.

She just nodded. 'Think we'll sleep pretty good tonight; brains blown and all that.' Her smile turned wry. 'I still can't quite believe it.' Her gaze was on the door to the garage.

Beyond the door was the family portrait that she and her older brothers had spent a lot of time looking at. It wasn't Owen's gorgeous ocean eyes they'd been focused on, but the fact that their parents had been smiling and happy and looking natural with both things. And, yet, behind that was obviously an affair.

It was understandable how disconnected the kids suddenly felt about everything. Perhaps it was good that I wasn't trying to stay tonight; I could be just an added complication right now.

I started, suddenly realising Megan had spoken and I'd not heard her at all. 'Sorry, Megan, what was that?' Felt a bit of embarrassment on my face.

'Just asked if you could… When you come over tomorrow morning, could you bring some eggs?'

I'd definitely missed something here.

She flushed, mumbled that she wanted to bake something. 'But everything takes eggs and I think we've only got one left.'

'Ah… sure, okay.' I gave a smile. 'You know, I seem to remember Owen saying once ages ago that you like to bake.'

'Yeah, I do. Haven't for ages though.' She suddenly looked a bit puzzled over that.

I squeezed her shoulder. 'I'll bring a dozen. Will that be enough?'

'Definitely,' she said. 'Thanks, Andrew, I'm so grateful.'

I knew that was for more than the eggs, but I just said, 'It's all okay, Hon. Call me anytime if you need to talk. Tell the boys too.'

Megan nodded.

'Alright,' I said, and opened the front door.

It was actually hard to step through and keep walking, but I did.

[Twelve]

Owen

I was washing the dinner dishes when the doorbell chimed. My first reaction was glancing at the microwave clock—7:51.

Megan dropped the tea towel on the bench, grumbling, 'Why do sales people always come so late?'

I watched her go, then turned back to the dishes.

Next thing I heard, 'Melissa?' delivered in total surprise. I was already hurrying to dry my hands, Jamie getting up from the couch when Megan added, 'Ah, Dad.'

That sped me and Jamie up, arriving at the door from both sides, making Megan jerk.

'What are you doing here?' I asked, heart jumping because dad's visit last week was coming back raw in my memory.

'You shouldn't be here,' Jamie put in, tone telling me he was remembering too.

'I came with Melissa,' dad said.

'Why?'

Dad turned his gaze on me and I saw his eyes narrow just a little. Before he could speak, Melissa took a part step closer, jiggling the dark-haired baby in her arms. 'I asked Chris to bring me. The other day was a shambles. I wanted to meet you all properly.' She directed dad a look we'd seen mum give him when she was annoyed.

Megan swallowed.

Dad gave a jerk of his head. 'I'm here to clear the air a bit, to… apologise for not revealing I was married again.'

We three kind of just stood there staring. Then the little boy held out a squishy ball to Megan, giving a wide smile.

Jamie and I were frozen as Megan choked on a breath and reached out. She took the ball, squeezing it, face reddening though I wasn't sure why. 'Th-thanks,' she got out.

My turn towards Jamie felt robotic. He looked just as shocked, but I think he understood the situation as well as I did. Megan had been instantly charmed, and because of that I felt like we couldn't make them leave. 'Um,' I said, 'come in. Would... you like a drink?'

Melissa smiled. 'No need to make us anything...' She stopped. 'My gosh, I don't know any of your names. I'm so sorry.' She gave dad a peeved look.

'My sons, Owen and Jamie,' he said, making us both shift a bit. 'And my gorgeous daughter, Megan.'

Megan went more red, eyes glimmering.

'Owen... Jamie. Megan.' Melissa looked at each of us as she spoke. 'Hi.'

We all got out something and I took another step back, hand out to indicate the way to the lounge. 'This way.'

'Where're Lisa and Matty?' dad asked.

'At a camp,' I heard Megan respond behind me. 'It's so peaceful without them.'

When I turned, Melissa had a slightly puzzled look on her face. Did she not know there were five of us? Sounding wry, dad expanded on Megan's comment, making Melissa smile. She sat when dad encouraged her to one of the couches, setting the baby on his feet between her knees. Megan sat on the other couch, still holding the ball, and Jamie took the single chair, looking really stiff.

Feelings totally proved when he said, 'So, clear the air.'

'Jamie.'

I flinched back, unsettled that dad and I had said that at the same time. Jamie looked startled a second before a weird grin came over his face and he seemed to relax. But, even relaxed, it was clear he waited for dad to speak.

Dad didn't immediately, just looked back at him and then glanced at Megan who just couldn't seem to take her focus off that stupid ball.

Melissa talked softly to her son when he made a noise. His little hand was out like he wanted the ball.

'Megan,' I said.

She jerked, glancing up. I angled my jaw and she followed the direction, flushing. 'God, I'm sorry.' She jumped up and held the ball out. 'I forgot I…'

The kid couldn't walk but he leaned as far as he could. Megan was going bright red, like she realised he couldn't come to her. She took a step, then another, bent to hand over the child's toy. 'Here you go.'

He latched onto her hand, reaching for the ball with the other. When he had his fingers on it, he didn't let go and return to his mother. He smiled at Megan.

'Can I… can I pick him up?'

The choking sound was Jamie's, going pink as he tried to suppress the cough.

'Of course, Megan,' Melissa said.

So, she did.

For a moment, the room only contained my sister and the child in her arms. She tickled him, making him giggle.

'—told you his name is Samuel. Sam.'

I refocused. Megan was looking at Melissa who was smiling.

'Sam,' Megan repeated. 'It suits you,' she told the little boy, fingers smoothing through his dark curls.

For a weird beat I flashed on that photograph we'd found—of me in that man's arms and mum beside us. I got my hand up to cover whatever sound was charging up my throat.

'S-so…' I got out after a second. 'Why didn't you tell us you'd married again?'

Megan actually frowned at me, like I was ruining her moment. She moved away from the couches, taking Sam around the room, pointing things out.

I looked at Jamie, could see he was as startled as me at her actions, given how she'd been last week. But he simply shrugged and turned to dad. 'You've been back almost a month. How did having another family slip your mind?'

Dad's mouth went even, but Melissa set a hand on his leg. 'You do owe them an explanation, Chris.'

God, this was weird, seeing her there beside dad, hearing her speak. Trying to reconcile that she was here because she was his wife. I forced in air and glanced at Jamie again. Somehow he now sat relaxed in the chair, though a muscle twitched along his jaw.

'I needed to see how everything was first,' dad said.

My skin prickled, but I forced that back and looked at Melissa. 'Did you know about us?'

'Yes, Owen,' she said.

'Right from the beginning?' I asked, knowing she'd know exactly what I meant.

'Not then, no,' she said with a shake of her head. 'Look, I know—'

'Mel,' dad said over her, 'you don't need to explain anything.'

She frowned at him. 'We should be open, Chris, or we're

not going to make it as a family.'

Jamie let out a snort. 'We're *not* a family.' He glanced at me and added, 'We don't want dad back after so long.'

I bit my lip to keep silent. He had right to speak but I hoped he'd stay civil with it.

'But, Jamie, it'd—' Melissa cut herself off.

She looked hurt. I felt sorry for her, realising she really had been kept in the dark, but I was still with Jamie. We didn't want dad back; it was time we started saying that openly.

Dad sat silent. Stiff but also sort of relaxed. Definitely a different man to the one we'd come to know in recent visits.

Know. Would he…?

'Owen!' Jamie said, startled.

'I'll be back in a second,' I said, walking away.

Had he known the man in that photo? The man we thought was my real father? I wasn't totally sure I wanted to find out, but if we *were* clearing the air then we might as well do it fully.

When I came back to the lounge, I noticed Megan had taken Sam out to the deck and Melissa was just stepping out there after her. That was good; I hadn't really wanted my sister around for this bit.

Jamie was rigid in the chair, worrying me about what had happened in the two minutes of my absence. He didn't speak when he saw me. I held the photo face-up to dad. 'Do you know who this is?'

Dad took the photo. His eyes went wide and then narrow and it was clear that he did. Didn't expect him to let out a sigh. 'Your mother…'

When he was silent after that I said, 'You said you adopted me. Is it true? Is that man my father?'

I glanced at Jamie when he made a sound of shock;

probably never expected I'd bring up the subject here. His eyes were wide at me.

'I need to know,' I gritted out softly.

He gave a jerky nod, and turned back to dad who was sucking his lips in and out and rubbing his jaw.

'Yeah,' dad said, looking up at me. 'Your father.'

'Who was he?' I asked. 'Why? Where?' Although my heart crashed against my ribs I actually felt quite numb.

'I didn't meet him,' dad said. 'He'd already split from Cathy before I met her again.'

'Is he… still alive?' I heard myself ask.

'No idea.'

'Were they divorced?' That was Jamie, head cocked.

Dad ran his tongue around his teeth. 'Engaged.'

I was beginning to regret bringing the photo out. I wanted to take it off dad but couldn't move.

'You were a bastard child, Owen.'

'Dad, that's not nice!'

Dad eyed Jamie. 'True though.'

'Yeah, but…' Jamie trailed off, maybe because *I* hadn't reacted to that comment.

'Do you know his name?' I asked.

'Only the one you carry,' dad said. 'Your mother never said much about him.'

I cocked my head. 'You mean… Owen?'

'No, Whitney.'

Jamie and I shared a choking breath. Mum had always said my kooky middle name would have been my first name if I'd been a girl. (Imagine how funny Jamie found that!) Since it apparently worked for both sexes she'd kept it when I turned out male but had at least relegated it back in the list.

Dad glanced at us then returned his focus to the photo. 'Cathy refused to change it, even though he ran out on her.'

Jamie got to his feet and took the photo off dad. He let it go easily enough, leaned back on the couch, gaze on me. I did my best to keep my composure settled. Not over how I carried my father's name, really, but that what dad… *this* dad… had said was true. I *wasn't* his kid. Shit.

I let out a sharp breath, hauled in another, jerked when Jamie held the photo out to me. 'Go put it away.'

I did without argument.

Closing the top drawer of the dresser I suddenly recalled Jamie telling me that me and him, and the others, were connected through mum, even if my father turned out to be different. I realised now that we had another connection too—both our fathers had run out on mum.

Coming back to the lounge, I reckoned I could face any conversation with dad just now and stay in control. Partly because dad was calm himself and I knew Melissa was the reason for that. I looked about for her; still out on the deck with Megan and Sam.

Megan's interaction with the little boy today was world's away from her reaction last week, but I had this feeling that the offering of the ball at the front door had caused that. It'd hit her and she couldn't do anything but go into a motherly sort of mode. No… sister mode. God, that kid was her stepbrother. *Our* stepbrother.

I swallowed, opening my mouth to ask dad something I realised we should have asked ages ago but choking it back when Melissa came inside.

'Your sister's a natural with him,' she said with a warm smile.

Jamie and I looked at each other. He muttered, 'Plenty of practice.'

I bit my lip. Instead of letting him launch into why that might be, I turned to dad, Melissa just taking a seat beside him. As he smiled at her, my gut dropped. There didn't seem to be any way that she could know what dad had been like recently. Didn't seem like she knew he was under a (seemingly invisible) restraining order either.

'Owen?'

I jerked, found Jamie looking at me, brows up. Flushing, I realised I'd obviously made a sound—they were all looking at me.

I cleared my throat. 'Um… when you first came back, Dad, were you planning to live here with us?'

'Yes,' he replied. 'Along with Melissa and Sam.'

I was startled he'd answered so quick. Jamie went all stiff, but I spoke before he could. 'How, though? There's not enough space.' Wasn't even now—my brothers and sisters shouldn't be sharing rooms anymore.

'Well, I expected you'd move out when you turned eighteen. Go have your life.'

Ironic, him mentioning my age. I cocked my head. '*How* did you think that was even possible? Things changed massively when you left. How'd I be in a position to move out?'

My father's face seemed to go a bit dark. Melissa squeezed his hand as if she saw that too. Dad cricked his neck. 'Well, you could now,' he said. 'I'm sure you've got funds.'

He didn't growl that or anything but the way he said it I knew he was meaning Andrew or even some other manner. I gritted my teeth.

'In fact,' dad said, 'why *haven't* you moved in with that man?'

'Chris,' Melissa murmured.

Sam giggled outside which made me look that way momentarily, but he was out of my direct view.

'Owen?' dad asked.

I looked at him. 'You seriously want an answer?' My brows were way up my hair in surprise. 'Because of them.' Jabbed a finger in the direction of each sibling. 'Because Andrew can't be here at night because you're being—' Somehow I kept back those final words.

My brother suddenly let out a weird laugh and got up. When I scowled at him, he said, 'I asked you that once, remember? Why you hadn't moved in with Andrew already. Do you remember what you told me?'

'No, and I don't know why you're—'

'You said you wouldn't walk out on us like dad did.'

A bolt of something flashed my nerves, shock or possibly horror. I couldn't remember the conversation though I didn't try to refute it. Dad was frowning at Jamie, pulling out of Melissa's grip. Jamie can't have felt the atmosphere shift because he said, 'I'm glad you haven't changed, Owen. Thanks.'

While I just stood there, staring, he turned to dad. 'Can you keep Andrew out of this conversation? I'm tired of you belittling him and making stupid comments. He's done more for us than you have, and so has Owen. They both deserve your respect at the very least.'

'That man is twice as old as your brother,' dad said.

'I really don't give a fuck,' Jamie said.

'Jamie,' I warned.

'Well, I don't,' he told me. 'And neither do you, do you?'

'No, but—'

'But nothing then,' Jamie said with a tone of finality. He turned back to dad and Melissa. 'You guys should go. You're breaking the rules, Dad, even if we let you in. Heh, did you know that, Melissa? He's got—Argh, Owen, don't—'

I'd grabbed his arm and yanked him backward, hissing for him to shut up. He hissed back that she should know.

'Yeah,' I growled softly, 'but not like this.'

Jamie stood with teeth clenched. I didn't say anything more just pleaded silently that he calm down.

Beyond us I heard dad suggest Melissa go collect Sam and wait in the car, that he'd be out in a minute. I was sorry that she looked worried but I didn't speak up that she should stay. I wanted them both to go. Beside me Jamie was all stiff, but at least he was silent.

Melissa headed to the deck, laying on some line that they'd better get Sam to bed.

Megan was the one who actually carried him inside, giving him a jiggle that made him laugh. Jamie let out a tight breath beside me while I held mine; our sister looked relaxed and happy. She offloaded the baby, smiled when Melissa gave her a half hug and told her she was a natural.

'Ha, he's just easy to be around. He's such a happy wee man.'

Melissa gave a wry smile. 'He can howl with the best of them.'

She came toward Jamie and me and we both tried to not look so stiff. 'Hopefully we can do this another, more settled time,' she said softly.

'Yeah,' I managed.

Jamie gave a jerky nod.

She glanced at dad, who said, 'I won't be long, don't worry.'

He smiled, and Jamie turned his head away.

'Ten minutes' max,' Melissa said, half warning.

Dad agreed and silence held while Megan and Melissa went to the door.

Once we heard the door close, I said to dad, 'Does she even know what you've done? What you've been like? Does she know you're not supposed to be here without permission?'

'You all keep letting me in,' dad said, with a shrug.

My brows came together at that stupid truth.

'That's beside the point, Dad,' Jamie said. 'You shouldn't be on this property. That's what the restraining order says.'

Dad shrugged and said he wasn't unaccompanied, as if that negated the need for permission.

Megan came back to the lounge then, stopping Jamie and me from responding to dad's comment. Her brows were dipped together; she wasn't happy. 'What's going on?'

'Your brothers are reading me the riot act,' dad said.

'What?' she said, startled, swinging to see us both.

Jamie muttered something under his breath. She raised a brow at me.

'We only asked if Melissa knew about dad's restraining order,' I said. 'Seems not.'

'Why would—' Megan cut herself off, didn't quite look like she knew how to finish.

'The way I see it,' dad said, 'is that Melissa has nothing to do with that order. I don't see why she would need to know.'

I choked on a breath of laughter. 'Seriously? You think she shouldn't know that the father of her child is abusive to his other children and is supposed to, *by law*, not be around them?'

Dad stood, saying, 'Don't try to threaten me, Owen.'

'I'm not,' I told him, feeling oddly relaxed. 'I was asking a question.'

My sister said my name in concern. I cast her a quick look but turned back to dad without reassuring her. 'Answer me this, then, Dad, maybe it's easier. You don't actually care that a *gay* guy ran a red light, do you? Yeah, it's given you ammo in your attacks on me and Andrew, but really you're just relieved that *some*one ran that light. Gave you a way to be with Melissa.'

Dad swung and missed because Jamie yanked me backward, making me stumble. 'Are you fucking crazy?' he cried in my ear.

Our father stood with his hands at his sides, chest heaving, eyes narrowed to slits.

I shook off Jamie's arm. 'Tell us it's not true, Dad,' I challenged.

He stayed silent.

'Dad?' Megan whispered, eyes glistening.

'I'm *not* glad your mother's dead,' he rasped out. 'I'm *not* a bastard.'

I grabbed Jamie's arm, pinching. He let out a growl but at least he didn't respond to that comment.

'But I would have left, yes,' dad said, letting his glare settle on me.

Though I'd pushed for that, I felt gutted and couldn't speak.

'Didn't you love her anymore?' Megan asked. 'Or *us*?'

Dad's silence then felt like the world had stopped, which was weird because we hadn't felt his love long before this point anyway. Why would he leave if he *did*? Yet, hearing it… no, hearing the silence…

'I loved her,' he said, wiping his hair off his forehead,

seeming to sag just a moment. '*And* you, but I also loved Mel. When I told your mother, she wanted a divorce. She was going to take you kids back to New Zealand.'

'And you weren't going to *fight*?' Jamie sounded hollow.

Dad shook his head. 'I thought it best you all go back. You didn't want to be here anyway, and I wanted…' He closed his eyes a second. 'Mel told me she was pregnant and that made the decision easier. It seemed best for all and then…' He didn't finish.

'Then mum died,' I said, 'and you *still* left.'

'I promised Melissa.'

We all stared at him and then Megan said, faintly, 'We were your kids, Dad. You were all *we* had.'

'I felt too guilty,' he told her. 'Forcing you all here, then Cathy dying, and Christmas… I couldn't handle being around you any longer.'

'*We. Were. Kids!*'

Jamie and I grabbed Megan as she flew at dad, crying and repeating that phrase over and over. Dad stepped back, startled. I didn't know how that could startle him. What the hell did he think we'd feel hearing this, even if we didn't want him in our lives? And *why* couldn't he have been open about this right from the very start? It'd still have hurt, but I was sure that knowing all those things would have made a difference to all our reactions.

Jamie reeled Megan against him when I let her go and stepped forward, telling dad he wasn't welcome anymore. 'Please leave.'

'This is my house.'

'It's not now,' I responded. 'You gave all this up when you abandoned us. You shouldn't be here *at all*, but you also have no *right* to be here either, no right to even *think* you have any right. You cheated on mum! You cheated on us! We *don't* want you here.'

'You don't get a say in this, Owen,' dad told me. 'I am still your father.'

'Don't play that card when it suits you,' I responded, bitterly. 'You don't control me. And Andrew's *their* guardian.' I flicked a hand at Jamie and Megan. 'You don't control them either.'

'This house is mine.'

I snorted. 'Point proved, Dad. Nice.'

He scowled.

'I was talking about me and Megan and Jamie, and even Lisa and Matty, but you focused on the house.' I let out a half laugh. 'You're not our father, you haven't been for a long time. Get out.'

'Kid, you're—'

'Get. Out!'

Dad drew himself up straight. Behind me, Jamie muttered my name but I didn't take my gaze off dad.

'Just get out there to your other family, Dad,' I said. 'The ten minutes must be up by now. Melissa's waiting.'

Muscles flexed along his jaw and his hands squeezed into fists, but perhaps he realised that he wasn't going to get anywhere and definitely not with a show of force. He picked up his jacket and made his way to the front door.

I followed at a distance, needing to ensure he really did leave, hoping I could maintain my mask until the door closed.

'I will be back for what's mine, Owen,' he told me, hand on the door. 'There's nothing you or that paedophile can do to stop me.'

'Calling people names is a sign you know you won't win,' I told him, just barely holding back panic at that word.

His lips curled up in a sneer. 'Some words hold power, kid. Just wait.'

'Don't come back, Dad.'

His gaze went over my shoulder but I didn't turn to see who was there, just stood stiff.

'Sweet dreams,' he said to me and then was gone, the clunk of the deadbolt sounding extra loud.

My confidence whistled out between my fingers. I waited a second or two before moving forward to engage the chain, and then turned. No one stood there. Not sure if anyone had been there before, but I was glad I hadn't looked. It had felt like he'd only done that to distract me and I was over feeling his fists. One up to me.

I hadn't actually intended he strike out earlier at my words. I'd just suddenly wanted him to admit this whole gay hate thing was mostly a sham, that he pushed that angle simply because he was jealous and insecure about how well my brothers and sisters were doing and *had* been doing with me and Andrew looking after them.

But, pretty much as I'd started to speak, Melissa had popped into my head. She had nothing to do with mum's accident and death, but those words about dad's relief had come out with me feeling like I'd had a light bulb go off.

And… we'd got answers. Horrible ones, actually, but answers.

Megan sat at the table out on the deck but Jamie stood, arms folded, scowling. 'That was a huge fucking risk saying that stuff, Owen.'

'I know.' In fact, the adrenalin still coursing through me was now turning my confidence into a bundle of regret. I mumbled an apology.

'Shut it,' Jamie told me. 'We got answers.'

'Yeah,' I breathed, took a seat on the top step. Our parents had been going to divorce! 'Shit,' I croaked. 'If mum hadn't… we'd be back in…' I felt sick and wasn't sure why—at the shock of dad's words, at the fact we could be back in New Zealand if…

A fist squeezed around my heart, and I knew why. I'd not have met Andrew. I wouldn't have had to deal with some horrible stuff, but also I would never have met the man I wanted to spend all my life with.

'Call Andrew,' Megan said suddenly.

When I twisted to look at her, she hadn't lifted her gaze from between her sneakers.

'There's no point, Sis,' Jamie said, sitting beside her. 'He can't do anything.'

'He can come home,' she said with a bit of steel, now looking up—first at Jamie, then at me.

'He's at a conference,' I reminded her. 'He can't just come home.'

Megan rose. 'Then he shouldn't have gone. He knows what dad's like.'

'He can't fight all our battles,' Jamie said, earning a glare.

I got to my feet. 'The conference was important, Megan, and booked before dad even came back. And it's like ten or something in New York. I'm *not* waking him up.'

My brother and sister both eyed me since I might have said that firmer than needed. Megan was biting her lip like she was trying to hold back something, then stalked into the house.

Jamie cocked his head at me. 'I back you, Owen, but not if you're thinking to keep this from Andrew.'

I frowned; a part of me had been. 'I'll talk to him tomorrow. Ring Sergeant Morrison too.' I let out a sigh. 'Dad was right about one thing, you know. We do keep just letting him in.'

'Ah, no, *you* keep letting him in,' Jamie said, which annoyed me because it wasn't me who'd opened the door to him tonight. After a second he let out a noisy sigh. 'Don't know why he couldn't have fessed up all that shit when he first came back.'

'Me either,' I said. 'And we should have pushed. God, we're dumb not doing that.'

After a moment he said, 'I keep thinking of those fights before mum died. I don't remember hearing anything about Melissa. God, Owen, I can't believe…' He trailed off, stared out into the yard. 'How didn't we know?'

I mumbled something about secret-keeping being a Tremayne skill, and Jamie's gaze narrowed. I shrugged. 'At least we've got answers now.'

'Even if Melissa seems nice, knowing dad ran out on us, leaving us on our own, just to be with another woman and kid, after *all* that had happened doesn't actually make me feel like a box of birds.'

Jamie got that out somewhere between a growl and a snarl, and was gone inside before I could react.

I stayed where I was, feeling much the same, and then more so because of dad's suggestion that I could move in with Andrew now. After all his attacks on me and Andrew, trying to split us up, I couldn't believe he'd even said it. What a hypocrite. For a brief moment, I wondered what'd happen if I did. Wondered if my room would be turned into Sam's, and so my brothers would still have to share.

I winced at that. As much as I wanted to be with Andrew, I wanted to be with him *here*, not apart from my brothers and sisters.

Leaning over my knees, I imagined Andrew in a flash suit going to various presentations, meeting and greeting clients. Hopefully, putting us out of his mind for a while. Even though we'd talked several times about how important the conference was, before he'd left on Tuesday Anne and I had really had to do the hard sell to keep him on track for it.

I got that last week (mostly my reactions) unsettled Andrew, but I also got that he needed a break. Though he was guardian his hands were tied as to how much he could push on my siblings' behalf and I knew that was stressing him. My own up-and-down emotions weren't helping.

The conference gave Andrew the space to reconnect with his business, and it gave me space to reconnect with my confidence.

And eight o'clock wasn't so hard when he wasn't here to leave.

We'd been messaging each day, and even though they were only words on a screen it didn't seem that either of us was in a bad space. I wanted to keep it that way, not sure I had the guts to phone Andrew and actually speak to him. Hearing his voice would be infinitely harder than just reading texted words.

Even tomorrow seemed too close to have gotten all my control restored to be able to tell him that dad had shown up, tell him what we'd learnt, and then tell him 'bye' all without doing some sort of meltdown and worrying him.

Perhaps I could just reveal it all when he got home on the

weekend.

And tell him then, too, what I'd learned about my real father. I blew out a sigh. Nothing much really, but it felt sort of good to know for sure where that photo and dad's adoption claim stood. Was a bummer to also prove mum had really lousy taste in men.

- # -

On Friday, I went into the office for a few hours of respite from home. Dressing more tidy than normal put me in good spirits too, since it seemed to build up my self confidence that I had everything under control.

Of course, I also enjoyed getting back into casual clothes once home, and I was in the middle of doing that when my phone went. I scrabbled around in my backpack, froze a second when I saw Andrew's name.

'Hi,' I said, unable to stop myself sounding puzzled.

'Hey you, just had a moment of downtime. Wanted to hear your voice.'

That caught me off guard and I sank to my bed, feeling a bit of heat rising. 'Nice to hear you too,' I whispered.

I heard a chuckle. 'How's everything?'

'Yeah, all good,' I said. 'I went into the office for a few hours today. Less distracting there.'

We talked a few minutes on that and on his conference, then he asked how everyone was here at home. 'Anything new and unusual happening?'

I went still, understanding what that question actually meant. 'Who told you?' I asked.

'Owen, it doesn't—'

'*Who* told you?'

'Megan phoned me.'

My breath whooshed out and I didn't know quite how to feel, given I'd pegged Jamie for it.

'She was concerned,' Andrew began.

'*She* let him in,' I cried in a low voice. 'And it wasn't just dad. Melissa and the baby were there too. It actually went fine. She *shouldn't* have called you about it.'

'Why didn't you?' Andrew asked.

'Because I knew you'd worry,' I replied.

'Of course, I'm worried,' he responded. 'Because I know how much all this has been stressing you.'

'I can handle it, Andrew,' I said. 'I've handled worse without you.' Knew right away that had been hurtful, but true so I bit back the apology even though his silence was painful. 'It… was actually a good meeting,' I said, voice steady. 'We got answers and no one hit anyone. Megan played a lot with Sam. Can you please just… forget about it for now? We can talk tomorrow when you're home.'

'I'm going—'

'No!' I cried over him. 'Don't cut the conference short, Andrew. You can't do anything here and we don't actually need anything done. So, *please!*'

I drew in a breath, gave him long enough of a gap to say, 'Megan told me about your father.'

Puzzlement reigned first, then I realised who he meant. Somehow I just said, 'Yeah, that's cleared up. I'm okay with that. Please stay in New York and enjoy it.' Ridiculous thing to segue into since he'd think about it now that he knew everything. 'Andrew, I didn't call last night because everything was okay. It's *still* okay.'

I had a thought that begging him to not come home early would have the reverse effect—that he'd think I was hiding something. I drew in a ragged breath, leaning over my knees, hand over my eyes as they started tearing up.

'I expect there won't be a spare seat today anyhow,' I heard Andrew say, sounding a bit off. 'So… I'll keep to tomorrow. I'll see you then, Owen.'

I was opening my mouth to respond when I heard the beeping. Had to look at my phone to be sure he'd cut the call without waiting for me to say something.

I felt sick. All the calm I'd had since the visit ran out like an artery had been slashed. That was one of the horriblest conversations I'd ever had, and I launched to my feet.

Megan was folding some washing. Jamie lay sprawled on one of the couches playing with his phone.

'You had no right to tell Andrew.'

Megan jerked then stiffened. 'Yes, I did. He's my guardian. He needs to know what happened.'

'Not while he can't *do* anything!' I yelled. 'He's at a conference, Megan! He's there for work and to have a break and now he wants to come home early.' Even as I said that I heard his last words, the flat tone.

'He should be here,' Megan said, voice tight. She turned her stiff gaze on Jamie as he got to his feet.

'He can't do anything!' I growled.

'Owen, she—'

'Butt out, Jamie.'

He actually took a step back at my tone.

'You're not our guardian, Owen,' Megan said.

'I'm in charge when he's not here,' I gritted out.

'That doesn't mean you can stop me from talking to him.'

'No, apparently not,' I said. 'But I don't expect you to tell him *my* stuff, about *my* father.'

'Megan, you didn't.' That was Jamie, looking shocked.

Megan went more stiff. 'It all just came out.' Tone as stiff as her stance. 'You should have told him all of it last night, Owen. He's our guardian.'

'And he's my partner.'

I stopped after that unexpected response, feeling pain rise up my chest to my throat.

My brother and sister looked puzzled, like what did that have to do with this conversation? I didn't want to say what hearing his voice just now had done to my calm. How it had weakened enough to let my grief and misery in that he wasn't here and how hard it was trying to plug that hole so I could cope.

'Forget it,' I croaked out, turning away. 'I'm going for a walk.'

'Owen,' Megan began.

'Forget. It,' I snarled over my shoulder and picked up my pace.

My emotions were making my stomach unsettled, but being on a bench in the play-lot kept me in control enough not to gag.

I understood where Megan was coming from, that she had the right to talk to Andrew whenever she wanted. But she knew that this conference was about giving him space as much as actual work and so I was furious she'd told him everything. Definitely that she'd done it behind my back when she knew that *I* was going to.

Though... perhaps she'd phoned to talk, thinking I'd

already made my call.

I leaned over my knees, ashamed of my reaction but also feeling justified. And in all honesty I didn't really care that she'd revealed the bit about my real father; I'd reacted just because it was all tied up with everything else and I kept hearing Andrew's tone as he'd ended the call.

'Don't think I've ever seen you go at Megs like that.'

I turned my head. Jamie stood near, hands in pockets. Held my breath a moment, then, 'Why are you here?'

'Just out for a walk,' he said. 'Like you.'

I huffed out a breath and went back to staring at the stones beneath my feet. Didn't react when Jamie took a seat beside me.

After a moment he said, 'You didn't go to work dressed like that, right?'

'What?'

He didn't speak and I straightened to look at myself, grimacing when I realised the phone had gone half way through my clothes change and I now wore my work pants and shoes and an old t-shirt. I let out a sigh.

- # -

Twisting, teeth gritted, I forced my eyes open.

I wasn't lying on coils of rope in the back of a theatre, I was tangled in my own bed. For a second I stayed that way, catching my breath, feeling the cold sweat all over. But then I had to acknowledge the burning heat in another part of my body. A cautious hand told me the truth and I rushed out of bed, to gag horror into the toilet.

My eyes were squeezed shut with the effort, but tears still

eked out.

It was hard enough writing down my short career as a prostitute, I didn't want to be reliving it in my dreams too. Worst of all, as I sat back on my heels, I compared what I'd just dreamed with what I'd recently written.

'Stop it,' I hissed to myself and climbed to my feet.

My groin had stopped burning but I didn't go for a physical check this time. My heart had stopped pounding too and I wanted it to stay that way. Flushing the loo, I turned to splash water on my face, give my teeth a clean.

When I looked in the mirror I was relieved that I didn't look frazzled but I didn't exactly look like I wanted either—confident and in control.

I'd told Jamie a while back that I'd been dreaming more of last year since dad had shown up, but until tonight I'd not actually dreamed about the sex. My top lip curled in distaste and a hand came up to cover my mouth. The distaste was as much at myself as for what I'd done back then.

Letting out a muffled sigh, I wondered if I should just stop writing, even though I was pretty sure that I'd only dreamed tonight because of the horrible phone call with Andrew and the argument with Megan. Those sorts of things whittled away my peace of mind and allowed memories to twine about in my sleep.

Except, thinking about Andrew saying that of course he was worried about dad showing up made me re-hear Sergeant Morrison's comments about Andrew not being able to help me if he didn't know the half of what was in my head.

I sighed at my reflection. I wasn't sure I'd get the courage to actually give him the pages of writing, but finishing was still a good idea.

A wry smile found its way to my lips; writing this stuff down was counselling in a non-verbal sense. Sergeant Morrison would probably be smug if he knew I was doing it.

I didn't feel tricked about it, and writing the events hadn't been too draining. Hadn't made me feel *awesome*, but I accepted that I felt more in control approaching these memories with intent rather than just fearing they'd pop up. I was in charge, not them.

Though, I didn't appreciate this dream just now. The guy hadn't been harsh but he'd been insistent. If *he* popped into my dreams, then what would…

Andrew knew about my final customer, Jack Wheeler (a name that was never going to leave my memory no matter what), so I was planning *not* to write about him, but there'd been another before him who'd been forceful. Nothing like Wheeler, but he'd still infiltrated my sleep days afterwards.

My stomach jolted at a seriously unwanted memory and I pressed my lips tightly shut, trying keep back the urge to gag.

'Come on, Owen,' I rasped through a dragged-in breath. 'You're stronger than this. Those guys don't… control you. Didn't before, don't now.'

I stared at my reflection until I was sure I believed myself.

'They'll burn. It'll all be good.'

Dropped my gaze, didn't want to see if there was a crazy look in my eyes that went with that speech. I didn't mean the men physically, of course, just the pages I'd written on. After Andrew had read everything, I was going to burn the pages, and the men would fade away with the flames.

When I finally got out of the bathroom, I didn't head to my room but to the big one Andrew had been using. Not for ages, and we'd changed the sheets since then, but I was sure I'd still sense him and I wanted that right now. Knew being there would keep the rest of my sleep easy.

Jamie

Andrew was definitely not focused on the newspaper he stared at. He still held the pen he'd been doing the crossword with but now he was just making circles. Been making them a while since the pen had cut through a couple of pages of newsprint. His dark brows were drawn over his eyes in a sort of frown. He didn't shift at all when I sat at the picnic table opposite him.

Seeing him like this was kind of scary. He wasn't unaffected by everything, but it wasn't often we saw him show it.

I was just opening my mouth to call his name, when he jerked as if only just noticing me or noticing he'd been wrecking the paper. He made a noise of annoyance and set the pen down.

'Lost your touch?' I asked, nodding at the half-completed crossword.

He let out a sigh and then, as if *finally* realising what he'd been like and that I'd noticed, he drew himself up straight. 'What's up, Jamie?' His smile was genuine. How he called it up I don't know.

'Is Owen sick?'

'Pardon?' came out sharply, and the smile vanished.

That surprised me and I straightened, my smile dropping too. But then I carried on with where I had been going with the question. 'Ah, it's… Well, you know, you guys were apart a week, I'd have thought he…' I trailed off, a bit unsettled by how serious Andrew looked.

Owen was actually doing a puzzle with the kids at the dining table, rather than being glued to Andrew's side. Hadn't been like that much over the weekend at all, which was why I'd jokingly asked if he was sick, but Andrew's response made my gut drop. Had I just stumbled upon a horrible secret? '*Is…* he sick? And I mean…' I waved a hand.

I meant AIDS. Owen had been tested for that and Hepatitis months ago, with clear outcomes, but could tests fail?

This whole thing with dad and the restrictions and everything was really hammering my brother, but he'd been through stuff last year that I considered *much* worse and he hadn't seemed as affected as he did now. Could he be reacting like this because…?

I rasped in air, realising I'd been holding my breath as that thought had been going around in my head.

Opposite me Andrew sat really still.

'No way,' I whispered. 'No—'

'No!' he cut over me. 'Owen's not— He's not ill in the sense of a disease.'

I made myself smile. 'Okay, that's… cool.'

Andrew arched a brow and then sighed. 'This whole situation's just difficult, Jamie.' He pushed fingers through his hair. 'And, today… Well, I'm sure you know we had a disagreement last night about your father.'

I hadn't actually heard it, they'd been outside, but yeah I knew. Felt a bit guilty actually since I was as much to blame for not kicking dad out straight away as Owen was. On the flip side, I felt better knowing that the distance today wasn't a health thing. 'He'll get over it.'

Andrew gave a wry smile. I was probably lucky he didn't tell me off for my part in Thursday's events.

He picked up the pen and looked over the crossword. He didn't write anything, just shook his head. 'I really wasn't concentrating.'

I looked at the circles and the holes in the paper.

'I hate being apart from you kids,' Andrew said softly.

'Then just fire him, Andrew,' I said without much thought. 'That'd solve everything.'

Surprise flickered across his face, then he shook his head. 'I don't need to, Jamie. Not with the restrictions in place.'

'Yeah, and they're working *so* well,' I grumbled. 'Owen's having nightmares again, *you're* ruining newspapers.' I jabbed a finger at it. 'And that argument last night wouldn't have happened if you'd kicked Owen's butt out the door when this all started.'

Across from me Andrew was still, expression a mix of surprise and irritation, but that didn't stop me from saying, 'It's a shit-load of stress on *everyone*. It's… it's not fair, Andrew. If Owen stopped working for you, then you could stay over again and be a proper guardian.'

Andrew's gaze was sombre. I could see he was upset too but I didn't back down now that I'd let my inner feelings out.

'I've thought about it, Jamie,' he said after a moment, 'but Owen asked me not to.'

'Why? Can't he see we'd be safer if—'

'Jamie, it's not…' Andrew drew in a long breath. 'Look, I know that Owen not working for me seems a simple solution, but it actually isn't. Despite restless sleep, he's reasonably calm. I don't want to rock that boat by forcing him into a change of situation.'

'But you'd be with him at night,' I pointed out.

'That's not the be-all and end-all, Jamie,' he responded with a sigh. 'And it's also exactly what your father doesn't want.'

'Yeah, but if Owen's not working for you then you're not breaking any law, and dad can't do anything about whether you stay the night or not.'

'You father won't stop, Jamie.'

'I *know* that,' I said. 'And Owen turning eighteen isn't gonna make any difference either, but if he didn't work for you, dad can't do anything *legal now.*'

'Jamie—'

'This isn't f—'

'*Please,*' Andrew said, almost with a cry.

I sat back, mouth slamming shut. Andrew sat still a second, then dragged in a breath. 'I know this is a terrible situation, but please…' He drew in a breath.

I tried not to stare as he blinked his eyes clear. A boulder lodged in my throat, thankfully, because I was angry and upset and at least I couldn't say something stupid and make things worse.

If I hadn't watched Owen flipping the blade on his wrist last week, I might have pushed further for him and Andrew to understand it wasn't just them affected by this. But I *had* watched, and he had told me why he did it. Deep down I understood Owen was walking a fine mental line. Despite the unfairness of the situation, I didn't want him to cross that line.

Across from me, Andrew hadn't moved. I whispered an apology to him and he gave a small nod in return.

[Thirteen]

Owen

Andrew was the one who looked tired, but it was me who fell asleep during lunch on Tuesday.

I would have blamed Andrew because he'd had a lunch/work meeting and left me alone in the office, but when I opened my eyes and spotted him sitting on the couch opposite me his expression was only concern.

Should I leap up and look alert in case he had brought his client back with him? Should I pretend I'd just been resting my eyes a second? Should I—detach the pencil from my cheek where I'd fallen asleep on it. I rubbed the indent in my face as I shifted into a sit. 'Is everything okay?' I croaked.

Andrew ran his tongue over his teeth. 'You tell me,' he said softly.

'Pardon?' Puzzled, I bent down to pick up the sketch pad that had fallen to the floor, flattened out the creased page.

'Owen.'

I looked up at him, then did a swift gaze around the office. Just him and me.

I brought my gaze back to him. 'I must have fallen asleep,' I heard myself say, knowing there was no doubt about it. A glance at my watch showed me I'd slept almost two hours. 'Oh.'

'Hon, do you think you should see a doctor?'

'What?' I yelped out.

'I'm worried about you,' Andrew said softly.

'I'm not sick,' I told him. 'I was only asleep.'

'Deeply,' he murmured. 'I called your name several times.'

I frowned for no real reason, and got up, holding the pad. 'Your fault for leaving me alone,' I muttered.

Andrew drew breath, rose. 'Owen, please, I—'

'I'm fine,' I growled out. 'And you should look at yourself. You're the one who looks sick.' I shoved a hand over my mouth, but I realised that right then he did. Maybe it wasn't tiredness that made him look drained. I bit my lip. '*Are...* you sick?'

'No, I'm not,' he responded quickly. 'Just still recovering from the conference.' He let out a sigh. 'Sorry, Owen, I just... I panicked when I saw you. You looked so...' He didn't finish that sentence, instead asked what I'd been drawing.

'Nothing.' I held the pad against my chest.

'You're holding it like you want to hide something from me,' he commented softly.

I told him I'd just been drawing stuff. My breath hitched a little. Didn't know why I couldn't show him.

Andrew didn't badger me about it, just opened his arms and I stepped into his embrace, struggling to keep back a wall of sudden tears. His arms curved my back like safety belts and it hit me then that it'd been ages since we'd been like this.

The restrictions had seemed to make us afraid to show our physical affection openly, and over the weekend things had been strained because of dad's stupid visit. I squeezed my eyes tight, clenched my teeth to try and prevent fresh heartache finding voice.

Then he had to go and kiss the top of my head, and I was out and out bawling. Not a reaction that would reassure him I was perfectly fine.

Andrew just held me, didn't seem bothered the art pad and

my hands were sandwiched against his gut.

After a while I choked out, 'I want him to go away and leave us alone. We were doing okay, weren't we, before he came back? We were all happy.'

'Definitely happy,' I heard him murmur.

'Then why'd he come back and ruin everything?'

Andrew shifted his hold to my shoulders, pushing me back a little. I was almost too ashamed to look up and let him see my wet eyes. His hands didn't leave my shoulders. His gaze was sombre. 'Owen, was he violent went he showed up last week?'

I went still, puzzled, then realised how he'd taken my comments and my crying. 'No.' I shook my head. 'No, he didn't hit anyone, I just…' I let out a long sigh and gazed down at the house I'd drawn. I turned it to face him, causing him to look even more concerned, as I said, 'Why can't we have a dream place where we can all go and he can't follow?'

I let him take the pad when he reached for it, and he stood there for ages staring at my drawing. I almost wondered if he even recognised it as a house. He looked up at me and I saw that his eyes swam.

'Angel,' he said on a quiet breath. He pulled me to him again. 'I want so much to be able to give you that peace, to shelter you from all this pain and misery.'

His voice cracked on those last words.

'Andrew?' I whispered.

He just held me tighter, so that I felt his body shake once or twice like he was trying to hold it together.

I pushed him back a bit so I could see his face; definitely had tears in his eyes. I reached a hand up to wipe them away, but he caught me before I could. He brought my hand to his lips, kissed my knuckles. I heard a soft thunk as the pad dropped onto the couch behind him and then his other hand caressed down my cheek.

Our mouths met, hot and starved, and my fingers gripped around his neck to keep him close. My pants got tight pretty fast and I could feel his desire, but neither of us made any move toward a couch. A tight embrace and a deep kiss were the priorities right now.

Don't know how long it was before I sagged against Andrew, drained, and he whispered, 'I so needed that.'

I huffed out a breath and straightened to stand under my own steam. 'I'd like more.'

Andrew's eyes darkened momentarily but he said, 'So would I, but we can't here.'

'We could go to your apartment.'

He grimaced. 'I've a meeting at three. Too late to cancel now.'

I stomped a foot, which made Andrew laugh. He grabbed me to him and kissed my forehead.

'I'm serious about this,' I growled, pushing him back.

He grinned. 'We'll sort something out,' he said. 'Later in the week. A special meeting or something.'

I cocked my head. 'Promise?'

'Oh shit, yes.'

The sincerity in his voice and in his eyes almost made me cry again, but I hauled in a steadying breath and nodded. 'Okay.'

He chucked me under the chin then told me to go wash my face, and I flushed that I probably didn't look so hot.

When I came back out, Andrew was sitting on the couch

eyeing my design.

'You're getting pretty deft at this drawing game,' he told me as I took a seat opposite.

'You're just saying that.'

He snorted. 'Do you know how many comments I get about that?' He pointed toward his desk, to the framed drawing of the Pantheon I'd done months ago.

'What, like did a monkey do it?'

He laughed, but he knew I'd heard some of the comments. He tapped the drawing on his knees. 'Pretty soon everyone will be asking you to design for them, not me.'

'Hardly,' I got out with a laugh. 'Anyway… that only came out like that because it's what I felt.' When Andrew's brows came together a little I added, 'Besides, who'd want stuff designed by some emotionally unstable nitwit?'

'I would.' He smiled but his tone was serious.

'You're biased.'

'Always,' he murmured, gaze dropping back to the design.

I watched him looking at it, a little uncomfortable in fact that he was seeing something from my inner self. Deeper than the secret I'd carried about the carving knife. *Well*, I thought, *at least he hasn't asked if I did* that *last week*. I hadn't. It was at least two weeks since the last time, and I hadn't thought about it lately either.

I smiled when Andrew glanced up briefly, then looked at my watch. 'You've got half an hour before that meeting. Why don't you have a nap?'

He straightened, looked about to argue, but then said, 'Only if you promise to wake me in twenty minutes.'

'Of course.'

Even though I hated the lie, I didn't ring Owen back immediately and confess.

Tonight I needed a break, and it wasn't so I could take a client to dinner, it was simply so I didn't have to wind myself up to that time-slot where I had to bury all I felt and put on a brave face for everyone. Not today, after Owen had told me about his dream house.

Not after he'd told me *I* was the one who looked sick. I wiped a hand over my face. I didn't feel sick, just exhausted. When combined with Owen breaking down, the design, *and* the kiss, I just couldn't face having to tell him good bye tonight.

My beautiful young man had been fine when I'd told him I wouldn't be around this evening so I expected he'd taken the reason hook, line and sinker. He hadn't sounded *relieved* but I was pretty sure my full absence was infinitely easier on him than me being present and then leaving. I knew that messaging "good night" last week, instead of phoning and hearing him, had been a heck of a lot easier for me and I guessed it was the same for him.

Owen had told me to enjoy myself and that he'd make his own way in tomorrow. Basically saying I didn't need to get up early after a late night just to come and get him.

I put my head in my hands briefly. I wanted to get around there right now and hug him, make love to him, but I just sat in the office dealing with a stomach twisting into knots.

And letting my anger grow.

Perhaps it wouldn't, if I could find a speck of sympathy for their father or even belief that he truly wanted his kids back.

From my view, he seemed only acting to undermine Owen, attack him for everything he'd ever done, and turn him into the stressed and drawn kid I'd known a long time ago.

Worst thing was, the man was winning. Owen's reactions today showed me that, even if I didn't know already from the return of the nightmares that had been absent for months, the moments of hard-headedness followed by painful doubt, some nights smiling as I left, some not.

I wanted to tell Owen that I felt all those things too, the worry that we wouldn't make it through this horror, to let him know he wasn't alone. But I couldn't, beyond what he saw himself, sure that revealing it would only make him worse.

I blew out a breath; kissing him today had been a mistake, reminding me what was at stake. And now I'd promised him something later in the week. I didn't know what and I didn't know how, but I was going to keep that promise like my life depended upon it. Like Owen's did.

On the days that Owen displayed doubt and despair, I thought that his life *did* depend on me. He'd told me he'd only ever once considered actually using the carving knife, but I'd texted him that day to see how he was and he said that saved him; last year when he'd been waiting for the results of the HIV test. The distance between then and now barely soothed me, but I trusted him. He'd been honest about laying the knife on his wrist recently and the counting and why he did it.

Telling me today how he *really* felt meant so much.

And it helped settle the unease in my gut, except I still didn't pack up and go spend a few hours with him and the kids.

My thoughts centred on the cause of everyone's stress: their father.

He attacked for two simple facts—he was homophobic and he was jealous of how Owen had kept the kids together while he'd been off doing his own thing. They'd not gone without anything and certainly hadn't seemed to feel any lack where their missing father was concerned, and he was unable to deal with that.

His cruelty grew my anger, but I couldn't act. My position remained tenuous because of Owen's age.

'Just fire him, you bloody fool.'

I sat back in my chair and laughed.

Such a simple thing, but I couldn't do it, not even after that difficult Sunday chat with Jamie.

It wasn't just the ability to be together at night that Owen and I wanted or needed, it was simply being with each other on our own terms.

And I wanted to see Owen during the day, watch him at work applying his skills, teach him the ins and outs of my business. I needed that normalcy as much as I needed to be able to hold him intimately and not worry about repercussions.

Not firing Owen meant I couldn't be a proper guardian, but I just couldn't bring myself to do it. Definitely not when he'd pleaded with me not to fire him.

I made myself draw in a deep breath and check my emails, trying to use work to clear my head before it got so bad I dug the bottle of bourbon out of the cupboard behind me.

Owen

Jamie tapped on the door as I was unsuccessfully trying to get Matty to have some chicken soup.

'I don't like it,' our little brother grumbled, pushing the spoon away.

'How do you know you don't like it?' I asked. 'You haven't even tried it.'

'It's soup.'

'You *like* soup.'

'I don't,' Matty groaned. 'Go away, Owen.'

'I feel like I shouldn't interrupt this comedy,' Jamie said dryly from the door, 'but that was Andrew. You've got a meeting this avo, Owen?'

I'd started to frown at his opening line, but stopped. 'Shit, what's the time?' I swivelled back to the clock on the nightstand. 'Oh phew, plenty of time.'

'So… you do have a meeting?'

I stood, bowl and spoon still in my hands. 'Yeah, at one.' I looked from Jamie to the bowl to Matty, and back to Jamie. He started to straighten. 'Come on, Jamie, I need to go get ready and Matty needs to eat *some*thing.'

'Not soup,' Matty grumbled behind me.

Right now I didn't care what he ate, but Jamie must have seen my frustration. 'Get outta here then, I'll see to the shrimp.' He took the bowl and spoon.

Matty gave a weak cry of complaint over being called a shrimp but I didn't stop to hear how Jamie responded to it. As I rushed between bedroom and bathroom Jamie yelled out, 'Andrew said not to forget the logie plans.'

I paused a second, thinking *what?*, then went back to the business of having a shower and brushing my teeth. In dress pants and blue shirt, dragging a comb through my hair, I leaned back in my brothers' room. 'Loggia, it's a covered porch.'

'Sounds thrilling.'

Guess Jamie wasn't having much luck with the soup either. Matty stuck his tongue out at me. I smiled and said I'd be home about four.

'Whatever,' Jamie said. 'Matty, look, here's a piece of chicken, so it's not all soup.'

I backed away before I could see or hear Matty's response.

Just after one, with a long package in one hand, I stood outside a dark green door trying to control my nerves. Centipedes had been using my spine as the I-80 since I'd picked up the "plans". I'd been doing my best to look business-like, but was really only just managing not to be looking over my shoulder every few feet.

I had to wipe my sweaty hand on my pants before I could pull the key from a pocket and slot it into the lock. Once inside the dim silent entryway, I let out a nervous breath. My lips, though, were wiggling about and I finally let them curve into a very excited grin, relaxing as I shunted out worry and let in anticipation. Though I did try to keep tight rein; had to do one more thing before knowing that the plan had been successful.

Drawing in a steady breath, I crossed to the black door with the number four beside it. I fisted my fingers tight just to hide the tremble, and then knocked. Sounded like my heart was knocking an echo. The lock clicked and the door shifted. My heart stopped a moment, but then Andrew stood in the doorway.

'What's with this being late?'

I grinned at him, holding up the tube. 'Had to get the loggia plans.'

Andrew chuckled and stepped back so I could enter his storage unit.

The door closed behind me and I turned. Andrew arched a brow. 'That is one hell of a devilish grin you've got going there, Angel.'

His voice came out all rough and I didn't have one myself. I set the tube on the dresser, noticing that my fingers were still shaking. In fact, I felt fluttery all over. I hauled in a breath and then looked back at Andrew, for a second not quite sure how to proceed. Except, when he opened his arms, I was against him like glue, fingers hooked into the back of his shirt. His arms came around me just as tight.

Wasn't like I'd not seen Andrew for days, but today... *now*... I turned my head to gaze over the bed, shifted a little to see it better. Yeah, I was seeing right. The bed had sheets and a proper cover. I looked up at Andrew.

'We're going to be all class this time,' he said in a whisper.

I grinned. 'I don't mind being unclassy with you.'

Andrew pressed a quick kiss to my lips and then stepped back. 'So, you actually got some loggia plans?'

I didn't care that he wasn't taking me to the bed straight away. Just being here with him, knowing we'd get there eventually, was enough for me to be fully relaxed. We had ages anyway. 'Yeah. Jamie mentioned them to me.'

'Ah... I was trying to sound official.' He picked up the tube. 'What is it?'

'Poster for Matty. He's miserable.'

Andrew looked at me. 'Not feeling better then?'

'Well, not worse,' I said. 'Though I did leave Jamie trying to get him to have some of that chicken soup.'

Andrew sucked in his lips, probably imagining quite rightly

how that was likely to go. 'Blowing off your brother's welfare for a meeting.' He shook his head.

'I'm looking after my own welfare.' I stepped back to him. 'And yours.'

'Mm?'

I reached behind his neck, encouraging him down so I could kiss him.

Our mouths open against each other ignited the flame that I'd been trying to keep under control since yesterday when we'd sorted out this "meeting". My knees were already weak and I clutched at him to keep myself upright. And then a dose of reality washed over me.

Andrew felt me go still, and lifted his head. 'What is it?' came out in a croaked whisper.

My face was on fire. 'N-nothing, I just...' Hadn't given thought to this beyond being with Andrew in bed. I was dying for that, had been for *weeks*, but how was I going to do it? It wasn't the sex I was having a freak-out over; it was the undressing.

Shit, it was stupid but I still couldn't undress under his gaze. I wanted to and part of me had probably thought that this time I'd do it because I'd be so in the moment but... I couldn't. God, I was going to look a right dork asking Andrew to turn around now!

Way to kill the mood!

'You'd better strip yourself, Owen,' Andrew suddenly said. 'If I do it, you might lose some buttons. That'll be too hard to explain.'

I looked at him, startled. He smiled but I knew why he'd said it. He understood why I was suddenly all weird, and he was trying to make it easier for me. 'R-right,' I croaked out.

'No buttons, not good.'

He kissed the side of my head and shifted away, turning to the dresser that his grandfather had made. God, I loved him so much. I so wanted to say, 'Hey, turn back, I want you to see this' but couldn't. I shed my clothes quickly, heaped them on a box out of the way, and climbed into the bed, amusement zapping me at the fact I did actually need to climb. The bed, also made by Andrew's grandfather, was higher than a standard bed. Built for storage, Andrew had told me the first time I'd come here with him. There'd been boxes stacked under it then.

I hauled the smooth cool sheet over me but shoved the cover to the wall. When we'd last been here there'd only been blankets then and not even a pillow. I wondered if Andrew had sorted this out last night after he'd left us. Tried not to think that he'd been sleeping here as a sort of safe place.

As I shifted the pillow under my head, I looked to see how far away Andrew was from joining me, and a massive bolt of déjà vu slammed the air from my lungs.

Nude and full frontal and pretty much lined right up with my sight.

'Hm, licking your lips is a good sign.'

I felt so hot with embarrassment that Andrew had seen that I was sure I was going to set the bed on fire. 'Just get in,' I rasped, flinging the sheet back and shifting onto my side to give him room.

Andrew did, laughing, and took the sheet from me to get himself under cover. When he'd done that, he cupped a hand to my face. 'Anyone would think *you're* the one with the fever.'

'Sh-shut up-p.'

His hand slid around the back of my head, exerting barely

any pressure to get me to shift right in against him, lips locking. That hand then travelled down my back to curve around a buttock, squeezing slightly. I had no idea where *my* hands were let alone what they were doing. I felt his lips on mine, his hand on my butt, and how much he wanted me against my thigh and that's all I needed.

Then he rasped out, 'Holy…' and I realised where at least one of my hands was. Spread amongst the hairs at his groin and hooked around part of his stiff penis. Any other time and I'd probably have pulled back because, though I was fully and totally into our love making, my hands weren't usually that adventurous.

But today… instead of immediately lifting off, my fingers just stretched out and grasped more of him.

I kind of liked that he was panting.

He moaned my name against my lips and then rolled me under him. Cool air drifted down one side as the sheet slipped, allowing me to curve that leg around his hip. The other one was hampered by the sheet, but we'd made love in my own single bed before and difficult bedding had never stopped us. Certainly didn't now.

Andrew lifted a little to rearrange himself, huffing out a moan as I pressed fingers down his spine to his backside. My muscles all contracted at the first tentative press but then I let out a deep breath, arching up with a moan of my own as he slipped in.

'Okay?' he whispered.

'Very,' I got out on half a breath, tightening my arms around him.

His lips pressed to the side of my neck and then came back to my mouth as one arm circled beneath me. We had to give up kissing at one point because both of us were panting and in need of breath.

Andrew raised up so he was almost on his hands and knees as he thrust in against me. I think he wanted to see my face to make sure I was okay. I was more than okay and if my legs wrapped around his and my hands scoring his arms and back didn't tell him I was then at least my face would. I was smiling broadly, my gaze slightly blurred with bliss as I felt the orgasm build in me and saw the love blazing in his blue eyes.

Catching my breath, I reached to grab around Andrew's neck to bring him back down on me as my nerves all sang at once and I exploded against him, arching into his weight, feeling extra heat soaking me. My muscles were doing their own jig and then Andrew stiffened for a second before letting out a long low moan as he experienced his own pleasure. I hugged my legs around him even tighter, making sure he wouldn't pull out too quickly.

He didn't. He sagged onto me, breathing heavily, lips tickling just below my ear, that one hand still curving my butt. He quivered a little as his muscles finally settled, and then let out a long sigh. 'Owen,' he breathed. 'Owen, Owen, Owen.'

I hugged him, hot, sticky and totally serene. Emotion squeezed my eyes tight. 'B-best meeting you've ever asked me to attend.'

Andrew laughed, deep and genuine. 'Best for me too. Feel like my bones have melted.'

That made me totally smug.

Shortly after that he shifted free of me and just lay at my side, a warm arm over my chest. We somehow got the sheet over us and then I think we both slept.

I did anyway, because when I opened my eyes, Andrew was

ferreting in something by the dresser, wearing pants but no shirt.

When he glanced over his shoulder I smiled at him, making him grin and straighten. 'You look pretty pleased with yourself.'

'It's been a good afternoon,' I whispered, curling further into the sheet.

Andrew's smile made me feel like *my* bones had melted. I stretched and pushed up onto a hip. 'Do we have to go?'

'Nope, just didn't want to sort out our now very late lunch naked.'

'Lunch?' I leaned over to spy what he'd been focused on. A picnic hamper. 'Hah, thought that was just something else you had stored here.'

'It was,' Andrew said. 'But when I came last night to sort the bed, I spotted it and thought we'd do lunch since we'd work up an appetite.'

My face heated at his grin, and I shifted closer to the edge of the bed, aiming to grab my clothes without getting up. A soft packet landed just in front of me; wet-wipes. When I snuck a look at Andrew he was absorbed with the hamper, giving me some privacy for a quick clean-up.

'Thanks,' I murmured, moving to his side once I had underwear and shirt on.

'No… problem,' he said, arching a brow at my attire and smiling as he turned away.

I asked what he wanted help with.

'How about you tidy the bed? Then we can sit on it.'

So I did that and then we made ourselves comfortable, plates spread out between us with sandwiches and even two travel mugs of tea. 'Did you bring this all in last night?'

Andrew chuckled and shook his head. 'I brought it with me today. We'd be drinking cold tea and dry food otherwise.' After he'd taken a sip he said, 'I had planned for us to eat first but... you were too good an entree to pass up.'

I stuck my tongue out.

'I was also going to bring champagne,' he added, 'but decided that might be a bit over the top.'

'Hard to explain why I might be drunk after a meeting,' I mumbled around my mouthful.

'Indeed.'

'Next time,' I said.

His brows went up. 'You'd do this again?'

'God, yes,' I told him. Then, quietly, 'You... wouldn't?'

'Oh Owen,' Andrew said, 'I'd do this even with your father pointing a gun at my head.'

I swallowed. 'Um... okay.' I called up a smile. 'Kinda wish you hadn't... said that, but okay.'

'Sorry,' he mumbled, sipped at his tea. 'It's how I feel though, what I'd do for moments like this.'

'Me too,' I croaked out, trying to banish the image in my head because it scared the shit out of me *and* kind of turned me on. I reached for another sandwich.

Andrew let out a long sigh and leaned back against the wall. His lashes sheltered his gaze from me and I stayed silent. He obviously needed to gather his thoughts.

I scratched a knee, grinned as I realised just where I was and how, shivered as I ran the last hour through my head. Goosebumps rose on my arms and I rubbed them. 'How is it so cool in here all the time?'

Andrew jerked, making me eye him. His hand came down on my knee, fingers warm. 'Stone building,' he said. 'Cool in summer, colder in winter.'

I snorted. He slanted a smile my way that chased away the bumps. 'What?' I heard myself say. 'I'm dessert now?'

Andrew laughed out loud, but he didn't take his hand off me. Well, not completely; it slid off my knee and up my thigh. I licked my lips in anticipation, leaned toward him as he straightened up from the wall.

The kiss was long and deliberate, like we'd been put into slow motion or something, or maybe we were just savouring the fact we could kiss and no one was here to prevent it. Andrew's arm curved around my back as I shifted onto my knees to get closer. I had one hand planted on his thigh, fingers hooked into his pants pocket, the other touching warm skin at his shoulder. His free hand smoothed up and down the back of my thigh.

Ending the kiss, I sagged on a hip against him and he hugged me tight, steady breathing soothing all my fears.

'I love you,' he murmured against my temple.

'Love you back,' I said. 'Wish we could stay here forever.'

Andrew twined his fingers with mine, raised the clasp as if he was inspecting it. 'We're almost there, Owen.'

I let out a long sigh. 'I know.' It was just under two weeks until my birthday; we could hold out until then. 'We'll do this again, right?'

'Better believe it.'

'Good.'

Silence after that for a bit, then Andrew let out a breath. I shifted straight. 'You're going to ruin the moment, aren't you? Say it's time we have to go.'

'Yep, sorry.'

'It's okay,' I said. 'You've got work stuff and I...' I pulled a face. 'Guess I should get home and make sure my brothers haven't killed each other.'

Andrew smiled. 'That bad when you left, huh?'

'No,' I admitted, 'but it could be now.'

'I'm sure it'll be fine,' he said, sounding just a bit wry.

I got off the bed so I could start packing the hamper with the containers he handed me. 'Are you going to take this with you when you go?'

'No, I'll come back later,' Andrew said. 'Tidy that too.' He pointed at the bed.

Once we'd closed up the hamper Andrew picked up his shirt, making me turn away to shuffle on my pants and then socks and shoes.

'I'll bring the poster when I come over tonight.'

'The… Oh, right.' I eyed it on top of the dresser. 'I could take it.'

'Best I do, Owen,' he said.

I looked at him a second then asked if he thought someone might have been watching.

He shook his head. 'But we should still be careful.'

I gave a single head nod, and found butterflies starting to gather in my stomach.

'I'll be around as early as possible,' he said, changing the subject. 'Bring something for dinner.'

'Yep,' I said with a nod. 'That'll be good.'

'Meanwhile, you're going to have to stop looking so smug.'

My face heated.

'Go on,' he said, smiling. 'I'll see you later.'

I stuck my tongue out. I really wanted to stick it in his mouth but we couldn't stay here any longer. I made myself reach for the door. Before I opened it and took the first step back into reality I turned back to him. 'Thank you, Andrew,' I whispered.

He swallowed hard, didn't speak. Just nodded.

I smiled myself and then went out the door. In the dim entryway again I hauled in a big breath and let it out slowly. Did that a couple more times, then walked down the hall to the main door.

It's all good, I thought, *it's all good.*

I did a quick check that my clothes were all fine, then unlatched the door.

- # -

After we'd all said our good-byes to Andrew for the evening, I went to my room to get the journal I'd been reading. Just as I was stepping out again, Jamie blocked the doorway, making me jerk in surprise.

'Are you okay?'

'What? Why wouldn't I be?'

Jamie took a step forward, which meant I shuffled back into my room. 'Uh… well, smiling when Andrew leaves isn't something you've been doing a lot of lately.'

If he was here just to push buttons, he was going to have to try harder. I was in a great mood tonight. I just shrugged at him. When I sidestepped, he moved to keep in front of me. Alright, great mood slipping. 'What do you want, Jamie?'

He cocked his head as if he was consulting with himself on what to say. He said, 'Obviously a good meeting today, huh?'

A smile hit me before I could control it, and Jamie looked slightly alarmed. I managed to say, 'Yeah, good. Stuff sorted.' Memory was showing me how good and I really needed Jamie to get out of my room.

'I want Andrew here at night.'

Alarm crashed through me before I could separate my memory and his words, and then it was all about his words. 'He can't, you know that.'

'Then stop working for him,' Jamie said, 'It's that simple.'

'It's not, Jamie,' I replied, fingers tightening on the journal. 'I'm the one paying the bills, remember? If I'm not working, then—'

'Andrew can—'

'No!'

Jamie took a step backward even though I hadn't moved. 'I don't want us without him at night anymore.'

'He wasn't always—'

'I *know* he wasn't always here,' Jamie cut over with a growl. 'But that was before dad. I don't like us being alone. Andrew's our *guardian*, Owen. Stop being selfish.'

I recoiled, stepping back from him.

'Well, damn it, you are! It's, like, two weeks to your birthday. How many pay days is that? Is it even *one*?'

'It's not actually about the pay,' I said quietly. 'I can't not see Andrew during the day.'

'You'd see him at night,' Jamie pointed out.

'It's not the same.'

His brows went up.

'Jamie, I can't be here at home all the time. I just… I can't cope with that. I'm sorry.'

I stepped around him and left the room, struggling to get my happy back. Jamie didn't come after me.

The situation was shitty, I knew that. But being at home all day… I couldn't do it anymore, not if I had to act like everything was fine. It didn't matter that Lisa and Matty had lots of summer school stuff on, or that Jamie had picked up extra hours at Walgreens. It didn't matter that some of the days I'd just be on my own. I couldn't be *here*.

Sitting on a stool at the breakfast bar, I flipped through the journal, trying to call back my great mood. Behind me Matty and Lisa yelled answers to a TV quiz show. With their racket it was hardly surprising Megan had decided a bath was a good idea.

'Hey, you fake that sickness today?'

Glanced over my shoulder to see Jamie on the couch, eye on our little brother. Matty coughed. Wasn't put on, but he looked kind of sheepish.

'Mm hmm,' Jamie let out. 'Back to summer class tomorrow, I reckon.'

'I'm not *that* better.'

I huffed a soft laugh and turned back to the journal. Jamie'd been dealing with Matty half the day, and I was perfectly fine with letting that continue now.

'You need to get to bed,' I heard him say.

'But it's not that late.'

Jamie let out a snort. 'It's actually after your bedtime, Shrimp, and you've been sick all day.'

'You're mean,' Matty announced. 'Owen!'

I held still a second, then twisted on the stool. Matty was kneeling on the armchair, looking at me. Beyond him, Jamie was rolling his eyes. 'What?' I asked.

'I can stay up late, right? Cause I—'

'Nope, Matty,' I cut over him. 'I back Jamie.'

Matty's lips got incredibly pouty. Trying not to smile, I got off the stool and came forward. 'Well… maybe you have a choice.'

Matty perked up. I caught Jamie's gaze, and his lips pressed together. Despite our little argument earlier I hoped he'd run with the plan now. I focused back on Matty and said, 'You go to bed now and rest and be perfectly fine tomorrow. I think Andrew said something about dinner out.'

'Dinner out? Where would—'

'*Or,*' I interrupted, hand up, 'you stay up late tonight and spend all day in bed tomorrow recovering, with Jamie looking after you.'

'Yeah,' Jamie said, putting in a heap-load of enthusiasm.

Matty blinked, then leapt up. 'Good night.'

Lisa looked surprised as Matty hurried out of the lounge, but she shouldn't have. Dinner out was as good a bribe as any with Matty, though the threat of Jamie playing nurse again probably helped just as much.

I smiled after him, then thanked Jamie for playing the mean brother. He kept his reaction to just a brow shift, then turned to the TV, joining in with Lisa on calling out quiz answers. I headed down the hall to check that Matty really was going to bed.

Jamie

I picked up the phone, half expecting silence, ready to put it down again the moment I realised it. Except it wasn't a nothing call.

'This is Sergeant Morrison. Is this Owen?'

I cleared my throat. 'No, Jamie, do you—' I turned, looking for my brother; he was outside at the table with Andrew.

'Is Mr Gordon with you, Jamie?'

'Yes, of course.'

'Good, can I speak to him please?'

'What's this about?' I asked, even as I started across the lounge.

I wasn't exactly surprised to hear, 'Please just get him on the line.' Sergeant Morrison putting on his authoritative tone.

'Yeah, okay.'

Andrew and Owen were making words with the Scrabble tiles, no board in sight. Didn't notice me until I set the phone on the table. 'The sergeant wants to speak with you, Andrew.'

They both jerked, showing shock.

'I don't know what about,' I said when Andrew opened his mouth.

Andrew's gaze went to Owen who sat rigid on the bench, then he rose and picked up the phone. He was already moving away from the table, heading inside, as he said, 'Sergeant, what can I do for you?'

I slumped to the bench beside Owen as he twisted to track Andrew's movement through the window. Andrew was nodding, set a hand to his head briefly, but he didn't seem overly stiff or anything.

'Morrison phoning out of the blue really freaks me out.'

I glanced at Owen. He pulled a face.

'Could just be ringing to wish him a happy Father's Day,' I said.

Owen rolled his eyes, picked up the pencil he'd been using to score their weird game and began tapping it on the table.

'You never know,' I said with a shrug. 'This day is already awkward.'

My brother let out a soft groan but I knew he thought that too. Lisa and Matty had made cards for dad, even though no one had known if he'd show up. Matty had had to be prompted by Megan before he made a card for Andrew (though he did it cheerfully enough). The pencil started tapping the tiles with a click, click, click.

He stopped when he obviously noted me sitting straighter, twisting to see that Andrew had just come out onto the deck. He didn't have the phone anymore.

'What's up now?' Owen asked, reorganising himself to sit like me, back to the table. Guess he already knew their game was over.

'Your father is coming around.'

'What?' That was me and Owen together. Amazingly, neither of us jumped up.

'God, *why?*' I groaned.

'Because it's Father's Day,' Andrew said quietly.

The snap made us jump, and we stared at the two halves of pencil in Owen's white-knuckled grip.

'That's rich,' he said in an insulted tone. 'Why did *Morrison* ring?'

'To tell me about the impending visit,' Andrew said, sounding kind of careful. 'Your father sought his permission and he agreed.'

'Do you have to go?' I asked.

He shook his head. 'And the sergeant has told your father that I am here.'

Owen made a feral sound deep in his throat, but didn't speak.

'I need one of you to get the kids back from the play-lot.'

I frowned. 'What if we don't want dad here?'

Andrew didn't answer me; his gaze was on Owen as he stood and said, 'I'll go get them.'

For a ridiculous second I had no idea what he was talking about. Then I jumped up. 'I'll do it. *You* won't come back if you go.'

'Fuck off,' he said quietly.

'Christ, now is *not* the time to start an argument.'

Owen and I both started a bit at the flash of frustration. Andrew didn't apologise, just said that dad was due at three, which was in about forty-five minutes. 'Go on, Owen,' he said. 'Don't linger though, please.'

Owen grimaced, then asked if it was just dad or Melissa too.

'Both of them,' Andrew said. 'That's why the sergeant said he'd given his permission.'

'Heh,' was all the response Owen gave.

'Finally he's following the rules,' I muttered.

Owen gave a nod to that, handed me the broken parts of pencil, and went indoors.

Andrew and I maintained our silence until we heard the front door close. As I sat again, I said, 'You wanted me to go, right?'

Andrew looked stern a second then rueful. 'I did, yes.'

'Because you thought exactly what I said?' I pushed.

He let out a sigh, shifted past me a bit and started tidying away the Scrabble tiles. I didn't swivel on my seat to help. 'I wouldn't blame him not wanting to be here,' he said quietly.

'Me either,' I admitted. I didn't really want a visit myself, and I was oddly unsure about it because Andrew would be with us.

Not that I wanted him to go, but it seemed like ages since he and dad had seen each other and a lot of shitty stuff had happened since then. I glanced over my shoulder. Andrew's lips were pressed tight and he seemed singularly focused on putting the tiles incredibly neatly in the bag.

'You okay?' I asked.

Though he started, he smiled. 'Of course, Jamie.'

I didn't think he really was, but I wasn't going to push. The rest of the tiles got dropped in the bag without order.

As Andrew straightened, he suggested I go sort out tea and coffee stuff. I didn't want to draw out their visit by offering refreshments but Andrew said, 'Go on. And I'm sure we've got some biscuits we can put out', and I realised I didn't really have a choice.

I thought he might stay outside to take a moment but he came in after me and started to give the lounge a bit of a tidy.

As with all visits with dad, this one was awkward. I doubt any of us had expected it to be otherwise.

Well, apart from Matty. He was straight out thrilled to have his father present on Father's Day. The fact dad hadn't been around *last* Father's Day because he'd abandoned us didn't seem to get a look-in with the kid. I knew his excitement was wearing Owen's tolerance ice-thin. And given what Owen usually went through when dad visited I wasn't surprised to see that *he* wasn't relaxed at all.

Though… I think that was because of Andrew's presence, because he was waiting for dad to drop some random snide remark about Andrew and/or their relationship and/or his guardianship.

Andrew, on the other hand, was incredible. As much as his being calm and accommodating annoyed me, I couldn't deny that it helped keep everyone else good too. He and Melissa, after a little bit of hesitation on her part when she and dad first showed up, were chatting and smiling. I didn't think he was on a charm offensive, just that he found her to be a nice person, like the rest of us did even if we weren't admitting that openly. Their chatting brought Owen a little out of his shell.

Maybe because dad wasn't at the table with them. He was getting a garden tour by the kids who were showing off their gardening skills.

I let out a soft breath; gardening skills actually taught by Andrew and Megan. It amused me a bit that Andrew knew how to do gardening things given he lived in an apartment, but he seemed to really enjoy getting into the dirt with Megan and the kids. And he was as proud as they were when dinner included things that had been grown right here.

Megan had, like the last visit, taken on Sam-sitting as her main role. They were on a blanket under the tree, playing with brightly coloured blocks. I caught Andrew's gaze their way several times but he already knew that Megan had taken to the baby.

I was also at the table but choosing to listen rather than speak. Andrew looked at me a couple of times too; guess he was surprised I'd been keeping my thoughts to myself, but since dad wasn't sitting with us, it was fairly easy to do so.

Fairly easy to lose the calm in seconds too, I found out when Matty clambered up the steps and came rushing up to us. 'Dad's gonna put in a swing from the tree,' he said excitedly. 'Isn't that cool? I've wanted a swing for ages.'

'You've never mentioned a swing in your life,' I told him, aware that Owen straightened, looking like he'd been about to say the same thing.

Andrew looked startled.

'Yeah, I have,' Matty announced.

Behind us dad said, 'I'm surprised you've not built a swing

for the kids, Mr Gordon.'

'I haven't actually been asked to, Mr Tremayne,' Andrew said, lips imitating a smile.

'Well, guess it's not something a guardian would think of.'

'Chris, that's too much,' Melissa warned, turning to dad. 'Don't start something stupid. It's been such a nice afternoon.'

'Just making an observation, Mel,' he said, sounding like he'd just been observing how warm it was.

'Yeah well, *don't*, Dad,' I said, getting up. 'Matty's never bloody talked about a swing before. Don't try to make it sound like Andrew's done something wrong.'

'Jamie,' Andrew said, 'it's okay, your father can make his observations. That tree *would* bear the weight of a swing fairly well.'

Owen mumbled something, gaze on the mug he'd been playing with.

'What was that?' Andrew asked gently.

My brother lifted his head, eyes a bit squinted. 'It's not okay, playing you off against him for Matty's attention. And it's not fair. Dad, why can't you just accept matters as they are? Why do you always have to be mean about everything? If we don't have a swing, it's not Andrew's fault!'

Dad opened his mouth but Melissa rose and put herself directly in front of him. I didn't really catch any words but her tone was firm and insistent. Across from me Owen was actually scowling at Andrew who, for a moment, let upset show in his expression. Owen obviously saw it because he huffed out an apology. Andrew gave a brief shake of his head and then he was on his feet as Melissa announced that they were going to go.

She looked upset herself, but smiled at us. I felt a lump in my throat over suddenly conflicted feelings—anger that she'd split mum and dad up but also grief that she was as stuck in this horrible thing as much as we were. Andrew was talking but I focused on my little brother because he still stood there, now looking unsure about everything.

'Hey,' I said to get his attention, tried out a smile. 'Why don't you and Lisa gather up those cards you made dad so he can take them?'

I heard a sound from Owen but didn't look his way.

Matty nodded even though he still seemed a bit unsure, but then he was calling Lisa and pretty much dragging dad back inside. I knew dad's reappearance but not living here was confusing but how was it that Matty couldn't seem to read the situation like the rest of us? Was it because he was so young that he took everything at face value? And quickly forgot things again?

That meeting on Megan's birthday had been horrible and he'd reacted badly to dad, but since then that'd apparently been missing in his memory. Dad was simply dad, and all those months of him being missing and then finding out he really had just walked out on us didn't seem to matter to our younger brother.

It bugged me a lot. I trailed my hands back through my hair, watching dad, Lisa and Matty through the window, jumping when Melissa said, 'It was good to see you again, Jamie.'

I almost said, 'What?' but caught myself and said something polite back, trying not to sound stiff. Dad's shittiness wasn't her fault.

She smiled then reached for Sam as Megan brought him onto the deck. 'Thanks for entertaining him, Megan, you're a wonderful baby-sitter.'

Megan blushed. 'He's so easy to take care of.' She exaggerated a pointed look at me and Owen, but it made Melissa let out a soft chuckle and even Andrew smiled as he encouraged everyone off the deck.

Well, Megan and Melissa. Owen didn't look like he was budging for anything and I decided to stay with him. I didn't want to stand in a row of people fare-welling dad like it meant something.

- # -

Dinner didn't come with the nothing-is-wrong facade it usually did. Matty was in a huff because of the swing comments earlier and kept making this ridiculous *hrumph* sound. Owen ate with a rigid jaw, and I went outside just to avoid it all. I thought he might come too but he probably didn't want to leave Andrew alone to be railroaded into agreeing to put up a swing.

It was Lisa who came outside with me, telling me as she sat down, 'Matty's a dick sometimes.'

I almost choked on my mouthful. 'Jeez, Lis, tell it like it is.'

She rolled her eyes. 'Well, he's being dumb. All the times he's climbed that tree he's never mentioned a swing.'

'Yeah, we know.'

'It's just because dad mentioned it.'

'Yeah, know that too,' I said, trying not to grind my teeth. '*He* was being a dick also.' Winced that I'd said that in front of her.

'I still don't get why he doesn't like Andrew,' she said after a moment, glancing in at the window. From her angle she probably wouldn't see anyone at the table.

From where I sat, I could see Megan but no one else. I turned back to Lisa, unsure what to say. Aside from the bad visit on Megan's birthday, she and Matty hadn't heard dad really spouting off about Andrew (or Owen). And today had been the first time they'd met Melissa. I wasn't quite sure they got the whole connection there though they hadn't been backward in talking to her. And I'd seen Lisa sitting with Megan and the baby for a short while too.

I'd sort of expected at least one of them to question something about mum or Melissa's possible role as a stepmother, but neither of them had. Maybe they just didn't think about it. I wanted to ask Lisa right now but couldn't get the question out of my mouth.

Instead of saying something more about dad and his crazy things, she said, 'Andrew liked my card.'

'Yeah,' I said, smiling. I think Andrew had been a bit surprised to receive cards from Lisa and Matty but he'd looked really pleased too. Megan and I hadn't done cards but we'd both said "Happy Father's Day" to him. I definitely hadn't felt weird saying that because he *had* been a father to us, even with his hands tied.

'He said I had really good drawing skills,' Lisa said proudly.

'You do, Lis,' I told her. 'You, Megan, and Owen—all arty.'

Lisa blushed a bit, but I wasn't telling a fib. Andrew had been impressed with her rendition of his car. Or maybe he'd just been surprised *she'd* drawn it and not Matty! I bit back a smile at that.

Owen stepped onto the deck. 'Hey, Andrew's leaving if you want to say bye.'

'It's already time to—' I cut off as Owen shook his head.

'God, has Matty driven him to it?'

A wry grin sped across Owen's face. 'No, headache. Though *probably* Matty related,' he added in a mumble. 'He's got a big meeting tomorrow so I told him to go home early, get some rest for it.'

'Makes sense.' And a headache was as good an excuse as anything to escape our little brother.

Lisa and I followed Owen back inside.

Andrew looked a little embarrassed when he saw us but also tired, so getting away from us early was probably a great idea.

Megan hugged him at the front door. 'I know you would have been here anyway, but thanks so much for today.' She cleared her throat.

'Oh, Hon,' Andrew said, looked lost for words for a moment.

I wasn't sure if she was thanking him for being like a father or thanking him for being here and staying when dad and Melissa came. Possibly both. I was grateful for both and told him that directly.

Andrew let out a sigh, thanked me for my words, didn't try to say anything like how it was good we got to see them and the kids could hand over their cards.

He gave the kids a hug, Matty having spun his roundabout and was smiling again. When I glanced at Owen he just shrugged. Well, we were used to Matty's sudden changes of mood; by morning it was likely that he himself had forgotten all about this one.

Andrew opened the door and Owen followed him out to the car.

He was back in about five minutes, looking relaxed. I was impressed over that given how weird today had been. He didn't speak to any of us, just picked up the book he'd been reading and headed outside. Megan caught my gaze and I gave a shake of my head. No, I didn't know what was going on. No, I didn't think anyone should follow him. Megan let out a breath.

Lisa flicked on the TV and we let ourselves be entertained by channel surfing.

I realised Matty wasn't in the lounge about the same time he came rushing inside, crying. 'Owen's mean. I hate him!'

'Whoa, what?' I hooked a hand around his arm as he tried to get past me, glancing over my shoulder as I did so. Just in time to see Owen throw his book. 'Ah…' I turned back to Matty. 'What happened?'

My little brother balled his hands against his eyes. 'He t-told me dad wasn't g-gonna live here. That no-one w-wanted it. He told me to sh-sh-shut up-p-p.'

'Yeah, well,' I heard myself say, which made Matty step back. Before he could say that he hated me too, I said, 'Owen's just in a… weird space at the moment, Matty.' I didn't think I'd heard him be so blunt to Matty before; today had obviously battered his tolerance.

'I hate him,' Matty insisted.

'Okay,' I said. 'Haters gonna hate.' I turned away before he could speak again, stepped outside.

Owen hadn't moved to pick up the book, just stood with his back to me.

'You know you made Matty cry, right?'

I saw his jaw tighten but he did nothing else, didn't refute, didn't tell me to shut up, didn't turn. God knows what combination of words Matty had used to get Owen this way but he was clearly angry. I went forward to pick up the book, straightening the bent pages.

When I turned around, facing him, he glared at me. The evil eye didn't stop me seeing that he'd been crying too. Did stop me from getting any closer or making any further comments. Angry *and* crying wasn't a combo Owen had displayed lately, but it was one I knew. With him, it eventually led to something more physical and no one needed that tonight.

I walked past him, set the book on the deck, and went inside.

Megan was on her feet, concerned.

'Don't do it,' I said as she took a step. Owen needed space.

That made her stop a moment, but then she tilted her jaw and ignored my warning. She walked right up to Owen, said something with a sort of smile, and then hugged him. He stood stiff, hands at his sides, but I saw his head drop a bit to her shoulder.

She had her eyes closed and I felt like a sort of voyeur so I got away from the door, focused on Matty as he said, 'Did you tell him off?'

'What? No.' I perched on the couch arm. I dared myself to say that I was on Owen's side about this. Especially after today.

'He's a dick,' Matty announced.

'Okay, stop,' I said, grabbing him as he went by. 'Firstly, don't say things like that. It's not nice. Secondly, have you somehow forgotten what dad did to Owen, how he bruised his face? Have you forgotten how you screamed that you hated dad?'

Matty's mouth went all pursed but I couldn't tell if he was

angry or just trying to remember.

'With how nasty dad's been to Owen, and to Andrew, how can you possibly think that Owen wants dad here?'

'He's *dad*,' Matty said with all the logic of a child.

'Yeah,' I said. 'And he's the one who walked out on us only four months after mum died. He's the one who took more than a year to even let us know he was still alive. He's the one who—'

'Enough, Jamie.'

The words were quiet but I cut off as if Owen had shouted over me. He stood just in the door, book in one hand, Megan stopping at his side. They were both red-eyed. I swallowed, but Owen wasn't angry anymore; he gave me a ghost of a smile and focused on Matty, who looked like he didn't quite know what to do—run off, yell, cry, something else.

'You're too young to get it, Matty,' Owen said, 'but today wasn't a fun day.'

'I had fun,' Matty said, puzzled.

'Yeah, but Andrew—' Owen cut himself off. He rubbed at his eyes a second and then shrugged. 'I'm going to bed.'

'What?' I croaked out, startled.

'I don't know how to explain it all, Jamie,' he muttered. 'And I don't wanna get into an argument. I've got a headache too.'

'Want me to make you a hot chocolate?' Megan asked.

Owen gave a crooked smile. 'No, I'm good.' He looked down at the book, then back at her, murmuring, 'Thanks.'

She just shook her head.

Owen glanced at me and then headed out of the lounge, all of us staring after him. I wanted to ask Megan about what I'd seen outside, but didn't because I knew *I* should have been the one to stay with Owen. I turned to my little brother. 'Bedtime for you, too.'

'But I don't have to get up early tomorrow.'

'It's still bedtime,' I said, not budging.

'You're as mean as Owen,' Matty said.

'Trying to be,' I told him. 'But you've not called *me* a dick yet, so clearly Owen's better at it.'

Megan's breath caught, but Matty just poked his tongue out. He wandered out of the lounge without another word and I turned to my sister who stood staring. I let out a breath. 'I'm with Owen on this one, Megs.'

'Me too,' she said after a moment. 'I just…' She shook her head. 'This is really hard.'

I couldn't tell her it was going to get easier; seemed like that was too far a stretch.

[Fourteen]

Owen

I glanced over at Andrew, smiled that he was slouched, head on his chest, asleep. He'd looked tired earlier but hadn't listened when I said he should just go home. Wasn't like he had meetings to stay for.

He was still snoozing when I started to pack up. Good, he'd gotten at least two hours' decent sleep. I didn't want to wake him, but also didn't want to leave without him actually knowing I'd gone. I called his name. No response.

When he didn't respond to a slightly louder call, I shifted closer and poked his arm. Nothing.

Harder poke, louder call.

Nothing.

My heart jumped into my throat as I peered closer at him. *Was* he just asleep?

I leaned down, holding my breath so I could hear his. Didn't hear it, but I felt it against my cheek. Faintly. I grabbed his arm and shook him, and when he started to slide down the couch at my movement I cried out Anne's name like she'd hear me.

Letting Andrew go, I dashed around the couch, heaved open the office door. 'Anne, I can't wake Andrew. He's breathing but I can't… can't wake him.'

I hadn't really stopped to see that she was actually behind the reception desk, but she was. She didn't speak, just saw my worry, and hurried into the office with me. She couldn't get Andrew to wake either.

'Keep trying, Owen,' she told me. 'I'm going to ring 911.'

'What?' I croaked.

'It's okay,' she said in a steady voice. 'Just keep trying to wake him, I'll be back in a second.'

She could have used the phone on Andrew's desk but I got the feeling she didn't want to make the call in front of me and panic me even more.

I got Andrew into a more comfortable position on his side with a cushion under his head, doing my best to rein in fear that he was totally unresponsive and might have been all this time without me noticing. Wedging myself onto the couch beside him, one hand crunched around his and the other squeezing and rubbing his upper arm, I closed my eyes, unable to look at him but also attempting to keep my eyes dry. Kept telling myself *He's just asleep, he's just asleep.*

But who slept like this? Who didn't wake up after such prodding and poking and name-yelling?

Anne returned and sat on the coffee table, squeezed my knee when I asked her why he wasn't waking up. 'Sometimes sleep is just that deep, Owen,' she said softly. But she looked worried and she *had* called the emergency number. 'Do you want me to get you some water or something?'

I shook my head. Turning back to Andrew, I pinched his arm, trying not to think how many bruises I was giving him. 'Andrew?' I couldn't yell with Anne right there even though I wanted to scream his name. 'Come on, please w-wake up.'

Muscles shifted under my hand, making me lift it a second before clamping it back down hard. 'Andrew!'

Anne called his name too, leaning forward to pat his pale cheek.

Andrew made a sound not unlike the sort Jamie made when

he didn't want to be woken, but where it'd normally make us back off with him, I squeezed Andrew's arm harder and Anne called his name again, sharp this time.

He groaned and shifted his face inward toward the cushion, then mumbled if it was time to go.

'Y-yes,' I choked out. 'S-so wake up-p.' I held my breath in an attempt to keep my relief from turning into tears.

'This overtime really has to stop, Andrew,' Anne growled at him.

I looked at Anne. 'Overtime? He's not…' I trailed off when I realised she wasn't talking about just now. I looked down as Andrew's fingers wiggled in my clawed hold. I relaxed my grip just a bit, and his fingers came around mine instead of the other way around.

Andrew's eyes opened but were semi-focused. After a short breath he mumbled he felt like he could sleep a hundred years.

'No way!' I cried. 'Keep your eyes open. Don't close them!'

His gaze sharpened on me just a bit, and then slid over to Anne and I think he realised then that there was something serious going on. He started to shift, like he was going to get up. I pressed down on his shoulder and Anne told him to stay still. 'I've got medics coming,' she said. 'In fact, they should almost be here. I better go wait for them. Owen, don't let him up.'

I shook my head and then she was gone.

Andrew breathed my name.

'Y-yeah?'

'Don't let me g-go.'

I chomped on my lip like the sudden burst of pain would stop my eyes filling at how weak he sounded, at the stammer, at the *words*.

'I won't,' I whispered, even though it was actually his hand holding mine in the vice-like grip now. I ran my free one up his arm and across his shoulder, kept up that circular motion, as we waited for Anne and the medics.

- # -

'Is that a new shirt?'
'What, this old thing?' Andrew plucked at a button. 'Nope, had it for ages.'
'Oh,' I said. 'Just looks different.'
'Probably because I actually ironed it,' he said with a smile.

This morning's conversation came back to me as I sat at Andrew's bedside. The shirt had looked different not because of the ironing but because it sat differently. Andrew had lost weight. Not a physical illness like cancer, but the same reasons as his collapse earlier: he hadn't been resting or eating properly.

'Why didn't you tell me?' I asked.

But Andrew was asleep, leaving me to run through the horror in my head.

He'd been so concerned about ensuring the rest of us were okay, me especially, that he'd not properly looked after his own stress. Guilt stabbed at me that I hadn't seen past his smiles. And, last week, I'd seen him naked but hadn't noticed the weight loss, which was crazy since I'd been looking hard enough.

Hated myself for not having really processed how hard this situation was on him. Hated him, briefly, for having hidden it from me. Swapped back to hating myself because I shouldn't have *needed* him to tell me. I ran my fingers over his hand.

'I'm sorry I'm so weak.'

Unable to be with us at night, Andrew hadn't wanted to be in his apartment apart from when he really needed to sleep. So, after he'd left the house each night, he'd gone back to the office to keep his mind occupied. That client dinner he'd had last week? Didn't exist, he'd just stayed at work.

I'd let Andrew down. We'd been together properly eight months. I should have been able to read him better. I should have realised he'd put everything he had into helping me and the others. I should have *known* he'd bury what *he* felt.

'I will from now on, Andrew,' I whispered. 'I promise.'

I didn't let Andrew's hand go when I heard the click of the door, just twisted to watch a young guy wheel in a tray.

'Oh, still asleep, huh?'

'Yeah.' Swallowed the croak. 'The doctor thinks a while yet.' I glanced back at Andrew. 'Which is only good.'

'Well, I'll leave this here. It's a fresh salad so it won't go cold.'

I nodded. 'Thanks.'

'You're welcome to it,' the man said. 'If you want. I can always bring another later.'

I gave a jerky nod, and my thanks this time was crooked.

He raised a "no problem" hand and left, pulling the door closed.

I glanced at my watch. Just about to go six, dinner time. I didn't actually feel that hungry, and then frowned at Andrew. He kept going on at me about my eating; seemed a tad off that he'd not been taking his own advice. Though… we both ate at dinner and generally shared lunch in the office. I let out a sigh, and rose to pull the trolley closer.

Lifting the dome lid revealed a pasta salad with spinach, tomatoes and bacon pieces. Seemed pretty flash for a hospital meal; mine hadn't— I clanged the dome down in an effort to cut memories of my own time in hospital. I turned my back on the trolley, took up Andrew's hand again.

- # -

Andrew sat in the armchair in his hospital room, dressed and ready to go home, but having to wait for a final blood result to come back before he was fully cleared to go. He looked a hell of a lot better than yesterday, smiling when I gazed at him.

I managed a shy smile back, but I wasn't over the fright he'd given me by a long shot. And we had a fair bit of talking to do, but I kept away from that—right now wasn't a good time or place.

I'd come this afternoon to walk him home. He could have taken a cab to his apartment but he'd wanted to walk the few blocks, claiming the fresh air would do him good. I sort of thought otherwise, since it was smoking hot outside, but the doctor had agreed.

The doctor had also forbidden Andrew to return to the office until Thursday and I knew Anne had rearranged most of this week's meetings, even those on Thursday and Friday. He could do work on his laptop but I really hoped he'd just take the time off to simply sit around and rest.

'From tonight on, Owen, I'm staying the night.'

'What?' I got out, startled, because he spoke out of the blue. Then puzzled because… staying *where?*

'With you and the kids,' Andrew murmured. 'I can't be away from you anymore.'

'But…' I straightened up from the windowsill where I'd been leaning. 'Dad… the restrictions…'

'I know,' he responded, 'but I can't—'

'God, just fire me.'

'What?'

'Fire. Me!' It came out all but yelled, making Andrew rear back. I slapped a hand over my mouth so I couldn't take it back.

Then he said, 'I… I don't want to, Owen. I need to see you during the day.'

'You'd see me at night,' I croaked out. Couldn't believe I was saying that, echoing what Jamie had told me the other night. I sagged against the bed. 'I've been so selfish, needing the day too. Night's not a silver bullet like Jamie thinks, but you not staying is hard on *every*one, Andrew, not just you and me.' I looked down at my feet a moment, muttered, 'The others need you as much as I do. You *are* their guardian.'

'I know it'd get us out of a loophole,' Andrew said, quietly, 'but it won't make your father any less antagonistic.'

God, I was really channelling Jamie here because I said, 'But dad couldn't *do* anything. No law would be being broken, so he'd have no…' I dragged in a breath, felt drained all of a sudden. After a small silence, I said, 'It's only a week, Andrew.'

To be honest, that was probably the only reason I was mentioning the firing thing—because after all the stuff we'd been through the last two months, a week suddenly seemed like nothing. A duration that I'd finally be able to cope with.

I didn't *want* to be fired but I didn't want to argue any longer with Andrew about stupid restrictions which dad didn't give a toss about anyway.

Andrew didn't speak and then I said, 'I don't reckon the doctor will think being at home is a good idea. Hardly a relaxed place to recover.'

He pulled a wry smile. 'The company will be good for me.'

I gave a soft snort, looked down at my shoes again. Would be nice to have us all around tomorrow, but from Thursday… with him back at work, I'd be at home and I… I was just gonna have to *cope!*

'I'll work from home,' Andrew said.

'What?'

'I can do most things on my laptop, even Skype meetings,' he said. 'If Anne lets me,' he added with a wry smile.

I must have looked puzzled because he said, 'I don't want to be away from you during the day, Owen. Yes, it's just a week, and we'll have the night, but I want the day too. This thing'—he indicated the room—'has made me realise how much I need you.'

I felt a flush working its way up my neck. 'I n-need you too,' I managed. After a second, I inclined my head. 'So… you're agreeing to fire me?'

He let out a sigh. 'Yes.'

I came to him and dropped a light kiss against his cheek, feeling his arm squeeze briefly around my shoulder. I'd have sat on the chair's arm if we hadn't been waiting for the doctor.

My stomach flipped about, nerves pinging as I suddenly realised what all this meant; Andrew and I would be in bed together tonight. My eyes stung and I had to blink hard.

'We should have sucked it up and done this ages ago, you know,' I said with a croak. 'Would have saved a lot of stress.'

Andrew gave a small smile even as his eyes filled. I didn't feel total alarm over that; we'd already been told it was the exhaustion choosing another way to display itself. I think it embarrassed Andrew so I pretended I didn't notice.

Andrew

In my apartment, while Owen packed a few more things for me to take to his house, I officially fired him. Even though it was only for a week and I'd still be seeing him, it was bloody tough writing the letter of dismissal, printing it out and signing it. Tougher to give it to him when he poked his head in the study door.

He read it with a sigh, then nodded and folded the letter in half and then half again. Tucking it into a pocket he said, 'I look forward to sleeping in tomorrow.' Though he smiled, I knew he was still upset.

'I've got another letter here,' I said, patting the laptop. 'Ready to give you next Wednesday.'

Another smile but he didn't speak this time. He looked about the study and I stayed quiet, just watching him. His gaze came back to me and we looked at each other a long time. I heard him swallow hard, and then he said, 'W-what do you need to take from here?'

'Um,' was all I managed right then.

I came around the desk and enveloped Owen in a tight hug. He didn't pull back but he didn't put his arms around me either. After a moment I rubbed up his back and let him go. As I turned back to my desk I noticed a hand go to his eyes.

'Not much,' I said, returning to his question. 'Laptop and all its bits and pieces. A couple of notebooks, my diary.'

He nodded. 'Do you want to sort that then? I'm going to make a cup of tea.'

'Sure thing,' I said.

Once he was out of the study, I emailed the letters through to Anne with an explanation, so she could do the HR things. Then I telephoned Sergeant Morrison to let him know what was going on.

I wasn't sure he was a whole bunch pleased, but when I explained the last two days to him I doubted there was much he could do to prevent mine and Owen's plan. Certainly couldn't argue that we'd be breaking any restrictions.

'I presume the order against Mr Tremayne will stay in place?'

'Yes, Mr Gordon,' he responded. 'That has nothing to do with the restrictions.'

'Thank you, I am glad to hear it.' Winced at how stiff I sounded. 'Do you need a copy of the dismissal letter?'

There was a small pause and then he said he'd better have one for his records. He dictated an email address and I sent him a copy as soon as I cut the call.

Owen was sitting at the breakfast bar when I brought my work bag out. He poured me a cup of tea and encouraged me to sit on the stool next to him. 'I rang Megan to let her know you were coming home.'

'Oh, good plan,' I said. 'And we should stop by the—'

'No,' he cut me off. 'We're going straight home, no detours. There's plenty of stuff in the fridge for dinner.'

For a second I felt like a naughty school kid. Owen's lips curled up.

'I actually feel very well,' I said.

'Don't care,' he told me. 'Once the cab's dropped us at home, *you're* going to bed. And you're gonna eat there.'

'How're you going to enforce that?' I asked, amused.

He laughed outright. 'Not me. Megan. She knows the doctor's orders.'

'Do I detect a little bit of devil in you, Owen?'

He smiled into his tea, and my heart expanded. Even banished to the bedroom, it was going to be wonderful being home with Owen and the kids and not having to leave again.

Owen had been right about Megan. After an emotional greeting when I stepped in the door, she ordered me to bed and told everyone to stay away so I could have some peace. Everyone included Owen.

He smiled *told you so* at me and said he'd bring me a cup of tea later.

Whether he did, I didn't know since I slept the entire afternoon. That proved, of course, that the doctor had been right about getting rest. I felt better but I still had a way to go before I was fully functioning.

Sun slanted across the bed as I pulled myself more comfortable. Fortunately, where I sat I couldn't see myself in the mirror over the dresser. I doubted that the few hours of sleep had brought much colour to my face. Bristles rasped against the fingers I ran along my jaw, making me wince and regret not shaving as soon as I'd gotten to the apartment.

I'd do it tonight, sure that Enforcer Megan would let me up for a short time. I hoped to eat dinner with the kids, despite Owen reckoning she wouldn't let me.

Running my hands through tangled hair, I smiled at how amazing Megan was for someone so young. Sometimes I even thought she was coping with this whole parental mess better that her older brothers, but I really needed to talk to her directly about it. Ensure that she *was* doing okay.

The chance actually presented ten minutes later when Megan poked her head around the door. 'Oh,' she said, like she hadn't expected me to be awake. She offered a smile. 'How're you feeling?'

'I'm doing okay, Hon,' I said. 'Come in and talk with me a while.'

She didn't actually hesitate but kept the door ajar as if she was aiming to be brief in the visit. When I patted the bed she sat, the sun tinting her blonde hair even more golden. 'Are you really doing okay?' she asked in a whisper.

I nodded. 'Just need to refresh my energy levels and I'll be as good as new.'

Her expression showed a dash of doubt but I was sure that Owen had reported, fully, what the doctor had said.

'I'm really sorry for worrying you all,' I said softly. I hadn't expected to collapse so I'd worried myself too, but Owen had told me of his panic and how the kids had reacted when he'd gotten home last night. I hated causing them more anxiety.

Megan sucked in her lips a second then apologised that they'd all been putting me through stress.

'Hon, it's not your fault.'

She did a head shake/shrug combo.

After a moment of silence, I asked if *she* was really okay, adding, 'This has been a very hard time for everyone. Do you have what you need to be okay?'

Megan cocked her head, gaze showing a little bit of surprise. 'Yeah, I'm fine.' Her brows knitted a moment and then she smiled. 'Alana's invited me to go to California with her in July. I kinda… I'd like to go.'

'I'm sure that would be a wonderful break for you,' I said,

smiling myself.

'You'd let me go?'

'Of course, Megan,' I responded quickly. 'Well, as long as her parents agree.'

'She's already asked,' she said, with a bit of a flush on her cheeks. 'They want me to come along.'

'Then we'll get it sorted.'

Megan's brown eyes filled but she smiled as she wiped them dry. 'I really am okay,' she said. 'Just… this mess seems never-ending. I do want a break. We all need one.'

'Yes, we do.' Couldn't have done anything but agree, given where I sat.

Megan sniffed then rose, offered up another smile. 'It's great that you're going to be here from now on, Andrew. It'll really help all of us.'

'I'm relieved to be here too,' I said, emotion sending my voice a little crooked.

Perhaps that's what made her offer to give Owen ten minutes to see me.

I gave a soft chuckle. 'I'd like that, thanks. And a cup of tea, maybe?'

'Okay, but you'll be eating dinner in here. You know that, right?'

'I'd hoped to eat with you at the table,' I tried.

Megan shook her head. 'Tomorrow night maybe.'

I laughed. 'Owen was right that you'd be my rest enforcer.'

She stuck her tongue out briefly, but was smiling as she left the room.

I let out a long sigh. Megan really was a strong girl. I reflected that she hadn't had much choice for a long time now but I was so proud of her. A trip to California would be incredibly beneficial though, and I would definitely back her getting some time away.

Owen

It was weird being home with Andrew. Not that I didn't want that but to go from seeing him only at work or on the weekends followed by having to farewell him at night to now being able to sit with him on the couch twenty-four-seven if we wanted was weird.

I still felt like I was breaking a law even though I was now unemployed. That sticking point in the law and the restriction had been in our faces so long it was hard to let it go.

That was probably why we weren't sitting on the same couch now. Afraid, somehow, that doing so would break the spell. The same at night—even though we slept in the same bed very little happened there that'd indicate we were a couple. Wasn't like we *never* had our own space in bed but it suddenly seemed more awkward advancing our relationship now than when we'd been curtailed.

Even if there were times when it was just me and Andrew.

Mrs Carter was happy to have Lisa and Matty next door or take them places, and Jamie had picked up more hours because of a sick workmate. Megan was at home but she wasn't in our faces pretty much ever.

At least Andrew wasn't working himself sick. He'd obeyed his doctor's order that he wasn't allowed to work until Thursday, and when Thursday arrived he only did a few hours. Dealing with things that his partners or Anne couldn't complete without his input. He closed the laptop at noon and said, 'How about an outing?'

I had my nose in a book, actually reading this time, and responded, 'Huh?'

Andrew gave a small smile as he set the laptop on the coffee table. 'Today I'm released from being housebound. I want to get the car.'

I almost asked what car, but that was the Mercedes still in its park at the office. 'Man, I forgot that it wasn't here.' I looked at him. 'Are you okay to drive?'

'I've had enough rest,' Andrew replied.

Wasn't sure that really answered the question but I looked about and said, 'Shall we sneak out before Dr Megan stops us?'

He chuckled and rose, stretching. Might have been about to agree but Megan came in from outside carrying scissors and a bunch of flowers.

'Megan, Owen and I are going to get my car,' Andrew said. 'Is that okay?'

She looked at him startled. 'Why're you asking—' She turned a scowl on me and I held my palms up, trying not to grin.

Andrew didn't hide his own amusement. 'We should only be an hour or so, get a cab there. Will you be alright on your own?'

'Yeah, of course,' Megan said. She carried on into the kitchen and found a vase for the flowers.

Andrew and I looked at each other and then I popped onto my feet. 'Well, let's get going.'

Megan didn't actually talk to us again until we were just stepping out to wait for the cab at the gate. 'Hey,' she said, coming from the kitchen. 'Any chance you could go by a supermarket on your way back? We need a few things.'

'Sure, Hon,' Andrew said, taking the paper and putting it in his back pocket.

'Thanks. And don't tire yourself out, okay? Owen, make sure he doesn't.'

'You know you just asked us to do grocery shopping,' I said. 'That's not exactly a walk in the park.'

Megan bit her lip.

Andrew patted my shoulder. 'There's only a few things on the list. I can sleep in the car while you rush in and get them.'

My sister gave a tiny smile as I let out, 'Hmph.'

'I feel pretty good, Megan,' Andrew told her. 'But, don't worry. I won't overdo things. We won't be too long.'

She gave a tight nod, directed me a bit of a scowl, then went back into the kitchen.

I followed Andrew outside, hearing him draw in a deep breath. Wasn't like he *hadn't* been outside these last few days, but perhaps out the front of the house, waiting by the road, was more free than sitting in the backyard.

I squinted at him. He looked a little self-conscious but he smiled, making me smile back.

Andrew

I went into the office on Monday, a little embarrassed to face my colleagues after last week's spectacular health fail but pleased to be there nonetheless. Interacting with other adults, in part, but also because I needed some time away from the house and the kids. Mostly Owen.

Which felt like a strange thing to need, because I really wanted to be with him.

It was that want that I had to have some space from. Even

though there was no barrier to our relationship now, I just couldn't accept that in my head. My want and need of Owen fought against a part of my brain that said if I gave in then we'd be in danger. Whether that was the law or Mr Tremayne I didn't know, but it had been a constant niggle this last week and even harder over the weekend, waking up beside Owen and sharing lazy breakfasts-in-bed.

He'd not initiated anything overly physical himself so I gathered he felt a bit the same. I groaned as I sat at my desk, annoyed that I sat here thinking about things when it would have been so much better if we'd just talked. When I got home this afternoon, we'd have a sit down.

And a serious one too because there was another reason I was in the office. John Laurence, my lawyer, was coming to see me. I wanted him to confirm face-to-face that on Wednesday, when Owen turned eighteen, we'd be done with the law. I reckoned it would only be after that date that I'd get over those weird niggles.

My teeth worried my bottom lip.

Every time I'd kissed or touched Owen since those damn restrictions were put in place a little part of my brain had whispered *rape*. It had even during that wondrous afternoon we'd spent in my storage unit the week before last. I'd blocked it because Owen had been very clear that he was there with purpose, and I'd kept ignoring it because of that, because he didn't seem to link "illegal" with *that* word.

I loved him so much for his feelings that I did my best to keep my darker worries to myself.

Being with him this past week had been both heaven and hell.

I pinned everything on Wednesday as much as Owen did.

His father probably wasn't going to stop, but the hell I'd made for myself would.

I hoped.

- # -

As I sat outside on the bench after dinner, I thought about the plan I'd made in the office—that Owen and I would have a serious talk about where we found ourselves and our relationship. I'd had plenty of opportunity since getting home just after two, but somehow I'd not quite been able to say, 'Owen, let's have a chat.'

He'd been fine with me going to work and he seemed a lot brighter now I was home, so I wondered if he'd also appreciated the short break we'd had today.

I huffed out a soft breath of amusement. We were an odd couple in so many ways.

I, at least, felt better about the situation. John had said everything I'd needed him to say and even left it with me in writing on his firm's letterhead. Two copies, in fact, so one could be delivered to Sergeant Morrison. Wasn't sure he really needed one, but he did have a copy of the dismissal letter from last week so it was probably only right that he had John's letter too—to show Mr Tremayne if he continued to be stupid, more than anything else.

Behind me the younger kids were weeding their vegetable patch, doing it now because it was cooler. I enjoyed hearing them chat and when Lisa brought me a fresh baby carrot I wiped it clean on my jeans and ate it. She eyed me, breaking into a wide grin when I announced it was very tasty. 'Did you try one?' I asked.

'No, wanted you to have the first one.'

I got up and gave her a hug. 'You're a sweetheart. Come, let's find one for you.'

For the next quarter hour, I was down on my knees with her and Matty doing some weeding and partaking in a few more baby carrots.

'We better stop or we'll not have any left for tomorrow's dinner.'

'Should we pull them all out now?' Lisa asked.

I shook my head. 'Keep them in until just before we need them. That way they'll stay all fresh.'

'Okay.'

'You all kinda look like you're plotting something.'

We all jumped, having not heard Owen's approach. I noticed that both Lisa and Matty put their hands down to cover the leafy remains of the carrots we'd been eating. That made me grin. I got up, rubbing my knees. 'Just plotting tomorrow's dinner.'

Owen stepped up, slung an arm around my waist and asked what we'd be having. I let the kids tell him, just stood there loving the feel of him right by my side. Didn't realise I'd tuned them out until I received a poke in the side and heard, 'Your eyes are open but are you asleep?'

'No, rude boy, I'm not asleep.'

Owen grinned and I realised Matty was already on his way inside and Lisa was just rising to follow him.

'Make sure you both wash your hands properly,' I reminded her.

She nodded. 'We will.'

And then it was just us, pivoting so we could watch her cross the lawn and head into the house.

'They've really enjoyed this gardening,' Owen murmured beside me. 'Thanks for doing that with them.'

'God, no hardship, Owen,' I said, gazing down at him. 'I've enjoyed it myself.' I took his hand. 'Come on, our favourite bench awaits.'

I heard his soft breath of amusement, and he didn't hesitate to slouch against me once we'd sat. My arm hugged around him.

Megan appeared on the deck briefly, asking if we wanted a cup of tea. We both did, and I told her we'd come in when it was ready.

When it was just ourselves again, Owen asked if I was going to go into the office tomorrow.

'Not sure,' I said. 'Maybe for a few hours.'

He nodded against my shoulder then said, 'I miss it.' Gave a sort of laugh.

'You're not enjoying the sleeping in?' I managed in a light voice.

Another half laugh, but then he shifted so he could look at me straighter. I rested my arm along the back of the bench rather than let it fall. 'You will, um, hire me back, right?'

'Of course,' I said quickly. 'That letter's already written, remember. Just waiting for Wednesday.'

He squeezed an eye shut, rubbed it, nodding. 'That's good.'

I rested my hand on his knee. 'We're almost through, Angel,' I said softly. 'And we'll be all good from Wednesday.'

Owen didn't speak.

'What's on your mind? Something other than the job?'

Sucking in his lips, he shook his head. 'Just... tired. This thing's been going on for ages and ages, and I don't really feel like my birthday's only two days away.'

'Well, it is,' I said. 'And we've got a big party planned.'

Alarm spread over Owen's face.

'Okay, so a small party with just the six of us,' I admitted, squeezing his knee.

'Don't freak me out like that,' he told me.

I dropped a quick kiss against his lips, then rose. 'Come on, that tea's probably almost ready.'

'Andrew.'

Turning, I watched him stand, brush hair off his forehead.

'Can you… um, I know eighteen makes everything all good but could you ask your lawyer to double-check?' He pulled a face. 'I don't want to be blindsided by something else. I couldn't… *can't* stand the thought of that.'

My breath caught just a moment at his pain and then I told him about John's visit today. 'On Wednesday, Owen, you'll no longer be a minor in any capacity.'

Owen just nodded, a long one that I patiently waited to end.

Megan called out that the tea was ready.

'Thanks,' I called back and then held my hand out to Owen.

He lips pursed and I almost thought he was going to decline to come back into the house, but he stepped forward and slipped his hand into mine, squeezing hard.

'Thanks,' he said softly, presumably for me checking with John about everything.

'We're going to be alright,' I said as we crossed the lawn.

'Yeah.'

[Fifteen]

Owen

I woke on my birthday in my own bed, curled tightly in the bedding even though it wasn't cold.

The location was my own doing because last night I'd had a mini freak out about breaking the restriction. Which was dumb for two reasons—it was highly unlikely that dad would show up in the middle of the night to catch us out and, more importantly, there were *no* restrictions to break since I was currently unemployed.

Still, I couldn't quite shut down the unease. Andrew had accepted my craziness; it'd been Jamie who'd been pissed. Mostly because it meant he had to share with Matty again. He'd gotten quite comfortable in my room since Andrew had been staying.

We'd traded the "It's only one night" argument, stalemate as that was. Andrew was on my side, though, so it was *me* waking up in my room.

Feeling stupid more than anything, but as I lay there, looking at the golden outline around the curtains, I sensed relief starting to build.

I'd started thinking that time had slowed down and today would never show up, and even darker thoughts that *I* wouldn't make it myself. I'd not told anyone but a couple of times my early counting of blade flips had reached single digits. I didn't know if I'd actually cut flesh once I hit zero but I'd done all I could to not get there, bringing out as many fractions as I'd been able to think of in my state.

It'd probably only been the fact that the fractions had frizzled my brain that had stopped me hitting zero, but I also knew that I'd had enough *I don't want to do this* to bring the mathematical things into play in the first place.

I flung the covers back in an attempt to shove away those thoughts. From today the carving knife would be a distance part of my history!

I sat, stretching for my toes. 'Shit, I'm eighteen.'

Until dad had returned, turning eighteen hadn't been any sort of significant in my head. I'd already been leading an adult life and my emancipation helped with that feeling too. Now, turning eighteen seemed like an incredibly hollow victory, and almost fake.

Glancing around my dimly lit room, I found myself somehow surprised at what I had, like I was seeing it for the first time. I hadn't slept in here once Andrew had come home from his hospital stay, so it felt a bit like I was a guest now in my own room.

I yanked back the curtain to brighten the room further and got out of bed. As I grabbed some clothes to go take a shower the door clicked open and I heard Matty say, '—be awake, it's his birthday.'

Then he was in my room and squeezing my breath out in a hug. 'Happy birthday, Owen!'

'Thanks,' I rasped out, smiling.

He only let me go when Andrew stepped up to plant a kiss against my temple. 'Happy birthday,' he murmured.

'Breakfast's almost ready,' my little brother announced. 'Come out and open your presents.'

I looked at the clothes still in my hands. 'Can I…?' I raised my hands.

Andrew chuckled. 'Go ahead, Angel.'

'But be quick,' Matty told me. 'I'm starving.'

'Hey, whose birthday is it?' I asked with a laugh.

'Matty, go see if your other brother needs help making breakfast,' Andrew suggested.

He didn't need to be told twice.

'Jamie's making breakfast?' I asked, surprised.

'Yep,' Andrew said. 'Not doing too bad a job of it, either.'

'Heh.'

After that we stood silent for a moment, and I found myself feeling oddly nervous. Andrew had a contented smile on his face and when he reached for me, I dropped the clothes and looped my arms around his waist. We didn't kiss, just held each other. His breath came out slow and I knew he was as relieved as me that this day had come.

Maybe five minutes later, Andrew released me and stepped back. 'Better make moves before Matty returns.'

'Hah,' I said, but bent down for my dropped clothing. 'He's definitely excited.' Mind you, my younger brother seemed to spend a lot of time in that state. I eyed Andrew. 'We're not doing a secret visit to the MSI or zoo, right?'

He laughed. 'No, not at all. I think he's just caught on that today's a big day.'

'Tonight will be bigger.'

Andrew bit his lip. I flushed but I *did* have plans. Just hadn't meant to blurt out anything now! I saw his half glance at the bed and then he shook his head as if he was arguing with himself. I would have eagerly encouraged him but I reckoned, too, that if we delayed longer we'd get a walk-in by an impatient kid.

'I better go get clean,' I said.

Checking the floor to make sure I'd not left anything behind, I gave Andrew a smile then walked out of my bedroom. Felt smug at my outstanding level of control. Behind me I heard Andrew chuckling.

- # -

Jamie expected me to ring dad and shout, 'I'm eighteen, suck on that' or something like that, but I wasn't gonna go anywhere near that sort of thing. He told me I was pathetic but he agreed, at least, not to ring dad either.

I wasn't even sure dad really remembered when my birthday was, though he obviously knew on some level since everything that was going on was related to it. Maybe he'd not cared enough to know because he thought Andrew or I would crumble before we could get here. Almost had.

Even now, half way through the day, I worried about dad showing up. He'd phoned a couple of times since we'd seen him on Father's Day but not come around. I didn't know if that was Melissa's doing or not, but I was grateful. I'd have hated him coming over when Andrew was here trying to recuperate. Would have done my best to stop it, actually, since I didn't want Andrew to regress or anything. Or, worse, go to his apartment.

He sat outside with me at the table, looked up when he obviously felt my gaze. When I just smiled at him, he smiled too and then went back to a report he was reading. I looked forward to being back at work tomorrow; hadn't realised that I'd be so bored hanging around the house doing nothing.

No, not doing nothing—spending time with Andrew wasn't nothing, but also I'd spent a lot of time just worrying that this day was never going to come!

'Hey,' Jamie announced, stepping out onto the deck. 'You've got a phone call, Owen.'

I straightened and Andrew did the same opposite. 'Who is it?' I asked.

Jamie sucked at his teeth like he was debating about answering, then he put the phone on the table and said, 'Sergeant Morrison.'

'What?' I croaked, looked at Andrew when he let out a breath.

'Well, at least it's not dad,' Jamie said.

Yeah, but what if it was Morrison saying that dad had asked for permission to visit? I didn't want to pick up the phone.

'Owen,' Andrew said softly, 'do you want me to talk to him?'

'No, no it's okay,' I got out, couldn't let him fight *every* battle. I picked up the phone, a bit unsettled that Jamie took a seat beside Andrew. 'Uh, hello, Sergeant Morrison.'

'Hello, Owen. I just wanted to say "Happy Birthday".'

I actually turned to look at the phone, like it'd explain what I just heard. 'Um, th-thanks,' I managed, keeping my gaze on the table, face heating for no reason.

'I know these last two months have been difficult for you,' he said, 'as well as for your siblings and Mr Gordon. Birthday wishes from me are unexpected, I'm sure, but I wanted to let you know that I fully acknowledge the day.'

My eyes were starting to sting and I was doing my best not to need to wipe them. Andrew and Jamie were watching like twin eagles and I so didn't want to be crying in front of them while on the phone to Sergeant Morrison.

I hauled in the steadiest breath I could manage. 'Thank you,

Sergeant. I… I appreciate you phoning.'

'I am sure you are already aware, but the dual restrictions you and Mr Gordon have been under are now fully removed.'

'Y-yes,' I said. 'Andrew told me his lawyer confirmed that'd be the case.'

There was a bit of a pause on the other end and I almost expected him to ask to speak to Andrew. But all he said was that he himself was aware of Mr Laurence's confirmation. 'At this time, Owen,' he added, 'the restraining order against your father remains in place. Unless… you would like it lifted.'

I choked on a breath of surprise, glanced at Andrew who raised his brows and then at Jamie who cocked his head and said, 'What?'

'Ah.' I focused back on the phone. 'No, Sergeant Morrison, I don't want it lifted. Not just yet anyway.'

'Okay, that's fine.' After a short pause he asked if I'd heard from dad today.

I shook my head before remembering he couldn't see that. 'No, he's not phoned.' I didn't say that I wasn't even sure if dad totally remembered my birthday date.

'And you've not contacted him?'

'No way.' Rolled a glance at my brother as I said, 'Jamie wanted me to but I won't. He's not been around since Father's Day. I don't want him to think he can drop by or anything.'

'He still requires permission, Owen,' Morrison reminded me steadily.

I huffed out a breath, didn't say that dad seeking that on Father's Day had just been an aberration to his usual actions. 'Are *you* going to contact him?' I asked, suddenly curious about that.

'Yes,' he responded. 'I need to keep him informed about

the law.'

'Hunh. Guess that sounds normal.' Pulled a bit of a face at how stupid that sounded.

I think the noise I heard was amusement, or something close to it at least. 'I had better go, Owen, I hope the rest of your day goes well.'

'Thank you for ringing,' I said, a bit of a lump in my throat. 'It... it means a lot.' It actually did I realised and when the call finally ended I kind of sat there gripping the phone, struggling to get the lump back down my throat.

'So...' Jamie drawled.

'He wished me a happy birthday,' I said, setting the phone on the table and looking across at them both.

Both Jamie's brows were up but Andrew had only one arched, and then he gave a smile. 'That was nice of him.'

Jamie gave him a *what the?* kind of look, but I agreed with Andrew. 'And he confirmed, you probably guessed, that the restrictions are done with.'

'Yes,' Andrew said, nodding.

'But the restraining order remains in place.'

'Fucking A,' Jamie responded.

I rolled my eyes. 'He said that I could have that lifted, if I wanted.'

'No way, Owen,' my brother said.

'Of course not,' I told him. 'Didn't you hear that bit?'

His lips pressed tight. Andrew looked a little stiff but then he said, 'I appreciate that Morrison is not lifting that himself.'

We all knew it was because my age wasn't a barrier to dad's crazy brain.

Our chat was cut off by Lisa standing at the door, saying, 'The cake's ready but you have to come inside. Megan reckons the icing'll melt if we bring it out.'

We all moved, Jamie nudging me as we stepped inside. 'Get ready to have your ears sung off.'

Lisa and Matty had already treated me to a few rounds of Happy Birthday, but I was happy for them to sing my ears off again. Made the day even more special.

- # -

Heading to the bedroom with Andrew should have been nothing unusual, but tonight—the first one with me being eighteen and everything being undeniably legal—had me almost nervier than the first time I'd slept with him.

I stopped. 'You go on,' I said when Andrew paused. 'I need to check something.'

'You okay?'

'Oh yeah, I just…' I flicked a hand behind like that'd settle his concern.

'Okay,' he said and smiled.

Heat spread through me like my heart was a flamethrower. I turned away and headed back into the dark lounge.

I had a plan tonight, something for Andrew, and to steady my nerves I checked that all the bolts and locks in the lounge, kitchen and entry way were indeed in place, and that the door to the garage was also firmly locked.

Wasn't likely that dad would show up *now* when we hadn't heard from him at all today, but I needed to make sure that if he did then he wouldn't be able to get in.

Of course, I didn't want to think about him right now— this was my night, not his—but I also felt a tonne of relief. He could no longer use mine and Andrew's ages or relationship or anything else against us.

'Stick that, Dad,' I muttered as I checked the front door a second time.

Okay, no way dad could get in unannounced. I forced him out of my head and, after a quick stop at the bathroom, I went to the big bedroom, trying not to bite my lip as I recalled Jamie saying he was permanently taking over my room.

Andrew was in pyjamas, folding his clothes to put on the chair under the window. He turned when he obviously noticed me, but didn't speak. I stood there appreciating the pyjamas—not because he looked outstanding in them but because he wore them. This night wouldn't pass without sex but I really, really loved the fact he hadn't just assumed, hadn't just gotten into bed naked and ready to go.

'You alright?'

I started, flushing that I'd kinda tuned out. 'Yeah.' I cleared my throat. 'More than alright.'

Andrew gave a nod, looked like he wasn't totally sure. I came into the room and closed the door. He folded the last piece of clothing then turned, stopped when he saw me still just standing there. 'Is something wrong, Owen?' he asked a little roughly.

I shook my head.

'And you are…?' He looked at the bed.

'Oh yes,' I said. 'But I—' Shit, my nerves jumped right back to crazy. I grinned, then put a hand over my mouth so I didn't look fully bonkers. 'I want to show you something,' I got out behind the hand.

Andrew straightened. 'Oh… okay.'

'No, get in bed,' I said, pointing.

I had him totally puzzled, but he climbed into bed, sitting

back against pillows. Looked both hesitant and expectant. I came around his side of the bed where there was a bit more space. 'I've wanted to… do this for ages,' I said with a bit of a scratchy throat.

His brows came together in question, and I saw them lift when I started to raise my sweatshirt over my head. I dropped it on the floor beside me, straightened my t-shirt. When I looked at him I saw the beginning of understanding, almost an expression of wonder.

That made me smile as I took hold of the bottom of my t-shirt. I heard Andrew breathe my name as my vision was momentarily obscured and then the t-shirt dropped down onto the other top.

I ran my hands though my hair, like it being tidy was paramount, tried to ignore the fact my nipples were already pointing. Feeling shy and brave, I looked back at Andrew, and tears spiked my eyes because all I could see from him was love.

'Owen,' he whispered. 'You're beautiful.'

'You have to say that.'

He laughed out loud, swiped his hair back.

I had a moment's panic that he'd see my jeans getting tighter, but I was doing this because I *wanted* him to see. I wanted him to understand how much I was in this relationship with him, that everything I was belonged to him, that I was here right *now* because he was everything to me.

'Stop smiling,' I told him with a grin. 'I can't concentrate on this.' The button on my jeans.

He chuckled. '*Who* can't concentrate?'

That made my smile wider. My fingers finally worked in coordination and I got the button and zip undone. I had practised this moment because I wanted to watch his face as I drew down my pants, and yet the manoeuvre wasn't as easy as it looked. I'd fallen over twice when practising, but when I looked at Andrew now and saw his love and appreciation it felt like those two things were actually keeping me stable.

I barely wobbled. Andrew didn't blink, but his lips parted and I heard a ragged breath.

I shunted the jeans out of the way and straightened. Air brushed my skin like tiny wings, raising goose bumps. For some reason my nerves were kicking in again and I trembled as I stood in just my undies.

I wasn't afraid though.

Instead, the feelings flashing over Andrew's face made me feel like I could face down anything. A part of my brain admonished that I hadn't done this undressing ages ago, but I knew I hadn't been strong or confident enough. Tonight I was, and Andrew's reaction told me he was as in this moment as I was.

'Come here, Angel,' he croaked, arms wide.

'Not yet,' I whispered back, fingering the edge of my underwear. 'I need say something.'

He looked a bit like I was torturing him, but his hands dropped back to his lap. He swallowed. 'Go ahead, Gorgeous,' he said when I hadn't carried on.

I nodded but it still took a number of seconds before I had control of my voice.

'I don't tell you often enough,' I began, 'but you are my life, Andrew. Right from when we met you've been my rock, my safety belt, and all this recent stuff…' I swallowed. 'Still my rock.'

I was struggling to hold his gaze, having a harder struggle

when I saw his eyes seemed as wet as mine. He held out his arms again and I nearly caved, but I wanted to finish this for him.

'You've stood by me in everything,' I said on a whisper. 'You've *healed* me. That's why I can do this.' I drew down the last of my clothing, still keeping his gaze. I straightened up, unafraid of being nude in front of him, unafraid of being aroused. I wanted him to see me this way, to know that I was fully here.

Andrew was staring, and I had to drop my gaze as a wave of shyness washed over me.

'Owen.'

I looked up.

'Magical,' he said. 'That… *you* are absolutely magical.'

I felt one of my brows go up.

He cracked a huge smile. 'I am so flattered at how you feel. You're my rock too. I don't know the words to explain how proud you make me, how beautiful you are.'

I felt even more shy, and just a touch self-conscious.

'For the love of God,' Andrew croaked. 'Get over here so I can kiss you.'

He flicked the covers back, shifting to give me room. I got in, reaching for him.

I went into the kiss mouth already open, sinking into a state of nothing-exists-but-him-and-me. One of his hands curved over my shoulder, the other down my lower back, fingers pressing to my backside.

'Happy birthday,' I whispered when we came up for air, looking almost cross-eyed at each other.

Andrew chuckled. 'I feel like it is my birthday.'

I smiled at that, because it was just the sort of response I'd been aiming for. I traced a stripe of his top. 'I think you're overdressed for the occasion.'

His hand captured my finger. 'Oh, you do, do you?'

I leaned up and kissed the side of his jaw, my tongue leaving a trace of its own, breathing out, 'Yeah.'

'Hmm,' came out in a long rumble. 'You know how to undo buttons.'

My brows jumped up, partly in surprise. Andrew let his brows do the same, while his tongue wet along his lower lip. I let out a soft, 'Hah' and reorganised myself to kneel astride his lap. His gaze dropped until I lifted his chin. 'Don't distract me,' I told him, grinning.

He laughed, snatched a quick kiss, and then relaxed against the pillow.

I made my button releasing as slow as I could stand it to be, enjoying how hot Andrew's breath got, how his hands slid up my thighs, occasionally around my waist. His fingers didn't curve into my centre and I appreciated that. I wanted that touch tonight but I loved him for letting that be *my* move, well, my request.

Andrew

Owen stayed curled in my embrace all night.

My lips curved against his head where he was tucked against me, eyes squeezed tight to hold back filling. He'd cried himself, I think through sheer relief and exhaustion that the last two months of hell were done with.

I didn't think they quite were but I couldn't tell Owen that. I just relished that he took comfort in being cleaved to me, that he felt I was his safety belt. That he loved me.

Felt my body start reacting as I re-saw the undressing. Shit, Owen was gorgeous and not just physically. I couldn't explain just how I'd felt seeing him undress facing me, undress purposefully in front of me. I'd been hanging out for something like it for a long time. That he felt like it was *me* who gave him the courage and confidence to act sent me to Cloud Nine.

My embrace tightened around him. He let out a soft breath but didn't speak so I guessed he was still asleep. I lay with him feeling like I'd struck the lottery over and over and over.

What a twist of fate to bring our paths crossing last year. Something I still regretted the circumstances of, but never regretting *him*. My breath issued out in a long sigh as I listened to Owen's soft breathing, feeling like my heart was beating in time to it.

Even if Owen's father didn't give up, at least now I could stand properly with Owen and the kids, and from now onward I was living in this house full-time.

I shook my head briefly to get that man away from my thoughts. Centred my focus on all the parts of Owen that I could feel with mine—the heat of his skin, the softness of those parts my fingers grazed, the jut of a joint into my stomach—possibly an elbow because he had his arms curled between us.

I bit my lip, revelled in the moment.

- # -

The startled curse made me jerk. Jamie stood at the bench, cutlery drawer out, staring. He'd obviously not realised he didn't have the kitchen to himself. He tilted his chin when I arched a brow. 'Didn't expect to see you guys.'

Owen and I were both business dressed, empty plates in front of us. He actually sat drinking from his mug with his eyes closed. I let out an amused snort. 'It is a week day, Jamie.'

Across from me Owen didn't open his eyes. Jamie's focus was on him a brief second, lips beginning to creep upward. Instead of the comment I was sure he wanted to make, he tipped the drawer closed with a hip and said, 'So?'

Trying to keep back the breath of laughter, I managed, 'So, I reminded your brother he's got work commitments again.'

Jamie snorted. 'Is he even awake?'

Owen's eyes remained closed but a middle finger sprung up. Jamie grinned.

'And why are *you* up early?' I asked.

'Just wanted a drink.' He was still clad in sleepwear so I guessed the plan was to go back to bed with whatever he made.

Owen cracked open an eye, surveyed his brother, then closed it again.

'Your employee's a dud,' Jamie told me, turning away now that the jug had finished boiling.

My young man didn't speak to that, but forced both eyes open and straightened in his seat. 'I *am* awake.'

I just smiled back, thinking how I should have had us both take the day off and enjoy it. He dropped his gaze, blushing.

(W)HOLE

[Sixteen]

Owen

'Come on,' Andrew said early Sunday afternoon, 'let's go look at a house.'

It was so out of the blue all I managed was, 'A what?'

Andrew grinned. 'A house. You know, it's a building with rooms of various purpose, like a—'

'Shut up,' I said, shoving him. 'I meant "what for"?'

I thought he'd been doing the crossword, but since I'd actually been reading for once I hadn't realised he'd gone off that. He shifted the newspaper onto my lap and tapped the bottom right corner. 'It looks nice and roomy, don't you think?'

'Uh.' I looked down at the house that had apparently caught his eye. A black and white image told me nothing about colour but I instantly saw what had appealed to him. Not the "nice and roomy" but the fact it seemed to be a fairly old house with a newer second level that didn't look quite finished. His architect's brain had hooked on it. That made me smile. A big tree showed just to the left of the house and a garden of flowers edged much of a long front porch that met up with jutting ends of the house which were full of windows. A mortgagee sale apparently and good for someone with a flair for making a house their home.

I arched a brow at Andrew. 'Are you bored with designing other people's homes?'

He smiled, shaking his head. 'I just… No harm in looking, is there?'

When I continued to look at him, Andrew dropped his gaze. Since that was something he very rarely did I knew something was up. I twisted on the couch to eye him more directly. 'No harm,' I agreed slowly, 'but… Why? You're not thinking of selling your apartment, are you? That would be—' I cut off, eyes wide. 'No way, this… You're thinking about *this* house?'

'Hey, hey, calm down,' he said quickly, touching my arm as I started to rise.

'But…' I pressed a hand to my mouth to shut myself up, heart hammering, head whirling.

Andrew kept a hand on my arm, not tight, but the heat from his touch sizzled right up my arm for some reason. In the end I had to peel his fingers away, though I didn't let him go. 'Why…? What…?' I shook my head, then squinted up at him. '*Why?*

We didn't totally fit in the house and dad kept saying we'd have to leave but I hadn't realised Andrew had any thoughts about actually doing so.

Andrew's gaze was on our clasp, half obscured by the paper. I shifted the paper around to eye the picture again, jerking when Andrew picked it up and said, 'Come, I want to show you something.'

He rose. I stood too, feeling nervous now even though he didn't seem upset or anything. He headed out of the lounge, still holding the newspaper. I cast a glance outside where Lisa and Matty were chasing each other around the tree, probably annoying the hell out of Megan who sat on the bench fiddling with her badminton racket. Jamie was lounging at the table. He had headphones on, as usual, even though they must have made his ears stinking hot.

He glanced my way, obviously feeling my stare. I shrugged and turned to follow after Andrew.

He stood in our bedroom and when I joined him he told me to look around. 'What do you see?'

Puzzled, I glanced about. 'A bed, side cabinets, a chest of drawers and a mirror. What's—'

'What's yours or mine in here?' he cut over me softly.

'Um.' I shifted around him as if I needed to see more angles as I re-looked.

The bed was tidily made, and Andrew kept most of his belongings even more tidily in a suitcase by the chair. His glasses case was on the side cabinet that he used but besides that and the suitcase I didn't really see much of his stuff. Mine neither, bar a flash of pyjamas poking out from under the pillow.

Catching Andrew's gaze briefly in the mirror I saw that he looked way serious. I came forward. Even the dresser didn't really hold anything of ours; in fact, we'd never actually packed away anything of mum's or dad's which was why Andrew's clothes were in the suitcase. We'd just not bothered to clean out a drawer. The only "new" thing on the dresser was the box of photos Megan and I had found and then left there. I touched it, trying not to frown.

Eventually I had to admit that we hadn't made the room ours.

'Indeed,' he said, sitting on the end of the bed. 'Even though we've been sharing this room a long time, and all but permanently for the last two weeks. Everything here is your parents', Owen. The room, the furniture, even the sheets and pillows. They're not yours or mine, definitely not *ours*.' Andrew looked up at me still standing by the dresser with my brows sort of knitted. 'Do you remember that house you drew? The one for us all to live in happily?'

I cleared my throat. 'Yeah, but...' I didn't know what to say except I then said, 'You don't want to live here anymore, do you?'

Andrew rose. 'I'd live anywhere with you, Owen, but I...' He rubbed his jaw. 'I want somewhere away from the past, away from your father.'

I eyed him, concerned when his eyes started to look a bit shiny. I moved up to him, picked at his t-shirt. 'I want that too,' I said. 'I just... not made of money, you know, and the others don't seem to mind it here. Well, they haven't said anything anyway.' I looked up. 'Have they said something to you?'

He shook his head. 'Not outright, in any case.' He sighed, brushed a thumb down my cheek. 'Guess I'm just feeling selfish.'

I huffed out a breath. 'Not selfish.' Then I poked his chest a little harder. 'Why didn't you say something before now? We didn't have to sleep in here, you know.'

'I know, but...' Andrew didn't finish that sentence, instead enveloped me in a hug.

I pushed back. 'Don't hide stuff just for me,' I told him. 'Remember last time? That was *horrible*, Andrew, not knowing why you weren't waking up. Please just tell me things.'

He closed his eyes a moment, then sighed. 'I only want to make you happy and relaxed.'

To be honest, just now he wasn't going the right way about it. I looked around the room. It really wasn't ours and suddenly I didn't feel so great about sleeping in here. 'Come on, we better go take a look at that place.' I nodded at the paper on the bed.

Andrew glanced down at it, then picked it up. He looked a bit hesitant but smiled when I admitted I wanted my own place too. 'And it looks kinda cool,' I added, taking the paper from him and looking at the image again.

'Are you sure?' he asked quietly.

I nodded, and tugged him from the room.

I left him in the lounge with the paper, contacting the agent who was listed for the property, and stepped out onto the deck. How the kids were still running about in this heat I had no idea. Megan's racket was on the ground and she was lying on the bench, eyes closed. Jamie was still at the table, on the phone now, but I didn't hesitate to yell out, 'Get yourselves organised, we're going to look at a house.'

Jamie swore and then hurriedly spoke into the phone. 'Not you! Owen. Making a fricking noise.'

Over on the bench, Megan was up on her elbows. 'A what?'

I felt my lips go up but I didn't respond how Andrew had earlier. 'A house,' I said. 'You've all got ten minutes. You included,' I told Jamie.

'What? Why?'

I answered with, 'You included. Because I said so.'

Jamie got a pissed look on his face but Matty and Lisa were coming onto the deck, full of questions, and I heard him tell whomever was on the phone he had to go. They started to pester him with questions and he told them he knew fucking nothing, which made Megan growl at him for swearing. I headed indoors, pulling a sort of *oops* face at Andrew when I caught his gaze. He just smiled.

Then the kids were pestering *him*, each trying to see the newspaper. Seriously, sometimes it was like we lived at the zoo Matty loved so much.

But in ten minutes we were in the car. Didn't stop Lisa and Matty reeling off a list of things they wanted—pool, climbing frame, a moat and drawbridge and other weird stuff that made Andrew laugh and relax his grip on the steering wheel. Watching him out the corner of my eye I realised he was actually very serious about finding a new place, and that it was quite a gamble. Me, he had even if he moved to the South Pole, but if one of my brothers and sisters didn't want to move, then Andrew wouldn't push for it. Even if he had legal right as their guardian.

I caught his gaze and smiled at him. He took a beat to wink back, but at least he knew he had my support.

Jamie suddenly posed a question that hadn't even occurred to me. 'Where's this place we're going to see?'

'About half an hour away,' Andrew said. 'Still within Evanston city limits.'

I glanced back at Jamie as he said, 'That's a pretty evasive answer, Andrew. Are we going to the back blocks?'

Andrew grinned. 'I'm pretty sure you'll find we'll still be within civilisation.'

'Funny that you're worried about that, Jamie,' I told him. 'Woulda thought that'd be Megan.'

'Hey,' she grumbled.

Jamie and I shared a grin. Wasn't like Megan was always at the mall, but she did seem to like it a lot. I actually didn't mind anything that might be rural, and I was sure I'd seen something in the listing about a pond. Heh, Matty could be getting a moat after all.

'Is this place in the country?' Matty asked. 'Can we have sheep?'

'We haven't even seen the place yet,' Jamie pointed out.

'Well, when we do see it and it is in the country, can we have sheep?'

I let out a laugh, pleased to see Andrew smiling too.

Their conversation/argument carried on for about five minutes then Lisa said, 'I don't like sheep. We can't have any.' The death knell had sounded. I glanced over my shoulder; Matty was pouting. I had to cover my mouth to avoid him seeing my amusement.

As Andrew navigated onto smaller streets, I noticed the space between the houses was definitely getting bigger. We had a decent yard ourselves, but I was suddenly really liking the space out this way. Lisa and Matty would be able to chase each other around without the rest of us worrying about getting a noise control call.

Within another quarter hour or so Andrew nosed the Merc off the road onto a weedy gravel drive between two big stone gateposts. Though I'd seen the picture all I could suddenly see in my mind's eye was that Matty really was gonna get his moat! Then Andrew said, 'We're only able to look around outside' and cleared out my imagination.

I looked at him. 'Really? That's a long way…' I trailed off. Hadn't really been a long way, but seemed sort of a time-waster.

He pulled a half smile at me, then a grimace as Jamie muttered about wasting the afternoon.

'It's not wasted, Jamie, if we got you off your phone,' Andrew said, leaning forward a little so he could better see the unclear line of the drive.

We couldn't see the house but the gateposts and a winding drive were capturing everyone's attention. Andrew explained how the agent hadn't been available to open the house for us. 'We can do that another day if you want.'

No one reacted to that and I was sort of surprised no one had really questioned just why we were here viewing a house. Andrew's lips pressed closed a moment as if he was preparing himself for questions, but Lisa called out, 'I see it' and all attention went out the windows.

We came out of a stand of trees that was more overgrown than substantial and into the open on a drive that seemed to circle around in front of the house. Gravel still, I think, though mostly it sounded like the car was pushing over very long grass.

Andrew cleared his throat as he stopped the car. Silence held.

In front of us was definitely an old house with a new addition, and the two end wings had big curving windows. But that's about where the similarity with the newspaper ended. The roof over the porch sagged, the porch itself had no steps, and paint peeled everywhere. And it was a sure bet the gutter wasn't doing its job bent and broken on the ground. 'Jamie, give me the paper.'

He held it out wordlessly and I looked it over. 'Hah, didn't realise they airbrush house pictures.'

Andrew let out a funny noise and someone muttered, 'Back blocks.' Wasn't me, though Andrew eyed me. My grimace shifted into a smile as I said, 'It still looks kind of cool. What's your architect blood say?'

He laughed out loud, looked a little more relaxed. 'Okay… the place obviously needs some work done on it. No surprises really given it's a mortgagee sale.' He twisted to see the occupants of the back seat, all looking kind of puzzled and curious. 'Do you all still want to look about?'

'Sure, why not?' Megan said, with a shrug. 'We are here after all.'

'There's apparently a pond,' I said, looking back at the description. Yep, I had read that right earlier.

'Really?' Jamie asked with a bunch of scepticism.

Understandable, given any distinguishing landscape features were hidden by weeds and grass, but it flicked Matty's enthusiasm switch on. 'A pond?' he exclaimed. 'Cool. I can fish. Hurry up and let me out.'

If Megan hadn't gotten out he'd have climbed over her. Andrew hurried around, settling a hand on our little brother's shoulder. 'Hold up, Matty. No diving into the grass.'

On the drive, the weeds were thick and tall in places but negotiable. Off the drive, though, the grass hadn't been tended in a long time and some of it was up to Matty's waist.

'We'll look around the house first,' Andrew said. 'Sticking together. Nobody goes off on their own and gets lost, okay? There could be hidden obstacles.'

Everyone chorused agreement, though Matty sort of pouted. Andrew might have to keep a hold on him.

Megan pulled her ponytail over her shoulder. 'Andrew?'

'Yes, Hon?'

'Are there snakes?'

Suddenly we all stood a lot closer to the car, eyeing the ground at our feet. Andrew was quick to say he doubted it. 'But be careful anyway. Look where you put your feet—in the grass and on the porch.'

The porch itself looked fairly steady and now I could see that the roof sagged because it had detached, not because any of the wooden beams or posts were broken. The windows along the wall, with French Doors, were so dirty that if we wanted to see inside we were going to have to get up on the porch to do so.

I didn't worry so much about snakes hiding in the grass between the porch and us, but suddenly I was thinking of all the places that spiders could be. I could really only tolerate those the size of my small fingernail, but this place… I glanced around, biting my lip. The touch on my arm made me jump and release a cry before I realised it was Andrew urging me to start walking.

My freak-out caused a chain reaction and now Megan and Lisa looked extremely nervous and Matty had his back up against the car.

'Sorry,' I gasped, 'I was thinking—' Saying it out loud was not a good idea. 'Anyway… at least the picture was right about the flowers.' I gestured at the garden in front of the porch, hoping the attention would move off me.

Despite weeds starting to grow tall, the real plants were holding their own, and the yellow and red flowers were bright beacons.

'It's really quite pretty,' Megan said, gazing from the flowers to over the house.

Andrew offered a soft apology for startling me. 'I was just going to point out the columns.'

I looked where he indicated and saw, amongst the weeds, two stone columns about half way between us and the porch. I hadn't seen them in the photo but maybe they'd just been hidden by the grass. I took a couple of shuffling steps closer, eyeing the details. 'They're neat,' I said, turning back with a smile.

Jamie was rolling his eyes but Andrew looked pleased. Then he got everyone's attention again and pointed between the columns to the porch. 'The path goes between those so follow that line to the porch.'

'There were steps in the picture,' I said. 'Where'd they go? The picture can't be that old.'

Though… the picture had also not shown broken guttering or roofing. Andrew shrugged but said, 'I don't expect they just rotted away, so be careful when you reach the porch. Watch your step.'

Jamie led the way, with me following then Megan and the kids. Andrew brought up the rear. There were no broken or rotted steps to trip on; they simply weren't there. The porch stood about my hip level; maybe they'd been removed to deter opportunistic thieves? Gazing at the windows I couldn't see that any of them were even cracked. But maybe the place had a working alarm system or something.

'What about this?' Jamie asked, pointing upward.

Andrew looked the posts over, pushing against the nearest, then peered up under the roof. 'I think it's okay,' he said eventually. 'Looks like the roof has simply detached a little. These posts and the cross-beams are sturdy.' He eyed the porch a moment. 'It's in decent shape, but take care anyway. And don't touch anything you don't have to.'

Jamie and I hefted ourselves onto the deck, grabbing up Matty and then Lisa as Andrew boosted them up. Megan waved away his help and clambered up, looking satisfied with herself as she wiped dirt off her hands. She pushed Jamie when he said maybe she wasn't just a city girl after all.

They both went after the kids, and I extended a hand to Andrew. He took it though the height was actually no problem to him. He snuck my knuckles to his mouth for a quick kiss and then told me to go look down the other end from him. I turned away, feeling weirdly giddy and nervous in one.

The ends of the house were mirror images and the one I peered into seemed to show some fairly ghastly wallpaper and carpet. The room was a decent size, though, and I was sure the dark thing I saw on the internal wall was a fire place. I tried to recall if I'd noticed chimneys but realised that beyond the second story I hadn't taken notice of anything else about the roof.

I shifted to front of the house, which mostly seemed glass wall—French doors with more windows on either side. Obviously part of the renovation because they were metal-framed. Shading my eyes, I strained to see through the dirt.

Beside me Megan said, 'I think this bit's *all* new. With a kitchen at the back.'

I peered harder, across a huge open room with wooden floors to what was obviously a bench. Yeah, I think I could see cupboards and drawers and a range-hood. 'I reckon it's bigger than our whole lounge.'

Megan made a noise of agreement.

'The agent said the kitchen was new,' Andrew said as he came up to us, shading his eyes with a hand to peer in. 'That should also mean fresh wiring and plumbing.'

I glanced at him, then back in, but I couldn't make out anything more than I already had. I went past them to the other flanking room where there was a door in the internal wall, not a fireplace. No freaky wallpaper or carpet either, but wood floors and I think grey-painted walls with white window frames. Probably intended as a bedroom.

Between it and the French doors was the main door, set within a little porch-like structure of its own. Thin stained-glass windows flanked it with another over the top. I carefully wiped a finger down some of the red glass and then looked in. A long hall stretched out and ended, I think, with another door.

'I'm bored,' Matty suddenly said. 'Can we see the back now?'

'Kid, you gotta learn patience,' Jamie responded.

Just to push Matty's buttons, but Andrew got between them. 'We've seen everything we can possibly see here.'

Megan winked at me over Andrew's peacekeeping, and we both shimmied off the porch.

Andrew took the lead this time, moving carefully but steadily through the grass around the east side of the house. The elevation of the house and the over-achieving bushes ensured that no one really got a glimpse in the windows. He said, 'Bathroom' for one of them but we could all tell that because of the type of glass.

At the back of the house was another porch, running across the entire length. Though it was uncovered it was deemed safe enough to walk on, and even had a set of wide stone steps.

Peering in the windows of the left-side room, I saw the opposite wall was lined with bookshelves. A boarded-up fireplace was in the wall we'd just walked past and I had to lean around the side of the house to make sure. Yes, I had just totally missed the white-painted brick exterior chimney. I let out a breath and encouraged Andrew to come and look in the window. 'You could work here maybe,' I murmured.

I saw him glance down at me briefly before looking back in at the room. 'I could,' he said. 'It's nice and bright.'

Besides the window we were looking in, the fireplace was flanked by two more.

'Be nice to snuggle up in with that fire going.'

'Yeah,' I rasped, flushing as I coughed to clear my throat.

He gave me a squeeze and then turned when Jamie asked about bedrooms. I turned too; Jamie was standing out in the grass looking up. Andrew went out to join him, shading his eyes. Obviously both were looking at the new section.

'I can't recall,' Andrew said. 'But I suspect that's what that new build was for.' He lowered his gaze back to the ground floor. 'And at least two bathrooms,' he added, indicating the bevelled glass.

I moved along to the windows where my little brother and sister were valiantly peering in. I could make out something white, maybe a bath, but Lisa was saying, 'Bath, shower, toilet.'

'You can't see all that,' I told her.

'Well, that's what bathrooms have, Owen,' she told me right back like I was an idiot.

'Yeah, okay,' I said and wandered off.

This end of the house had two external doors. Both of them were solid wood so I couldn't do any more peering down hallways. Megan stood at the window of the end room.

'I like this,' she said as I came up. 'Look at those cupboards.'

She stepped aside to let me look in the bit of window she'd wiped clean. I saw a large, pale yellow room with a wall of white cupboards at the end. 'Hmm, don't think your clothes would fit in there.'

Megan jabbed me, grinning. I shifted away from her, looking up when Andrew called my name.

'We're heading around the next side,' he said. 'Come on.'

We had no better luck looking in windows than on the eastern side, though there was *another* bevelled window.

'How many bathrooms does this place have?' Jamie wondered.

'Apparently a lot,' Megan said. 'God, I'd *love* my own bathroom.'

'We'd love you to have your own, too,' Jamie said and hurriedly distanced himself from her jabbing elbow.

I slowed my walking, Andrew automatically doing the same. 'What's up?' he asked quietly.

'Nothing,' I said. 'Just… I've enjoyed this.' I took his hand.

'Me too,' he said after a few steps.

I glanced up at him. He seemed more relaxed right now than he had all day. 'How long had you been wanting to bring up the idea of a new house?'

His gaze flicked down to me and then up as we heard Lisa and Matty laughing. They were just going around the corner of the house. Andrew called out to be careful, and then looked back down at me. 'A wee while.'

'Why didn't you say something before now?'

He shrugged, swung our clasp out and in again. 'Guess I was afraid to.'

I remembered my earlier reaction, when I realised he was thinking about getting out of our house. No… not *our* house. 'I was just surprised earlier,' I said. 'I want our own real place too.' I twisted to look up at the paint-peeling wall, let out a bit of a laugh. 'I like this one.'

'So do I,' Andrew murmured. 'Despite the work that needs doing.'

I snorted. 'Come on, I saw your architect brain kick in when you stopped the car.'

Andrew chuckled but before he could say anything we stepped around the corner. Matty spotted us and immediately said he wanted to see the pond. I realised Jamie had a handful of his t-shirt, obviously keeping him from doing a dumb dash off into the grass.

'I don't think it's wise, Matty,' Andrew said.

'But you said—'

'He *didn't* say we'd go look for a pond,' Jamie cut over him. 'Which could be any bloody where in that grass. You go in there and you might never come out.'

'Jamie,' Megan began, but she didn't sound as warning as expected.

'I don't know where the pond is located,' Andrew said apologetically. 'And I don't think traipsing around in the grass is a good idea.'

'Are there really snakes?' Lisa asked timidly.

'Well, I don't know, but possibly. I don't really want any of us to find out for sure.'

Matty asked if he could have a pet snake. Jamie's mouth dropped open but Megan said, 'No' before he could speak.

Matty turned to me. 'Owen…'

'Hey, don't look at me. I'm with Megan on this one!'

'I thought you wanted sheep anyway,' Jamie said.

'Oh yeah,' Matty said and started to talk about them.

I leaned into Andrew. 'Dumb idea bringing him along.'

He chuckled. 'Okay, everyone, back in the car. We ought to get going on our really long journey home.'

Megan poked her tongue out at him, making him wink at her.

Once Andrew executed a careful turning manoeuvre with

the car, I watched the house slide out of view in my side mirror. 'Is this whole place fenced?' I asked, when we got to the gateposts.

'No idea, Owen,' Andrew replied.

Out on the road, I tried to follow a fence line but wasn't sure I lost it because of the trees and bush or because there wasn't one to actually follow.

As we got back to the more condensed part of Evanston, Jamie suddenly said, 'I'd like to look inside. I want to know what's in that second story.'

The others all piped up too, making Andrew say he'd see if the agent was free on Wednesday.

'But we go to camp that day, Andrew,' Lisa said.

'And it's the Fourth of July,' Megan commented.

'I'm pretty sure real estate agents work every day,' Andrew said, 'and we'll arrange the morning, Lisa, before you and Matty head off.'

That got satisfied agreement and he smiled, looking relaxed.

Jamie

It wasn't the real estate agent who tossed out our plans, but dad with a message left on our phone.

I delivered the news as I slumped to the chair. 'He wants to see us on Wednesday. Do lunch or something.'

'Why does he always ruin our good times?' Owen grumbled.

I pulled a face. 'He didn't mention *you*, just the rest of us.'

That made Owen sit straighter, frowning. When Andrew shifted beside him he turned his way. Andrew directed him the smallest smile then said, 'Perhaps this is a good idea, now that things are settled.'

I knew "settled" meant him and Owen being legal.

'Did dad mention Melissa?' Megan asked.

'Nope.'

'It would… be nice to see her,' she said quietly. 'I want to see Sam too.' She looked worried about how we'd take that.

I was surprised to not be angry about it, remembering how she'd been the other week. Owen didn't look angry either.

'Jamie,' Andrew said, 'why don't you give your dad a call and arrange something?'

'I kinda don't want to,' I responded.

'And we want to see the house,' Lisa said.

'We'll just have to arrange that for another day,' Andrew said with a smile.

'But we'll be at camp.'

Andrew's lips pressed tight a moment. 'We'll… sort something, don't worry.' He looked back at me and Megan. 'It'll be good for you to meet with your father and Melissa, now that all these…' His eyes squeezed shut momentarily, like he needed the dark to come up with the right word.

'Andrew's right,' Owen said before he could find that word. 'Now it's all legal, you guys should meet up with them. Things will probably be better.'

'Sure they will,' I got out.

Owen's eyes narrowed. 'If you put some effort in.'

I held my breath about effort because there was no use starting an argument. I got up. 'Fine, I'll call him, sort something.' I didn't go for the phone but out of the lounge, needed to sort my calm before anything else.

- # -

'Andrew was right, you know. You're on that phone a lot.'

I glanced up; Owen leaned against the door frame, hands in his pockets. Huffing out a *heh* sort of breath, I swiped back through the photos I'd been looking over and then turned my phone around. 'You'll be glad I had it.'

Owen's brows came together a bit and he eventually stopped leaning and came into the room. He eyed the photo and then he obviously got what he was seeing because he whipped the phone out of my hand and eyed it a lot closer. He swiped left and right, and then looked at me. Instead of commenting on the picture I'd shown him—of him and Andrew peering in a window, him with a fully smug look on his face—he said, 'Man, I didn't even think of taking photos.'

He let out a half laugh and sank onto the computer chair, still swiping.

'So, not a bad thing I had it after all, was it?' I challenged.

Owen glanced up and then went back to the pictures, tongue running along his teeth. When I held my hand out he relinquished the phone easily enough, saying, 'Can you send that one to me?'

I grinned. 'Sure, if you tell me why you were looking so smug.'

'That's all in how you took the photo,' he responded.

Chuckling, I sent it off in a message. Then I dropped the phone on the bed and said, 'Why'd we go look?'

'I think Andrew got bored with the crossword.'

I cocked my head. 'We went on a whole-afternoon trip to look at some random house because Andrew got bored with a crossword?'

'Yeah.'

There was definitely more to that decision, but Owen trumped me with, 'Did you sort something with dad?'

I bared my teeth a moment, then sighed out, 'Yeah. Lunch on Wednesday. But just me and Megan.'

'You told Matty that yet?' he asked, with a grimace.

'Nope.' I shifted cross-legged. 'I don't think Matty or Lisa should be there, Owen. It's not gonna be all sweet, like Andrew hopes.' I held up a hand. 'I'll be putting in effort, so shut your mouth.' He did, surprisingly. 'I mean, even though dad knows you're eighteen he'll still probably say something stupid. I don't want Lisa and Matty hearing that stuff anymore.'

'I'm not arguing, you know,' Owen put in.

I eyed him, and he shrugged. 'I don't like them being around him either, Jamie, but they're gonna be upset to miss him.'

'Just tell them they have to get to the camp meeting point early or something,' I said.

'Or you could tell them that dad asked for you and Megan especially,' Owen countered.

I screwed up my face at that.

'Ah, whatever,' he said. 'We'll deal with it on Wednesday.'

'What about the house?'

'What about it?'

'All that talk about going to see inside,' I prompted.

My brother's shoulders went up again. 'Not happening on Wednesday at least.'

'But... still happening?' I picked up my phone and looked through the photos again. 'Why did we go and see it?'

Owen didn't say anything about the crossword this time. With his gaze on the phone, he said, 'Curiosity. Architect, remember?' He didn't lift his head even though I was pretty sure my gaze was boring a hole in him. 'I enjoyed it,' he said after a short silence. 'Getting out and doing something together.'

He glanced up now and held my gaze, but I could see that I wasn't gonna crack him open to reveal the real reason.

'Fine,' I muttered and leaned back against the wall again, focusing on the phone.

Owen got up. At the door he stopped. 'Thanks for taking those photos.'

I managed to hold back most of my surprise at the comment, but felt my lips curl up. 'There's some good ones.'

'Yeah.' He hesitated a little longer but then left without saying anything else.

I stared at the empty doorway for a while, then went back through the photos where I'd managed to capture my brothers and sisters and Andrew. Smiling and laughing, enjoying themselves in most of them.

Whatever the real reason was for looking today, Owen had been right that getting out and doing something together had been fun. I swiped to the images of that second story, and sat for a while imagining what it would be like to have a bedroom that was truly just mine.

Heaven, I reckoned.

- # -

It was like I'd told Owen the other night; even though dad knew Owen was eighteen and the illusion of illegality was completely shattered, he'd still probably say something stupid.

The amazing thing was, he didn't say it until after lunch

when we were walking by the lake at Grant Park. We'd been together almost two hours by then, the start of which had included a quick ten minutes with Lisa and Matty before they got shipped off to the school to head away on their school camp. He'd given them each ten dollars to spend at camp.

The lunch had sort of felt like a weird double-date, with Sam next to Melissa in a highchair, but by the end of it everyone was actually quite relaxed. We'd chatted and smiled, even laughed at one point.

Still had a small pit of apprehension but I told myself to just keep being normal, that this visit was a good thing, and that acting stupid myself wasn't a good idea. It would feel decent to report back to Andrew and Owen that things were a lot more sorted.

Of course, it meant that, 'I expect your brother and that faggot are making the most of their afternoon' made me misstep and I had to do a fast manoeuvre to prevent myself ending up in the water.

'Chris,' Melissa said with a frown.

Dad shrugged like it was nothing.

'Dad, come on, why would you say that here?' I asked, striving to react without fireworks.

Beside me, Megan had her arms around herself, looking upset.

'Free speech, kid,' dad said.

'No!' I cried. 'It's hate speech, and it's not fair.'

'I'll call it how I see it, Jamie.'

I swallowed back the growl and said, 'Yeah, okay, you're entitled to an opinion. Everyone is. Here's mine. If you can't accept Andrew *or* him and Owen being together, then I don't want anything more to do with you.'

'Jamie,' Melissa began, concerned.

I stepped back, raising my hands. 'He's allowed his. I'm allowed mine.'

'Yes, but… let's please not ruin the afternoon.'

I actually bit on my hand to stop my retort about who was doing the ruining. Melissa was upset, pushing the stroller rapidly back and forth which made Sam start to cry. As she knelt down beside him, Megan got out my name. She didn't say anything else but I saw her pleading with me to stop.

Drawing in a long breath, I looked at the bite mark I'd given myself, rubbed it hard and then dropped my hands. 'Okay,' I said on a sharply exhaled breath. 'Let's…' Another breath out. 'It's just us five, *no one* else in the conversation.'

Melissa and Megan agreed instantly but dad cocked his head. God, I hoped he wouldn't say anything dumb because I didn't actually want to ruin this afternoon and I would if he said something dumb. He simply said, 'As it should be' and continued walking.

He'd gone several steps before I could make myself move, grinding out a half smile at Megan when she looked at me over her shoulder. Her gratitude made my gut twist, so did the fact she hurried up alongside dad and engaged him in chat about how the lake seemed like the beach back home. 'I swear sometimes I can smell salt water.'

I wasn't angry at her talking with him because I knew she was trying to find a smooth path too. But I was angry at the fact we had to play this "stay on the line" kind of game, that we were stuck between dad and Andrew.

No, I told myself, *not stuck*. Dad wasn't ever going to be my pick, but it still hurt that I had to play his game just so he wouldn't go off at Andrew or even at Owen.

Melissa walked beside me, neither of us really saying much aside from the occasional comment about the skyline. I offered to push the stroller for a while to give her a break and she quickly relinquished control. She swiped her hair back and dug out a bottle of water from her bag. 'When you combine Sammy with the stroller, it's quite a weight to be pushing.'

I didn't find it so but then I'd only just started.

After a few steps Melissa said a soft apology over dad. 'He's just envious that you like Andrew so much,' she said with a sigh.

I gritted my teeth, but couldn't stop myself speaking. 'It's not envy, it's homophobia.'

Melissa's lips sucked in and she turned her gaze toward the lake. I stayed silent. She didn't try another apology, and then we caught up with the others as they stopped to look at something or other. Melissa took back control of the stroller, wheeled it several feet so she could make use of the bench.

I walked to the edge of the path, was just about to drop down onto the next level so I could go look down into the water when dad said he expected Owen to move out soon. 'What? Why?' I said, turning back.

Megan looked just as startled at the sudden comment.

'We need his room for Sam's.'

I forgot what words were for a second. Megan just said, 'What?' in a completely puzzled tone.

'Your brother needs to move out. Let the *rest* of us become a family again.'

I swear dad wasn't speaking English. Megan continued to look as puzzled and then I shook my head. 'Wait… you want to move in?'

'It's not a "want", Jamie,' dad said. 'It's a "will".'

'No way,' I croaked. 'We're not… Andrew's still our guardian.'

'I will be seeking to have his guardianship dissolved. After all,' dad said, 'it's no longer required.'

'Oh, no way,' I said steadily. 'There is no way anyone will allow that.'

'I am your father.'

He must have been suffering heatstroke or something to sound that confident.

'Yeah, but you've done *nothing* to show us that,' I said hollowly. 'Nothing to show us you actually want to be with us. Everything has been against Andrew and Owen.'

'For your sake, kid,' dad said softly.

'No!' I cried. 'That's bullshit. You *know* Andrew has never done anything to us. You *know* Owen's with him because he wants to be. It really sucks that you're letting one crazy mistimed thing drive all this.'

'Crazy?' dad asked, hands on his hips. 'You think me being angry over the fag who killed your mum is crazy?'

'Yes!' I shouted. 'Who cares if that driver was gay? That shouldn't matter. It's a stupid fucking reason to hate Owen and Andrew.' I hauled in a steadying breath, but I still said, 'If the driver'd been Asian, would you hate Alana because she's half Japanese?'

Megan choked out my name, shock widening her eyes.

'Same diff,' I growled at her. 'Well?' I said to dad.

He was holding his breath.

'Yeah,' I said, nodding, 'totally unfair, right? Well, it's unfair to go at Andrew for the same reason. We didn't even know him back then, and Owen sure as shit wasn't gay.' Even now he barely admitted it out loud. I could see why! 'And *you* were cheating on mum at the time, Dad, so going on about the accident just makes you a hypocrite! You don't seem to get that all you're doing is ruining *any* chance of being in our lives officially. Not that we want you here!'

Megan yanked me out of dad's face, making me stumble. But it cleared my head a bit; I hadn't realised I'd been all but toe to toe. I pressed a hand over my face and turned away.

'Dad,' Megan said quietly, 'Jamie's right, you know. If you want to spend time with us, be a *father* to us, then you need to show that you do.'

'I have shown—'

'No. You. Haven't.' She spoke like she struggled to form the words. 'I wish you hadn't come back, Dad.'

'Megan,' he began.

I called her name too when she rushed by me. She didn't actually go far, but slumped to a bench a few metres away from the one Melissa sat frozen on.

My emotions were churning so much I wanted to be sick, but felt like that would give dad some satisfaction. I swallowed hard, gazed out over the lake to try and gather some zen, but it wouldn't come when I saw that Megan was crying.

I turned back to dad. 'Take your replacement family, Dad, and bugger off.'

'Hey, Jamie, I think that's enough.' Melissa rose, one hand on the stroller handle. I could hear Sam squawking. 'You're frightening—'

'Go away! You started all of this.'

I wasn't so wound up that I missed the flash of hurt, but I was too wound up to really care. 'Our mum died and you still—Grr, fuck *off*, Megan.' I wrenched out of my sister's grip as she tried to pull me away.

Tears were still streaming down her face. 'You're making this worse, you're making this *worse.*'

I heaved in a breath, rearranged clothes that she'd disorganised. She wiped at her eyes and Melissa's were wet too. She wasn't angry, just upset and concerned. Dad, though, just looked furious. If he'd shown a speck of anything caring, I wouldn't have been so angry myself.

'You're not our father anymore,' I told him. 'You destroyed that relationship ages ago. We don't want anything to do with you.'

'That faggot has turned you all against me,' Dad got out. 'He's—'

'Andrew's got nothing to do with this,' I said over him. 'But the way you've treated him and Owen just strengthens what I feel. Come on, Megs, let's go.'

'But,' she began, though didn't try to get out of my grip.

'Jamie, wait,' Melissa called. 'Don't let…'

I stopped, making Megan whisper my name. We held gazes a second and I saw all her distress and stress. I fought back words I wanted to say, tilted my head and got out, 'Sorry it's like this, Melissa.' Started walking again before she could speak.

Dad didn't say anything, at least not loud enough for us to hear.

I looked at my hands as I walked, my fingers were shaking I was that angry.

Megan sniffed as she hurried along the path with me. As upset as she was, I knew part of it was because of Melissa and my words to her. I couldn't apologise though. Melissa might not have known dad was married when she'd first met him, but she had by the time mum died.

Right now, my anger felt justified.

The train ride and walk had me all good again by the time we got home. I hadn't made Megan promise to say nothing about how the visit had ended, but she simply agreed with me that lunch had been pretty good and everyone had stayed civil during it. 'Sam had tomato for the first time. It was really funny watching his reaction.'

I knew she didn't keep quiet about the lakeside walk because she thought it should totally stay out of sight; she expected *me* to spill the beans. I kind of didn't want to because Andrew looked relaxed over the lunch stories.

Finding out that the bridges he'd hoped would be mended with the visit had been shattered further wouldn't sit easy with him. But right now he didn't seem to suspect that we'd left dad and Melissa on a bad note. Saying he was proud of us made me wince, but even then he took that as me being embarrassed over hearing it.

I was embarrassed but not for the reason he thought.

Owen stayed remarkably quiet during the conversation and I tried not to look at him so much. Didn't want him to start thinking about our conversation on Sunday and my prediction that dad would say something dumb, and question me about it.

As Andrew was putting away the hose after watering the garden, I chose to broach the subject of the afternoon in a very roundabout way. 'Owen said we went to look at that house on Sunday because you got bored with a crossword.'

Surprise flickered across his face, and then he gave a half smile.

'That can*not* be the reason,' I said steadily.

Andrew inclined his head. 'It wasn't. Owen obviously didn't tell you?'

'Second time I asked, he said it was curiosity because you're an architect.'

'Well, the photo did catch my eye,' Andrew said. 'But, I'd been thinking about houses for a while already.'

'So… *your* decision?' I asked. 'Not Owen's?'

'That's right,' Andrew agreed, 'so please don't niggle at him over it.'

I heard the even tone and inclined my head, eyeing the dripping plants in front of me. 'Secrets are not a good idea in this family,' I muttered, understanding the irony of spouting that right now.

Andrew almost looked amused a second, then he said, 'It's not necessarily a secret but I guess you wouldn't likely notice. The fact is, Jamie, I'm not comfortable sharing your parents' bedroom with your brother.'

I took a step back, pulling a face. 'I don't—'

'It is somewhat annoying how your brain goes straight to sex,' Andrew told me, and he wasn't joking.

'It doesn't,' I defended myself. 'You just… what you said…' I raised my chin. 'What did you mean then?'

'That the bedroom isn't ours, that virtually nothing within the bedroom is ours. Even though I've been living here for the past two weeks it doesn't feel… right.'

'Are you going to go back to your apartment?' I asked, shocked. Worried too, hearing that after the conversation with dad this afternoon.

He shook his head. 'No, not at all. I'm here with Owen and with you guys. I *want* to be with you. I just find this house a little uncomfortable, given the last few months.'

I scratched my head. 'Owen knows this?'

'Yes, we've talked about it.'

'So… we went to look at that house for a reason then? To find somewhere else to live?'

'To just look, Jamie,' Andrew said. 'Felt like a breath of fresh air, as they say. I would not try to uproot you all just on my feelings.'

'Pfft.' I glanced around at the yard, gazed up at the tree, seeing in my memory the big ones at that house. Remembered it was me who'd suggested looking inside.

Andrew stood silent, watching me, looked concerned when I glanced back at him. 'You know Owen would go with you to the moon,' I said. 'And I don't think the rest of us would fight much about following.' I let out a sigh and admitted that sometimes it hurt being in this house. 'The memories and stuff. Don't tell Owen I said that.'

'I won't,' Andrew said, 'but you boys really need to start being open with each other.'

'Heh,' I said. 'Anyway, you may wanna do more than just look. Dad reckons he's gonna move in soon.'

'What?' That came out sharp and then I revealed how the last part of the visit went.

I expected a bit of a telling off, but Andrew just held a hand to his forehead for a moment, blue gaze nailing me.

'I couldn't stop myself,' I said, swallowing as my voice started to crack. 'He's totally psycho, Andrew, just doesn't get…' I shook my head. 'Melissa said he was just envious but he's taken it way beyond that.'

'He didn't hit you, did he?'

I shook my head rapidly. 'No, no fists thrown at anyone.' I think I smiled. 'So… you know how you were going to arrange a look inside that house? I think it's a *really* good idea.'

Andrew looked like he was working through what to say that wouldn't come out furious or rude.

I chanced his control by asking him to not tell Owen any of this. 'He probably suspects, but I'd rather that's where it ends.'

Andrew drew in a long breath. 'Yes,' he said slowly, 'keeping this from Owen is a good idea. And I'll contact the agent tomorrow, see if we can get inside on Saturday.' He gave a small smile. 'But no telling the kids when we hear from them. They'll be severely disappointed.'

I snorted, then rubbed a stinging eye. 'Secret-keeping is our strong point.' What a hypocrite I was saying that now after telling him earlier that secrets weren't good. I let out a noisy breath.

Andrew sighed. 'Ah shit, I'd hoped today would…' He shook his head, called up a stronger smile.

It made me smile back but I wasn't sure what it was about.

Seventeen

Jamie

Having pizza for dinner was so much smoother when we didn't have Lisa and Matty competing to come up with the weirdest toppings. Tonight we were arranged around the coffee table enjoying three pizzas with plain old regular pepperoni or chicken toppings.

Rain bucketed down now and then, which was why we weren't out at the picnic table, but it was quite a nice soundtrack as we ate and talked. The occasional rumble of thunder from the summer storm wasn't half bad either. Kinda fitted in with my emotions today.

The roof arched out maybe two feet but the deck itself had no cover. Andrew had probably already designed one several times over in his head, but didn't mention it. He was chatting to Megan about her going away for a week with Alana and her family.

A sly grin at Owen didn't garner a response, even though I reckoned at the back of Andrew's mind he was angling at giving Owen and himself some alone-time.

But even if they got rid of Megan—who did need something 'normal'—they'd still have me around. Though, I'd picked up more hours at Walgreens, enjoying seeing my bank account rise and enjoying the actual work. Turns out that it's nice being around other people and not have to worry for a while about my family.

And... if this thing with Sarah turned out true then I couldn't go away anyway. I wouldn't run if it turned out she *was* pregnant. I had no idea what I'd actually *do*, but running wasn't an option. She had an appointment to see her doctor next week, and since she didn't seem overly freaked out I was doing my best not to be either.

Though I kinda was—that I'd left her earlier, even if she'd told me to go, that I sat having pizza with my family trying to figure out if I should say something or not.

Picking up a new slice, I realised no one had been looking at me like I was acting weird. Obviously I was better than my brother at hiding emotions. I glanced over at him sitting beside Andrew, relaxed, and fought back a smile. They'd barely been out of each other's sight since Owen's birthday.

For some reason that turned my thoughts back to Wednesday. The lunch with dad and Melissa had been pretty decent and I'd almost started feeling like things were becoming good between us. Except it'd all gone sour because dad couldn't let go over Owen and Andrew, and we hadn't heard from them in the two days since.

I knew Megan was conflicted over it all because she really liked Melissa and Sam but they were with dad and we didn't want *him* anywhere near us.

Andrew had made me report to Sergeant Morrison, probably just to keep him in the loop, but I hated it. How long would this go on? That we'd have to keep the law updated on our stupid father who couldn't seem—

'Everything alright, Jamie?'

I glanced at Andrew, then realised everyone was looking at me. God, I must have growled or something. 'Yeah, fine.' I stuffed the rest of the slice into my mouth.

'Pig,' Megan said.

No matter how we laughed at her, she ate pizza with a knife

and fork. Owen eyed the cutlery in her hands. When I caught his gaze, he grinned but held his tongue.

'There is nothing wrong,' Megan said, noticing us, 'with displaying good manners.' She used an incredibly prim tone, ruined it when she stuck her tongue out as Owen cracked a laugh.

I had a hand over my mouth so I couldn't spit anything out before I had a chance to swallow.

'Too much of a stretch for you, I know,' she told me.

'Remember how she used to eat fish and chips, Jamie?' Owen asked.

Knife and fork.

'Hey!'

'Little Miss Manners,' I responded with a laugh.

'It's not actually that amusing,' she said in a dark tone, but looked like she was struggling not to smile.

Owen winked at her, and that defeated her struggle. Grinning, she picked up the rest of her slice and ate it that way.

'Who's the pig now?' I asked.

'Can't beat them, join them,' she said around a mouthful.

She looked like she was enjoying herself and Owen was still smiling. Beside him, Andrew reached for another slice, looking pleased. Beyond them I noted that the rain had shifted into something softer even as thunder rumbled faintly. The storm was definitely moving away; in an hour it'd probably be gone and the heat would have dried off the wet like it had never been.

Still, it'd be nice to have a covered deck.

'Sarah thinks she might be pregnant.'

I startled myself as much as them because when I'd opened

my mouth I'd been planning to ask about the deck. Now Andrew and Owen sat opposite, still and staring, and Megan gawped at me from the other couch. Andrew cleared his throat.

'Um,' I said. 'That… don't know… um.' Shit, what could I say?

When I saw Owen shift I looked up but his gaze wasn't on me. He was still surprised, but not apparently at me. Same with Andrew.

Just as Megan and I were turning, we heard, 'On your feet, Paedo.'

No one moved and no one spoke. I wondered if they were all thinking the same things: where had dad come from and where the fuck had he gotten that—

Holy shit, dad had a freaking serious-looking gun.

All those pizza slices sat really awkward in my gut.

'Deaf now, Mr Gordon?' dad sneered. 'Do you need a little incentive?'

He raised the gun and all four of us popped onto our feet. I grasped Megan's wrist and yanked her close to me, making her cry out in shock. On the other side of the coffee table, Owen had his hand clamped around Andrew's wrist, and I guess that was because he'd taken a step between the couches, must have been aiming for the open space.

Owen was white and full of horror, but Andrew looked crazily in control of himself.

'Mr Tremayne, you have two seconds to get out of this house.'

I couldn't help but gape. Andrew had a gun pointed at him, yet spoke like he didn't.

The man who claimed to be our father looked taken aback,

but then his lips curled. 'You think this is *fake*?' He made a show of inspecting the weapon.

I felt fingers grip into my t-shirt; Megan, barely breathing. I shifted a step to put her more behind me.

'You have no legal right to be in this house,' Andrew said.

'It's *my* house,' dad replied. 'And you're not welcome in it, Boy-fucker.'

'Don't call him that,' Owen growled, forcing Andrew to take hold of him since he'd started to push past.

'Shut up, you whore.'

'Dad, that's—' I cut off as dad swivelled to me.

Megan gulped behind me, not because of the gun I didn't think but because of the utter conviction in dad's gaze that he reckoned he had all the right. 'It's okay, Jamie, Megan,' he said. 'You'll be safe soon. This paedo won't be—'

'Andrew's not a paedophile!' Owen shouted, shoving past Andrew and into the clear, putting himself in unimpeded sight line with dad. He was scared, but I could see that fury was a far stronger driving force.

Dad lining up the gun and Andrew stepping beside him trying to move him back didn't stop my brother. 'Why can't you grasp the facts? I am *eighteen*, nothing can stop us being together, and Andrew has never done anything to the others. The sergeant's warned you about making false claims, Dad! Go *away*, you are not. Welcome. *Here!*'

Those last words came out with finger stabs, and my stomach twisted in fear that he'd push dad too far.

'Owen, I—'

'*He's not taking you*,' Owen hissed over Andrew.

The gun fired, making us all cry out in some way. I tucked Megan completely into my embrace but dad hadn't actually shot someone. Bits of ceiling floated down on top of dinner.

Beyond the couch, grey-faced, Owen had such a grip on Andrew's arm I could see the pressure from where I stood.

'No one seems to be getting the point.' Dad's tone was like he'd actually just said, 'Hey look, the rain's fully stopped.' He eyed Andrew. 'Mr Gordon, you *will* come with me.'

'No,' Owen cried, though Andrew hadn't actually moved.

'The next bullet's through your whore, Mr Gordon.'

Owen had been trying to tug Andrew back but now he went dead still. Dad's tone had been pure promise. Behind me Megan whispered our brother's name. I might have managed a swallow.

Andrew carefully pried Owen's fingers from his arm. Owen didn't fight the removal, just let his hand drop like it was too heavy to keep raised, shock dilating his eyes really wide.

'I can't let him hurt you,' Andrew murmured.

'But—' Owen didn't say anything more, almost like he had no energy left and it was all he could do to stay on his feet.

Except, then he said, 'Take me.'

'Owen—'

'Take me,' he cried over Andrew at dad. 'Take me instead, Dad.'

'I don't want you around my kids, true,' dad said. 'But *he's* going first.' He angled the gun, and Andrew took a step.

'No,' Owen rasped out, reaching.

'It'll be okay, Angel,' Andrew told him in a soothing tone I had no idea how he called up.

'He's gonna k-kill…' Owen choked on a breath. Panic was starting to take control.

'Too right!' dad said.

Megan made a noise of shock and yet she and I stood like

dummies. What could we do anyway? Andrew was calm; afraid, obviously, but looked like it was more for us than himself. Did he have a plan?

Owen was beside himself, trying to stop Andrew, telling dad to take him instead. Total admiration for my brother washed over me. Megan moved, but since she wasn't bolting I didn't turn to see what she was doing.

Andrew got out of Owen's grip again, and once he'd moved closer to dad than him my brother fell still and silent, as if reality was suddenly too much. Dad had partially turned, with his back half toward me. Should I—

My breath snagged when Andrew caught my gaze and gave the barest shake of his head. Dad swung to me and Megan briefly and we both took a step back, but he was already turning again.

Andrew hadn't moved in that small opportunity.

'P-please, Dad…' Owen croaked.

'Get moving,' dad told Andrew, totally ignoring Owen.

Andrew swallowed, glanced at my brother, and I could see what he felt—love, pride, concern.

This wasn't fair. Surely there was something we could do? Why the fuck didn't I have my phone with me? 'Megan,' I rasped, 'your phone…'

But she wasn't close anymore. I hadn't seen her move but she was on the other side of the chair now, out of reach. She looked as blank as Owen, had probably moved without even realising it.

Andrew was still sidling toward the door, dad keeping his distance. Owen shuffled a step or two, and I found myself moving too, like I was being pulled along by a string. I feared for my brother because if this ended the way it seemed it was going to then he'd never recover.

That made me say, 'Dad, don't be stupid. Are you willing to ruin your other family's lives too?'

Owen turned a *what the fuck?* look on me. I raised my hands, hadn't known *that* would come out.

'Yeah,' Megan said, glancing back at me. 'Sam's not even two yet. Are you going to let him grow up without a dad? Is that what you do now? Just abandon children?'

He actually turned to her. I don't think any of us could have described his expression. 'I'm getting rid of this boy-fucker for you, Megan.'

'What?' I yelped since Megan just stared. 'You're crazy, Dad! Sick. Why don't—'

'Jamie,' Andrew said over top of me, and I shut my mouth.

I didn't know how he was so calm, but I got what he was saying even without saying it: don't aggravate. I forced myself to nod, take a step back even. I hated the gratitude in his gaze right then.

My gaze shifted to Owen; he could have been unconscious with his eyes open, for all I knew.

Our father waved the gun in a "get moving" gesture, and turned to follow Andrew toward the door.

Owen breathed out hard, and then sharply in. I turned and saw Megan leaping at dad. I got out half her name in total horror, dad part turned, and then Megan was on him swinging her arm.

Dad let out a yell and stumbled to his knees, firing as he did so. Andrew fell and Owen screeched his name, launching forward. Megan scrambled back from dad, and then I saw what she'd done.

The big knife we'd used to slice the pizza stuck out of dad's shoulder. He was struggling to get up, to get the gun raised. Near the door, Andrew was actually on his feet. He had Owen around the waist and was dragging him away from the shattered side window.

'Andrew,' I croaked, pointing, unable to move myself.

Andrew clearly had all his faculties, stomping down on dad's hand, making him yowl in pain. He kicked the gun away and I heard it crash off a wall somewhere in the hall. Then he shoved Owen my way, telling us to call the police and the EMS, and wrestled dad who was struggling and swearing even with that knife.

I grabbed Megan up off her knees where she'd dropped in shock and hauled her into the lounge out of the view of the struggle. 'I stabbed dad,' she said. Pressed both hands over her mouth.

No way she was phoning anyone.

I looked at Owen; he looked like he was defrosting—trembling shock giving way to horror and anger and fear. I didn't think he was up to much either, but then he told me to sit with Megan and went to the phone.

I dropped beside our sister as she rocked over her knees and wrapped my arms around her, closing my eyes so I couldn't see the ruins of our dinner.

Dad was still mouthing off in the hall. I didn't hear Andrew speak. Was he okay out there? Had he been hit? The glass had shattered, but had *he* been hit?

Over at the bench, Owen talked scarily normal, giving details, the address, confirming the number of people. He gave other random things too, as if whomever he was talking to wanted to keep him engaged.

Once I'd told Jamie that people were coming I headed for the hall, needing to get a change of pants.

I saw dad's legs and one of Andrew's first. When I shifted into a clearer view I saw Andrew with a knee in dad's back, one hand pressing his head to the ground and the other his shoulder. The knife was still there.

Except, that wasn't what ended up capturing my attention, it was the gun. Andrew had kicked it away from dad in those manic seconds and it was down the hall, not far from my old room. A big black thing, like a menacing spider, and I couldn't take my eyes off it. Dad had threatened Andrew, he'd threatened me, he'd *shot* the ceiling. Fresh panic flooded through as I remembered the second shot. The side window at the front door was all but gone, glass spiking from the edges but mostly on the carpet.

It was raining again.

Dad made a sound. My attention went to him then back to the gun.

'Owen.'

I didn't take my gaze off the weapon. Dad had been—

'*Owen!*'

I stopped and looked back at Andrew. His face was red from holding dad in one place, yet his focus was all on me right then. 'Did you ring for an ambulance?'

'Yes.'

'Okay, good.' He managed a small smile, pressed harder on dad's head when he tried a struggle. 'Can you go and unlock the front door?'

'Why?'

'To let the EMS team in,' Andrew said calmly.

I glanced up toward the shattered window. Couldn't they just use that?

'Owen.'

I refocused on Andrew.

'Angel, please… Go unlock the front door.'

'But I…' I waved a hand at the hall, suddenly remembering I'd been aiming to change my wet jeans.

'Please.'

Real concern in his voice now, so I nodded and started to move.

'Around through the kitchen,' he said quickly.

I paused, then swallowed hard.

'Go on,' he said softly, nodding over his shoulder, and I realised he didn't want me directly in dad's sight.

My throat closed up and I gave a jerky nod, then hurried around through the kitchen to the door.

Dad muttered something half muffled. I didn't hear Andrew respond. I wanted to help him, but didn't know how other than flip the deadbolt so the EMS and police could get in. *Dad must have had a key*, I thought as I did this. We'd not heard his arrival at all and the door and lock weren't broken. I nearly hauled the door open to see if his car was in the drive but instead rapidly stepped backward and hurried back to my brother and sister.

Jamie had Megan tight in his arms. She wasn't crying. In fact, both of them looked at me and I simply stood there looking back, not knowing what to do or say. I wanted to cry and scream and shout. I wanted to fire the gun at dad. I wanted, most of all, for Andrew to hold me and swear to never let me go.

My gaze riveted to the dust on our pizza, memory replaying us joking about how Megan ate hers. I pressed a hand over my mouth, willing my stomach not to release its contents.

The sudden long high cry of a siren stood the hairs on my arms, and I couldn't stay where I was, sprinting out of the lounge to release my terror into the toilet.

The sounds of authority in the house kept me there, even when I had nothing else to bring up.

'Owen.'

I jerked sideways. The newcomer was Sergeant Morrison, looking full-on in his uniform. I stayed back between the vanity and toilet, scared, but also not. But mostly scared.

'Are you hurt?'

I shook my head. He looked sceptical, but I hadn't been physically hurt.

'Will you come out to the lounge, please?' He sounded weirdly calm, and my brain realised he was that way for me, because I was backed into a corner and shaking so hard he could see it.

'I need to change my pants,' I blurted and charged forward.

The sergeant let out a sound but didn't bar my escape.

Possibly he didn't quite trust me though, because he stood just outside the door when I came out a few minutes later in clean and dry clothing. He looked at me, brows together, but didn't query the change. And I wasn't about to verbally admit the extent of my cowardice.

I took one step, but stopped when I heard dad mouthing off. He was still here?

'Your father is contained,' the sergeant said quietly. 'He can't reach you.'

I gave a jerky nod and started to walk. He moved to be on

my right which actually part shielded the view in the entry way as we came out of the hall. I got a glimpse of dad on his feet, surrounded by both medical and police staff. Somehow he still found a gap to spy me and I shifted sideways.

Sergeant Morrison set a hand under my elbow, but I wasn't running, just… shrinking from the utter hate in my father's gaze.

I hadn't realised I'd stopped moving until the sergeant encouraged me on, and told me to take a seat next to Jamie. Instead, I looked about for Andrew, afraid to see him being treated by a medic. He wasn't; he stood over at the kitchen bench talking to a police officer in a safety vest. He had his back half to me but maybe he felt my stare because he turned. His smile was small, but full of love.

I bit my lip, nodded even though he'd not said anything, and turned to thread my way to the couch, past a cop sitting on the other one. Jamie clamped my wrist as soon as I was near enough and dragged me down, not letting me go once I'd sat. He had Megan in a similar grip though she sat silent and limp. I leaned across Jamie and squeezed her knee. She glanced at me, eyes wet and round.

She was my hero for what she'd done.

Tears ran down her face but she covered my hand briefly, then Jamie shoved me back out of his way, and we faced Sergeant Morrison sitting in the chair opposite.

'I understand you're all in shock,' he said gently, 'but I'd like an outline of what happened. Alastair'—he indicated the cop—'is going to take some notes so please be clear and stay on track.'

He looked at me like he expected me to do all the talking but I really didn't want to. I didn't want to recall any of it, and when we heard the click of the front door and finally silence from dad I leaned back into the couch like I was trying to disappear.

'I did it.'

I jerked and stared at Jamie. Morrison frowned my way, as if he thought I was letting my brother take the rap for what I did.

'*I* did it,' Megan spoke softly. 'Sergeant, I was the one who stabbed dad. He was going to take Andrew. I couldn't—' She cut off.

Morrison's gaze was keen, but he had to see that of all of us she was the one feeling the guilt.

'You saved Andrew,' Jamie said. 'You shouldn't—' He shut up as he realised the sergeant's gaze had shifted to him. He lifted his chin and continued. 'Don't feel guilty, Megs. You did the best thing ever. He'd have come back for Owen, too, you know that.' He settled an arm around Megan's shoulders and hugged her.

'He threatened you, Owen?' Morrison asked.

'Yeah,' I said. 'But... only to g-get Andrew moving.' I looked over but he was still talking with the cop and not looking our way. 'I told dad to take me instead but he w-wouldn't.'

Morrison's jaw dropped just a second and then he held a hand up. 'Can someone please tell me from the beginning what happened?'

'I stabbed dad!' Megan said forcefully.

Which wasn't the beginning, of course, though Morrison had cocked his head at her, probably wondering.

'Oh God,' she breathed. 'What if he *dies*?'

Jamie opened his mouth and I crunched his wrist with a

hand, making him growl, 'You think it too.'

'Megan!' I whispered at him. Our thoughts weren't helping *her*.

Jamie stiffened a second, then inclined his head and I let him go. He cleared his throat. 'We don't know how dad got in, we didn't hear him. We were in the middle of dinner.'

The dusty meal still sat in front of us. I glanced up, found myself wondering how much it would cost to repair the damage in the ceiling. 'Dad shot it to prove the gun wasn't fake,' I heard myself say.

I could see Morrison's gaze on me but the hole, larger than I expected from a bullet, fascinated me all of a sudden. Would the bullet have hit the actual roof?

Morrison cleared his throat but didn't tell me to focus. Instead he said, 'The garage door is open, we—'

He cut off as the three of us all went, 'What?'

I glanced at my siblings. Yep, as stunned as me. We hadn't heard the door moving, but also we'd thought it was locked. Or maybe it was just that none of us had tried it in ages. The internal door just had a push-button lock but I had no idea if that had been activated.

'Your father had an electronic opener in his pocket.' Morrison's brows came together. 'I am presuming he didn't tell you.'

'Why the fuck would he?' Jamie blurted.

He was unsettled, looking like he was going to jump up and go see for himself so I ringed his wrist again. He looked briefly at my grip and then he was telling Morrison and the other cop how the ceiling damage had come about. In such verbatim recall that it scared me.

When Jamie reached the part where I'd offered myself to

dad—over and over, in fact—Morrison's gaze levelled on me. 'I admire your courage, Owen, but that was a very dangerous thing to do.'

'I couldn't just…' I sagged back against the couch again. I knew it had been stupid but I couldn't just let dad take my partner without doing something. Except, in the end I'd really done nothing; paralysed with horror and fear as Andrew had moved further from my grasp. It had been up to my fifteen-year-old sister to save Andrew's life, *my* life even. I swallowed hard but my nose and eyes still stung.

'Don't tell him off,' Megan said, sniffling. 'He was amazing. Dad was calling him names and threatening him and he still tried to deflect him.'

Sergeant Morrison sat very still for a moment, then said, 'I understand that, Megan, and I am not surprised that Owen acted that way. However, confronting a gun-wielding person is a very dangerous idea.' He looked at me and I realised that he actually wasn't angry, just very concerned.

My gaze dropped to my hands.

After a moment the sergeant took us back to telling what had happened.

'Well,' Jamie said. 'Given that dad did that.' He pointed a finger upward without looking. 'Andrew didn't really have any choice.'

'And that's when… when I offered myself,' I said, 'but he didn't want me. Not then anyway. He said he had to get… rid of Andrew first.' I glanced up. Jesus, why was Andrew talking so long with that cop?

'Dad kept calling him a pae—'

'Don't,' I said sharply.

'What…?' Jamie began.

'*Don't* say that word, Jamie,' I ground out. 'The sergeant knows it anyway. *I* don't want to hear it again.'

My brother bit at his lip.

'Jamie, you can be explicit when you give your formal statement,' Sergeant Morrison said. 'But for now, as Owen says, I am familiar with the words your father has been using.'

Jamie made a noisy swallow, gave a jerky nod. As he opened his mouth to continue the tale, I decided I couldn't be apart from Andrew any longer. Jamie and the sergeant spoke my name but no one grabbed me. Andrew turned as I neared and enveloped me in a tight hug even as he still talked.

I breathed him in, heard the staccato of his heart. Cowardly, probably, to run to him instead of staying with Megan and Jamie but I needed Andrew right then. Needed to know he was alive. Needed to know he was still with us, with *me*.

Jamie

Andrew was smiling when he came back to the lounge. I wondered how long he practised it in the hall.

I appreciated the attempt to project a sense of calm and confidence, but it would take more than his smile to get us there. Owen had been curled up on the couch, arms around his knees, since the cops left. Talking but not really functioning, hadn't even taken any role in boarding up the window by the door. He was going to need something bloody powerful tonight to prevent a nightmare.

Shit, so was I!

Owen didn't unfurl as Andrew came to take the chair opposite us.

Andrew's gaze shifted to me. 'Jamie, could you stay in with

your sister tonight?'

That sat me straighter, even made Owen shift a little.

'Um, yeah.' Pulled a face as I admitted I didn't fancy being on my own either.

My brother completely unfurled, opened his mouth.

'We're safe here,' Andrew said before he could speak.

Owen's mouth stayed open a bit and then he swallowed, glanced at me.

Dad had cops keeping him company tonight and he was in hospital anyway, but I shared Owen's nerves. But instead of revealing them, I just nodded. Then I mumbled about being shattered and I rose and left the room.

After several minutes listening to Megan's choppy breathing, I sat up. 'Megs, you're not beating yourself up over this, are you?'

Her breathing cut off totally for a second and then, dimly, I saw a hand move up to her face. I fumbled for the lamp on the table between the beds, and suddenly we were lit up by Elsa and Anna from *Frozen*. Couldn't stop the grin since the lamp was actually Megan's not Lisa's.

Lying with her hand over her eyes, Megan mumbled, 'I stabbed dad, Jamie, of course I—'

'No fucking way,' I cut her off, making her wince.

My sister had a little bit of normal spark in her though because she mumbled something about swearing. I pretended I didn't hear the hitch in her voice. 'Seriously, Megan, you saved Andrew's life.'

She lifted her hand slightly, tilted her head to look my way. Her eyes squeezed shut and then she pushed upright, didn't bother to get her hair away from her face so I could see it.

'Sis, you know that's true,' I got out. 'Dad would have killed Andrew, and the way he looked at Owen…' I choked on a breath. I had this really scary feeling that we'd been incredibly lucky dad had only shot the ceiling.

'He's our father,' Megan croaked out. 'How can he behave like that, like we don't matter, like he thinks we'd forgive and forget all he's done?'

'Father in name only, Megs,' I ground out. 'Andrew's our… Well, shit, he's been more our dad than dad *ever* was since we came here. I mean… I get that dad was all guilty about mum and Melissa and the kid, but he still totally ran out on us when we needed him most. Remember all the shit Owen put Andrew through? And… well…' I scratched my head. 'Me too. And all this recent stuff has been so fucking crappy too, but he is *still* here. He's *always* been here for us.'

Megan was nodding, still half leaning over.

I got out of bed and crossed to hers, making her straighten when I sat down. 'You saved Andrew's life,' I whispered. '*And* Owen's. Don't beat yourself up over it.'

Megan looked at me, biting her wobbling lip. Her eyes filled.

'We owe you everything,' I all but mouthed and then pulled her into a hug.

She sobbed. I understood her feelings, but the dad she'd stabbed today, the dad who'd broken in and threatened us with the gun, the dad who *would* have shot Andrew—that man… he was so different from the one who'd returned two months ago that I almost couldn't believe he was the same man.

I squeezed my eyes tight to prevent their watering.

I joined Owen in his old room.

Oddly, when he was distressed, the smaller bed seemed to comfort him. I didn't mind the single bed because it meant I had an excuse to hold him close. Though, I would have done that tonight in any case. And obviously so would he; the squeeze of his arms seemed extra strength, as if he was maybe afraid I'd disappear.

I drew in as quiet a breath as possible, adrenalin pushing through my nerves as I flashed back to early evening. 'G-god,' I whispered. 'I'm so lucky.' I kissed Owen's forehead.

That seemed to be the signal to start his tears. He'd been in control all evening, but oh so quiet. Shock, I knew. The control was gone now and he was sobbing into my chest, babbling too. 'He was g-gonna shoot you. K-kill you! How c-could… could he do that? How could—'

He punched my chest and I took that hand and held it, wrapped my other arm around him. 'Sssh. It's okay, Owen, it's ok-kay.' Darn… if I broke down that'd only ramp up his distress. I held my breath.

'It's not okay!' He squirmed until I finally had to let him go, then pushed upright, pressing against the wall. 'He was going to kill you and I didn't stop him! He was taking you away and I just stood there. If Megan hadn't… I'm so useless, I—'

'Stop it,' I said sternly, making him press back a little more. 'You jumped in front of me for god's sake, Owen! You *offered* yourself for me. Don't you *dare* tell me you're useless!' I had to consciously stop myself from stabbing my finger at him.

'But he was still going to take you!'

Owen's own fingers were scrunching up the sheet over his

knees. I covered his hands with mine and he froze a moment, and then his eyes filled again.

'Listen to me, Angel,' I got out in the steadiest voice I could manage. 'Nothing would have stopped your father. He was too far gone, but you are *so* brave for trying and I am so in love with you for it.'

I slowly raised a hand and he didn't stop me from brushing his hair off his forehead and then leaning to place a kiss there. 'You are the most important and wonderful person in the universe, Owen, and I love you.'

I had to take a moment, even as I managed to keep his gaze. His lips kept sucking in and out and I knew he was struggling to keep the bad feelings back.

'Owen,' I whispered, 'I would go with your father any time to save you.'

His whole body was trembling and his indrawn breath shuddered. And then he said, steady but soft, 'I don't want to be saved if it means I lose you.'

His forehead came to lean against my shoulder and I put my arms around him, hands rubbing his back as he gave a couple of heaving sobs.

I had my teeth clenched to keep back my own grief and relief and everything else I was feeling.

'I peed my pants.'

'Mm,' I murmured, throat constricting, 'came pretty close myself.'

He sniffed. I got us both shuffled horizontal and then I just held him. His head was tucked under my chin and I felt my top getting wet. I wondered if he could feel my tears wetting his head.

Owen

Come morning I was in decent control of myself. Felt lighter too because dad wouldn't bother us again. No one would strip Andrew's guardianship after yesterday.

I didn't wake Andrew, but carefully extracted myself from the bed and went along to my sisters' room. I gave the door a light knock but opened it without waiting for a response. Sticking my head in the gap I saw Megan sitting up, arms around her knees. The curtains weren't quite closed, as if she'd wanted a bit of light but didn't want to disturb Jamie. He lay on his stomach, facing the wall.

'Hey,' I said softly, coming to sit on the edge of Megan's bed. 'How'd you sleep?'

'Okay,' she answered with a little bit of a croak. 'You?'

I did a shrug/nod combination then blurted, 'Shit, Megan, I owe you big! Andrew would be dead if you hadn't acted. You *saved* his life.'

Megan stared at me a second, then lowered her head, fingers pulling at the sheet.

'Don't feel bad, Megs,' I croaked out. 'You did a good thing, and I'll owe you forever.'

My sister looked up, tears in her eyes, brows sort of bunched up. 'I *stabbed* dad, Owen, I can't… I'm a criminal.'

'Are you fucking kidding?' That was out loud before I could stop myself, but Jamie didn't even shift. 'Megan, no way! You saved Andrew's life! You did what I couldn't, you've got so much more guts than me! I just stood there but *you* acted. You stopped him from taking Andrew, from destroying me, from ruining all our lives. Hell, Megan, you're my hero!'

Her expression was weird, as if she was trying to believe

487

but couldn't quite get there. I held my breath and then said, 'What you did saved us all.'

'Fucking *A*.' We both jerked at the sudden words, and Jamie rolled over. 'I said it last night, Sis; you shouldn't beat yourself up over this. And I'm as grateful as Owen that *one* of us had the guts to act. Not that I think you didn't,' he directed at me. 'Fuck man, dad was all prepared to shoot you and you wouldn't budge. If we're talking cowards here, that's me. I did *nothing*.'

'That's not true,' I whispered.

Beside me, Megan drew in a breath. 'What if he presses charges?'

'He hasn't got a leg to stand on,' Jamie replied.

'But I stabbed him in the back, Jamie. He didn't know.'

'So? Defence of another.'

'And he *was* warned,' I reminded her. 'Jamie calling your name turned him.'

'I regret that.'

Megan looked at Jamie sitting there defiant, and swallowed deeply. The knife would have gone to a whole different place had dad not turned. Jamie shrugged. 'I know you think the same, Owen, so don't look at me like that.'

I held his gaze, but didn't argue.

'You see, Megs?' Jamie got out, sounding a bit gravelly. He cleared his throat. 'You did good.'

Megan shifted in the bed, making me glance up at her. Her smile was weak but at least she was smiling. 'Yeah.' Barely audible.

I squeezed her knee, deciding I'd talk to Andrew about getting her some counselling. 'I'm gonna make some tea. Any takers?'

'Yes, please,' Megan said.

'Coffee,' Jamie said. 'Fried eggs wouldn't go amiss.'

'What am I, your servant?'

He actually grinned at that, which made me smile as I left the bedroom.

When I made it back to my old room with cups of tea for Andrew and me, he was sitting on the edge of the bed, curtain open behind him. The relief that flooded his face almost made me speak out. As I placed the mugs on the chair by the bed he rasped out, 'I thought you were gone. I thought he'd taken you.'

'What—'

I managed nothing else before Andrew had me around the waist and was holding me tight between his knees, sobbing over my shoulder. I didn't even have my arms free to encircle him or to hold onto him for balance as he pulled me tighter against him. My knees jammed into the edge of the bed as I tried to avoid falling. I croaked out his name but he didn't let me go.

My heart galloped with rising fear at his distress, which was about the most open I'd witnessed, with just a little bit of concern for myself because the hold was beginning to hurt. 'Andrew,' I rasped out, 'ease up a little.'

'Sorry, sorry.' He started to rise, must have thought he'd caused a bad memory.

'Stay,' I told him, pushing him back to a sit. 'I just wanted free so I could do this.' I climbed onto his lap, ankles hooked behind him, arms wrapped around his shoulders. Pressing my face against his neck I murmured, 'I'm here, I'm never going away. I love you.'

Arms encircled me.

Andrew quietened down a long time before I decided it was probably good that I got off his lap and let him stretch. I spied the cups as I did so. 'Heh, we should drink these before they get completely cold.'

As I reached for one, Andrew suggested we make a fresh pot and sit outside.

'Yeah, that—' I cut off as I turned. Andrew was on his feet but it wasn't him that had my heart stop. Dad was at the window, gun in his hands. 'Watch out!' I cried and shoved Andrew backward.

The window shattered with a shriek, something slammed into my left shoulder and I was suddenly on my butt. Instinct had me immediately scramble upward. Andrew lunged toward me as dad aimed again. 'Stay back, he's gonna—'

Andrew was saying stuff I didn't comprehend and then I found myself dumped in the bath. I couldn't coordinate myself to even sit up properly I was that thrown with the sudden change in location.

'Stay there,' Andrew ordered. 'You've been shot, you're bleeding.' He yanked towels from the rail and thrust them against my shoulder, grabbed my right hand and pressed it to the pile. 'Hold these tight.'

'But dad's gonna—' I cut off, seeing how white Andrew was, how wide his eyes were.

'Owen, please,' he said, 'just… hold—'

'What the fuck's going on?' Jamie cried from the door.

Andrew twisted on his knees as if he was going to try and keep my brother back, but I was gaining my coordination and I didn't want to be stuck in the bath. Andrew turned back to me, one hand tightly around a wrist, trying to keep me down, the other hand pressed to the towels since I'd stopped doing that myself.

Jamie was in the bathroom with us now, Megan behind him. Andrew was telling her to shut the door. She did, but it made Jamie repeat himself and then, 'We heard something shatter, what—'

Dead silence then because I'd managed to twist somehow out of Andrew's grip and the towels had fallen onto my lap. Blood covered my shoulder, the towels too. Megan screamed. Andrew grabbed Jamie and yanked him to his knees, making him squawk. 'Keep him still, Jamie, *please*. Keep weight on the wound, I'm going to the phone.'

'What?' Jamie said. 'But… what…'

Andrew grabbed up a towel, pressed it to my shoulder and put one of my brother's hands there too. Jamie didn't fight and I was still myself, cold at the fear in Andrew's eyes. Then he was on his feet.

'No, Andrew, he'll shoot you, he'll—' But the door was already closing.

'Fuck's sake, Owen!' Jamie heaved against me, forcing me to sit. 'Stay still.'

'Jamie, dad's out there. He s-s-shot… He's g-gonna…'

'Dad?' Jamie breathed. '*Dad?* He shifted, looked back where Megan stood like a statue.

Taking advantage of his distraction, I twisted but all that got me was a wicked wrench of pain through my shoulder and I stilled a moment, realising that I hadn't really felt any pain until then. And then I whispered, 'Let me go.'

I knew Andrew had gone to confront dad and I had to somehow stop him.

Jamie remembered me and put extra pressure into holding me down.

Behind him Megan whispered, 'Wasn't he in a hospital?'

Jamie swore.

A muffled crack came to us. Jamie jerked with the shock and couldn't get hands on me in the right places to hold me down. I shoved at him and Megan got out of the way before I could actually haul her away from the door. I ran, shouting Andrew's name, but of course he didn't pop out of my bedroom or the kitchen to answer me.

The cordless phone lay by the closed front door, making me stop a second. Had he rung the cops, after all?

I nearly bent to see if anyone was hanging on the line, but all of a sudden sirens broke the silence and flashing lights flickered through the glass on the left side of the door. As I grappled with the stupid deadbolt, I heard Sergeant Morrison yelling, 'Put the gun down, *put the gun down!*

Andrew

My lovely young man wasn't brilliant at taking direct orders, so I wasn't surprised that he ignored the sergeant yelling at him to go inside. Unfortunately, he ignored me too, instead stepped onto the lawn and came toward me.

Owen looked fierce. His hair caught in the breeze, lifting in places. His ocean eyes were bright, wide and narrow at the same time. His jaw was set. He meant business. I heard him whisper, 'He's not h-having y-you.'

The stammer made me look properly. Panic and pain were what made his eyes bright, his face was white, and he trembled. His left arm hung at his side and blood coloured more of his top than before.

'Owen,' I began.

He shook his head and faced his father. The man stood with his back against my car, gun in a left-handed grip. Pain kept twisting the corners of his mouth, the only sign that he was carrying an injury.

'Dad,' Owen got out, 'you've done enough damage. Please stop.'

Tremayne wrinkled his nose. 'Shoulda put a bullet through you yesterday. Wouldn't have just wasted that one.'

That one—the one in Owen's shoulder right now.

I drew in a breath, gearing myself to react or speak, but Owen shifted a step—out of my easy reach—and said, 'Killing me or Andrew won't get you anywhere. You won't g-get c-custody of the others. The s-sergeant's here, Dad.'

'Yeah, but getting rid of that boy-fucker is enough.' A stiff jaw jerked at me. 'And you'll just be a bonus, you good for nothing little fag.'

'That's enough!' I growled out before I could stop myself.

Owen began to turn and a shot cracked around the lawn. Both Owen and I jerked, stumbling. I started to crawl to him but he wasn't hit again. His terror was all for me, eyes everywhere, fingers grabbing at me, but I wasn't hit either.

I wasn't sure if he had even noticed Sergeant Morrison wasn't the only officer on the property or that there were two cars with their lights flashing. One of the officers had shot the gun from his father's hand, and he was now on his knees, holding his wrist. Sergeant Morrison approached cautiously, ready in case the man could still be armed, and then Owen jerked away from me.

I cried his name in reflex, but he hadn't been hit or

anything. His father's gun had been flung not too far away and I'd not noticed until Owen dived for it, too slow to grab him back. He scrambled onto his knees, and then upright, holding the gun in both hands.

'Owen, *no*,' I cried, jumping up.

'Put that down!' the sergeant barked.

Beyond Owen, Megan and Jamie stood frozen on the porch.

'Go on then,' Tremayne said, spiteful despite his obvious pain. 'Shoot your own father.'

For a long moment Owen just stood there. I was terrified he'd collapse and somehow shoot himself. More terrified that he'd intentionally do it. But... I could also partly see his expression. Anger ruled. Despite the damage to that left shoulder, he was steady on his feet and he held the gun straight.

When he spoke, it was quiet but deadly. 'You're not my father, you said so yourself. Doesn't matter anyway. You have n-no idea the p-pleasure I'd...' He hissed in a breath.

'You don't have the guts,' the man said and climbed to his feet, right arm hanging a little. I hoped that stab wound was hurting the hell out of him.

Morrison yelled at him to freeze. Another officer was in grabbing distance now, probably holding back because of Owen who'd taken a step backward at his father's movement. He had the gun only in his right hand now and seemed to be focused on his bloody sleeve as if he'd only just noticed it.

'Drop the gun, Owen.' Morrison said it gently, moving carefully and slowly forward at the same time.

Owen jerked to attention, bringing his left hand back up. But he got it only so far before letting it drop, grimace on his face. His father, leaning against my car, smirked.

'Don't want him k-killing Andrew,' Owen got out.

'He won't,' the sergeant said, using a bit of force. 'But you, Owen, you'd be committing murder.'

I froze. Megan let out a squeak. I realised she was hanging onto Jamie as if holding him back. I looked at him more closely. Terrified and angry—like his brother—and so not a good combination. I called for them both to go inside.

'No fucking way,' Jamie cried. 'Shoot him, Owen!'

'*Jamie!*' Megan shrieked, eyes wide.

I was afraid he'd leap down the path and grab the gun. Instead he flung his arms around his sister and held her tight, blocked her view of us.

I took advantage of Owen's slight distraction to try again. 'Owen, if you shoot him I will definitely lose you. The sergeant will arrest you and you will go—'

He glanced at me with wet eyes. 'I want him to s-s-stop.' He brought his hand up to wipe his eyes. The gun hand. That seemed to startle him but the next thing his arm pointed straight out at his father.

'Owen, please,' Megan called out. 'We need you. *Please* give the gun to the sergeant.'

'He doesn't deserve to live,' Owen replied.

'Angel,' I said, 'if you do it, *he'll* win. We will all be parted.'

'You'd better do it, Faggot,' their father sneered from the car. 'Or that paedophile's gonna get his bits cut off and fed to him.'

Owen had been wavering, but at that… I saw hate drown every other emotion, and began to cry out, heart leaping into my mouth. Sergeant Morrison took a step as if he was about to lunge and then Owen lowered the gun. That seemed to make everyone freeze.

'You're not worth a bullet. You're not worth anything anymore.' His tone was one I hoped to never hear directed at me. 'You had a family who loved you, Dad, and you cheated on all of us. Maybe if you'd been loyal, mum wouldn't have been out in the car that day she had the accident. Blaming everyone else for what you did just makes you a loser and a shitty father. We don't want anything to do with you. Just leave us alone.'

I wanted to go to him but he hadn't dropped the gun, and though he seemed suddenly calm he could easily still lift the weapon.

He looked down at it, brows knitting a bit. Tremayne made to move but two officers swarmed over him, hammering him against my car. Morrison swiftly took the gun from Owen, disabling it as he said, 'It's alright, it's over now.'

'Okay,' Owen responded and crumpled to the lawn.

I scrambled to him, Jamie and Megan reaching him a close second. We were all in a huddle until I asked Megan to fetch a blanket for her brother. Jamie followed her, muttering there were too many people about for PJs on the lawn.

[Eighteen]

Owen

When I opened my eyes, it took a moment staring at the ceiling before I recalled why I didn't recognise it. I felt no pain but I couldn't really feel my arm either. A lady in a white coat was standing at the bedside, checking something or other, but my focus slid across the room to Andrew who had his back to me looking out a window.

'Andrew?' I had to repeat it to get sound, but he didn't turn. His shoulders seemed a little hunched. 'Is he crying?' I asked the doctor who glanced up, puzzled. 'Why's he crying? Is he dying? Am *I* dying? Oh god, I've lost my arm, haven't I? That's why—'

'Owen, calm down. Calm. Down.' The doctor set her clipboard on the bed and took hold of my right shoulder, keeping me back against pillows, while I made a pathetic attempt at struggling. 'Nobody's dying and you haven't lost your arm, but *keep still.*'

A whipped glance showed I had no needles or drip bags, *and* both arms, and relief aimed a punch that made me focus on breathing rather than freaking out.

The doctor kept one hand on me for a second, but let me go after I whispered out an embarrassed apology. She gave a small smile. 'I'm Dr Kartik, by the way, and I can assure you that surgery went perfectly fine on your shoulder. However, you still need to treat the wound with respect; that means rest.' She gave a bit of a smile as if she wasn't unused to patients having silly reactions when they woke. 'I'll give you ten minutes, Owen, and then it's no visitors.' She held a hand up as I started to protest. 'They can come back tonight, *if* you're deemed up to it.'

I knew what that meant. Arguing and complaining or trying to get out of bed would see visitors banned. 'I'm not gonna get out of bed,' I mumbled.

I'm sure Dr Kartik made a 'hmph' sound before she turned away, crossing the room to Andrew who had not turned this whole time. She spoke too quiet for me to hear, but he nodded and held out his hand.

Dr Kartik shook it with a smile, then came back to the bed and picked up the clipboard. 'If you start to feel pain, press the buzzer, alright?'

I glanced where she pointed beside the bed, and nodded.

'Good, I'll see you later.'

It wasn't until she'd left and closed the door that Andrew turned. He smiled but it didn't look straight. That could have been my brain, but as he came across the room to me I was with it enough to see that he had been crying.

'I'm ok-kay,' I croaked out, trying to reassure him.

He mouthed my name, eyes shining, and then he was right beside the bed. He looked like he was going to take the seat that was there but I lifted my good hand and he interpreted that just how I wanted, leaning down to give me as much of a hug as he was able in the circumstances. I breathed him in, throat restricting. His own breathing was choppy and his lips wiggled when they pressed to my cheek.

Andrew cut the hug short and took the seat, putting some papers down on the bed near my feet. He wiped his face with the other hand. 'God, I am so glad to see you.'

I just smiled at him, hoping he knew how glad I was back,

hoping he knew that being with me right now meant the world.

He started to say something but my gaze had slipped to the papers. Probably he'd been reading work stuff while waiting, though the paper looked kind of different. And words on that top one weren't typed but written. Pencil. My gaze narrowed as if that'd let me see the writing but the way my stomach was jiggling I was pretty sure I knew what I was looking at. 'That's… the stuff I wrote?'

Couldn't stop it coming out puzzled because how did that end up here? And why had Andrew been reading it? I mean, I had wanted him to but…

'You don't remember telling me to find it and read?' Andrew asked softly.

'No,' I said. 'But my head…' I felt a loose smile turn up my lips. 'You probably heard me before. I'm a bit…' I gave a half shrug; obviously I wasn't fully with things and I didn't remember a whole bunch after Morrison had taken the gun off me. Glancing toward the window all I saw was a cloudy sky. 'It's still today, isn't it?'

'Saturday, yes,' Andrew said, fingers encircling mine.

I heard myself whisper that was good and then my gaze was back on the papers. 'You've read it then? All… of it?'

He nodded, looking that way briefly.

'S-sorry.'

'Oh, Owen, you have nothing to apologise for.'

Making my partner read the story of my prostitution while I was having surgery seemed like something I should apologise over. I mumbled why I'd written it down, and that I was too cowardly to tell him.

'Don't say that,' he said raggedly. 'You've got great courage just *writing* this, Owen.' He reached out and tapped the paper. 'I just wish you'd never needed to. I wish I'd saved you from all of it. You've been through too much.'

Seeing Andrew's eyes filling made my heart ache; I always felt so inadequate at comforting him. Turning our clasp so I was once again the one doing the holding I lifted his hand to my lips, forcing him to lean closer to me and away from the papers. 'You make me okay,' I rasped out. 'Every day.'

He closed his eyes, but didn't try to pull out of my grip.

I still believed that it was dad's attacks that brought those men back to my dreams, but as I'd been writing about the encounters with them I realised that I really did owe Andrew. I hated him knowing what I'd done but since my demons weren't as buried as they once had been, I didn't want him in the dark anymore and not knowing how to cope when *I* couldn't.

But, also, I didn't want to start discussing what he'd read or how we'd ended up exactly where we were now, so I said, 'Andrew, I want to be with you the rest of my life.'

He jerked as if I'd woken him, and his smile was as much sad as happy but then he straightened a little. 'I want that too, Owen. I want nothing more in this world. I was so terrified I'd lose you today.'

I bit my lip. 'I'm gonna be okay, and dad… he'll *never* part us.'

'No,' Andrew said, with a grim smile, 'he won't.' He stood and leaned over to kiss my temple.

I shifted a little but he didn't then aim for my mouth. Instead he took a full step back. 'Your brother wanted to see you, so I better give him a few minutes.'

'But—'

'Just a few minutes,' Andrew said over me. 'And we'll all come back this evening. You just need to behave so Dr Kartik lets us in.'

I felt embarrassed that he'd heard what the doctor had said. He smiled then picked up and folded the pages of writing. Didn't speak as he did that but I knew he'd put them back where he found them, and keep it all secret from my siblings. 'I'll see you later, Angel.'

'Yeah,' I got out around a lump in my throat.

Jamie

I'd asked for a minute with Owen, but when Andrew came to let me know that minute was now he almost had to push me toward the door. Sitting in the waiting room had sent me right back to last year when I'd waited for Owen to wake from another surgery, and I suddenly wasn't sure about seeing him now.

'He's looking forward to seeing you,' Andrew said quietly.

Despite what was in my head, that made me snort (though not entirely with amusement).

'You can do it this evening…'

'No, now's… good.' I gave Andrew a half smile and pushed open the door.

Now wasn't so good for my brain, but I still understood that facing Owen today was a world away from the last time I'd seen him in a hospital bed. He looked tired, but his face wasn't blown up by the ugliest black eye known to man. And there were no scratches and bruises on his arms and hands, no drips.

'Hey,' I managed, dug my hands into my pockets.

'Hey,' Owen responded, fingers picking at a sling which I guessed was there for support.

He was propped up, sheet and blanket to his waist, against a single pillow on an angled bed. Bandages showed where the hospital gown sagged over his collarbone. Dr Kartik had told us the surgery went perfectly fine and Owen would retain full use of his arm. No bones broken, no nerves damaged.

'I hate that this is becoming common place.'

Owen started, eyes wide. Blue-green as usual, but a little bit murky. I grimaced but didn't take it back. Twice in less than a year was common place, and I *hated* it. I looked at the chair near the bed but didn't take it, even though I was forcing my brother to look up at me.

'Um,' he said. 'Are you okay?'

'Of course I—' I cut off, shaking my head. 'No, I'm nowhere near okay. Dad *shot* you! And, shit, I egged you to…' I sucked in a breath and flopped onto the chair, which made him shift a little and look totally unsure about me. I leaned my forehead on the bed a second, heaved in a breath and straightened. 'I thought that seeing you in hospital the last time was the scariest thing and then later that you might have AIDS, but…'

'Jamie.' Owen reached slowly for my nearest hand.

I wanted to pull back but didn't, just let him curve some fingers around mine. 'I'm okay,' he said.

Since I couldn't speak all of a sudden, I just nodded and hoped that with the light behind me he wouldn't see my eyes watering. I dragged in a big breath and sat straighter but kept my arm stretched so he could still clamp my fingers. 'Okay, right, I'm good now. Sorry about that.'

Owen shook his messy head. 'I g-get it.' His smile was soft, tired. 'I'm not a fan of this either.'

He looked down at his lap, I looked down at my spare hand picking at the pale-yellow knitted cover.

After a second he murmured an apology.

'What?' I croaked. 'Why are you apologising? Today was… Don't be fucking stupid, Owen.'

He picked at his teeth, gaze down.

'I wish I had your guts,' I whispered.

I'm sure he almost suffered a whiplash, his gaze swung about that fast, eyes less murky now. I turned the clasp so that I squeezed his fingers. 'What you did today, with dad pointing that gun, trying to get his attention off Andrew… That was the most fucked-up thing I've ever seen, including yesterday, but it was *so* amazing too.'

My brother just stared at me. I probably shouldn't have been surprised about that.

'Owen, dad *shot* you, there was blood everywhere, and you still—' I found I couldn't continue.

'Well,' he croaked. 'I… I love Andrew.'

I just stared at him, at the absolute knowledge in his gaze.

'Fucking A,' I whispered, shaking my head and smiling at the same time.

The door clicking had us both turn. Andrew leaned in. He seemed hesitant at first but smiled when he saw us. I felt a bit shame-faced how I'd been when I'd first come in. 'Time to go?' I asked.

'Yeah,' he said. His gaze lifted to Owen. 'Get some rest, Owen. We'll be back later.'

Owen nodded. I squeezed his fingers, then rose. 'I'll bring some cards or something.'

'Okay,' he said, with another half nod, rubbed an eye.

He was probably as tired as he looked, and I reckoned that if I hadn't been talking he'd already have fallen asleep.

'Love you,' Andrew murmured quietly from the door.

That got a shy glance from my brother followed by a ghost of a smile. I rolled my eyes, making his smile a bit stronger. I gave the bed a pat and then headed for the door, pushing Andrew out the gap and closing it after me.

Owen

If I had visitors Saturday evening I so didn't know it, sleeping pretty solid until the next morning. When Dr Kartik dropped by to see how I was doing I didn't ask her about it, just went with answering her questions. My calm eked out when she told me that Sergeant Morrison would be dropping by shortly.

I winced—that took me right back to last year when he'd sat at my bedside asking me questions and not really liking my answers. At least… at least this time I wouldn't have to describe anyone for a sketch artist. I pulled a face.

'I can't put him off, Owen,' Dr Kartik said. 'He dropped by last night but you were having a good old sleep and I didn't want you disturbed.'

Managing a reasonable smile, I said, 'It's not that, it's just…' I shook my head. 'Kinda never expected to be in this situation again.'

She squeezed my hand. 'Would you like me to stay when he comes?'

'No, it'll be okay.'

My words seemed to make Dr Kartik a little hesitant but then she nodded and rose, glanced at the tray she'd rolled out of the way when she'd arrived. Breakfast—bacon and eggs, which had been really great but a bit tough to deal with one-handed.

'Good to see you finished breakfast off.'

'I was starving,' I told her. 'And it was really nice.'

'We do try not to feed gruel,' she responded with a chuckle, making me flush a bit. 'Now, I better get onto my rounds. If you feel a bathroom need, use that button to call for a nurse. First time on your feet I want someone with you, okay?'

'Okay,' I responded automatically, deciding I'd do my best not to feel a bathroom need.

'The sergeant should be here in a half hour or so, and I believe your family will be back later this afternoon.'

I nodded.

'Use that button if your pain levels increase.'

'I will,' I told her.

Dr Kartik left me then, obviously satisfied that I was sensible enough to request help if it was needed.

- # -

When Sergeant Morrison arrived, I thought he'd get out his notebook and ask me a bunch of questions. But all he asked was how I was feeling and if he could take a seat.

'Ah, sure,' I said. 'And I'm feeling fine.'

'Dr Kartik told me that surgery went well,' he said, getting comfortable on the chair.

'Yeah, she reckons I won't have any lasting damage,' I said. 'But I'm grateful I'm right-handed. I have to wear this sling at least until the end of next week.'

Morrison nodded. 'That'll be to keep your shoulder steady while you heal.'

He almost had this tone that said *A miracle's more likely to occur than you wearing that for two weeks.* I couldn't call him out because I'd already had thoughts about when I could do away with it. He smiled, probably knew what I was thinking too.

'Sergeant Morrison,' I said after a moment, 'This is over, isn't it? Dad's gone forever?'

'It will be over, Owen, yes,' he responded.

'But… dad?' I asked when he didn't go on to mention him.

'He's currently in hospital, but—'

'Not *here?*'

Morrison swiftly reassured me he wasn't, and I leaned back against my pillow, making myself settle down.

'He's in Stateville, and will likely stay there.'

'It's a prison?'

'Yes, it's a prison,' he responded. 'He's been charged with attempted murder and various— Owen?' He leaned forward. 'Are you okay?'

'Yeah, yeah,' I got out, trying to make myself be less stiff. I dragged in good air so I didn't sound like I was gasping. 'I just… Attempted murder is kinda…' I wasn't sure why hearing that shocked me so much, since I'd been on the receiving end of the attempt. I guess to hear dad's intention in black and white just hit way hard. I dragged in more air, then managed a smile at the sergeant who looked like he regretted telling me.

He arched a brow.

'Does Andrew know about it?'

'Yes, he and I had a long talk last night.'

I nodded. 'Good. That'll relieve him a lot, dad no longer being around to call him those horrible words.' I looked down at my fingers curled in the sling. I stretched them out then curled them again, mumbled, 'I was going to shoot him. What he said last about Andrew just…'

'I know,' Morrison said softly. 'I saw your face change.' His lips pressed together a second. 'I definitely did not expect you to lower that gun and start talking. That took immense maturity and courage, Owen. I'm proud of you.'

I winced a little, but didn't spoil his praise by saying I'd just not wanted dad to win. Instead, swallowing back a croak, I asked, 'Is it *really* over now?'

'It will be, Owen,' Sergeant Morrison answered, didn't say he'd already told me that.

It was something I was gonna need to hear over and over before I could accept it. Even under guard dad had been able to sneak out yesterday morning.

'Was anyone else hurt?' I asked.

'No, no one else was hurt.'

'That's good.' Then, even though someone probably already had, I told him about hearing that second gun shot.

'Mr Gordon said your father fired into the ground. It was just before we arrived.'

'Why don't you ever call him Andrew?' I asked suddenly.

'Best to maintain professionalism, Owen,' he responded after a beat.

I gave a one-shouldered shrug.

Morrison eyed me a bit longer but I wasn't going to comment. Instead I asked about giving a statement. One of his brows went up and then he said, 'I'll take it tomorrow.'

I looked at him, puzzled.

'We've got Mr Gordon's and your siblings' to go through. Yours waiting another day won't be a problem.'

I nodded. Tomorrow was good for me, actually, because

hopefully by then I'd be over the total embarrassment at how many times he'd had to take my statement. God, tomorrow would be the *second* time in a hospital room. I hoped I didn't look as embarrassed as I felt.

He patted the bed briefly, then looked at his watch, rising. 'I better be on my way. I'm glad to know you're feeling okay.'

'I am,' I confirmed. He smiled and turned away. 'Sergeant?'

'Yes, Owen?'

'I'm sorry for all this.' I wafted my hand about like the hospital room meant everything. 'Right from the *start*.'

'Thanks, Kid, but there's no need for apologies. I'm just glad that yesterday turned out better than—' He cut off but it wasn't because we were interrupted. He rubbed a hand through his hair. 'I'll see you tomorrow morning.'

I nodded, let him go without pestering. Knew where he'd been going with that anyway—the day had ended with no one dying. Maybe he thought that was a miracle. *I* did.

- # -

Jamie was my first family visitor, but he confirmed Andrew and Megan were here; they'd just take individual turns. Probably so I didn't feel overwhelmed.

I didn't mind that because what was suddenly in my head probably didn't need a wider audience. 'So, is Sarah pregnant?'

Jamie looked at me like I had two heads. 'Uh,' he said, 'don't know.'

Obviously not a subject he wanted to talk about it, so I said, 'You know about condoms, right?'

He arched a brow. 'Ah... asks the guy who was tested for *AIDS*.'

Guess I'd opened that door myself. My chin tilted up. 'And you didn't *learn* from that?'

'Man,' Jamie said, 'I can't believe you're on the high horse here.' He shook his head. 'Anyway, Sarah's not sure herself. She says she's a bit late.'

'Late?'

'Yeah, her period, you know? She said she's usually clockwork, give or take a day or two, but it's about two weeks now.' Jamie folded his arms. 'You know I'm only talking to watch your face, Owen. It's priceless.'

I'd hoped the drugs were keeping me pale, but guess they couldn't quite mask the discomfit.

'Serves you right,' Jamie muttered.

'I was serious,' I croaked out. 'Jamie, it's… big.'

He drew in a long breath, holding my gaze. 'Yeah, I know, but she thinks it's probably just hormones or something. She's been stressed lately with ballet exams and that audition for the dance company.'

I nodded like that sounded normal. Jamie pulled his hair back. 'Shit, can't believe I blurted about it the other day.'

'Has Andrew said anything?'

Jamie shook his head. 'Think it's completely gone out the window for him.' He looked relieved, then gave a grimace. 'I should thank you for that.'

'Hah.' I looked down at the sling a moment.

'She's seeing her doctor sometime this week,' Jamie volunteered. 'Guess we'll know after that.'

I nodded, still didn't look up. Was doing my best not to do a 'What the fuck were you thinking?' thing because I really had no standing at all, and didn't feel like Jamie telling me that to my face.

Jamie sat sucking at his teeth then said, quietly, 'Hey, don't bring it up with Andrew, okay? It's my… thing.'

We looked at each other and then I shook my head. 'I won't say anything.'

'Thanks,' he mumbled and then asked if I'd had a visit from Sergeant Morrison.

'Yeah, earlier,' I said, happy to go with the subject change. 'Told me dad was in prison. Well, in hospital in a prison.'

'Told us that too. Have you given your statement?'

I shook my head. 'Tomorrow. He said you guys have done yours.'

'Last night,' Jamie said. 'He must be getting sick of doing that.'

We shared a wry glance. 'Well, should be the last time,' I said.

'Fucking A,' he responded between gritted teeth. Picking at a thread on the blanket, he said, 'On a side note, the neighbours don't have any entertainment.'

I cocked my head.

'We're staying at Andrew's,' Jamie said. 'Crime scene and all that at home, you know.'

'Ah, yeah.' We'd boarded up the window by the front door but my bedroom window was now shattered and there was probably blood all… I swallowed hard.

'Dr Kartik says you'll be released mid-week, so we'll go back home then,' Jamie said. 'Things will have been made good by then.'

All I could do was nod. Then I asked about Lisa and Matty.

'They're at camp, Owen.'

'I know that, I just wondered if they'd been told or something.'

'Fuck no,' Jamie said. 'They won't be told anything about anything.'

Which was what I wanted myself, so I didn't argue. I looked up. 'You said neighbours before. How many… on Friday…?' Maybe none had noticed since police cars at our house had become a regular thing. The ambulance though… 'God, we didn't make the news, did we?'

'Yeah, we did,' Jamie said.

I groaned. 'We're gonna be asked to move away.'

Jamie let out a bit of a chuckle. 'Wouldn't say that's a bad thing right now.'

I eyed him.

'Andrew went home this morning to just check things and there was a media car outside. A reporter was talking to some guy I think lives down the end of the street. Had a dog with him.'

'Oh God, not *him*.' I pushed my hair back off my forehead, told Jamie about the couple walking the dog who'd seen me and Sergeant Morrison talking on the drive after Megan's ruined birthday.

Jamie bit back a grin.

'It's not funny, Jamie,' I said. 'I don't want this stuff out and about. It's horrible!'

'Well, it's too late,' he said. 'It's out and about, but from what I've seen so far there's no footage of the actual… thing.'

'Thing?'

My brother looked at me like I was dumb. 'Yeah, you waving a gun around and everyone trying to make you drop it.'

I winced back against my pillow, drew my knees up.

'Sorry,' Jamie said with a bit of a croak. 'But… yeah, no

footage of that. Social media footage anyway. Sergeant Morrison said one of his officers was wearing a badge cam.'

'Oh, *God*.'

'Apparently it's usual for an armed offender call-out,' he said. 'You know what? We're lucky Matty wasn't home. He'd have been asking everyone if their gun was real.'

'Yeah, he probably would have.' I scratched my head. 'Crazy kid.'

'Hey,' Jamie said after a short silence. 'It's all good now, Owen. Done. Over with.'

I nodded, swallowing back a lump.

He leapt up. 'Gonna go before you make me cry. See ya!'

My brother was gone before I could even start a response.

Andrew

Owen beamed at me when I walked in.

'Hey, you,' I said, leaning to give him a quick kiss. 'You're looking more with it today.'

He let out a soft laugh. 'Feel more with it. Even ate all my breakfast.'

'Wow.'

Owen stuck out his tongue. When I sat down, he reached out and I let him take my hand. His beautiful blue-green eyes were bright this morning and he definitely didn't look as murky as yesterday. Probably still tired though, so I aimed not to take too long since Megan actually wanted to *talk* to him when she came in after me.

'Sergeant Morrison says he calls you Mr Gordon to be professional.'

'Hm, that's a good way to be,' I said.

'That's not what I meant to say,' he mumbled, reddening, swatting at my hand. 'He said dad was in prison and that all this stuff is over.'

The pain and anger and relief in Owen's eyes was hard to see. 'Yes,' I said, 'he told me that too.' I refrained from saying that I'd believe it only when it really came true.

As if he understood my thoughts he whispered, 'I need to believe him, Andrew. I can't be afraid anymore.'

I swallowed a lump, whispered back that he didn't need to be afraid, and raised his hand so I could kiss his knuckles. He shifted from my clasp and reached out for my neck. I leaned forward, half off the chair, so he could hook me in closer. I should have stopped him doing that, worried about the wound, but I wouldn't deny him a kiss if that's what he wanted.

Not long into it, both of us acting like we'd been starved of this sort of action for weeks, Owen was leaning back against the pillows and I was balancing on my hands either side of his hips so I didn't squash him with my weight.

Fingers began tangling into a belt loop; fingers that belonged to the hand that belonged to the arm in the sling, and they shouldn't be moving or exerting any sort of pressure that might affect that shoulder. I closed my hand around Owen's and gently freed his fingers, pushing back on my other hand to put space between us. His grip in my collar tightened but then he let the hand fall, released a sigh as he did so. I didn't expect him to call me a spoilsport.

I snorted, sat back in my chair, shifting a little for comfort. 'A hospital room is not a good place.' I waggled a finger at him.

He drew his knees up, causing a blanket tent. 'I'm willing

to practise.'

That made me let out a loud chuckle. 'No way,' I told him. 'You are not egging me into making a fool of myself. Do you want Dr Kartik to walk in on something? She'd ban me from visiting you.'

Owen grinned then, open and pure.

I smiled back, heart expanding with how much I loved him.

He cocked his head. 'I could tell her you're my best bet for recovery.'

I laughed. Before I found myself doing something so very stupid, I asked if the sergeant had taken his statement.

Owen sat silent and then, 'Well, that was freaking mean, bursting the bubble.'

'Sorry, Angel, but I need calm us both down. I don't want to be banned.'

He pulled a face, then gave a half shrug. 'He's coming back tomorrow to do the statement. Said one more day wouldn't make a difference. Jamie said an officer had a badge cam, or something, so he probably doesn't even really need my statement.'

'Jamie said what?'

Owen looked at me, puzzled. 'You didn't know? He said Morrison told him they used cameras in armed offender call-outs.'

'Oh… right, I knew that. Just didn't understand "badge cam".'

He gazed at me but at least didn't tell me to get up with the word play or whatever.

'Use of cameras is a great idea,' I said. 'Though I'm not that pleased to be recorded in my pyjamas.'

That got a smile out of him. He said, 'If I gave you a ring, would you wear it?'

I nearly went, 'A ring, what?' His eyes were dark, serious, more green than blue at the moment. Somehow I stayed on the chair rather than getting up and doing something daft. 'I would, Owen, yes.' Managed not to sound suddenly giddy.

'Good,' Owen murmured. 'You'll try to look surprised when I give it to you, right?'

I stared. 'You've got one already?'

He flushed. 'Yeah. Ages ago, actually.'

'You got me a ring ages ago?' I murmured.

Owen breathed out, 'Yeah.' Looking really shy, he added, 'Been trying to come up with a good time to offer it, but…' He pulled a face.

'Can I bring it to you here?' I asked.

'Ah… that kinda defeats the purpose of *me* presenting it.'

'God, yes, sorry.' Smiling, I rose so I could kiss his temple. 'In your own time, Owen. I'll be patience personified.' I didn't sit again. 'We're only allowed an hour total. I better let Megan have some time.'

'Yeah, okay,' Owen responded, giving a small smile.

I actually didn't want to leave, but Megan needed to see her brother, and the longer I stayed the more likely Owen would be able to egg me into something that could turn out embarrassing and disastrous.

Owen

The second Megan stepped through the door, her breathing choked and tears streamed down her face.

I had a moment's fright that something bad had happened in the seconds between Andrew leaving and her arriving, but then she was reaching for a hug. I held her as tightly one-armed as I could, struggling to keep myself dry, saying over and over, 'I'm okay, I'm okay.'

'I kn-know,' she sobbed, 'and l-last time was… was worse, b-but…' A huge breath dragged in just by my ear and then she unhooked from me and stepped back, wiping her eyes. Her lips curved to a small, embarrassed smile. 'Sorry.'

I shook my head as I swallowed back a lump. 'Don't be,' still came out like a rasp.

She looked down at the edge of the bed and I didn't know what to say so silence held for a few minutes before I ventured to ask if she was okay.

Another blocked breath and more silence before Megan started to nod. 'Yeah,' she got out softly. 'Because *you* are, because dad has…' Now she shook her head, and took the seat by the bed. 'Far out, Owen, I don't know what—'

When she cut off, I reached out and she let me take one of her hands.

'It's all going to be fine,' I said, sounding as sure as I could. 'Dad's gone, in jail, Megan. He won't be coming back. The sergeant said so.'

'Yeah, I know, he told us all that.' Megan pushed hair behind an ear. 'It's not *that*, so much, but…' She gave a half shrug. 'All that he did, and not just yesterday. And Melissa phoned me.'

I went still.

She looked up, brown eyes showing guilt. 'I've had her number for a while.'

The ability to react appeared to have disappeared, so all I did was stare.

'I should have said something, I know,' she whispered, 'but

I didn't think…'

Even though I was shocked, my brain was suddenly wondering about Melissa and how she was reacting to what dad had done. My stomach took a bit of a twist as I realised that his actions would affect her and Sam as much as they'd affected us. Dad was her *husband*.

Megan wiped her eyes. 'She's our st-stepmother, Owen.' She put a hand over her mouth briefly then looked at me properly. 'No m-matter how horrible all this is, she's still our—'

I didn't know what to say.

My sister let out a long, steady breath. 'I know Jamie feels she's part to blame for everything, but she's s-suffered too, you know, and Sam's just two. Dad…' She straightened her shoulders. 'Dad screwed them over too and I just think… Well, Melissa's always been nice.'

I drew in a breath and made myself ask, 'How is she?'

'Um, shaken.' She nodded as if she could totally agree with that. *I* could. 'But more concerned about us, *you*, than herself and Sam though.'

I bit at my lip.

'I… want to see her, Owen,' she said quietly. 'I know she's not… *mum*, but…' She trailed off, looking helpless.

Grief tightened my throat. I recalled Megan telling me once that she had Alana's mum if she needed to talk, but I guess that Melissa showing up married to dad, with a child, had made the lack of a real mother suddenly apparent again. I hadn't really felt that loss *or* that connection to Melissa, but Megan was right. Technically, Melissa *was* our stepmother. I understood how that link would act on my sister.

I straightened, startled to find Megan suddenly right by the bed, flushing a bit that I'd tuned her out. 'W-what?'

'Can I see her, Owen?' she asked. 'And Sam?'

'Why are you asking me?' I croaked out.

'Because you're my *brother*,' Megan said. 'And if you don't… want…'

I swallowed hard. 'Megs, if you wanna see her, then see her. I would never—' Had to swallow again.

I remembered her playing with Sam those times and him smiling and giggling. For a short while it'd been like there was no hurt or doubt or loss weighing her down. And with all that had happened, all that she'd *seen*, I couldn't deny her something that helped.

Megan's eyes were shiny. 'Really?' she whispered.

I nodded. 'Maybe… we *all* could meet some time.'

Sniffing and nodding, Megan leaned forward to hug me.

When she pulled back, she returned to the chair and looked like a whole weight was off her shoulders. And, as we sat and talked, I realised I didn't mind that she'd been growing a connection with Melissa. In fact, I thought that meeting up would probably be a good thing, help us to truly realise that dad's actions hadn't affected just us.

[*Nineteen*]

Owen

Dr Kartik gave me the green light to go home on Wednesday morning.

I wanted to be at home, but also didn't. I kind of hoped Andrew would take me to his place, but that was dumb. We couldn't *all* fit there easily.

When Andrew came to pick me up, I was dressed and sitting in the chair by the bed, arm in the sling. He was given the run-down of things I should and shouldn't do, even though the doctor had already told me. Maybe she thought I would ignore the instructions. I sort of wanted to because my arm ached being in the sling all the time and I *really* wanted a shower to wash my hair. I'd only been allowed to do cursory washing and my hair was gross.

Except, showering was on the banned list until Sunday because I needed to keep the bandage over the wound dry for a while yet. Andrew wouldn't entertain us even trying to find a creative solution. He just assured me we'd get my hair done over the sink.

I pulled a face in response, then got up. I could have carried my backpack but Andrew hoisted it over his shoulder once he'd put in the packets of painkillers.

After a few more instructions, Dr Kartik let Andrew take me out of the hospital. I winced in the bright light but relished the fresh air on my face. He dumped my bag on the backseat and then helped me get in, carefully putting my seat belt in place. 'Okay?'

'Yeah,' I replied, trying not to finger the sling.

We didn't really talk much on the way home, the silence resting comfortable between us. Then as we turned into our street I asked if the window had been fixed. The possibility that I'd be confronted with a boarded-up bedroom window bugged me. I kept my gaze on the dashboard but noticed Andrew glance at me. 'Yes,' he said, 'both of them.'

I nodded, chewed my lip. My stomach was uneasy and I closed my eyes as the house started coming into view. A whirring sound came to my ears and I opened my eyes, mouth dropping as I saw the family car in the driveway, blocking the view of the bedroom, and the garage door rising.

Andrew cut the engine and looked at me. 'You okay?'

'Y-yeah,' I got out. 'I didn't... didn't realise the car... Where did you find the keys?'

Andrew unclicked his seat belt and said, 'I didn't. I ordered some new ones.'

My brows went up, but I restricted myself to, 'Huh.' Then, 'And it works?' I released my belt, did my best not to bang my arm with it as I did so.

'Nope. Dead battery. I had to push the car out.'

'Why did you bother?' I asked, puzzled. 'You should have just called a mechanic.'

'I have called one,' Andrew replied, 'but they can't get here until later.'

I looked at him.

'Angel,' he said softly, 'I didn't want you to have to walk up the path.'

I dragged in a breath, understanding, and whispered, 'I love you.'

Andrew leaned over and kissed my temple. He murmured

he loved me back and then got out of the car. He helped me out, hand at my good elbow as I straightened. 'I'll get you settled in bed and then get your bag.'

'Couch?'

'Let's try to get through at least the first hour obeying Dr Kartik's orders,' he answered wryly. 'There's too much stimulation in the lounge.'

Probably true, so I didn't argue. He stayed on my left side so I didn't get a good view of the new window beside the front door. Didn't see into my old room either; that door was closed.

He got me settled in what had become *our* room, then fetched a glass of water. As he gave it to me, I said, 'You're gonna have to help me with baths.'

He smiled. 'Looking forward to it.'

'It'll probably be easier if you join me, you know.'

Andrew chuckled as he flipped the spare half of the cover over my lap, and it was so good to hear that my eyes stung a bit. 'Owen…'

'I'm okay,' I told him. Couldn't reveal that coming home from hospital this time was somehow more difficult than coming home after Wheeler's attack. I didn't quite get how it could be, given *that* attack had been physically so much worse followed by a longer hospital stay. Without the ability to really understand it myself I didn't want to upset Andrew by saying weird stuff. I cracked a smile. 'I'd ask you to sit with me but I think I'm gonna be asleep soon.'

He eyed me and then said, 'I'll sit with you anyway, Angel.'

\# - \# - \#

On Friday, Andrew came home just before one.

'Everything alright?' I asked once he was in the house and the door was relocked. He was doing lesser hours this week but one o'clock still seemed pretty early.

'That's what I want to ask you, Owen. Come on, you shouldn't be on your feet too long.' He walked me to the lounge where I sat on the couch and he on the coffee table in front of me. 'Are you alright?'

'What? Of course, why—'

'Hon, you rung me a lot today.' His smile was off as he rubbed his hands together. 'Normally I wouldn't mind but it was clockwork.'

'No way,' I said immediately. 'I didn't ring that much.'

Andrew cocked his head, and his smile was still not brilliant. 'You rang every hour, Angel, *on* the hour. That's why I started answering "Hi Owen". I knew it would be you.'

I sucked in my lips as memory showed me doing a lot of phone work. My gaze dropped to my knees.

'What's up?' he asked softly. 'Are you bored? Scared?'

I started to deny that last thing but my head was already nodding. Out came a whisper that I didn't want to be alone. 'Not in this house.'

Andrew leaned forward and squeezed my knees, making me lift my head. His blue eyes seemed extra dark. 'You're safe here, Owen. Your father's locked up.'

'Doesn't matter.' I was still whispering, barely able to keep eye contact. 'All the things he did, he did *here*.' I hunched up my good shoulder in a shiver. 'I don't want to be alone, Andrew, and I don't want to be here. Can I go to work with you tomorrow?'

Andrew cocked his head. 'Tomorrow's Saturday.'

Shit… so it was. I swallowed. 'We could still go.'

'Oh, Owen,' he said on a sigh. 'The office isn't a good place for you to be, weekend or not. You're supposed to be resting.'

'I *can't*,' I squeaked, force in a deep breath to get my voice back. 'I know it's weak but I can't… here…' I chomped down on my lip like pain there would stop my eyes getting wet. This was even more stupid since I'd managed okay yesterday on my own; I didn't really know why today was so different. Maybe because it was Friday the Thirteenth? Maybe because it was exactly three months since dad first phoned?

I happened to be looking down at Andrew's hands on my shaking knees. He lifted his hands and the shaking stopped, making me realise it wasn't me doing the trembling. 'I'm sorry,' I got out.

'*I* should be the one apologising,' he told me. 'I did all that car manoeuvring on Wednesday, but hardly thought how you might be *inside*. Hell, I haven't even thought about how your siblings are doing. When they get home we'll talk about going back to the apartment.'

'We b-barely fit t-there.'

'We'll fit just fine until we sort something else out.' Andrew's steady smile settled me a bit. 'Okay?' he asked when I hadn't said anything for a while.

I nodded.

'Okay,' he murmured, and then got to his feet. 'How about we get you back to bed?'

'No.'

'Thought you might say that,' he said wryly. 'So I'm willing to make a deal. *You* go back to bed and *I* make us a cup of tea and then keep you company for the rest of the afternoon.'

A brow rose before I could control it.

'Clothed, of course,' he said with a grin. 'Can't run the risk of you egging me on. I do not want to be explaining to the good doctor how your stitches came to be ripped.'

My face heated just a bit that he'd understood my raised brow. 'Guess I can control myself.' Smiled at his chuckle. 'But… it's okay you leaving work sooner than expected?'

'Being the boss always has perks, Owen,' he said.

'Do you pay yourself for these short days?'

Andrew laughed outright and helped me up. Didn't answer my question, just asked how I was feeling pain-wise.

'I'm okay,' I said. 'Bit of an ache but nothing major. I'm not due for more pills until four.'

He didn't look like he disbelieved me. 'This way then.'

Andrew

When my cell phone rang, I found myself with déjà vu. Owen asleep in bed, me sitting beside him doing some work, phone near in case someone in the office needed me.

Depressingly, this time *wasn't* because we'd left work early to spend the afternoon making love.

With my arm around Owen as he slept, I had limited moves open that wouldn't wake him, if the phone itself didn't because I couldn't find it immediately. Felt like minutes before I found it under several papers. 'Jamie!' I force-whispered. 'What's up?'

There was a pause then, 'Why are you whispering?'

'Owen's asleep,' I said, glancing downward. Mercifully still true.

'So you *are* home then?'

'Yes. Why, where are you?'

'In the drive,' Jamie said. 'I was surprised to see the car. Rung to check that everything's okay.'

'Yep, things are fine,' I told him. 'Just decided to leave work early. How about you save some money and come talk face to face?' I almost expected a sly comment but he just said, 'Yeah, bye' and ended the call.

Dropping the phone on the bed, I glanced down at Owen again. Still asleep against my shoulder, long lashes shadowing his cheeks. I brushed hair off his forehead, pleased that my sigh didn't come out crooked. Flexing my arm a little to ease some stiffness made him shift but not waken.

Half a minute after hearing the front door being used Jamie stepped into view. 'I wondered if I should come with my eyes closed.' *There* was the sly comment. 'But I see he's just catching flies.'

Owen's head was tilted back now, mouth slightly ajar. I suppressed most of the smile. 'How was your day?'

'Same old, same old,' Jamie responded. 'How was yours?'

'You do see that I am fully dressed, and that your brother has an arm in a sling?'

Jamie turned away with a wide grin. Over his shoulder he asked if I wanted anything.

'A cup of tea wouldn't go amiss.'

He gave a nod and was gone.

'Cheeky so and so,' I murmured.

The head on my shoulder shifted and Owen croaked, 'I wasn't catching flies, my nose is blocked.'

'Hey you,' I said as he straightened off my shoulder. 'How'd you sleep?'

He swiped his hair back and yawned, then tilted his gorgeous ocean gaze to meet mine. 'Always better when you're with me, Andrew.'

I dropped a kiss on his temple. A tiny smile curved his lips.

'Hey,' I said, 'do you want the tea Jamie's bringing?'

Owen shook his head, then shrugged down until he was horizontal. His cheek came to rest on my thigh and I noted his eyes closed almost immediately.

'Hmm, your shoulder okay with you lying like that?'

Since he was pretty much on his side, turned into me, his slinged arm rested across my legs. 'Yes.' He didn't open his eyes.

I didn't think he'd move even if I chose not to agree, so I just tucked the covers around him. He drew in a long breath but said nothing, and I reached for the journal I'd been reading before Jamie had phoned.

As if he realised I wasn't going to make a fuss, Owen shifted again, getting his right leg beneath my partially raised one and then his left leg over top. I couldn't quite understand how he found that comfortable and I was sure one or both of us would end up with numb limbs, but I let him do as he wanted. In fact, I was perfectly happy to have him cleave to me. If I was sure I wouldn't get some comment from Jamie, I'd have shrugged down and let Owen cleave even closer.

Instead I tried to concentrate on the journal.

When Jamie brought me my tea, he said, 'He allowed to lie like that?'

Dr Kartik had told us as flat as possible. 'He said it was okay,' I responded.

I knew what Jamie's smile meant—that I'd let Owen lie any which way he liked, even if it hurt. For a moment I thought I also saw pain in the smile and I nearly asked him how he felt about being in this house. Managed to hold it back; it was a conversation I didn't want to have sitting in bed.

At the door he turned back to me. 'When are you supposed to be picking Megan up from Alana's?'

'Uh, at five. Why?'

Jamie pointed at the bed.

'What?' I asked, puzzled.

'Him,' he said, still pointing. 'He's like ivy. You'll need to start the separation process long before you need to leave.'

I realised then what Jamie was talking about. Owen *was* pretty much entwined with me. I chuckled, saying I was sure I'd be fine and that *he* could move right along.

Jamie snorted, and left us in peace.

- # -

'Andrew, why do you love me?'

Given it was out of the blue after forty minutes it was amazing I simply jerked rather than let out a yell. I didn't have time to speak before Owen added, 'Your life's totally upside down because of me.'

I looked down at him still folded around my leg. 'I love you *because* of that, Owen, and everything else besides.'

His slanted gaze showed scepticism.

'Owen,' I said softly. 'You're my world, always have been. Nothing has changed that. I love you for everything.'

His lips curved into a tiny smile. 'Same.'

I supported him while he shifted into a sit. His knees nudged my leg and his unrestricted hand ventured to curve my thigh, fingers picking slightly at the wrinkled material. I held still, trying not to feel the heat from his palm seeping right through my pants.

His fingers pinched a little into my leg, then he smoothed the material and let his hand fall to his own lap. 'I'm still having a bath tonight, right?'

The question threw me for a second then I agreed he was. 'And we need to change the bandage too.' I wasn't looking forward to that a great deal, not wanting to see the wound.

'You'll join me?'

'Yes, I'll be— Hang on.' I cocked a brow, watching his face start to gain colour. He wanted me in the bath with him. Even as I was saying we wouldn't both fit and that I couldn't really take care of him, my imagination was showing me how it might go. I hauled in a ragged breath, coughed. 'You'll be in the bath. I'll be there if you need me, but that's got to be it.'

Owen poked his tongue out, then rubbed his shoulder a little.

'Is it sore?' I asked immediately.

'No,' he said. 'Just… can't wait to be out of the sling for a bit.' He lowered his gaze, lashes shadowing pale cheeks.

I caved. 'How about we do another deal?'

He tilted his head.

'You eat everything I put on your plate at dinner,' I said, 'and I'll find some way to make bath time a good time.' Mental eye-roll at how ridiculous that sounded.

Owen obviously liked it though because he accepted immediately and we shook hands. With his face dusting pink, I wondered what he was imagining. Whatever it was, he obviously had faith in my abilities because he'd know I was really going to load up his plate. In recent weeks, he'd been eating less and less and I'd failed big time in encouraging him to see someone about it. While the shooting was going to take decent time to fade, I hoped that with his father out of the picture, his stress would fade and his appetite pick up.

I felt a little mean encouraging him with a promise I didn't yet know how to fulfil, but I also felt that his accepting meant that he really needed more from me than just keeping him company. I let out a sigh.

'You don't have to…' He trailed off.

'Oh believe me, I want to,' I said, smile more solid. 'I just… Well, it's a lot of pressure.'

Owen blinked and then grinned, and I leaned over to snatch a kiss, pulling back before he tried to keep me close.

'How about you get some more rest? I need to go and pick up Megan.'

His happiness slipped a little, but then he said, 'Yeah, okay.'

I paused a second, waiting, but he started to slide back into the bed. Once he was comfortable on his back I carefully got out of the bed and tidied up my papers.

- # -

Whenever I usually said, 'Okay kid, bath time then bed', I was speaking to either Lisa or Mathew. It felt distinctly odd saying those words tonight to Owen, but he went off without argument to start the bath while I fetched the medical supplies Dr Kartik had sent him home with.

In the bathroom, steam already misting the mirror, I helped Owen remove the sling and his pyjama top with little shoulder movement. The grey bandage carried general dirt around the edges, while a fading bruise coloured his skin like an odd tan. Dr Kartik had recommended the bandage remain on for the first decent wash and I was okay with that. Seeing the bandage was enough on its own right now.

Owen shimmied out of his pants and turned for the bath, giving me a rear sight that had me biting my lip. I still didn't know how I was going to make this bath time a good one for him, but just seeing him nude was doing it for *me*.

'Need help?' I asked when I realised he'd not actually taken a step into the bath.

'Nah, I'm okay.' Didn't glance over his shoulder, just manoeuvred into the water, right hand pressed to the wall. He straightened up, facing the taps, and then carefully lowered himself.

I ended up taking hold of his left arm so that he didn't exert any pressure on it. He hissed in his breath as the water rose up his skin, making it red. I dipped fingers in and winced. He'd run the bath high and hot. 'I don't think this heat's a good idea, Owen.'

'It's fine,' he replied through clenched teeth. 'My back's sore from all the lying around. This will help.'

I didn't bother arguing, but I had him promise to tell me if it got too much; didn't need him getting light-headed and adding to his injury by fainting. He stretched his legs out and leaned back, left arm carefully laid along the side of the bath.

'You aim to be here a while, huh?'

Owen glanced up, eyes bright. 'You promised me a good time. I'm hoping you'll join me.'

I choked on a breath, grinned. 'We'll see,' I told him. 'First let's get you all squeaky clean.'

His lips moved into an exaggerated pout. 'I ate all that food you gave me.'

I laughed outright. 'I saw the whole show, don't worry. But part of the reason for this bath is to clean you, so let's get working on that.'

Owen smiled and levered himself straight again. Though he sat with his eyes closed, he was quite relaxed as I ran my soaped-up hands over him. His skin was hot even where it wasn't submerged and I kept my senses on his health. I wasn't entirely convinced he'd let me know if he started feeling dizzy.

'Can you do my hair?' he asked softly. 'I really hate it like this.' He ran a hand through it, making it even more messy.

I leaned up to grab the shampoo, sure I could manage this particular wash without getting the bandage too wet. The rinsing was a little fraught since I didn't want Owen shifting so he could lie flat. In the end I sucked up water with a face cloth and wrung it over his head. We got there in the end and I used a dry facecloth to lightly towel his hair off.

'A shower would have been so much easier,' he said with a sigh, using his good hand to wipe his hair back off his forehead.

'Yep, but we're good guys following medical orders,' I told him. A shower wasn't on the 'can do' list until Sunday.

Owen directed me a peeved look. I smiled and asked if he still wanted me to join him.

'Yes.'

'Alright, well, we'll need to let some of this water out. You didn't account for my flab when you filled it up.'

'You don't have flab,' he told me.

His tone wasn't jovial, so I just reached in for the plug, wondering if I should release water and then turn on the cold tap for a bit. It really was still hot and Owen's skin was pretty bright and his face had a sheen. He raised a brow at me when I just looked at him without saying anything. 'Just thinking,' I murmured, turning back to the plug.

I let the water out a couple of inches, deciding that would

probably be enough to not overflow when I got in.

'Scoot forward a bit, so I can sit behind you.'

As Owen did that, I quickly stripped then got into the bath. Sitting, I could see it was nowhere near as suitable for two as my own spa but when Owen glanced over his right shoulder I told him he could move back if he wanted. He didn't hesitate but wiggled his way close, forcing my legs wider as he started to wedge between them. He stopped before he got completely against me, which was probably a good thing, but then leaned carefully back. I angled his bad arm along the side of the bath again so the weight wasn't hanging from his shoulder then circled both my arms around him.

Breathing in his clean smell, I whispered that I loved him.

He didn't speak but his smile told me everything I wanted. Gripping one of my arms, he used the leverage to really wedge himself against me.

I clamped my lips closed as I reacted physically to that touch, hoped I wouldn't pant when I next had to breathe. Owen let out a sigh. 'This is nice.'

'Yes, it is,' I said after a moment, and it was; soothing warmth, his weight on me, his fingers running over my hand. I pressed my lips against his head and closed my eyes.

I felt Owen turn his face into my neck, his steady breathing leaving cool patches on my hot skin. My arms relaxed so I wasn't holding him so tight, and water sloshed as he rearranged himself to be more on a hip. It did mean that left arm came off the side of the bath, but he didn't go wild with it, just curved it against himself and I bolstered it in place with my own arm.

My other hand slid when he moved and I was pretty sure the crease I could feel beneath my fingers was that between hip and thigh. I'd have curled my hand back somewhere slightly safer, except Owen directed it right to his groin, causing the same reaction in both of us.

'Owen…' I was a little unsure about it since touching him this way remained something he wasn't quite comfortable with.

'I want you to,' he said softly. 'You don't have to… to do anything, just be there.'

I hesitated a moment, then nodded. 'Okay, Angel.' I relaxed my hand, and actually did my best *not* to feel because I wanted to stay in control. Making love in the bath was out of the question, and getting us both hot and bothered and going nowhere wouldn't make this bath time pleasurable.

He let out a sigh, said his shoulder was okay when I asked about it.

After a moment he murmured, 'Thank you, Andrew.'

'For what, Owen?'

'Indulging me,' he answered. 'For doing it all afternoon, for being here with me now. I appreciate it.'

'Sweetheart,' I murmured, 'I'd do anything and everything for you.'

'I've been selfish today,' he mumbled.

'No, you haven't.'

Tilting my gaze, I saw his small smile. 'Thank you anyway.'

I kissed his temple in reply and settled back to stay with him until the water cooled.

It didn't seem we got even five minutes before there was a single knock on the door and Jamie called, 'Andrew, John Laurence is on the phone for you.'

Owen sucked in his breath as we both jerked and I yelled for Jamie to tell him I'd ring back later. 'I'm busy here.'

Water sloshed as Owen shifted straight, and we heard Jamie groan, 'Aww, gross' and slap the door.

I twisted to look at it but he didn't come in. 'Your brother's got a dirty mind,' I grumbled.

'Heh,' Owen let out. 'We are in the bath together.'

'He can't know that detail,' I said, laughing.

Since Jamie didn't interrupt us, I guessed he'd gone to give my lawyer the message. Owen sat between my knees, hand cupping his elbow.

'Think it's time you got out.'

'But it's still hot.'

'Mm, and you're already red enough,' I said.

I told him to stay put a second so I could get out and help him. After a cursory dry, I wrapped my towel around my waist, pulled the plug and turned back to Owen. He was as wrinkled as a prune, and he swayed a little as I got him to his feet. 'Okay?' I asked.

'Yeah, just a head rush.'

Steam rose from him as he stood on the bath mat and did a brief one-handed dry with the towel I'd given him. I wrapped it around his waist when he asked, and then he sat on the closed toilet while I did my impression of Dr Kartik.

Because Owen could see my face I strove to keep my emotions in check as I peeled away the old bandage. I hadn't seen the wound in its stitched state and, in fact, I wished I could do all this with my eyes closed. I hated that Owen had this bruised and puckered wound with spidery black threads, hated that his *father* had done the damage, *hated* that I hadn't protected him.

Owen was my life and I felt I had failed him, though he'd told me he didn't feel that way.

A few minutes later I smoothed fingers over the new bandage. 'How does that feel?'

'Okay.' He hadn't angled his gaze for a view at all nor asked how the wound looked.

'Good. All sorted then.'

'I didn't bring a change of clothes,' he said in response, throwing me a little.

'Ah.' I looked around; his clothes were on the floor in a messy pile beneath mine. 'Me neither.' I got off my knees. 'I'll go bring you fresh PJs.'

'No, I'll come too,' Owen said. 'It's too hot in here now.'

In the bedroom, he perched on the end of the bed and I went to hunt down his clean pyjamas. Once he was clothed, I said, 'Right, now into bed.'

He shook his dark head. 'I want to stay up for a bit. And I'm… I'd like some fries.'

I stood a moment, just staring. 'Did it only *look* like you ate what was on your plate?'

'I ate,' he said. 'But I… I'm hungry.'

I know I looked amazed at his response but I agreed I'd cook him some fries. Hell, I'd cook him a three-course meal if he asked for it, since asking for food was so rare. I dressed and we relocated to the lounge, Owen settling into the single chair. His brother and sister eyed him.

'Andrew,' Jamie spoke. 'I told Mr Laurence you'd ring back. He said it wasn't urgent and that tomorrow would be okay.'

I nodded. 'Thanks, Jamie. Can you go and fetch your brother's sling? It's in the bathroom.'

'Do I really need it here?' Owen piped up. 'I'm okay without it.'

I hesitated, but he did have his arm nestled against the chair, ensuring his shoulder wasn't taking any weight. 'Alright, while you're out here.'

He smiled. Jamie dropped back to the couch. I realised it was probably Megan's presence on the other couch that prevented him mentioning *my* change of clothes from an hour ago. Though, Megan had returned to her book and wasn't taking much notice.

Except when I said, 'I'm cooking up some fries. Do you guys want any?'

'Fries?' she got out, brows up.

'Your brother's hungry.'

They both looked at him, surprised. I ruffled his hair and headed for the kitchen, ear half on the banter behind me but tuning it out when I heard nothing that sounded off.

Owen

I sat hugging my bowl of fries.

Andrew smiled when I snuck a glance his way, but he seemed preoccupied. I hated to think he was recalling my shoulder. I really didn't like his focus on it and that he felt guilty it had happened. I didn't think anything I could say would change those feelings, so was determined to do all I could to remind him how grateful I was for him and how much I loved him.

The ring I'd told him about would help, but I hadn't yet found the right time to present it. I let out a sigh around my chip munching. Peripheral vision showed him glance at me but I didn't look up.

He broke the silence with, 'Tomorrow we're going to move back to my apartment.'

Megan looked up from her book. Jamie muted the TV. 'Why?'

'Because of me,' I said before Andrew could answer.

My brother and sister looked my way, then back at Andrew. He gave a half shrug/half nod gesture, and then directed me an encouraging smile. I think I made his day whenever I actually revealed my feelings. I said, 'I don't like being here anymore. It just… doesn't feel like home.'

Megan cleared her throat. 'I'm not really comfortable either.' She looked sort of apologetic and embarrassed at the same time.

Jamie's gaze swung to her.

'You can't tell me you don't feel… odd, Jamie,' she said softly.

Jamie straightened, turned his gaze on the muted TV a moment then actually hit the off button on the remote. 'I wasn't…' He shook his head. 'Even with those windows fixed, and that fixed,' he added, poking a finger upward at the ceiling, 'we're living in a crime scene. I don't particularly like it.'

We'd all looked up when he pointed. Aside from that patch of ceiling being quite white compared to the rest, you'd never have known it'd had a hole shot in it.

'I'm sorry I didn't realise this earlier,' Andrew murmured.

'That's dumb, Andrew,' Megan said. 'We should have said something ourselves.'

Jamie sighed. 'Yeah.'

'Right, then,' Andrew said. 'Tomorrow we'll go to the apartment, and from there we'll figure out what to do.'

That puzzled me a moment until I realised he was thinking beyond tomorrow. If none of us wanted to be here, then where could we live?

Even though Megan would be away with Alana from Monday, Lisa and Matty would be home Thursday and the apartment was just way too small. And how would we explain the move to them? They knew absolutely nothing about what had happened. We'd agreed to keep it that way as much as possible, but being at Andrew's apartment for no apparent reason could be hard to explain.

Andrew patted the chair arm. 'Bed time for you, I think.'

'Whaat?'

'You look half asleep sitting there.'

'I'm awake,' I told him and shrugged myself upright.

My sister let out a bit of a *pfft* sound, shaking her head when I frowned at her. Jamie just turned the TV back on and tuned us out. I was tired, yeah, but I'd been enjoying the company; it kept my mind off things.

Didn't bother arguing, though, just went with Andrew to the bedroom. Once I was comfortably in bed, he leaned down and kissed my forehead, murmuring he'd be in soon.

'Hope so.'

Andrew

Owen wasn't asleep when I came in later. The night light down his side of the bed showed me that.

'I knew those fries were a poor idea,' I commented as I changed. 'They've got you too wired to sleep.'

'I'm just not tired,' he responded.

The tone belied otherwise. I kept my sigh silent. His ability to sleep through the night had been blown part by his father, and not even sleep aides we'd tried a couple of times seemed to help. I still thought that a counselling session might help but I was too tired and upset myself to take on that fight just yet.

Easing into the bed, I turned onto my side toward Owen and saw that he had his gorgeous face turned to me. 'I enjoyed that bath,' I said.

He smiled but instead of responding to that he asked if I'd phoned my lawyer back.

I shook my head. 'It can wait until tomorrow, not urgent.'

'Oh.'

I could tell he wanted to ask what it was about but it was not something I wanted to discuss right here and now.

Fingers fumbled for my hand and I let Owen draw my arm across him, obligingly moving in against him, knowing my breath caressed down his throat. I wanted all of a sudden to be even closer but I couldn't start something that I knew I couldn't finish. That wound of his was still too tender. I closed my eyes, popping them open again when he asked if the others thought he was weak not wanting to stay here in the house.

'No, Owen, you heard them. They don't want to be here either.'

'Yeah, but...' He trailed off with a long sigh.

I shifted my arm so I could tuck him closer into my embrace. 'Angel, you're not weak. Nobody expects you to act like nothing's happened. And I should never have brought you here after the hospital. I never thought... just never thought, so so stupid—' I drew in an unsteady breath. 'I've let you all down so badly, you especially.' I rolled onto my back, face turned away, trying to breathe normally.

'Andrew!' Owen cried. 'You *know* I don't feel that way!'

Fingers curved tightly around my left hand.

'What about your brothers and sisters?' I croaked out. 'Jamie said so many—'

'No!' he growled over me. 'Everything you did was to protect us.'

I turned my head back his way, saw that he was up on an elbow, rolled to face me. 'Your shoulder,' I began.

'Fuck my shoulder,' Owen replied heatedly.

My mouth opened but he didn't give me time to speak. 'Never, *ever* think you're at any sort of fault. You. Aren't! You're their saviour, and you're *my* saviour. Always.'

His mouth on mine stopped my words this time and I responded like he'd given me a lifeline. When I managed to haul back, I realised I had Owen on his back and a hand down his pyjamas curved around his backside. I froze a second, got out a ragged breath when Owen said, 'Please don't stop.'

'I… I have to.'

'My shoulder's fine,' he said. 'You know it'll cope.'

I closed my eyes tight a moment, willing my hand free from his pants, doing my best to fight how much I needed him, trying to pretend I couldn't feel how much he wanted me. It took more effort than I could have imagined to disengage and roll onto my back.

'You're going to owe me bigger than that bath time,' Owen said.

My laughter came out sounding a bit sob-like. He clasped my free hand with a tight squeeze, whispered he loved me.

I turned my head, found him looking up at the ceiling, beautiful face in profile. I croaked out that I loved him back. His lips curved and his eyes closed.

[Twenty]

Owen

For the first time in Andrew's apartment, I felt stuck.

I was pretty much banished to the bedroom, to rest, and by Sunday afternoon there was only so much gazing at the condo across the street I could do before I got sick of it. Same with reading and playing Solitaire.

My shoulder was really only sore because of the damn sling but Andrew didn't want me risking it. I could rotate my arm fully without much hindrance but he was sticking like glue to the doctor's orders.

I let out a noisy sigh.

'You're a grumpy ass for someone being waited on hand and foot.'

I jerked, scowled at Jamie as he came into the room and closed the door. I rubbed my brow; maybe after tomorrow's visit with Dr Kartik I'd be allowed more physical freedom.

'Sarah got her period.'

'What?' I yelped.

My stupid brother grinned at me, making me embarrassed. I straightened, got out, 'Why do *I* care?'

'It means that she's not pregnant.'

For a moment I was lost, then memory rushed me back a week to his startling pronouncement that Sarah thought she might be pregnant. It was *that* that had stopped us hearing dad's arrival that day. I cleared my throat. 'Ah, that's good.' Didn't know what else to say.

'Yeah.'

When Jamie just continued to stand there, I said, 'Isn't…
it? I mean…'

Jamie slumped to the side of the bed, fingers crunching into
the cover. His brows were bunched up, jaw tight.

Shit, was he trying not to cry?

I ventured to ask if Sarah was alright.

He glanced at me. 'Yeah, of course.' His brows scrunched
up again. 'She's really relieved, but… I think, upset too.'

'About… about not being pregnant?' I wasn't able to keep
the surprise out of my voice.

Jamie pulled a face. 'Yeah. Well, she didn't actually say it
but I think…' He leaned back, eyeing the ceiling.

'And… *you?*

'Relieved,' he spouted immediately.

I think he held back "but" by sheer will.

Jamie straightened, swallowing. 'God, Owen, it's so dumb
but I *am* disappointed. And I really don't get why. There's no
way we could—' He put his face in his hands.

'Have you told Andrew?'

'Fuck, no,' came the muffled response.

'Sooner or later he's gonna remember what you said.'

'You promised you wouldn't say anything,' Jamie said,
looking at me.

'And I haven't,' I responded. 'But that doesn't mean he
won't remember.'

'So, I don't see why *I* have to jog his memory,' Jamie said.
'I don't want a sex talk.'

My brows went up in surprise. His came down. 'You think
he *won't?*' he challenged.

I cleared my throat. 'Yeah, mostly likely will.'

'I so don't want it,' Jamie said. 'I kinda want to forget it all.'

'Leaving him in the dark's not a great idea.'

'Don't think *you* can talk, Owen,' he responded. 'Isn't leaving people in the dark your speciality?'

I tried not to sound pissed when I replied, 'You forgot already the shit that caused?'

Jamie ran his tongue over his teeth.

'What about Megan?'

He looked puzzled a second, then said wryly, 'Am pretty sure *she's* not hiding anything.'

'I didn't mean… *She* heard you, too, Jamie. Might pay to say something in case Sarah does first. They're friends, remember.'

Jamie cocked his head as if thinking about that. 'Fuck it,' he said with a groan and got up.

'Are you going?'

He stopped, startled.

'I'm bored out of my brains,' I admitted. I reached for the cards. 'Come on, at least one game of something.'

Jamie hesitated, then climbed on the bed and sat cross-legged. 'Snap.'

'I can't play that one-handed. Go Fish.'

He rolled his eyes but held his hand out for the pack, shuffling expertly once he had it.

Half way through the incredibly exciting game, Andrew poked his head around the door. Jamie took that as a sign he could leave.

'Hey, we're—'

'Your next sitter's arrived,' he said. 'I'm done.'

'But… you're a dick,' I grumbled.

Jamie just snorted, patted Andrew's arm when he reached him. 'You're It,' he said and left, swinging the door closed after him.

Andrew glanced at the door then at me. 'What was that about?'

I shook my head, then patted Jamie's pile of cards. 'Play with me.'

His lips curved into a grin at my choice of words. Sitting on the edge of the bed, he picked up Jamie's cards and looked them over. 'What's the game?'

'Go Fish.'

Andrew nodded, looking back at his cards. After a moment he said, 'This hand's a dud, I can see why Jamie left.'

I snorted, earning a smile. 'You could entertain me another way.'

'You know we—'

'I meant *singing*,' I cut over him. I *had* meant singing but it was annoying that he just wouldn't consider a more horizontal form of entertainment. Especially since this morning I'd been allowed to shower. Obviously that meant my shoulder was pretty good. Maybe after tomorrow…

Andrew looked wry. 'Don't you have a bit of an issue with clothing when I sing?'

'That was only once,' I retorted, going red.

He grinned. 'I've only sung for you once. That makes the likelihood rather high, don't you think?'

'Pfft, the others are here.' I said that with a *so there* tone, like it was a sure bet that Megan and Jamie's presence would stop me stripping if he did happen to sing that particular song.

He laughed. 'Maybe later.'

Feeling like I'd won an important battle, I turned back to my cards. Seeing Andrew smiling in my peripheral vision made me feel even better.

The song in question was The Hollies' *Boulder to Birmingham*. I had no idea why it had made me strip. Maybe those few opening lines? Maybe the refrain at the end which Andrew did really well?

Whatever it was, the blood had zipped to my groin. Oddly, it hadn't been the first song he'd sung that afternoon a few days after my birthday. I think maybe the third. Anyway, I'd stripped in front of him and he'd made love to me on the lounge floor.

As I stared at about that spot now I could feel my body reacting. *Really* had to shut down those thoughts and memories. Especially since it was Megan and Jamie laughing their way through a song, not Andrew singing. Beside me, he leaned forward to pick up a handful of popcorn and another memory hit me. 'Hah.'

Andrew eyed me. 'What's up?'

I flushed. 'Just… remembering something.'

'Ah, okay.'

I watched, smiling as he ate the popcorn.

We'd had Garrett popcorn since, but on the night I was now thinking about it had just been me and him here in the lounge. I'd blown an argument with Jamie totally out of proportion, as usual, and bolted all the way here from home. Andrew'd actually found me sitting outside the building as he'd come back from buying the popcorn.

I let out a soft breath. We'd had sex that night—the second contracted time—but something far more important had happened. He'd told me he loved me.

I'd been—

'Snap out of it, Owen,' Jamie butted in. 'That smile's kinda creepy.'

Embarrassment boiled my face, further when Andrew said, 'Oh, I thought it was cute.'

'Shaddup,' I got out to both of them, and stuffed my mouth with popcorn.

My brother smirked, accepted a glass of water Megan held out. Looking over the coffee table, I saw that Andrew and I already had glasses. Damn, I'd obviously been zoned out a while. And I couldn't stop the smile.

Despite the telling-off Megan had given me that long ago night when I'd gotten home, the few hours here had been pretty good. I hadn't been in love myself at that point, but I'd had no fear of Andrew's feelings. In fact, I'd been flattered and satisfied.

I still was. A thousand times more so.

I turned to Jamie. 'Just relishing that I'm no longer a prisoner.' I jerked my head in the bedroom direction.

He choked on a snort and Andrew rolled his eyes. He was smiling though.

Andrew

Owen's ocean gaze fixed on me like I was his anchor and his fingers were twisted into the empty shirt sleeve lying on his lap.

Dr Kartik obscured my view of the wound as she carefully snipped and released the stitches, but I could tell each time she did because Owen's lips would press momentarily tighter.

I smiled encouragingly and continued to tell him about the work meeting this afternoon. Wasn't anything exciting or overly important but I knew he needed me to distract him.

'Almost done,' the doctor murmured.

Owen let out a breath, glanced at her. 'Good.'

'You're doing well, Owen,' she told him. 'And this is looking very nice.'

His gaze flicked to me; she obviously saw that and gave an explanation of what "nice" meant in medical terms. Owen flushed a little, then murmured, 'Will it scar?'

'Yes,' she said, 'but it'll be tidy. I expect it'll end up only noticeable if you're really looking.'

'That's good,' he murmured.

As Dr Kartik turned her attention back to the final stitches, she said, 'It's due in part to you looking after the wound. I can tell you've been wearing that sling religiously.'

Owen let out a wry chuckle. 'Not my doing. I'd have taken it off ages ago if it wasn't for Andrew.'

The doctor glanced over her shoulder at me, smiling.

'I did my best,' I told her.

'Thanks, and I hope you can continue for a few days more.'

I raised a brow as Owen groaned and said, 'I still have to wear it? Why?"

'Because, no matter how good the wound looks, we want to support it through the few first days of being uncovered and de-stitched.' She smiled at him. 'I don't want you to forget about it and do something wild.'

Owen bit at his lip. 'I'm right-handed,' he said. 'That'd be the side I'd go wild with.'

The doctor laughed, turned to look at me again. 'You've got a battle on your hands, Mr Gordon.'

I chuckled. 'Yes, I expect so.'

Owen stuck his tongue out at me while Dr Kartik couldn't see him. I knew he'd hoped to be free of the sling by Thursday when Lisa and Matty came home, but it looked like we were going to have to make up a story after all.

Dr Kartik snipped the final threads, bringing Owen's focus back that way. He wrinkled his nose, teeth in his lip, but then looked down at his shoulder.

When the doctor leaned across her tray for a small tube of cream, I got to see the wound. A bit red and still clearly a wound, but weirdly not as large as it had seemed when the stitches were there. Dr Kartik held the tube out to Owen who eyed it for several seconds before taking it. She explained the cream needed to be put on three times a day and she wanted to see him do it right now. Presumably to ensure he could.

'Uh,' Owen said, cleared his throat.

When he looked at me, I didn't offer to do it for him; this was something he was going to have to cope with. He looked like he was thinking *Damn* but then twisted the cap off the tube and followed Dr Kartik's instructions.

Owen's expression displayed discomfit, and I suddenly wondered if he'd had to do the same sort of thing with the scars on his chest or that one through his brow.

A fleeting glance at the exposed part of his chest didn't reveal a scar, but I already knew they'd settled into something hard to find unless specifically searched for. For a moment I wanted to bring up the topic of counselling. Owen had been sleeping well these last few nights but I wondered if caring for this new wound would interfere with that.

I held my tongue, though. I expected Dr Kartik would support me but the dual pressure could backfire.

Perhaps Megan might have a quiet word about it when her own session ended.

That girl—God, I was proud of her. How strong she was

but also how she could let go her own pride to realise counselling wasn't a sign that she was crazy or unable to cope. I hoped *both* her brothers took notice.

I started, realising Owen and the doctor were looking at me. 'My apologies. If you spoke, I totally missed it.'

Owen had a weird smile on his face, still clutching the tube and still half dressed.

Dr Kartik smiled. 'I just said that we're done here, and I won't need to see Owen again unless something concerns you over the wound.'

'Oh, okay, that's good.' I rose and took the tube when Owen held it out.

He stood too and got himself carefully dressed, then only half rolled his eyes when Dr Kartik helped him back into the sling.

'Preferably until Friday,' she said. 'Especially when standing. You can leave it off at night, and during the day if you're sufficiently supported while sitting.'

Owen nodded, looking resigned. At least he was able to have showers now. I expected he thought the ones he'd had yesterday and this morning had been Heaven, a sort of freedom he'd been lacking recently.

- # -

Half way home from picking Jamie up after his shift at Walgreens, he said, 'Andrew, I need to tell you something.'

My grip tightened on the steering wheel momentarily, but I managed to say, 'Okay' in a normal voice. Glancing at him showed a set sort of expression. 'Do you want me to find somewhere to stop?'

'What? No. No, this is…'

He trailed off and when I glanced his way again I saw he'd turned his head to watch the buildings slide by on his side. He didn't seem enthusiastic about speaking and I guessed he'd been debating with himself for quite some time about even *starting*.

I found a place to park safely and asked something I'd been meaning to bring up for a few days. 'Jamie, is Sarah pregnant?'

His head whipped around. 'God, Owen told you! He promised—' He cut himself off, and let go of the belt across his chest as if he'd just realised he had a two-fisted grip on it.

'Owen's not said anything,' I said. 'Why…?' I shook my head, then said quietly, 'So, she's pregnant?'

'No!'

I was unprepared for that being delivered in a shout, and also felt puzzled. 'Why would you think Owen told me she was pregnant?'

Jamie looked at me and I saw confusion on his face too. 'What? I don't…' He let out a groan, rubbed his face. 'She's not pregnant. I told Owen yesterday morning and he promised not to tell you. I thought… thought he'd broken…' He trailed off again, cleared his throat. He seemed to sag in the seat.

I sat silent. Jamie was obviously rattled and he didn't need me to be annoyed on Owen's behalf right now.

We sat perhaps ten minutes in silence and then Jamie let out a long sigh. I opened my mouth and he blurted, 'I don't want a sex talk, Andrew.'

'A what?'

'A—' He cut off, clearly seeing I was startled. 'Nothing,' he said and looked out his side again.

I worked my jaw, knowing I had to be extremely careful with my words here. 'Jamie, you're old enough to know the consequences of your actions, so I'm not going to give you any sort of talk. But I would like you to start giving your brother a bit more credit. He has your back, you know.'

Jamie let out a snort and then sniffed. 'Shit,' he croaked and had his hands over his eyes.

I heard myself say, 'I'm here, Kid, talk to me.'

His response was a cross between a laugh and a sob, but he did uncover his eyes. Didn't look at me, just peered out the window again. Well ahead of us but still easy to see was the sloping flank of my building. I found my thoughts going back to yesterday, when I'd taken over the card game from Jamie. Neither of them had acted like it but I suspected that's when Jamie had revealed the result to Owen.

I let out a soft sigh. 'Are you okay? Is Sarah okay?'

'Yeah.'

I waited but Jamie said nothing more.

'Shall we… continue home then?' I asked after a moment.

He blew out a big sigh. 'Yeah. Sorry.'

'What's the apology for?' I asked, staying my hand on the key.

Jamie shrugged, pulled a face, shook his head.

I dropped my hand. 'Jamie, are you upset about Sarah *not* being pregnant?' I couldn't stop that coming out just a little bit puzzled.

'Shit, no,' he responded quickly. Then added, 'Yeah, a bit. God knows why cause I really don't want that sort of thing. And telling her parents? Jeez, that would have been… Owen's already given me a condom talk.'

'What?' I croaked out, fully startled.

Jamie scratched his head and then told me about last week's discussion in the hospital. He sounded amused, angry and upset all in one.

'Well, then,' I said when he fell silent. 'You definitely don't need me to give you a talk.'

I smiled when he looked at me. He rolled his eyes then leaned back against the headrest. 'Hopefully Megan will have more brains than Owen and me when she hits sixteen.'

There was a curve to his lips but he sounded lost. I fought against telling him he should sit down with someone professional, just started the car.

Before I got us moving again, I said, quietly, 'This was the something you needed to tell me, right, nothing else?'

Jamie choked on a huffed breath, pulled himself a little straighter in the seat. 'Yeah. Coulda picked a better time. Sorry.'

'Any time you tell me things is a good time, Jamie,' I responded. 'For all of you kids.'

'Yeah, I'm not doing counselling,' he responded right back. 'Even if Megan reckons a weight's off her shoulders.'

Jamie had still been at the house this morning when we got back there so Megan could pack for her trip with Alana. She hadn't revealed much about the counselling she'd attended while Owen was getting his stitches out, but *had* said she felt better for talking to someone.

'I wasn't doing a sideways suggestion,' I said with a sigh.

He gave a stiff nod.

We spoke of nothing serious for the rest of the drive, but Jamie stiffened a bit as the elevator climbed. As we walked around to my door I told him that what had been discussed was between him and me only. He inclined his head, mumbling, 'Thanks.'

'How about you invite Sarah for dinner one night when we're back at the house? It'd be nice to see her. Seems ages since we did.'

One of his brows cocked up, and he seemed to have some difficulty swallowing. 'S-sure,' he got out.

He looked so young for a second that I pressed an arm around his shoulders in a quick hug. I did not expect him to turn right into me and push his face into my shoulder. I heard a snuffly sort of breath and wrapped both arms around him. 'Kid, it's okay, it's okay.'

I wasn't sure if Jamie was actually crying but it was rare that he turned to me for this level of comfort, from any of his siblings even, so I just stood there, one hand gently rubbing his back. Fighting back words about counselling.

'Come on,' I said after a little while. 'If Owen's not having *another* shower, what say you run yourself a bath and relax?'

Jamie squinted. 'Why would he be having another shower?'

'Seems to think they're Heaven or something,' I said, fishing my keys out of my pocket.

'He's weird,' Jamie muttered.

'Sure, but at least he won't smell.'

My grin encouraged a half one onto his face.

A wider one appeared when we stepped into the apartment and found Owen on the couch watching TV.

'Go on,' I said to Jamie, nodding down the hall.

He went without a word.

Owen looked at me and I said Jamie'd had a busy shift lifting boxes. 'Going to relax his muscles in the bath.'

'Oh.'

'How about I make us a drink and we can relax our muscles

right here on the couch?' I held up a hand. 'That was not a suggestion for anything so don't look at me like that.'

'Spoilsport,' Owen grumbled.

'Doctor's orders,' I reminded him.

'She's a spoilsport too,' he said.

I laughed and went into the kitchen. Instead of staying on the couch, Owen came and sat on one of the bar stools. He seemed to enjoy watching me doing kitchen things.

Jamie

It was probably unusual, Owen and me seeing the counsellor together, but neither of us would have gone on our own.

Megan had said she felt like a weight had sort of been lifted—talking about her stress to others and not burdening family—but Owen and I had still been against it.

I really didn't think I needed to go but I wasn't so sure any more about Owen. No matter what he said, with the last couple of months being one horror after another, and memories from last year impacting his sleep, he had to be a powder keg waiting for a spark.

Andrew, however, had refrained from forcing him (or me) to counselling and had stopped suggesting too.

Then, last night, he'd *asked* Owen to go.

I'd thought my brother would immediately refuse but he sat silent, fingering the sling. Then I'd popped out, 'I'll go with you.'

He'd looked at me then, so long that I struggled to keep eye contact. Then he'd breathed out, 'Okay' and turned back to his dinner. He hadn't looked that comfortable the rest of the evening but I was sure he understood he'd just destroyed the demon that made Andrew stressed and uneasy about his continual refusal.

Anyway, now Owen and I sat beside each other on a soft red couch, with the counsellor on the opposite one. I was sure she'd been given a brief about Owen, maybe about me too. I didn't know if she was the same one Megan had seen on Monday morning before she'd gone off on holiday.

We'd been talking about dad—what he'd been like before he ran out on us. I guess she'd been letting us find out where our anxiety and everything was rooted. Well, I reckoned *that* was way back during the discussion about us moving here in the first place but we didn't mention it.

Owen was answering questions and engaging in some to/fro with me but he'd not really started anything. He fingered the sling like it was an annoying itch that just needed to be scratched. I spent time forcing myself not to reach out and stop the fiddling; he probably didn't realise he was doing it. We were *all* going to be glad when he no longer needed the damn thing.

Despite my own misgivings about seeing a counsellor, I was feeling relaxed. Wasn't sure if it was because Owen was with me or not, but it was kind of nice to talk stuff and not have to worry about upsetting Andrew further or even angering Sergeant Morrison. When he found out about this visit he was going to think a miracle had occurred.

After a moment, Ms Schaeffer asked us to consider our main emotion when we thought about our father. She looked at Owen first.

Given the odd expression on his face I wasn't sure if he'd answer, or could even narrow it down. Then he said, 'Regret.'

My brows came together in puzzlement.

'Regret that I didn't shoot him.' Delivered soft but steady.

Ms Schaeffer sat straighter, but she didn't speak.

Tears blurred my brother's blue-green eyes and I could see him struggling for control so he could speak. He dragged in a raspy breath and said, 'For what he was going to do to Andrew, for sh-shooting me, for everything he did… did to my brothers and… and sisters, I should have shot him.'

Owen's eyes streamed like a flash flood, mouth hitched open as he obviously strained to breathe around crying, leaning over his knees. His slinged arm was crunched between chest and knees but if it hurt I didn't think he noticed. He was crying so hard he almost wasn't, barely making a sound, like whatever he felt was so huge that it squeezed his vocal chords.

Then a breath scratched in like it'd found a gap. A second one followed and then whatever had blocked sound shattered and Owen was bawling noisily and messily.

It really only took a couple of seconds to get to this point after he'd spoken but it had felt slow motion, and I sat there staring, not knowing quite what to do. I'd seen my brother crying, sometimes I'd caused it, but this was something else. My throat constricted. Should I—

'Leave him,' came the quiet command.

I stopped reaching, glanced over at the counsellor. She gave me a tiny sympathetic smile. 'Let him work through this.'

I nodded, but felt odd leaving him to bawl as if he was on his own. Then again, he probably wasn't conscious of us right now. I found myself telling Ms Schaeffer what I'd said that day of the shooting, how I'd egged Owen on briefly. 'I feel guilty about it,' I mumbled, 'but I'm not surprised *he* feels regret.'

What I *was* surprised about, still, was the fact that, despite what dad had said, Owen had lowered the gun and talked, that he'd done that even after everything that had happened. Which made me unsurprised, with almost two weeks separating us from that day, that Owen's main feeling had turned toward regret. And I understood why he was crying now—for the fact he hadn't shot dad *and* for the fact that he felt regret about not shooting dad. A dumb conflict but my brother had always been complicated.

I just hoped that breaking down here would give him some release. Dad was gone, anyway. The rest of us were generally okay, and he and Andrew were rebuilding their relationship.

Owen straightened, taking my attention. His eyes were wet and red-rimmed, nose running until he wiped his sleeve over it, and his mouth was red and puffy. He looked a freaking mess but his gaze was clear as he looked at me. 'What's your main emotion?'

He said that with calm curiosity and I stared just a bit, before understanding that that violent damn burst had helped him somehow.

'Um, I don't really know.' Then I shrugged. 'Puzzlement, I guess, at why dad did all that, why he continued. Even when we knew about Melissa and Sam.'

Owen chewed on his lip, but we both knew they'd had no part in this except for being victims too. I rubbed my fingers down my jeans. 'It was like he didn't think he was doing anything wrong, like he'd get away with it, like—I don't know—he'd just go back to them as if everything was all good.' Ran my nails down my jeans this time, not able to look up. 'I just don't get how he got to this last point.'

Dad had shot my brother, had *meant* to, and that was… My brain was never going to be able to understand that.

Which was dumb because we'd all seen and heard news reports of hate crimes, and they weren't all stranger-related. Just still somehow didn't comprehend how dad could go so far.

And yet, I could comprehend. Like Owen had challenged dad once, I didn't think homophobia was the driving force of dad's action. It was just a means to an end when he found that we weren't welcoming him home, that we hadn't lacked for anything after he'd left us bar himself. And it had been very early on that we'd stopped lacking him.

Dad hadn't been able to cope that we'd done fine without him and didn't want him back, at least not as if he'd just been gone on a week's holiday.

How had he never understood that his actions after mum had died, the slow pulling away, and the physical leaving and never contacting us even once drove our reactions?

Who could ever believe that children in that situation would welcome back the parent that put them in that situation?

And then to go all stupid about Owen and Andrew, and become violent and frightening...

My head hurt with all that whirling around inside it.

Dad really just simply hated that we kids, led by a sixteen-year-old, had survived and thrived. I felt a wry smile on my face; Owen and I still had healing wounds courtesy of each other that broke open now and then, but we were a better family, a closer family, for everything we'd been through.

'I feel like I should thank him for leaving us,' I muttered.

Owen's brows came together but all he did was sigh, and he hadn't really reacted to my chosen emotion either. I guessed he struggled with all that too, how dad had morphed into a terrorist.

'I want to go home,' I said.

Owen looked at me, surprised, probably because *I* was the one wanting to bail first. I grimaced. 'I meant New Zealand.'

That only made him more surprised. Then he seemed to realise we could count all his teeth bar the missing one and shut his mouth. His gaze lowered to his knees.

'You do too, huh?' I murmured.

'Yeah,' he said after a moment. 'Well, anywhere away from here, away from the house.'

I fully understood Owen's PTSD feelings about the house, but I was also unsettled with the revolving door, too, since we'd been going back and forth between the house and Andrew's apartment a lot recently. We were back home again because Matty and Lisa were returning from camp this afternoon, and we intended they stay as far removed from the drama they'd missed as much as possible. Being at Andrew's would be hard to explain away easily, and we didn't all fit there comfortably anyway.

Owen had hoped their return meant he could do away with the sling, but Andrew had simply said they'd say he had a sprained wrist or something.

Wasn't sure what we'd say when they asked about dad's next visit.

Owen had been reasonably settled in the house since we'd moved back, though I suspected that was only because he'd been going to work with Andrew. He'd refused to stay at home, even if I was there. We'd have to sort something though because I still had my extra shifts, and we couldn't foist the kids onto Mr and Mrs Carter *every* week day.

I looked at my brother; he had a weird smile on his face. Then he said, 'Remember that house we went to see? With the tall grass and the new second story? That would have been nice.'

'Mm.' I was somewhat surprised I didn't have to try hard to recall it. 'Wish we'd gotten to see inside.'

'Yeah,' Owen agreed. He looked at me straight then, still a visual mess, but his gaze was serious. 'Thanks, Jamie.'

'Wha-at?'

'For doing this today. For—' He cut off, face going red as if he'd just remembered we weren't alone. He stammered an apology to Ms Schaeffer.

She smiled. 'No need to apologise, Owen. You and your brother talking is just what I was hoping for.'

Owen flushed further and I felt myself going a bit red too, then I nudged him. 'A for effort.'

He elbowed me, but he was smiling.

Andrew was going to be *so* relieved.

Owen

This is dumb! Set one foot in front of the other, that's all you need to do.

But I was stuck there on the edge of the lounge, unable to move.

Wasn't because Lisa and Matty were there watching TV, having finally run out of camp stories. Wasn't because Jamie slouched on a couch and I was embarrassed about things he'd heard in the counselling session. He had his headphones on anyway.

Pots clinked in the kitchen where Andrew was starting to sort out dinner. My heart beat in time with the clinking, and the ring curled in my fingers felt all hot.

Up until the moment I took the first step out of the hall,

I'd been fine—all fired up to give Andrew the ring I'd told him about. But the public space just seemed to suck my courage.

I let out a breath then jerked when I heard, 'Waiting for an invite?'

Jamie'd pushed back the nearest-side headphone and was looking at me, brow up. I cleared my throat to respond and stopped when Andrew stepped into view.

'Hey,' he said softly. 'I thought you were resting.'

'I was,' came out automatically, almost defensively. I forced back thickness from my throat. 'Can we… can we talk?' I pointed outside, doing my best not to go all red at his surprise or at Jamie's when I turned and saw his expression.

I didn't wait for Andrew to respond, just forced myself to walk, letting out a sigh when I stepped out into the afternoon sunshine. Too hot on the deck though so I moved onto the lawn, half shaded by the tree.

As I stood there, hearing steps after me, I glanced at the house—the bedroom windows were dirty.

A memory hit me as Andrew came into my peripheral vision. The day he'd named my favourite cloud formation (no clouds today at all) and we'd had a weird one-upmanship game over home verses apartment living. Part of that had been about cleaning windows.

I turned to Andrew and smiled. He actually looked taken aback a second.

'Remembering something,' I mumbled.

'A good something, I presume.'

'Yeah.' It was the day I'd started to realise that my feelings for Andrew (Mr Gordon, as he'd been then) were moving beyond gratitude.

'That's good,' I heard him respond softly and I realised he was a little unsure standing here.

Saying "Can we talk?" wasn't exactly a thing I did, and probably hugely unexpected after a counselling session. And, actually, I *didn't* want to talk. 'Close your eyes,' I said, 'and hold out your hand.'

He did, holding out his right.

'Other hand,' I whispered.

Andrew's brows gave an amused/puzzled kind of wiggle but then he stretched out his left hand, palm up.

I retrieved the ring from its fist cage, suddenly thinking this manoeuvre could be difficult without two fully functioning limbs, but I stepped right up and tweaked my hand out of the sling just enough to turn his hand over so it was palm down.

Glancing up showed Andrew's eyes still closed. His lips were pressed tight and he held himself just a little tensely. Silence probably wasn't helping, but I couldn't speak right now. My voice would have shaken as much as my hands as I guided the silver band onto Andrew's ring finger, smile flashing at the perfect fit and how amazingly solid it looked there on his hand.

His right came up and clamped mine before I'd even finished, his breath whistling out. I looked up at him; his gaze at me was full of emotion.

'S-stay with me forever,' I whispered, heart pounding.

Andrew breathed my name and then kissed me, hands cupped to my face. I stepped up close and his arms went around me, cheek now pressed against my head. 'Forever and always,' he said.

When he stepped back, inspecting the ring, my eyes were glistening. I smiled when he glanced at me, trying not to give in and cry. I'd done enough of that today already. Andrew drew me in again, this time kissing my forehead. 'I am so lucky to have you.'

I mumbled out something of the same.

'Come sit,' he murmured. 'My legs are jelly.'

We went to the bench, and I held up his hand so I could see the ring. The moment I'd seen it in the shop I knew I had to get it for Andrew. Circumstances had delayed the presentation though and I kicked myself for the further delays as my confidence had weakened and fear had grown.

'It looks good,' I croaked.

'Best piece of jewellery I've ever had,' Andrew said softly.

'Sorry it took so long.'

'Angel,' he breathed. 'I told you I'd wait forever.'

'I just want you forever,' I said, twisting the band around.

His fingers covered my fiddling hand as he murmured, 'You have, Owen. Don't ever worry about that.'

I leaned my head on his shoulder and he disengaged his hand so he could wrap his arm around me, carefully because that was the sling side.

[Twenty-One]

Owen

'This is not the way to work,' I announced.

'No,' Andrew agreed. 'We've got an appointment with the sergeant first.'

'What? Why?' My heart went from leisurely beats to racing in three seconds.

'He has a few things to tell you.'

'And… he couldn't phone or… or email?'

Andrew cast me an amused look but I could see that below that he was all serious.

'Do you know what it's about?' I asked.

'Partly.'

'Then, you can tell me, right?'

Andrew shook his head. 'Best heard from Sergeant Morrison himself, Owen.'

Poxy way to start my first day back at work.

When Andrew parked the car, I was almost calm again, but then I spotted his lawyer walking toward us. 'Why is…? Are *you* in trouble?'

'No,' he said. 'And neither are you. But there *are* some legal matters up for discussion.'

Totally unsettled now, I went to pick at the sling but I no longer wore it. I almost missed the weight of it around my neck.

I followed Andrew out of the car, said, 'Hi' to Mr Laurence when he greeted me, then went with them into the station.

Andrew had barely announced us to the lady at the desk

before we were being escorted down the corridor toward the sergeant's office. I'd thought I would never have to visit here again, then stopped dead. 'Dad's not here, is he?'

My stop forced Mr Laurence to take a swift sidestep. I mumbled an apology to him but my focus was on Andrew. He didn't seem concerned or uptight so I was pretty sure dad wasn't, but I couldn't see what else might be going on that would need a chat with the sergeant *and* Andrew's lawyer.

'Your father's not here, Owen,' Andrew said calmly. 'But… some of the discussion will be about him.'

'Why?'

'The sergeant is better placed to answer that,' he told me, holding his hand out to encourage me forward.

I still looked about for dad once we were in the office, but it was just us and the sergeant, who came forward and shook hands with all of us. Me included, which I think was a first. Nerves had me playing with the cuff links my sisters had given me for my birthday.

We all sat around the small table, and Sergeant Morrison cut right to the chase. 'It turns out, Owen, that your parents had the house in both of their names and that your mother willed you her half upon her death.'

'What?' I said, because that wouldn't have even made a top one-hundred of things I thought we'd be talking about. I turned to gape at Andrew; he looked back sombre. 'What does that mean?' I rasped out.

'I believe it means,' he said quietly, 'that you own half of the house.' He didn't glance at Mr Laurence so I expected they might have already had a chat.

'But… what? I didn't…' I turned back to the sergeant. 'I didn't know. Why…? How…?' I shut my mouth.

'It appears that the lawyers were instructed to keep that silent until you turned eighteen,' he said. 'A legal adult.' He sounded a bit grim about that, and I felt that myself given all the other crap I'd had to deal with *before* turning eighteen.

'I get the age thing,' I said, 'but why keep it silent?'

'Ordinarily, it wouldn't have been,' Mr Laurence said, quietly, making me turn to him, 'since dealing with such an asset as a house goes through the courts even when it's will-related. However, your mother left explicit instructions.'

I stared at him, trying to understand. 'But... *why?* I mean... she and dad were going to divorce and we were going to go back to New Zealand. Why would she give me half of the house if—' I cut off. Had she *not* meant to take me?

I flinched at the hand at my back. Andrew murmured something but didn't take his hand away, and I appreciated the touch now. Something *real*.

The lawyer directed me a sympathetic smile. 'Apparently she made that change while in hospital.'

I swallowed a ragged rock. My breathing sounded as ragged as I tried to get my head around that. I tried to remember what the doctors had told us. A blood clot, I think, had caused her death. Mum couldn't have known about that. Surely, if they'd known they'd have been able to *do* something.

The three men stayed silent while I struggled to maintain control of my emotions and to make sense of what I'd heard. Holy *shit*... mum had gifted me part of the house! I looked at Andrew.

'What is it?' he asked quietly.

'Could I have gotten us out of that house ages ago? Sold it or something?'

Andrew shook his head, which was good because if he'd

have said, 'Yes' that would have been painful. Having a means to get us away from dad and not knowing it was too horrible to think about. I turned to Sergeant Morrison. 'Did… does dad know about this?' I didn't remember *any*thing about a will. 'He kept telling me the house was *his*, he never said anything about it part being mine.'

My eyes stung at that betrayal. Andrew's hand rubbed a small circle on my back.

'Your father knows about this, yes,' the sergeant said. 'I do not know why he didn't tell you once you turned eighteen,' he added when I opened my mouth, 'but he wants to sign his half over to you as well.'

My mouth dropped open.

Sergeant Morrison looked at Andrew, making me do the same. Andrew seemed a little stiffer than earlier, and that put me on edge. 'I'm not breaking up with you just to get the house,' I told him evenly.

He jerked as if I'd startled him and for a moment I reckoned I saw grief, but then he smiled. 'I'm sure your father has not asked for that.' He didn't sound particularly sure.

'There's no way,' I said, spinning back to the sergeant. 'I'm *eighteen.*'

He held his hand up briefly. 'Mr Gordon is not involved, Owen,' he said. 'However, there *is* a condition.'

My skin prickled.

'Your father wants you and your siblings to visit him.'

'No way.' My hand went to my shoulder. 'No *way*, Sergeant,' I said, shaking my head as he sat there watching me. I looked to Andrew for support.

'*I* won't force you,' he murmured. He gently clasped the hand at my shoulder and lowered it.

'Owen,' Mr Laurence said, gaining my attention. 'No one can make you go, but a visit *is* a condition of the title change.'

'Can he do that?' I croaked.

'Yes.'

'That's m-mean,' I replied. 'I don't want my brothers and sisters to—'

'It's not them,' Mr Laurence cut over me. 'Related to the condition, that is. Your father wants them to visit, certainly, but it's *your* presence that the title swap rests upon.'

'That's so… not fair,' I breathed out, feeling my stomach lurch. I twisted free of Andrew's hand and pressed against my shoulder again. 'He shot me, how can…?' I sucked in a breath. 'That's f-force.' I turned to Andrew. 'I can't… I c-can't…'

Andrew scooted his chair close and put his arms around me as I struggled not to hyperventilate. He talked over my shoulder to the others but my breathing was so raspy in my ears I didn't catch what they were saying.

The brief glimpse of total freedom ran around in my head being chased by dad with a gun. How could he *do* that to me? Hadn't he had his fill of terrorism?

'I don't want the house.'

Since Andrew hadn't let me go, I doubted they heard so I pushed back from him and faced them all. 'I don't want the house. I don't want mum's part and I don't want dad's. I don't want *any*thing from him, and I *don't want to see him.*'

They remained silent.

'I'm sorry,' I said. 'You've probably been working on this, but I can't do it. I cannot see the man who tried to destroy everything I love. I cannot take a gift from him like that fixes everything. And none of us want to be in that house anyway. I'll gift my part to charity or something.'

Instead of running from the room like I might once have done, I sat there looking each of them in the face. I was shaking but hopefully that wasn't too noticeable.

Maybe thirty seconds of silence followed that, then Andrew murmured he was proud of me.

I gave a small smile but part of me was suddenly thinking it'd been a selfish reaction. Would having the house provide more stability for my brothers and sisters? I swallowed hard; didn't want to let doubt in. I turned to the sergeant. 'Please tell dad we don't want his half.'

He gave a nod, but didn't speak.

To Mr Laurence I said, 'If I truly do own half, could you look at ways I could sell it or give it away?'

He didn't glance to Andrew for direction, but kept his gaze on me. 'I will, Owen.'

'Thank you.'

I could feel tears starting to sting so hauled in a big breath. Forced a smile as I said to Andrew, 'Take me to work. I don't want everyone to think I'm already skiving off on my first day back.'

Andrew gave a soft chuckle and nodded. 'Let me know, Sergeant,' he said, 'if there's anything else you need from us.'

'I will,' came the reply.

We all got up and there was a whole bunch more handshaking, and then we were out into the morning sun. I relished the fresh air on my face. While Andrew and Mr Laurence had a quiet chat, I went up to Sergeant Morrison.

'What can I do for you, Owen?' he asked, with a glimmer of a smile.

'Um, I don't want… That is…' I pushed my hair out of my face. 'If my brothers and sisters want to see dad sometime, I don't want just now to have… uh, ruined that.'

The sergeant's brows came together momentarily, but I held his gaze. 'We'll deal with that if and when it comes up.'

I nodded. 'Okay, thanks.'

'Owen,' Andrew called.

I turned to find him with his door open.

'Go on,' the sergeant said. 'And remember to take things easy first day back on the job.'

I nearly stared in surprise, not least because he was now actually smiling.

My face heated and since my voice stuck in my throat all I could do was nod. I hurried away to the car, flashing a shy smile at Andrew when I caught his gaze.

As we headed down the outer drive, the John Hancock appearing in and out of view, I said, 'You said you partly knew what that visit was about. Which part?' I wasn't angry, just curious.

'The will part.'

'How long?'

'Only since last night, Owen,' Andrew said. 'And I didn't tell you then because you'd not have slept.'

Stupid truth that I couldn't really argue against. Instead I said, 'Did Mr Laurence tell you?'

'Yes,' he said. 'After our conversation about finding another home, I asked him to see if he could find out about the current one.'

'And dad's… Well, him being in prison means nothing? No forfeit or anything?'

'No. As long as the mortgage or taxes are being paid, it's still his. Or, in this case, partly his.'

'And partly… mine.' I let out a breath. 'This is insane.'

'It's definitely something.'

I looked at him properly. His gaze was on the traffic but I could tell from his words, his tone, and the sombre expression that he was shaken.

'Does it… mean something bad for *us?*' I asked softly.

A brow went up and he looked at me. 'No, not at all.'

'Oh… good.' I said. 'It's just… you don't seem…'

I heard his breath release in a sigh. 'It's not what your mum's done, Owen.'

'Oh.' Dad. Still upsetting us even though he was locked up.

'That's a cruel thing he's done.'

'Yeah, but I don't want the house so…' I shrugged. As we came up Michigan Ave, I said, 'Don't suppose we can go…' The black bulk of his building slid past. 'You're mean.'

Andrew eyed me. 'I thought you were afraid of skiving off.'

I stuck out my tongue. He gave a soft breath of amusement, and I was actually kind of grateful. Work probably would do a better job of distracting me right now.

- # -

Though I'd been in the office a few days last week, I hadn't been working. I'd been there just to be out of the house. So, by lunch time I was pretty exhausted and lay down to have a nap.

Should have known Andrew'd just let me sleep, but I was still embarrassed to wake and see the clock say 2:10. I pulled myself straight, swiped my hair tidy, and then rose.

Andrew looked at me over his glasses, chewing on his lip. I patted my hair again just in case that's what was amusing him.

I grumbled that he should have woken me.

'You weren't snoring,' he said. 'I wasn't being distracted.'

'Pfft.' Shifting my shirt straight, I went back to the tilt desk where I'd been tidying up some plans. As I sat I let out a soft thanks, glanced over to see a contented smile on his face. 'Was actually kinda good,' I said, picking up a pencil. 'I think I've got a plan.'

Andrew cocked his head, gaze flicking to the desk.

'Not this,' I said with a smile, poking the desk, 'but the house.'

He sat straighter in his chair and removed his glasses, expression going serious. Looked a bit puzzled when I smiled because this morning's meeting at the station hadn't had much to smile about. I rubbed my brow with the pencil end and said, 'If John says I *can* give my part of the house away I'm going to give it to Melissa.'

Andrew drew in a breath but didn't speak, as if he was afraid to.

I arched a brow. 'Not... a good idea?'

'On the contrary, Owen,' he said a little roughly, 'it's a wonderful one. But... are you sure? I mean, giving as opposed to... selling?'

'Yeah,' I said. 'Melissa might not actually want it, I don't know what's going on between her and dad, but it seems dumb to make her *buy* if she does. And if she then wanted to sell, then... Well, I don't care.' I glanced at the plan in front of me then back at Andrew. 'Is that dumb?'

'No,' he said. 'It's a brave and generous decision.'

His dark blue gaze continued to hold mine and I cleared my throat. 'I hear a "but",' I said wryly.

He let out a soft breath and shook his head. 'It's not my

decision to make, but I would like to see you make *some*thing from the house.'

'I'd rather... Oh. Hm, yeah, didn't... think.' I ran my tongue around my teeth. 'Kinda hard to buy a new place if I don't have any money.' I scrunched up my face, feeling stuck. Even though mum had left me her share, I would still totally walk away from the house, but that wouldn't exactly get us a new place to live. Nor would gifting it. 'Bugger.'

'We'll come up with something,' Andrew said with a smile. 'And I doubt any decision has to be made instantly.'

I sagged a little, feeling like my brilliant idea had a leak and was slowly squeaking out air.

'How about,' Andrew murmured, picking up his glasses and putting them in their case, 'we pack up for the day and go to the apartment?'

'What? Why?'

He chuckled. 'Didn't you beg me to detour there this morning?'

A mad flush stopped my ability to speak. Andrew grinned, let one brow arch up. 'So...?'

'So, let's pack up already,' I rasped.

He laughed out loud.

Andrew

'I've been thinking' was always a dangerous way to open a discussion, but it turned out that Owen was half asleep against my shoulder and I got only a mumbled sound instead of a smart retort.

Instead of letting him just doze off again, I said, 'About our house quandary.'

Another mumble, but he pushed himself upright. 'Our what?'

'Housing problem,' I said. 'I can sell this place.'

'What?'

Definitely awake now, and staring with blue-green eyes wide in disbelief. 'But…' Owen looked around the bedroom before returning to me. 'Shit,' he said, 'you're serious.'

'Yes.'

'Why, though? You told me once you'd bought here as soon as you could. Why would you sell?'

'Hon, we can't all live here.'

Owen's brows knitted and he rubbed a hand over his scarred shoulder. Unconsciously, I think. 'I don't get…'

I waited but he didn't speak again. After half a minute, I said, 'Like you, Owen, I want a place where we can call home. And… if we've got a home like that, then why keep this apartment?'

'But you love it here.'

'Yes,' I said nodding, 'but I want to be with you and the kids as a proper family. I wouldn't need this anymore.'

For a moment it looked like Owen's eyes were filling and I wasn't sure what over. I knew he loved the apartment too, but it really would be superfluous.

'What if you worked late or something?'

'There's hotels,' I told him. Flashed back to the night I'd met him—in the bar of a hotel I'd been staying at because the plumbing wasn't working here.

Owen didn't look convinced. Obviously he was still trying to get his head around my suggestion.

'It'd get a good price,' I murmured, squeezing his sheeted knee. 'Allow us to find something that'll suit everyone.'

That made Owen's eyes go wider than before. 'You'd sell just so *we*… Andrew, I don't…'

'Hey,' I said softly, lifting his chin to keep eye contact. 'I want to do this for you, Angel. For *us*.'

He squinted at me.

'I've been thinking about it for a while,' I told him, drawing my knees up. 'Remember when we went to see that half-done house?'

'That was ages ago!'

Three weeks wasn't ages ago but a heck of a lot had happened to make it feel so. 'Well, even then I had thoughts about selling this place.'

'You didn't mention it then,' he said, sounding a little bit accusatory.

I shook my head. 'No, because I was *only* thinking and we were *only* looking.'

Owen picked at the cover over my knee, then rested his head on it, arms curving around my leg. The move exposed the beautiful shape of his spine and since he didn't yank up the sheets to cover himself I didn't either. I traced the curve with a fingertip, murmured, 'What are you thinking?'

His face was turned from me and from the angle I couldn't actually see if his eyes were open.

'Just looking at the view,' he murmured. 'Do it again,' he added after a second. 'Your finger.'

So I traced again, going further down, then back up. I heard him let out a long sigh and then he said, 'You'd really sell?' Didn't turn to look at me.

'Yes,' I said, using multiple finger tips this time. 'Anyway, the building's losing its name later this year. I couldn't live here then, could I?'

He twisted, exposing a great deal more of himself as he leaned back against my leg. 'I thought these were the East Delaware apartments, not John Hancock.'

I pulled a face at him, making him grin. He lifted an arm to hook around my neck and bring me forward for a kiss.

Owen

I hadn't quite expected total silence after revealing this morning's visit to the police station and what I'd learned about the house.

I'd purposefully chosen to speak after the kids had gone to bed but Jamie and Megan *still* just stared, and then both turned to Andrew as if for confirmation. He simply nodded.

I felt a bit sorry for Megan because she'd gotten home from her trip with Alana only an hour ago, and she'd already been blindsided by Jamie telling her that we'd faced up to a counsellor. Her wide-eyed gaze came back to me. 'You own half... this house?'

'Apparently,' I said, still stunned myself.

'And you could own all of it if you went to visit dad?' Jamie said.

'Yeah.'

'But you're not going to,' he said, getting a tint of anger in his voice.

'No.'

'Why not?'

'I already said why,' I responded, trying not to grit my teeth.

'You'd cut off your nose to spite your face?'

'It wasn't *you* he shot!' I slapped a hand over my mouth, hadn't expected the words or the savage tone.

Jamie reared back and even Megan looked like she wanted to back away. Out the corner of my eye Andrew shifted but didn't speak.

'S-sorry,' I rasped out.

Jamie's chin tilted up. 'I… get it. I just…' His gaze slid to Andrew briefly and he didn't carry on.

'I don't want to be in this house any longer,' I said, calmer. 'And I don't want *any*thing from dad.'

'We don't either,' Megan said, eyeing Jamie a second, 'but what…' She inclined her head. 'What'll happen to it? And where are *we* going to go?'

Jamie looked at her, puzzled, like he hadn't thought that far ahead himself.

'Mr Laurence says I can gift my half away, if I want.'

Megan's brows knitted. 'Gift it?'

'Yeah, like… mum did,' I said quietly. 'I was thinking… Melissa.'

My brother and sister both straightened, Jamie letting out, 'What?'

'Well, she's still… Jamie, she's still married to dad. I don't know if that will change but doesn't it make sense she'd have the half?' It did in my brain, whether they divorced or not.

Jamie just turned to Andrew who said, 'This is not my decision, Jamie. It's your brother's.'

'I know, I just… thought you might have talked some sense into him.' He mumbled that bit but I heard anyway.

'I back Owen's decision,' Andrew said. 'It's strong and courageous.'

Jamie muttered something fully under his breath but before he could say something louder Megan said, 'Melissa does think it's a good neighbourhood. Well, she does,' she added when Jamie looked at her.

He just shrugged and turned back to me. 'What about us? Like Megan said, where will we go if this goes ahead?'

'Obviously, we'll have to find somewhere,' I said.

'Where? When?'

'As soon as we can, I guess,' I said. 'And I don't know where.'

'I don't really want to change schools,' Megan said quietly. 'Or leave my friends.'

'Me either,' Jamie said, looked like it had come out automatically rather than thought out.

I glanced at Andrew and he smiled. 'I'm sure there's a perfect place around here waiting to be found.'

'And you'll be living with us, right?' Megan asked, a little hesitantly.

'Yes.'

Relief flashed across her face.

'How can we afford this?' Jamie asked. 'If we're talking buying?'

He eyed me and I chewed the inside of my cheek, mind on the brief discussion with Andrew this afternoon.

Andrew didn't hesitate to speak here. 'I'll be selling the apartment.'

'What?' my brother and sister yelped together.

'What the fuck, Owen?' Jamie said to me.

I started. 'What do you mean "What the fuck, *Owen*"? I didn't make that decision.'

Andrew hugged an arm around my shoulder, chuckling. 'I had to argue half the day to get Owen to accept common sense.'

I jabbed his side at the duration exaggeration. He smiled

down at me then looked back at Megan and Jamie. 'We're a family; there is no reason to keep the apartment.'

They just stared at him and then Jamie breathed, 'Well… shit.'

Megan frowned at him but he clearly didn't have any other reaction. She turned to us but she ended up saying nothing either. Andrew squeezed me again and I gave a weak smile that I'd been the only idiot over this.

I was just thinking we'd come to the end of this whole conversation when Jamie said, 'Does dad know you've turned him down?'

'Yes,' I said, unable to stop that coming out rigid. 'At least…' I twisted to look up at Andrew.

'Yes, John told me he'd relayed your decision to your father's lawyer.'

'What's the response?' Jamie asked.

'Hasn't been one, as far as I know,' Andrew said. 'In any case, that's done for now. *We* need to focus on finding ourselves a new home.'

A shiver slipped down my spine at "new home". I felt the stress and anxiety of the last few weeks leaving me, being replaced by anticipation.

'As long as I get my own room,' Jamie said, 'I don't care about anything else.'

Megan let out a breath, nodded.

Andrew chuckled. 'Yes, the main priority is enough bedrooms for everyone.'

Except him and me. The realisation that we'd have a room truly for *us*, like a married couple, made butterflies dash about in my stomach. I felt Andrew's lips press to my temple and I flushed, realising I'd made a sound.

Jamie rolled his eyes but didn't pop out a sly comment. Megan looked like she was already viewing houses in her head.

'How about,' Andrew said with amusement, 'everyone writes down a wish list so we can look with knowledge?'

Megan blinked. 'Good idea.' She headed out of the lounge, presumably to get paper and pens.

Jamie made a huffing sound and simply went outside. He had his phone out but he was more likely texting Sarah or Sean than writing a list.

'You too, you know,' Andrew said to me.

I looked at him in surprise.

'It'll be our house,' he reminded me. 'We all need to be happy.'

I nodded. 'Hey,' I murmured, 'are you *sure* about the apartment?'

'Yes.'

His gaze didn't waiver, not that I was really trying to stare him down. 'Thank you,' I whispered.

Andrew smiled and dipped down to kiss my lips. 'To be with you, Owen, I'd sell everything.'

He wrapped me in his arms, letting me feel the solid thump of his heart.

'Hey, do you think—argh, jeez get a room!'

Andrew and I had our mouths nowhere near each other; we were just standing together, his arms around me. They went tighter for a moment, then relaxed again. I smiled that Andrew didn't actually step back.

Jamie pulled a face, then raised his phone. 'That house we looked at the other week… Do you think it'd still be for sale?'

I reached for his phone; clearly he hadn't deleted the

photos. He let me take it and I swiped through a few before giving the phone to Andrew. His brows went up a second and then he murmured, 'Hell, I didn't even think of taking photos.'

I guess back then the whole desire to find our own space was just beginning, and we really had only just been looking out of curiosity.

'I liked it a lot,' Jamie said. 'And if we're really going to move, then…' He trailed off, shrugging when we looked at him.

Andrew was swiping back and forward, peering closer now and then. He let out a soft breath at one, angled the phone a bit when I leaned in. It was the photo Jamie had shown me that night—Andrew and me at a window, me looking smug. I felt my face heat up. Andrew grinned, then gave the phone back to Jamie who said, 'Do you still have the agent's number?'

'I'm not sure,' Andrew said. 'But I should be able to find it easily enough.' He cocked his head. 'If the house was still on the market, I'm guessing you'd like to look inside?'

'Yeah.'

'Inside what?' Megan asked behind us.

We all turned to see her with a writing pad and pen.

'That house we went to see before dad— Er.' Jamie grimaced, looked down at his feet a second.

Megan glanced at him and then Andrew and me. Andrew gave her a small smile and said Jamie had taken photos of that visit. 'He was just wondering if it was still on the market.'

My sister looked like she was about to ask why but then she drew in a breath and let it out. She looked at the paper and pen in her hands. 'Am I wasting my time with this?'

'No, Hon,' Andrew said with a chuckle. 'Still write up that list. You two as well,' he told me and Jamie.

'Sure, but…' Jamie trailed off, rubbing the back of his neck.

'I'll find the agent's number, don't worry,' Andrew said. 'If the house is still available, I'll get us a time to go through it.'

'Thanks,' Jamie mumbled, looking embarrassed. He glanced at his phone and turned around to go outside again.

'I am somewhat amazed,' Andrew said quietly, 'that he even remembers it.'

When I looked at him I saw his brows were knitted together, concerned. I wasn't quite sure what over but I wanted to take his mind well away from possible between-then-and-now thoughts. 'What would be on your wish list?'

'Mine?' he asked, surprised. He glanced from me to Megan, who ripped off some paper and held it out to him, saying that he should write one too. 'Ah,' he said, clearly on the spot.

I went to the junk drawer in the kitchen and found some extra pens, brought them back to the others, catching the tail-end of something about trees. Megan rolled her eyes. 'That's what Matty will write. What do *you* want specifically?'

Andrew huffed out an amused breath and then said, 'It's very simple, Megan. That you and your sister and brothers are happy and relaxed.'

Megan's eyes filled almost immediately and she gave Andrew a hug. Andrew smiled at me over her shoulder. I mouthed *Love you* at him, making the smile get more contented looking.

- # -

I stood in the middle of the corner room, eyeing wooden

bookshelves, an ornate boarded-up fireplace, and freaky wallpaper and carpet. Behind me I heard Andrew moving about the room but I couldn't watch him. I needed a moment.

Rubbing a phantom pain in my shoulder, I let out a soft breath at how whirlwind this week had been. Sort of funny that I thought of it like that, because we'd had a lot of whirlwind weeks lately, but this one had gone from me finding out I half-owned our house to Andrew's apartment already being sold. And now, Saturday afternoon, the six of us were looking through this large, old, and half-renovated house like we were hoping to find treasure.

I blew out another breath. So far, the house had seemed *all* treasure. From everything in it to still actually being for sale.

My gaze went slowly around again; the space would be big enough for a couch as well as Andrew's two desks and the chair from his study. And, while we didn't exactly own a lot of books, *he* had a full bookshelf that would easily fit in here.

'I like this space, Andrew.'

'Mm,' he said as he wrapped me in his arms.

I leaned back into his embrace, closing my eyes for a second as I imagined what it'd be like in here on a winter's night with the fire going.

'Smiling like that is a good sign,' I heard him sigh softly.

Giving a small chuckle, I turned in his arms to look up at him, liking the feel of his hands sliding down my back to my butt. He gazed back, obviously content just to stand here with me for a while. Then I whispered, 'Be honest, can we afford this place?'

Andrew continued to gaze down, silent, and then he nodded. 'Yes, Owen, we can.'

'Because of your apartment?'

'Yes.'

He'd not mentioned what it had sold for but I guessed a decent amount. He hadn't been surprised, either, at how quick it had all happened; the East Delaware apartments were obviously still hugely sought-after. I let out a breath. 'I'm going to owe you forever for this. For a house, I mean.'

'No, you're not,' he murmured. 'No owing at all.' As I was opening my mouth, he pointed to his ring. 'This is all I need, Owen.'

I looked at it, biting my lip—trying to keep my eyes dry and other parts under control. Andrew lifted my chin and leaned in for a kiss. A quick one but with enough heat to sizzle my blood. He grinned when he straightened. 'Woo, dangerous living,' he said. 'Come on, before you get me into trouble.'

I snorted and grabbed up his hand, feeling the cool band briefly against my own fingers, tugging him from the room.

Despite not having a built-in cupboard, the room beside the study was probably a bedroom, the third on this ground floor. This would probably end up as Lisa's room since we were pretty sure Megan had already claimed the one on the opposite corner to the study. It had a whole wall of cupboards and in-built shelves and drawers. Of course, it had pale yellow walls so it wasn't likely Jamie'd go after it.

The other bedroom here on the ground floor I already thought of as mine and Andrew's. Quite aside from being light and airy with the bay windows, it had a closet you walked through to get to a private bathroom.

Venturing back into the hall I said, 'You know, we haven't seen anyone in a while. And it's really silent.'

'I'll bet dinner they're all upstairs,' Andrew said, jerking a thumb over his shoulder.

'Come on then.'

At the top of the stairs a door lead into a small bathroom. Further around the landing was a good-sized, unlined room with a large window looking out over the front of the house, and the door at the end of the landing revealed where everyone had got to. This room was also unlined; obviously it was the second story that'd been the money killer for the previous owners.

Megan glanced over her shoulder as we entered. 'Hey, come and look at this view.'

We came, but not fast enough for Matty because he pulled me forward the last few steps, worriedly stating that he couldn't see the pond. Neither could I—the house might have been cared for while it was empty but the grounds certainly hadn't had the attention. The tall grass and weeds we'd had to wade through twice now stretched out into the trees, and even from this height I couldn't see the road that I knew ran along over to the left.

'I'm sure it's somewhere, Matty,' I said. 'You wouldn't put it in a description if it didn't exist.'

On my other side Jamie said, 'We think it might be over that way. Where that shed is, you see?'

Andrew and I followed his pointing finger and spotted an old red shed.

'So, that would be a boating shed?' I asked sceptically. 'How big is the pond supposed to be?'

Andrew shrugged.

Guess that'd only been revealed once the grass had been cut. Andrew's attention turned to inspecting the frames, the windowsill of the other window, even the cupboard at the other end. I watched him, a little worried still about money.

The apartment could have sold for a million, for all I knew, but the cost of this house and the renovations still needed wasn't going to be piddling. Could you even *use* these two bedrooms without proper walls?

I was just opening my mouth when Andrew asked Jamie and Matty if they'd even seen the rest of the house. 'Or did you come straight up here?'

'Of course, we've seen it,' Jamie said. 'The kitchen was super impressive with that dishwasher.'

Andrew grinned, rolled his eyes when he caught my gaze. As *we'd* looked over the huge living space with the giant bi-fold French doors and the brand new kitchen I'd told him that everyone would think the dishwasher was awesome.

'But we like it up here,' Matty said. 'This is gonna be my room, and Jamie's is the other one.'

'Is that right?' Andrew asked, amused, ruffling Matty's hair. 'How about you girls? Have you seen the whole house?'

They both said they had.

'The carpet's freaky,' Lisa added. 'Would we have to keep it?'

Everyone looked at their feet, but the floors were just plain wood.

'The wallpaper in those rooms, too,' Megan said. 'Just as interesting.'

Andrew smiled. 'If they're functional, then they could stay for a while. The priority would be up here, I think. Including curtains.'

I don't think any of us had realised the lack of curtains, which was odd given the lack of real walls.

'Anyway,' Andrew said, 'we ought to get back downstairs. The agent will be wondering where we are.'

He encouraged everyone out of the room and down the stairs, squeezing my shoulder when I glanced back at him with a smile.

As we carefully got down from the porch, the agent left her car. 'So what do you think?'

Everyone spoke at once, making Andrew cry, 'Hold up, everyone, you'll deafen her.'

She smiled. In fact, she seemed quite calm about us all.

Andrew, with his hand on Matty's shoulder now as if he was forestalling a rush off in the general direction of that shed, said, 'Sorry, can we take another five minutes for a chat?'

'Sure,' she said. 'Take all the time you need.'

Andrew shifted us all back to the columns, smiling when I mumbled, 'Ionic.' Jamie nudged his elbow into my side, grinning when I eyed him.

'Okay,' Andrew said. 'What do you all think? Should we get serious about this house?'

Megan: 'Definitely serious. I like it a lot. It's got a nice feeling.'

Lisa: 'Me too.'

Matty: 'I want my own room and the pond.'

Jamie: 'I'd move here in a pinch.'

Me: 'I want to live here.'

Andrew looked around at us, but I doubted he was surprised at the responses. The surprising thing was that he didn't immediately react. I cocked my head. 'You *don't* like it?' I asked, hesitantly, sure that wasn't so.

'Oh, I do,' Andrew said. 'I just...' He cleared his throat. 'Seeing you kids so excited...' He smiled bright, looking from me to the others, hugging Megan to his side when she stepped up. 'I think this could be made into a wonderful family home.'

Jamie nudged me again, so I shoved him back.

'And it's such a big space, in and out, that you two could really avoid each other,' Andrew said, light but even at the same time.

Jamie let out a snort of amusement, which I echoed.

Andrew gave a short shake of his head, then looked around at us all. 'So, shall we officially inform the agent that we're interested?'

After our enthusiastic agreement he turned back toward her.

[Twenty-Two]

Jamie

For all the stuff we'd left behind at the old house for Melissa, we still had a stinking huge lot of boxes to unpack.

I sat on one of them and eyed the rest. Man, were they multiplying as I watched?

'Get up,' Megan said behind me. 'I need that one.'

My whole body protested as I rose. Didn't ask what was in it because we'd diligently labelled everything. *Bedding (single).* Which was, in fact, all the bedding we'd taken since Andrew and Owen had the bed from the apartment and Megan and I not only had new beds but new bedding. Megan shoved a wad of sheets at me. 'For Matty's bed.'

'You want *me* to make it?'

She gave me a look, but all she said was, 'I think he already grabbed the cover and pillows.'

Clearly dismissed, I headed out of the box room. Upstairs, I found that the cover and pillows were indeed present in my brother's room but he wasn't. Instead of just dropping the sheets on the mattress I decided I'd make the bed after all. It'd get me out of unpacking boxes for twenty minutes at least. Longer, when I realised I had sheets left over and could make the other bed too.

Though… I wondered how I'd manage given that it was now a top bunk. The single beds that me, Matty and our sisters had used had never been put into their bunk arrangement but both kids had chosen to go that way now. Guess it was an easy way to look like you really had your own room while retaining a spare bed for when friends stayed over.

That thought made me give a wry smile. It was really only *now* that we had the space to allow friends to stay over. I snorted as I scrambled up onto the top bunk with the sheets. If Sean or Lincoln stayed, they'd be sleeping on the camp stretcher!

Once I'd made the bed to a reasonable level of tidy I hefted myself back off the side and turned to see Owen just stopping inside the door, eyes wide.

'What?'

'Just…' He came into the room. 'Weird seeing bunks.'

'Weirder making that one,' I muttered, poking a finger toward the top bed.

'Why did you?' he asked, coming forward to pick up one end of Matty's duvet as I picked up the other.

'Megan gave me two sets, so…' I shrugged. Didn't tell him that it was ten times weirder making a bed *with* him.

He gave a *yeah, makes sense* kind of noise and tossed the pillows onto the bed. Then he looked around the room.

In the freaky quick time since the sale had gone through both these top bedrooms had been finished off and curtains had been put up. No carpet but we each had cheap rugs from Walmart for the time being and the rooms at least looked like rooms now.

Owen ran his tongue over his teeth, then moved to the south-facing window, the sun flicking up bright brown in his hair.

I walked up beside him, not speaking.

Andrew had focused first on these bedrooms rather than the outside, bar the sagging roof over the porch, so the grounds still looked like a jungle beyond what various vehicles had crushed.

Matty had already been reminded twice today that he was NOT allowed to go running off to find the pond. He'd tried to kick me when I told him we should put a harness and leash on him, but I reckoned Andrew was beginning to consider it. I huffed out a breath, making Owen shift a little and glance at me.

'What're you pestering me for, anyway?' I asked.

His eyes narrowed briefly but he didn't sound peeved when he said, 'Just wanted to see…' He didn't finish, just turned and leaned against the windowsill, arms folded. He looked around the room, still large despite the bunks, side cabinet and chest of drawers. A new beanbag sat invitingly next to me. I shoved it with a foot, making Owen glance at it as the beans all rustled.

Andrew had been incredibly generous with his money, but I knew it was *Owen's* that had bought most of the little individual things for Lisa and Matty. I glanced at my older brother; he had a funny smile on his face. I elbowed him. He shoved me and straightened, still smiling. Without speaking, he left the room.

I stayed by myself for half a minute, then followed, realising I ought to find where my bedding was and then corral Matty into helping me make the bed.

When I couldn't find the right box I went in search of Megan to ask, and when I found her I sort of wished I hadn't. Aside from the bunk beds, the bedside cabinets and the girls' dresser, we'd only taken one other piece of furniture from the house. Mum's writing desk.

We didn't use it ourselves, and I wasn't even sure anyone

had looked inside it since mum had died. Not even when it was being wrapped for moving to see if anything within also needed wrapping. That was completely dumb of us, but it wasn't Megan looking inside the desk that had me choke on my breath. She was just putting mum's vase back on top of it.

A stab of grief flashed through me, remembering Owen saying that we couldn't leave mum behind, that she'd already been abandoned twice. He'd sounded really hard-nosed when he'd spoken but I think that was just to keep himself dry-eyed.

Megan glanced over her shoulder and seeing her eyes swimming made mine follow suit. I wanted to back away, not quite ready for this particular thing, but then her mouth curved up in a small smile.

I walked forward, slung an arm around her shoulder when I reached her and she dropped her head against me, sniffling. I let out a long sigh. 'Mum'll probably like the paisley,' I heard myself say. 'Bet she had carpet like this in her childhood.'

Megan whacked my chest. 'That's the sixties, she wasn't born then.'

I released a soft breath, pleased with the little bit of amusement in my sister's tone. I gave her a squeeze then stepped away, smoothed fingers down the slope of the desk. 'Did you look in here?'

Megan shook her head as she wiped her eyes.

'We probably should one day.'

'Yeah, but...' She gave a big sniff, a half smile, and seemed to pull herself together.

Because of that I asked if she'd seen the box with my bedding, and she turned away from the desk. 'Yeah, I think so.' She walked away, leaving me there at the desk. After a heartbeat I followed after her.

By eight, we had the house all closed up and had dispersed, knackered, to our new bedrooms. Though I'd been using Owen's old room at home, it was weird walking into mine and accepting that it was truly just mine. I didn't have to share with anyone.

Almost weirder was the fact that Matty and I had a bathroom to ourselves, though I was sure we'd get used to that quickly.

I gave a knock on Matty's open door. 'How're you doing?'

He stood at the window in the deep gold of evening. 'Look at all these stars, Jamie, they're cool.'

I crossed the room and looked out. High up, the sky was dark enough to let the twinkling stars be seen. 'Cool, alright,' I murmured, letting my gaze slide lower over the jungle below. I released a quiet breath. Man, I liked it here.

'You think dad sees these stars where he is?'

I nearly choked on my breath. 'Uh.'

Matty looked up at me, obviously expecting me to answer.

'Um, yeah, I guess so,' I said. 'Most people across the country can see these stars, Matty. Dad would be… no different.'

I held my breath, hoping that would satisfy him. Since we'd come clean on why dad wouldn't be visiting any time soon, having also had to reveal why dad was in prison in the first place, Matty and Lisa had been pretty quiet on him. I hadn't expected them to *not* think about dad, but I was totally thrown that Matty had asked about him now.

'You could write to him, Matty.'

My little brother and I both jerked at the quiet words, swinging around to see Owen standing in the doorway. The lingering evening light showed his tiredness but he seemed relaxed. I knew my mouth was open but I couldn't shut it any more than I could speak.

'Can I?' Matty was asking. 'Do we have the prison's address?' He started away from the window, heading for the desk we'd brought him.

'I'm sure we could find it,' Owen said, sounding wry. 'But not tonight, okay? I reckon you're so tired you wouldn't be able to spell your own name.'

'I would, too.'

'Matty, just leave it,' I said softly. 'How about you get into bed right now, and tomorrow morning we'll work on a letter?'

Matty looked like he wanted to argue, but then he rocked out a smile, said, 'Yeah' and headed for bed.

I caught Owen's gaze a moment before I hauled the curtains closed, plunging us mostly into darkness. His shadow stretched out across the floor. As I crossed to the door, he wished Matty a good sleep. I echoed it, and Matty mumbled something back.

Owen turned and headed for the stairs.

'Hey,' I said quietly, following. 'That was a nice thing to do,'

He shrugged, scratched his head. 'I can't tell him he *can't* talk about dad. And dad would probably… like a letter.' He swallowed.

'Mm.'

'Sleep well, Jamie.'

Owen started down the stairs. I leaned over the balustrade. 'Hey.'

He looked up, a little wary. I grinned down. 'Sleep well,

yourself.'

His eyes squeezed up a little, but I saw the smile as he continued downward.

After a moment I flicked off the hall light and headed for my own room, falling into my big new bed with a sigh. I choked up a little, and held my breath to keep my control. To get my thoughts away from Owen and dad and Matty writing a letter, I made myself do a virtual tour of the house counting all the boxes we had left to unpack.

Owen

First words I heard in the morning were, 'Did you get *any* sleep?'

'Huh?' I croaked, rolling over, not bothering to untangle the bedding as I did so.

Andrew was sitting, a book in his lap, the lamp on the cabinet letting out dim yet obviously useful light. 'You tossed and turned half the night. Kneed me several times.'

I pushed myself up, now kicking the sheets free. I tried to keep back the peeve from my brows but this wasn't quite what I'd expected waking up the first morning in our new house. 'Should have said something,' I muttered, 'or gone to the couch.'

'I'm not complaining, Owen,' he said. 'Just concerned. Were you uncomfortable being here?' His hand smoothed over the cover between us.

In *our* bed in *our* room.

I shook my head

'It wasn't me snoring, was it?'

'You don't snore,' I responded, frowning.

'Okay.' Andrew set the book aside. 'That should have come with a smile but you don't look anywhere near close to it. What's up?'

I didn't want to worry him so I just said, 'It was nothing, just silly things.'

'Silly things don't keep a body awake all night,' Andrew said gently. 'Was it a nightmare?'

'Dad.'

'*What?*'

I drew my knees up, encircled them with my arms, teeth gritted that I'd spoken. Andrew was dead still beside me. 'It's just…' I sighed. 'I was thinking about how much I already like it here, how everyone's happy, how cool *this* room is.' I looked around, lips curling up at the space that hadn't shrunk even with all the furniture. 'And how we could be a real family here. Then dad kind of butted in and I couldn't get him to leave.' I mumbled the rest—that I'd wondered what we'd do if he somehow came here and then how the new sounds of the house kind of became footsteps.

Andrew's hand closed gently on my arm. 'Your father cannot reach us here, Angel. You're safe. We all are.'

'I know,' I whispered. 'Guess I was over-tired.' I definitely didn't feel rested, and he probably wasn't either if I'd been physically restless. 'Sorry.'

'Ssh, no apology needed.' He leaned over and kissed my temple. 'It's only seven. I doubt the others will be up for ages, so how about you try to sleep now? I'll keep you safe.'

I'd been about to say, stupidly, that I wasn't tired but his final words warmed me. I nodded. Instead of leaning into his side, I slid myself horizontal again, forehead pressed against his thigh, fingers picking into his pants at his knee. I heard a sound of amusement, but all he did was tuck hair out of my face then bring the covers up around my back.

When I woke and dug my way out from my cocoon, Andrew was still beside me. He was doing a crossword now, but he set it aside. 'Hello, how are you feeling?'

A little groggy, in fact, but I pushed my hair back and smiled at him. 'Really good.' I pushed myself up so I could kiss his cheek. 'Thank you.'

He leaned into my lips, telling me it wasn't a hardship on his part. He got another kiss for that, and then I realised that a tray lay at the foot of the bed with a dirty plate and cutlery and I shifted in the bed to get a closer look.

'Scrambled eggs,' Andrew said. 'You were out to it and I didn't want to wake you.'

I looked back at him, and then over to his alarm clock. 'Ten?' I yelped out.

Andrew turned to glance at the clock and seemed entirely satisfied when he looked back at me. 'Good few hours' sleep,' he murmured.

'Did you get more?' I asked. 'Or did you sit here with me all this time? You must be bored out of your brains.'

He smiled. 'Sitting with you in our bed is not boring, even if *you're* just sleeping. Of course,' he added, dropping his voice, 'if you feel like you want to pay me back, you're welcome to do so.'

I stuck my tongue out and turned away, but my brain was already going down that track. Andrew chuckled behind me, making me flush that he probably knew what was on my mind. Then he told me I better go get something to eat. 'That stomach of yours is deafening.'

It *had* been rumbling a bit.

'Eat up big,' Andrew recommended as I tugged a sweatshirt over my head. 'Megan's probably got more hard labour planned today.'

I rolled my eyes. 'I note she didn't come to turf *you* out of bed.'

He laughed and patted the newspaper. 'I was occupied.'

I snorted and left the room, feeling a whole lot more relaxed than when I'd first woken.

Andrew

Though we'd finished our late lunch a good half hour ago, none of us were showing any signs of getting back to work.

There were still multiple boxes to be unpacked—all the things we hadn't needed immediately—but there was no real urgency. We'd all slept in properly set-up bedrooms last night, the kitchen was functional, and we had the leather couch and chair from my apartment to relax on.

My dining table was hidden under several more boxes so all meals thus far had been at the breakfast bench or on the couch, and today's lunch was spread out on the front porch. Lisa and Matty sat on the edge, swinging their legs.

I leaned against the folded-back doors, ankles crossed and eyes closed, thinking about the new study. The furniture from my old study was in there but just haphazardly placed for now. I felt a smile on my face at how I was quite happy to not do anything that looked like business work.

After a moment I dimly heard Jamie saying, 'Looks like both our slave drivers are asleep. Guess that means we can relax.'

Near me Owen let out a soft laugh and I felt a hand curve over my lower leg. I didn't mind if they both thought I was snoozing. And, clearly, Megan was too.

She had been the busiest over the last few days and I knew why. As much as she wanted to get out of the other house she'd found it hard to do so, to let go the memories. She'd admitted that there weren't exactly many good ones but I understood her feelings. It was still their first home here and it carried an attachment that was hard to let go.

Megan had been the main slave driver here just to keep that upset at bay.

Lisa and Matty didn't seem to have the same feelings; they were just excited about the house and grounds.

Mental note—organise someone to cut the grounds.

We'd ventured into the jungle this morning in the direction of the supposed pond, just to stop Matty going off on his own adventure. We had a bit of a track now but I wasn't keen on the idea of anyone forging their own paths in the grass and weeds.

Matty's enthusiasm had taken a bit of a hit when we'd found the pond. Actually, found where it should have been. It was mostly a weed-filled swampy hollow.

I tried not to smile; the kid was a hundred percent into anything he did, even a panic. My assurance that we'd work on the pond had, at least, settled him down. Jamie had pointed out there were plenty of trees he could climb instead of babbling about the pond, and that had caught the kid's attention.

Just not, I hoped, while Owen and I were out this afternoon. I'd seen Matty climb the oak back at the house and knew he was capable, but these were new trees and would take time to learn.

Shifting my consciousness a little, I heard Lisa and Matty talking—not about the pond or trees, but about vegetables. The kids had created a vegetable garden at the old place, and it pleased me they wanted to carry that on here.

'Hey, Andrew, when—'

'Ssh, he's asleep,' Owen cut over in a soft call.

'I'm not,' I said, blinking my eyes open.

The boys and Lisa all looked at me. Megan was definitely asleep, curled on her side.

'Sorry, Andrew,' Matty said. 'I didn't mean to wake you.'

'It's okay, Kiddo, I wasn't really asleep.' I shifted straighter against the doors, smiled when Owen gave a shake of his dark head. I turned back to Matty. 'What was it you were after?'

'Plants,' he said. 'We wondered if you could get some when you went out.'

'Vegetables,' Lisa clarified. 'We want to start a garden like at home.'

'Sure,' I said, cutting in on Jamie who was opening his mouth. 'How about you both write up a list? Owen and I'll see what we can get.'

'Do we even have a place for a garden?' Jamie asked.

'Perhaps you all could find a spot,' I suggested. 'Being careful, of course.'

That got the kids enthused and they went inside looking for paper and pens. Jamie shrugged. 'Better than unpacking, I guess.'

He glanced at his sister but she was still in the land of nod despite the chatter and the fact it can't have been that comfortable a space to lie upon.

I tilted my watch. 'We should probably start to get a move

on,' I said to Owen.

He nodded, but it took another ten minutes before either of us got up.

Didn't think it was the coming visit with Melissa that stopped us, just reluctance at having to move. Owen put a hand to his back, mumbled something about a spa bath and stepped into the house.

I looked back at Jamie, still sitting. 'Don't let your sister sleep too long.'

'Because she'll be crabby when she wakes?'

'There's that,' I said, smiling. 'The sun will start to cook her, and we don't need that.'

Jamie sucked at his teeth, but didn't respond.

I turned to go put on tidier clothes and got presented with a list of vegetables by Lisa when I came back to the lounge. Owen peered at the list too. 'You guys are ambitious. That's a lot of plants.'

'Well, we've got more space here,' Lisa said.

Owen couldn't argue with that. He tucked feet into shoes and I followed him out to the porch. Megan was still sleeping, Jamie still sitting. The kids returned to their spots on the edge of the porch. I guess sitting and relaxing was the number one priority, rather than finding garden space.

'We'll only be a couple of hours,' I said. 'But ring if you need anything.'

'Will do,' Jamie agreed.

Owen and I dropped off the porch—my mental check list raising *steps to porch* higher than *pond*—and walked the well-trodden path to the Santa Fe. I breathed out a sigh. The Santa Fe had been great for shuttling between the houses with various boxes and things, but I was so looking forward to driving the Mercedes home.

Owen got into the car biting at his bottom lip.

'You don't have to come if you don't want,' I said quietly.

I saw his teeth go in harder for a second before he smiled. 'It's all good. Was just… thinking…' He didn't say what about.

'You've got the house keys, right?'

'Yep. Got the Merc's?'

I smiled. 'Yes. And I've checked several times to be sure.'

Owen grinned. 'It's cute how you and Matty are obsessed.'

I laughed out loud, managed, 'I think your brother beats me in that game.'

'Sure.'

Directing the big car down the flattened track, I simply smiled. I *was* looking forward to getting my car back. Didn't quip that I was sure Owen looked forward to it just as much.

Melissa pulled up just as we were getting in the front door. I went to greet her while Owen stepped inside, saying, 'I want to do a final check.'

I let him go, suspecting reality had given him a jolt and he needed a moment.

I met Melissa on the drive, gave her cheek a kiss in greeting. 'How have you been?'

'A bit sleepless,' she said. 'Sam's got an earache and he's very grumpy about it.'

I glanced past her to the car but couldn't see anyone occupying the baby seat.

'He's with a sitter,' she said. 'Couldn't have brought him today. I'd like to start here with a good impression.' She sounded wry, and it probably wasn't all because of a screaming baby.

We'd steered clear of those other possible reasons whenever we'd met over the last couple of weeks, and we did it now too. I encouraged her inside. 'Owen's just doing a final check.'

As we walked up the path, I handed her the car keys. 'It's been running very well, and there's a quarter tank left.'

'Are you sure about this, Andrew?' she asked, taking the keys hesitantly. 'The house *and* the car?'

'The car's registered under your husband's name,' I said, trying not to sound stiff. '*We* cannot keep it.'

Melissa nodded, gave an audible swallow. She dropped the keys in her bag.

Owen came out of the hall, stopped a second as if surprised then continued forward. 'Hi Melissa, how're you doing?' He didn't resist being hugged, didn't flinch from a kiss on the cheek.

'I'm well,' Melissa said. 'Though I was just telling Andrew I'm a bit sleepy. Sammy's screaming his way through an ear infection.'

'Doesn't sound like fun,' Owen responded.

'Not for either of us,' Melissa said wryly. 'But you guys must be tired too. Moving is exhausting.'

'Yeah, but—' He indicated the furniture in the lounge. 'We haven't had to do a *lot*. Mostly unpacking boxes.'

'I'm so very, very grateful to you, Owen,' she said, voice catching. 'The house is amazing enough, but the furniture too. That—' She put a hand over her mouth.

Owen looked uncomfortable but he said, 'We didn't need it. You can't imagine what stuff Andrew had at his place.' He cast me a tiny smile.

'Well,' I said, '*that's* a polite way of saying I have a lot of junk.'

He snorted, gave me a little shove, then turned back to Melissa. 'We didn't need this stuff, honestly, and it would have been dumb to sell it, right?' He didn't wait for her to agree or not, just carried on. 'The main bedroom and my old room still have furniture too, but the other two rooms are bare. And we did take some things from here,' he added, walking to the breakfast bench. 'Baking things that Megan couldn't live without, favourite mugs, that sort of thing.'

We'd also depleted the fridge, freezer and pantry but Owen didn't mention that. Though we were giving the keys to Melissa today, she wasn't planning on being here right away. Didn't make sense to leave her rotting or out-dated food.

Owen was still talking—not nerves, I didn't think, just eagerness now to get this all done.

Melissa stood with him at the bench as he went over the list of names and numbers we'd gotten together for her. The Carters next door, the insurance companies (she already had the documents), *our* new phone number.

I was proud of the kids for including Melissa in their lives, comfortable with it myself. Megan had already said that she was available for babysitting over the rest of the summer break and beyond.

I was gazing at the space above the TV that had never been filled by another picture when the clink of metal jerked me to the present.

Owen had set his house keys on the bench. He splayed them out. 'Front door, French door. Back door via the garage.' He tapped the grey device beside the keys. 'The opener for the garage door.'

'Okay.' Melissa smiled, but didn't reach for them.

'There's a bunch of spare keys in the top drawer,' I said, stepping forward.

They both jerked like they'd forgotten my presence.

'Yeah,' Owen said. 'Plenty of them.'

'Oh, okay.' Melissa touched the set in front of her but still didn't pick them up.

'I hate to rush this,' I said after a moment, 'but Owen and I have a date with a supermarket. We better get going.'

A broad smile lit up Melissa's face. 'Guess I should go relieve the babysitter.' She picked up the keys now, clutching them tight, and we headed for the door.

Standing beside the Mercedes, Melissa gave Owen a hearty hug. 'Thank you, Owen,' I heard her say. 'I hope you… enjoy your new home.'

'Thanks,' he croaked. 'I am already.'

I gave her a hug when she turned to me. 'Do let us know if you need any help when you move in.'

'I will, thank you.' Her smile wobbled for a second then pulled straight.

She walked out to her car and I beeped the Mercedes open, making Owen jerk and spin about. An embarrassed grin turned up his lips when he saw me smiling. 'Coulda warned me,' he muttered.

I chuckled, then waved as Melissa tooted the horn and pulled away.

We stood for a little while once she was out of sight, each in our own thoughts, then Owen walked around the car and opened his door.

I was willing to take the blame for us nearly ending up in a ditch, even though I wasn't driving, but it had to be Andrew's for starting the sequence that put us right here in the backseat of his Mercedes out of sight on a dirt road.

Not that I was bothered by the situation.

As we'd gotten in the Mercedes after Melissa had driven away, Andrew had looked at me and said, 'I'm so proud of you, Owen.'

I'd sort of shrugged in acknowledgement but the heat from his praise and the depth of the love that had been in the tone grew until, half way home after the supermarket visit, I'd said, 'I want to make love.'

'Mm mm, sure.'

When I'd looked at him, brow up at the response, I saw that he had most of his concentration on the road. 'I mean it, Andrew.'

He glanced at me, obviously meaning to take just a short moment, but he must have understood then that I wasn't just spouting words. '*Now?*'

'Yeah.' I let that roll out long off my tongue.

That's when he nearly steered us into the ditch; staring so much that the wide corner came up and startled him back to the road. I wanted to apologise but right then his surprise and fluster and strange grin were just stoking my need hotter.

Andrew breathed out, 'Are you serious, Owen?'

An out if I wanted one. 'Yes,' I said.

He cleared his throat. 'Okay.'

And so here we were, on the backseat, upper clothing still on. Andrew had had to get the front seats forward to give us more room, but being intimate wasn't an easy feat. I enjoyed it though, heart racing, clinging to Andrew's shirt to keep him close enough to kiss, feeling the leather back of the seat all the way along my leg that he had pressed out of the way.

I arched up under him, went to wrap my less restricted leg around him but found I'd got it between the front seats and I was sort of stuck. I started to laugh, making Andrew push back to crouch in the gap between front and back seats.

'Sorry, sorry,' I got out, up on my elbows as I rearranged my limbs.

'This really isn't a great place,' Andrew commented wryly. 'We'd have been better off outside.'

'No way, not out in that long grass,' I said. 'Might've been bitten on the bum.'

Andrew snorted and shifted to sit properly now that I wasn't taking up so much space. His shirt fell over his lap, tented so I knew he was still aroused. I started to move so I could kneel astride him, but first had to sort out the remains of hampering lower clothing. Probably wasn't romantic at all, but Andrew seemed pleased when I finally made it to his lap. He was slouched a bit so my knees weren't jammed into the seat, and I could feel him taut beneath me as I shifted for comfort. He snatched a kiss on my lips and then kissed his way down my throat.

He murmured, 'Lift up a little' and I did so, letting him rearrange himself. 'Down,' he said. 'Carefully.'

I did, relaxing as I felt myself filled. He let out a long sigh, matching my own, and kissed me long and slow, his arms curved around my back. Clenching my muscles made him suck in a breath and stop kissing for a moment. We looked at each other, cross-eyed.

'I love you,' he rasped out.

I just smiled and returned us to the business of making love, flexing my muscles around him until he let out a sharp breath and came. His arms tightened around me, and when he sagged back he pulled me in against him. Both of us were breathing heavily.

'So...' he said a bit raggedly after a few minutes, 'what induced your blatant disregard for public decency?'

I pressed my lips to his throat briefly, then shifted so we were no longer connected though I didn't make any move to get off his lap. 'You told me you were proud of me,' I said. 'And what public? It's just you and me here.'

Andrew laughed, stretched to kiss my forehead. 'Really? Because I said I was proud of you?' His blue eyes hooked mine and I could only nod. 'I'm sure I've said that before.'

'Yeah, but...' I trailed off, unable to articulate just why this time was different. Then I tapped his chest. 'You didn't stop me.'

'I'll never stop you,' he told me earnestly. 'Just...' His smile was wry. 'Somewhere not so damn awkward next time.'

'You did alright.'

'Okay, stop right there with that grin. I *do* need the strength to drive home.'

Jamie

When the Mercedes pulled up by the columns, Owen and Andrew didn't immediately get out. Looked like they were having a conversation, Owen turning to look into the backseat. Andrew shook his head, laughing.

'Yay, they're home,' Matty said. 'I wonder what plants—'

'Hold it,' I said, grabbing his arm as he went to leap off the porch.

'But—'

'Just chill,' I told him. 'Let them at least get out of the car.'

Matty grumbled but when I let him go he stayed put.

Owen and Andrew eventually removed themselves from the car, turning to the trunk. That's right, getting groceries had been one of the afternoon's missions. I called out if they wanted any help.

'We're good,' Owen called back, then followed up with, 'Matty, come get your vegies.'

Phew, they hadn't forgotten the most important task. Having spent the afternoon looking for good vegetable plots with Lisa and Matty, which included pulling out weeds, I didn't want to hear they'd forgotten the kids' list of plants.

Matty jumped off the porch. Instead of watching, I turned back into the house and relaxed on the couch.

Not too long after that, Owen clambered onto the porch with several bags, pulling a face as he adjusted his hold.

Rolling my eyes, I went to help. 'Where'd Andrew get to?'

'Matty convinced him to go look at the ground you guys found,' Owen said, relinquishing several bags. He winced as he straightened and then headed inside. 'Shit, I'm glad we didn't forget those vegetables. Get the feeling Matty would have skinned us.'

'*I* would have skinned you,' I told him, setting my bags on the bench and started to sort out what was in them. 'We spent ages out there finding the right spot. I'm pretty sure I weeded the whole damn backyard.'

Owen grinned. 'At least for now he's forgotten that pond.'

'Hunh.' I cocked my head. 'How was Melissa?'

'Yeah, good,' he said as he put two bottles of milk in the fridge. 'Bit overwhelmed, I think,' he added, looking over his shoulder. 'The house was one thing, but the car too…' He shrugged. 'Anyway, glad it's done.'

He came back to the bench, gazing over what I'd taken out of the bags but didn't make any moves to put anything away. His brows came together for a second and then he brushed both hands back through his hair. 'I was sort of worried about being there,' he mumbled, not looking at me. 'Well, about leaving. But all I felt was relief.'

'Understandable,' I heard myself say.

Owen glanced at me then and I just lifted a shoulder. I'd felt the same yesterday as we'd followed the removal truck down the road.

'Hey,' I said, 'I'll finish this off. You go find Matty before he comes and drags you outside.'

He rolled his eyes but grinned and headed out of the kitchen, one hand pressed to his back.

Owen

I had the best night's sleep in a very long time, and when I woke I simply lay there listening to Andrew's soft breathing. Tried to keep my lips relaxed but they kept curving into a grin. Andrew murmured when I let out a long, shaky sigh but he didn't waken. I shifted carefully from the bed and padded out to the kitchen to make a cup of tea.

The house was amazingly quiet. Getting used to the fact we had so much space that we weren't constantly in each other's faces would take time. Outside, the front yard shone gold with the morning sun, Andrew's Mercedes there like an old friend.

I felt a lump in my throat unexpectedly and coughed to clear it.

As the jug finished boiling, I detoured back to the bedroom to see if Andrew was still asleep. Nope, he was actually pulling back the curtains.

'The Merc's still there, don't worry.'

He jerked and turned, saying he hadn't been checking that. The wry tone told me otherwise.

I grinned. 'I'm making tea. Do you want a cup?'

'Of course,' he said, starting forward.

'No, get back in bed. I'll bring a pot.'

I didn't wait to see if he obeyed just went back to the kitchen. Since he didn't show up, he obviously was taking orders today. I grinned to myself as I reboiled the jug and sorted the teapot and cups.

As I carried the tray into the bedroom, Andrew asked how I'd slept. 'You look brighter this morning.'

'In your arms I sleep like a log,' I responded, letting him take the tray so I could get back in beside him.

He smiled and said he appreciated me keeping my knees to myself this time around. Lucky for him he was positioning the tray or I'd have shoved him. Somehow he still managed to plant a kiss on my cheek.

'Don't distract me,' I said, grinning, as I reached to spin the teapot about a bit.

Andrew simply smiled. When we both held a cup and the tray sat safely down by our feet, he said, 'I'm glad you slept well. What you said yesterday morning worried me.'

'Don't let it,' I told him. 'Just a bunch of first night jitters.'

He was opening his mouth to speak when my stomach let out a loud rumble. I winced.

'That's a great sound, you know,' he said. 'One rarely heard.'

'All this fresh air,' I told him. 'And hard work.' I rubbed my stomach. 'Guess I should have sorted breakfast, rather than this tea.'

'Let's finish this first,' Andrew said as I started to shift.

I sat back, but when my stomach gave a ridiculously long howl I couldn't stay still any longer, not with Andrew right there getting an earful. 'Right then, breakfast. What do you want?'

The look that came over his face sent mine suddenly hot.

'You can't have *me*,' I told him. 'You'll need strength for boxes and stuff.'

He chuckled.

'But… if you're good, I could be on your lunch menu. Maybe under that big tree by the pond?'

Andrew gave me a slow glance up and down that made me take a step back to try and keep myself in control. 'Are you suggesting work *and* play, my dear young man?'

'M-maybe.'

He pursed his lips like he was thinking about it. 'Consider the suggestion accepted,' he said after a moment.

I rolled my eyes, grinning when he winked at me. Got myself out of the bedroom before I could change my mind about being his breakfast.

Although I'd offered myself up as part of the lunch menu, when I headed toward the pond at about one I carried a container of sandwiches and a bag with a flask of tea and two travel mugs. A blanket was precariously tucked under one arm too.

Over the previous few days we'd made a good track between the house and the pond, though as yet we hadn't brought in an industrial mower to take care of the grounds. As I reached the tree, noting a blanket had already been spread at the base, I was pleased we still had long grass. If Andrew and I did get a little adventurous we'd be hidden from the house. From the upper story too because of the tree itself; funnily enough, an oak just like at ho—our *old* home.

Andrew had his back to me as he stood at the pond's edge, probably wondering just how we were going to manage to turn it back into one. The designation wasn't that valid right then due to the lack of decent water and a great deal of mud and other plant-life.

Matty had been upset when he'd first seen it so getting it back to being a pond was high on the "fix-it" list.

I set down my items, then stepped along the beaten track toward Andrew. He smiled over his shoulder when he obviously heard me and I felt heat start spreading around my veins. He reached a hand back and I gladly took it as I stepped up beside him. He leaned to kiss my temple.

'Think we could get away with filling it in and making it more lawn?' I asked, eyeing the mess in front of us.

'Depends upon whether we want to live with Matty's wrath,' Andrew replied, wry.

I reckoned he'd forget about it eventually, but instead of saying that I murmured, 'It's going to be a lot of work.'

Andrew nodded. 'It sure will, but it will be wonderful when it's fixed up.'

I squeezed his hand in appreciation that he would take on the work (or fund someone else to take on the work). He smiled down at me.

'Come on,' I said, taking a back-step and turning, tugging him with me. 'I made lunch.'

'I thought you were lunch.'

I stuck my tongue out at him, trying not to let the heat rise even as I said, 'Yeah, but *I* can't have me, can I?'

Andrew laughed, rubbed a hand up my back.

Under the tree, he spread out the second blanket to give us a bit more space. I took the lid off the container of sandwiches and announced, 'Egg.'

He actually looked puzzled a second and then he smiled and picked up one. 'Egg's my favourite.'

Which was why I'd made them. And… 'You made me an egg sandwich that very first time I stayed at your place,' I mumbled.

Andrew stopped with the sandwich half way to his mouth, eyeing me. 'Yes,' he said slowly, as if his consciousness was half on me in front of him and half in memory.

I caught myself doing a weird nod like I had to agree with him even though he hadn't asked me anything. And then I whispered, 'Thanks.'

After a beat, he croaked out my name, swallowed hard and repeated it with a bit more sound. He set the untouched sandwich on the container lid. Instead of reaching for me like I thought he was going to he shoved a hand into one of his front pockets. That totally threw me and then all I could really do was stare as he held out his palm. On it lay a silver ring.

'Owen,' he rasped.

'Wha-at?' Flushed hard at that stupid response. I cleared my throat but then couldn't speak.

Andrew closed his eyes a moment, lips pressed tight. Then he gazed at me across the container of egg sandwiches and totally blew my mind with, 'Will you marry me?'

I looked from his face to his hand and the ring lying there, then back up again, then down again. Might have done that several times before I could pull myself together. I dragged in some air, whispered, 'Are you serious?'

'I have never been more so, Owen.' He tipped the ring onto its edge, then picked it up. It shook, catching light even though we were mostly in the shade.

I enclosed the ring-holding fingers in mine and leaned forward to press a kiss to Andrew's cheek. 'Yes,' I said against his warm skin. 'Yes, yes, yes.'

'Yes?' he got out.

'Oh *hell*, yes!'

I came over all shaky too and between us we managed to lose the ring for a moment, before Andrew found it between sandwiches and dug it out, sucking off a bit of mashed egg. My grin was as wobbly as the rest of me when he reached for my left hand. The ring fit just as perfectly as the one I'd gotten him, and I couldn't put into words how I felt seeing it on my finger. I released a whistled breath, feeling giddy.

Andrew raised my chin and I saw his whole face had become a smile. He took the rest of my air in a long, heated kiss and I clung to him.

A low growl made me freeze. My heart started to hammer for an entirely different reason but then Andrew was laughing. So… obviously not worried about some beast hiding in the grass?

'My stomach,' he managed. 'S-sorry, Angel.'

It wasn't until he reached for the sandwich that I realised what he meant—his stomach had growled. I snorted. 'This is why I made a *real* lunch,' I told him, picking up a sandwich too. '*I'm* hardly gonna settle that particular beast.'

Andrew almost choked as he laughed and chewed at the same time. I flushed, hadn't meant to speak quite like that, but couldn't stop myself grinning.

Later, wrapped in the blankets for privacy while we caught our breath, I whispered, 'Andrew, do you *really* want to marry me?'

'I do,' he responded.

'That's pretty cool.'

His lips pressed to my temple. 'I think so too, Owen.'

Smiling, I cuddled further into the man I was going to spend the rest of my life with. My sleepy gaze angled to the amazing mackerel sky streaking toward the horizon, and I knew I was finally home and healed and whole.

Acknowledgements

Amy — I am so grateful for your enthusiasm for both novels, and for driving me to Madison so I could check out the gardens, the Capitol and the zoo!

Lauren — your coaching and feedback remains infinitely valuable to me and to my writing.

Nick — brilliant title, thanks!

Mum — Your insight and feedback has been amazing. And, of course, thanks for the threatening sky darkening up the cover!

Legal Fiction and **Trauma Fiction** - Facebook groups for writers, filled with wonderful people who don't bat an eyelid at what you ask.

About the Author

Jade lives in New Zealand but most of her characters don't. She's trying to encourage a change.

She has been writing since she could make letters with a pencil, though *Threatening Sky* is only the second novel actually FINISHED. She's now looking forward to progressing the stories of other characters who've been keeping her company over the years, whether they be short stories or novels.

Jade is trying to be more consistent with blogging on http://www.sjadecastleton.com (where you can meet a couple of her other characters), and she welcomes contact through email: jade@sjadecastleton.com. (She has a twitter account but is even slower tweeting than blogging.)

Stories by Jade:

Mackerel Sky (novel) – https://www.amazon.com/Mackerel-Sky-S-Jade-Castleton-ebook/dp/B07DS3GT4N

Fire Red Leaf (short story) - https://www.amazon.com/Fire-Red-Leaf-Jade-Castleton-ebook/dp/B07N2MMYKH